THE MAN

IN THE

LIGHTHOUSE

ALSO BY ERIK VALEUR

The Seventh Child

ERIK VALEUR

Translated by Mark Mussari

THE MAN
IN THE
LIGHTHOUSE

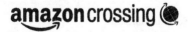

Text copyright © 2015 Erik Valeur and JP/Politikens Forlagshus A/S
Translation copyright © 2017 Mark Mussari
All rights reserved.

Previously published as *Logbog fra et livsforlis* by JP/Politikens Forlagshus A/S in Denmark in 2015. Translated from Danish by Mark Mussari. First published in English by AmazonCrossing in 2017.

Published by AmazonCrossing, Seattle

www.apub.com

Amazon, the Amazon logo, and AmazonCrossing are trademarks of Amazon.com, Inc., or its affiliates.

ISBN-13: 9781503942639
ISBN-10: 1503942635

Cover design by David Drummond

Printed in the United States of America

PREFACE

The Ominous Dream

The Omen came to him in his dreams one night, as he slept, smiling as all children do when they sleep.

The woman. The sea. The woman's hands reaching for him, as if beckoning him toward her.

Viggo Larssen awakened, with a small shout, to his dark room. Even back then, he could already sense what the dream meant—and why, as an adult, he named that dream the Omen.

He never told anyone about the fearful dream, neither his mother nor his grandmother, and certainly not his grandfather, who suffered from a persistent, mood-darkening migraine and who was renowned throughout their modest neighborhood for his peevishness.

After all, they were adults. They would never understand. They already thought he was peculiar; that was the word adults used to describe him. They were afraid of the unknown, of anything different, of visions they could not explain. That sort of thing belonged elsewhere and must never come anywhere near their neighborhood.

Viggo Larssen kept his disturbing dream private. Periodically, the dream would return. The hands. The sea. The woman who looked like his mother. A dark shadow whipping the water into a white froth around her feet. Yet he always awoke before the shadow lurking beneath the surface ever made it into the light.

Even at such an early age, he sensed that his nocturnal visions demanded a deeper level of thought than anything else he had encountered in his short life. He somehow felt that no one could possibly draw any kind of comparison with his strange dream, and that he would be alone in his experience. Thus, he buried his fear deep inside himself, as children often do.

When, at fifteen years old, he recognized his dream in someone else's description, it was due neither to decades of research on his behalf nor to any newly sharpened mental prowess, but instead solely to what Destiny has only ever been the sole true expert in—surpassed by neither God nor the Devil—*chance*.

What normally separates events in time and space suddenly unites them in a completely unanticipated way, creating a pattern that no eye can detect and no thoughts can explain. But one that Viggo Larssen still knew existed.

By the time the dramatic events at Solbygaard Nursing Home in Gentofte ended his self-imposed isolation, he had long since grown up.

PROLOGUE

THE WIDOW'S DISAPPEARANCE

Office of the Prime Minister
Thursday, January 1, 2015,
late in the evening

The prime minister shook his massive and, as some wicked tongues might say, grotesquely large head.

Then he rested it in his huge paws, which were big enough to span it.

A news journalist (allegedly using a craniologist as his source) had once estimated that the head in question weighed more than a medium-size bowling ball. You could almost hear thoughts crashing around behind the prime minister's granite-hewn forehead, unable to find their way out.

Long ago, the prime minister's mother had given him a series of illustrated booklets about the trapper Davy Crockett; absurdly enough, the burly man now resembled the wounded bear of those drawings. Rising up on its colossal hind legs, summoning a mighty roar that soared up, up toward the sky, the bear had been drawn with a furious, wordless pain, giving the dying giant an almost human appearance.

Yet not a sound came out of the chief executive's thick lips, his face clenched in rage. For prime ministers rarely roar in any official capacity. Nor in private, either, for that matter.

Instead, he stood and paced once around the desk in a large, aimless circle before returning to his chair and sitting back down.

The chair, its seat and back made of Congolese buffalo leather, was a gift from an African delegation that had not anticipated their host's impressive weight; the relatively fragile piece of furniture creaked under the huge body.

The man across from him remained seated. His head was the same shape (though not exactly the same impressive size) as the chief executive's. Clearly, the two men were closely related, both resembling the parents who had passed on these powerful genes. Their eyebrows were similarly gray and stern, their foreheads towered over their broad noses, and their hairlines had all but disappeared, except for a crescent-shaped wreath encircling each head.

The younger man leaned forward reassuringly but without speaking, since he was, after all, only the country's second in command.

The brothers' respective positions as prime minister and minister of justice, since 2011, made everyone think of the two murdered brothers of the Kennedy clan. The press had quickly embraced this idea, christening the two Danish politicians and their brood of ambitious sons and daughters, "the Blegman Dynasty."

Just like the Kennedys in the 1960s, Denmark's first famous political dynasty had an imposing widow at its head. Her husband, a tyrant by any estimation, had died at a relatively early age, and since then she had reigned over the family.

At almost ninety years old, Widow Blegman still enjoyed the status of a queen, even though the brothers had been forced to move her to Solbygaard Nursing Home in the wealthy community of Gentofte after she had fallen seriously ill with a pernicious case of pneumonia that would not release its grip; however, her time at the home, with its beautiful tall trees in a parklike setting, had apparently done her some good.

And yet the Widow was the problem this evening.

"Where is she?" asked Palle Blegman in his unusually deep voice; he had since his earliest youth been nicknamed "the Bear" by friends and enemies alike.

The younger of the country's two most powerful men, Poul Blegman, answered. "I don't know."

None of the comments that followed were suitable for publication or even worth hearing outside the high-ceilinged room, the finest in the kingdom, which people somewhat disrespectfully called the Bear Cave. Here, at the height of desperation, the brothers' voices had the same deep rumble that resonated in their chests long after their last syllables were spoken.

"He must have some *goddamn* theory," said the Bear.

"He's a *fucking* pedant—he makes a virtue out of working tirelessly . . . and slowly, *much* too slowly," replied his brother.

The object of their contempt was Copenhagen's most accomplished policeman, whom the nation knew simply as the Homicide Boss. Of course he had been placed in charge of the investigation, which grew ever larger by the minute and would soon involve much more than just the nursing home in Gentofte and the surrounding wealthy suburbs. This investigation had only one person as its target: their mother.

The policeman's skill was indisputable. The brothers had called him immediately, but their patience had lasted only a few hours.

"He's *shitting* on us . . ." Once again, the younger Blegman brother placed outraged emphasis on the swear word.

The prime minister sat back down again and covered his face with his hands.

"I'll call him."

"No." Palle Blegman shook his enormous head twice; more than ever the two men resembled a pair of Davy Crockett's giant bears. "I'll do it myself."

There were journalists who, smirking, had privately christened the Blegman dynasty "the Cave Bear Clan," though none of them would dare write that in their newspapers or say it on television. Even in a country whose press incessantly strove to appear brave and critical, there was still something menacing about the two brothers—something that made otherwise merciless critics retreat with fear for their lives.

The prime minister reached for the telephone.

***

Office of the Homicide Boss
Thursday, January 1, just before midnight

The Homicide Boss was an unobtrusive man. Though not particularly tall, he was likewise not short and stocky. He was neither too heavy nor too thin, neither too dark nor too fair, and had it not been for a distinct air of authority (which, at times, struck those around him as hostile), he would have been the archetypal nondescript Dane.

To place such a calm and balanced man in police headquarters in the heart of the capital—as the leader, no less, in the fight against the ugliest crimes humans were capable of committing—might seem paradoxical, yet everyone knew he was the very best at what he did. The Homicide Boss shook his head for at least the tenth time that night and turned toward his deputy assistant, who was never called anything except Number Two.

"It's completely insane. Who decides to abduct an old woman from a nursing home—and what in the world would be their motive?"

As expected, Number Two's response was immediate. "Money." His deputy assistant was unknown outside police headquarters, and even within headquarters, many people no longer remembered his real name. Most of the time, he rarely contributed to discussions. In his silence he was an effective investigator, and his boss's favorite and only confidant.

They had attended police academy together and, as new cops, had gone on evening patrols in the city's most sinister alleys.

"Ransom?" said the Homicide Boss. "Maybe. Terror . . . no. If so, they would have cut off her head and hung it in front of city hall—or blown up the whole nursing home, no?"

Such a brutal scenario made the deputy briefly close his eyes, perhaps imagining the smoky ruins of the nursing home. Behind his seemingly impenetrable facade, he had a reputation for being far more sensitive than his superior. Their shared office at police headquarters was not particularly spacious, furnished with only two easy chairs, a rosewood desk, and a pair of light walnut office chairs with comfortable arms.

"The clan—the *dynasty*—is affluent, but there are other, much wealthier families. And yes, they have great power but"—the Homicide Boss shook his head yet again—"no, it doesn't make sense. We all know that she's old and weak. The entire public knows that. So if anyone wanted the Widow *dead*, they only needed to sit back and wait a few months. It doesn't make sense."

It was the third variation on the same theme in less than half a minute, and Number Two could already detect his boss's hatred for his unknown adversary—the very hatred that famously motivated him. His boss's predecessor had once observed, somewhat pompously, "One hunts a beast but captures a person," but that's not what his current boss thought. Now, beasts were *beasts*, even if some bleeding-heart judge or an overly forgiving God foolishly showed mercy. Such nonsense belonged in courtrooms—or in the hereafter—both places far from police headquarters.

The first police who arrived at Solbygaard Nursing Home had found the Widow's small two-room apartment in perfect condition. On the windowsill stood a birdcage with a slightly frightened golden canary sitting on its topmost perch. A small pile of New Year's newspapers and a single magazine were on her coffee table; everything appeared peaceful and calm.

There was no sign of a struggle. No one had seen her leave her apartment, and no one had seen anyone go in. On the other hand, that wasn't so odd, since the staff spent most of their time in the spacious office across from the dining room, generally with the door shut, so they could work in peace. Mounds of paper lay scattered among coffee cups, timetables, forms, charts, and spreadsheets, all waiting for attention. Evaluation and control of the aging population were becoming their central tasks—or at least their most time-consuming.

Half an hour later, the two police chiefs arrived at the scene; it was the prime minister's mother who had disappeared, after all, and the prime minister was demanding action.

First, they sealed off the Widow's small apartment, then her floor, then the entire building, and finally the sprawling parklike surrounding area. It had been barely an hour since the Blegman brothers had sounded the alarm. Their mother had invited them over at six o'clock; when they arrived, she was gone, and she hadn't been seen at dinner just before, either. The brothers claimed that the door to her apartment was ajar, and naturally that detail had to be addressed. It was not like the dynasty's first lady to leave anything ajar, least of all the door to her home.

In their search, the evidence technicians had almost immediately discovered a small piece of yellow plastic, about the size of a hand, lying on the windowsill. It was found between two elegant porcelain figurines of Hans Christian Andersen and Søren Kierkegaard, alongside pictures of the Widow's three sons, the youngest having died as a child. They had carefully eased the rather curious discovery into a sterile evidence bag. It didn't look like anything an older woman would use as a decoration.

Ten minutes later they found another piece of plastic, of exactly the same type as the first, this time under the Widow's pillow. This had seriously disturbed them. Were they a sign of senility, which might then explain her disappearance, or had someone brought the yellow pieces of plastic into the apartment—and if so, why?

The third possible clue, discovered by the eagle-eyed deputy police chief, proved to be the most peculiar; naturally, Number Two had already determined its possible meaning. He only had to ask the nursing home's terrified supervisor a simple question before the foreboding that had grown inside him with each passing minute took hold. He no longer had any doubts.

He now *knew* that something had gone very wrong in that apartment.

His boss immediately decided to keep his second in command's discovery confidential, a decision that was communicated to the nursing home supervisor in such urgent tones that her nervousness manifested as bodily tremors. She immediately became unfit for work.

The technicians carefully removed the third and final discovery from the drawer in the Widow's bureau, where Number Two had found it.

The large leather folder that had caught his eye was brown and faded, and by all accounts appeared quite old, but the writing on the little piece of cardboard clipped securely to the front was in black ink and clearly far more recent in origin. He had studied the two words for almost a minute before he moved.

Will, signed.

That second word was what had heightened his growing feeling of unrest. There was something definitive, irrefutable, about that word, as if the signing itself had been of utmost importance.

However, when he carefully opened the brown cover, the real reason for his concern emerged. The old leather folder was empty.

If there had ever been a will, it was gone.

***

Afterward, the two police chiefs drove back to headquarters to consider everything and to piece together an initial theory about what had happened. Was the Widow's disappearance merely the unfortunate consequence of a lack of supervision at yet another nursing home hit by budget cuts—or simply the result of a confused or slightly senile woman's suddenly impulsive behavior? Neither scenario seemed likely. All the exterior doors were locked securely, precisely because of confused residents with dementia; anyway, the Widow was mentally as sharp as a tack.

She had even told the staff that she was expecting a visit from her sons.

The Homicide Boss didn't care for the other possible scenarios. At the very worst, it could be kidnapping for ransom (he hated that thought). Or it could also simply be an act of revenge against the reviled dynasty. Or something else entirely, something completely unknown.

Though they had no answers, they sent out a terse press release based on demands from the police director's office, a few floors up.

Seconds later, or so it seemed, the phone system in police headquarters collapsed, and the press began its daylong siege of both Solbygaard and the police's office at the Central Station.

The Dynasty's Grand Old Lady Vanished—Possibly Kidnapped, proclaimed all the major news outlets. This revelation was followed by a hefty stream of Facebook and Twitter updates with accompanying rumors and doomsday theories, the entire nation apparently caught up in an intoxicating emotional blend of titillation and horror.

"No one has come forward . . ."

". . . with threats or demands—for anything." The Homicide Boss completed his second in command's assessment of the situation.

Just then, the red telephone to his right rang: the number was known by only a small handful of executives and politicians, and neither of the two policemen had any doubts about who was calling.

The roar would now come over the line, issued from the highest halls of the realm. This case would receive greater priority than any in the nation's history.

Placing two chronically choleric brothers in the realm's highest positions (two tyrants, if ever there were) was one thing—but abducting their mother on the first day of the new year, without any explanation, would ignite a sustained and unstoppable fury.

The Homicide Boss caught his subordinate's glance before he straightened up and lifted the receiver. Over the past decades, they had endured numerous crises and conflicts together—ever since, as newbies, they'd had to confront Vietnam War demonstrators, Hells Angels, and revolutionary house squatters. Back then, the enemy indicated their position with prior press releases and mounds of ammunition. It was no longer that simple.

Both men thought about the evidence found in the Widow's abandoned rooms, evidence that had to remain hidden from the world until otherwise necessary. Hidden also from the terrifying man who in a second would be venting his frustration and demanding immediate solutions.

They had to maintain control over an investigation they had already sensed would become the strangest case in their beleaguered police careers.

***

The Lighthouse on the Cape
Thursday, January 1, midnight

At exactly the same moment, out by the old lighthouse on the tip of the long peninsula, a man stood with both hands buried deep in his pockets, watching the moon over the dark water.

The yellow disc hung low and clear over the place that had seen countless shipwrecks through the centuries. Most of them had been unavoidable, a confluence of unfortunate circumstances, a few of the caliber no one in the area today would mention to strangers.

The lighthouse rising above his head did not seem especially tall, but its one shining eye—when still in use—had been seen from as far away as twenty-five miles. Nevertheless, those dark waters held nightmarish tales of ships and crews coming too close to shore, then being ensnared by the winds rushing over the cape's cliffs and out across the water, whipping the sea into foam with their otherworldly howls and then grabbing the unlucky seafarers before they could react, pulling them down into the deep.

Turning away from the moon and the water, the man traipsed the few steps back to the lighthouse's garden, which was overgrown with scrub and wild bushes: blackthorn, buckthorn, hawthorn, and elder.

There was a little stone bench next to the lighthouse door. He sat there, his hands still in his pockets, and leaned his back against the whitewashed wall of the tower.

When the fading orb of heaven was finally swallowed up by the clouds—a few seconds before midnight—he was still sitting there, motionless, his eyes closed, almost as if the wind and the sea and the deep rumbling sound of the waves against the rocks didn't even exist.

If he was cold, no one watching could tell.

PART I

HELL'S DEEP

CHAPTER 1

The Lighthouse on the Cape
Friday, January 2, morning

By the time the story of Widow Blegman's mysterious disappearance exploded onto the media scene on the second day of the new year, I had been living as Viggo Larssen's neighbor for exactly three months and three days.

The case made the entire country quiver in terror-induced pleasure. Ours was a country obsessed with becoming ever more cozy and comfy, a need that is measured as *happiness* in international studies, recently underscored by the most frenzied and consumer-driven Christmas season ever. For such people, sudden catastrophes arrive like a refreshing breeze from another world, a spine-tingling yet much-needed respite from everyday life.

Leaving my rickety red woodland home, sliding and half running down the slope to the deep hollow where the trees thin, I glimpsed the white tower on the tip of the cape. I don't think I could ever tire of observing it, leaning as it did in that slightly menacing way, as if the wind and the white spindrift were pushing it back against the rocky coast on which it had been built.

There was a strange depression in the landscape here, as if a giant had stepped across the hollow in ancient times, leaving behind a single violent footprint in the cape's soft soil. From the very first day, I called it the Giant's Footprint.

Throughout the hollow, there were still remains of primeval forestlike shrubs. Venturing farther into the woods became a laborious, almost painful struggle among the enormous trunks, craggy branches, blackthorn, dog rose, and hawthorn. It was almost as if a rainforest from the Amazon had been planted here at Fyrskoven on Røsnæs.

When the fog creeps up over the fields in the early morning, resting like a gold-and-white halo over the landscape, the Røssers—as the people of Røsnæs call themselves—know that winter is coming to an end. Later, when the sun finally breaks through in those summers not washed out by rain or trapped beneath drifting clouds, clusters of nature lovers come wandering or cycling through Ulstrup then out along the winding road toward the Lighthouse. Here, the fields sprawl over the hills and down the valleys, past cliffs where attentive hikers can spot exotic plants, such as shade-seeking primrose, nodding pasqueflower, and rough saxifrage. Those who are truly attentive might even see a rare butterfly—such as the ochre satyrid, black copper, or French skipper—or hear the small fire-bellied toad, whose call sounds like distant church bells. In the autumn, after a violent downpour rips yet another chunk off the steep cliff where my house is built, you can see large flocks of migratory birds on their long journeys south.

As for the inhabitants on the cape, I think they've been satisfied living and dying exactly as they do, up on the rocky cliffs, in the thickets among the massive ravaged branches, which in the evening twilight resemble withered limbs. When winter storms sweep in from the northwest, even the heaviest of the fallen pine branches let themselves be moved, ever so slightly, to new positions in the landscape, stretching reluctantly toward heaven before once again slipping back into the soil, engulfed by the shadows.

The white tower stood steadfast on Sjælland's most westerly point, on the tip of what looked like a crooked protruding finger pointing resolutely toward the west, in the direction of the island of Samsø and Jutland. If you shifted your gaze just slightly toward the northwest, you were staring directly out to the place where the seabed suddenly changed beneath the waves and rose up, up toward Røsnæs Reef. Parish records, gravestones, and oral legends told stories about shipwrecks and drowned seafarers that fully justified the name people had given the place in ancient times.

Hell's Deep. That's what they called it.

I heard the name for the first time from the old woman whom locals knew only as the Sea Witch. She told me the day she handed me the keys to the ramshackle house in the thicket east of the Lighthouse.

I had rented it dirt cheap from her for four months. Only an outsider would move into a house that stood there literally swaying beneath the tall pine trees, far out on the cape's steep northern slope. During every major storm on the peninsula, gusts of wind lopped off yet another chunk of the house's crumbling foundation. From my kitchen window, I could look directly down into the abyss, down into the black water and onto the waves with their foamy white crests.

My landlady released the rusty key chain (which looked as if it hadn't been used in years) and briefly held my hand tightly in her crooked fingers.

Then she released her grip and pointed toward the lighthouse, standing in silhouette between the branches and pine trunks, and said in her hoarse voice, "There is the Lighthouse, it has been there for a hundred years. And out there"—the old woman stretched her finger even farther out toward the horizon—"out there is Hell's Deep. Don't ever forget it . . ." She froze for a moment, before returning again to that strange, low whisper. "Remember that you must never go near that place, no matter what happens."

I took note of the warning without really understanding what she meant. Although serious shipwrecks had become increasingly rare as the years passed, hundreds, possibly thousands, of unfortunate sailors lay on the bottom of the ocean. So said the locals—and so said the manager of the Daily Market in Ulstrup, the first person I spoke with in town.

The plump, almost pear-shaped man—I immediately felt at ease with him as I rarely did with strangers—had shaken his head when he heard about my stay in the Sea Witch's house, as if only a lunatic would do something so strange.

I ignored that, just as I'd learned since birth to ignore unpleasant facts. One's personal actions were not always explainable, even more rarely logical, and strangeness was not a characteristic that offended me. I was not, nor had I ever been, afraid of living anywhere, not under tall trees, not on some crumbling foundation, not even in an extremely odd house, and certainly not by the sea.

He promised me a weekly delivery of food and necessities; he would drop off my goods at the foot of the cliff, where I could then carry them across the torn-off branches and up the hill to my wobbly home. It would work.

I didn't need anything else.

That's how my months began in what I can only describe as my completely new life. I began exploring my very first day, partly out of curiosity and partly because I knew there was no time to waste.

**

I had come to the cape in late September, and the first few days I did not make my presence known.

Even on the coldest days, I would see Viggo Larssen out in the sea air, sitting motionless on that little stone bench next to the lighthouse door, before he got up to make his hours-long afternoon trek along the shore, out to Bavnebjerg's Cliff, then back again.

Of course he was older and taller (and thinner) than when I had last seen him, at a cemetery in Søborg when he was fifteen years old. I had been only a child then. That meeting was brief, confusing and permeated by his sorrow; it had been no place to meet someone.

Now, what amazed me most was his immobility. He barely turned his head, hardly moved an arm or a leg; he simply sat there for hours, leaning back against the wall of the lighthouse, staring out over the ocean, sometimes with a bottle of wine and a glass sitting on the bench beside him. I used to be able to guess—almost predict—people's thoughts, even before they spoke or moved, but I couldn't with Viggo Larssen, no matter how hard I tried.

I watched him, unnoticed, for almost a week, without fail. If life had taught me anything, it was patience, the patience my long-ago foster mother had considered boundless, violent, almost disturbing.

On the sixth day—a day when the October sun hung over the cape against an icy-blue background—I made my decision, took a deep breath, and rose out of the shrubbery covering the border of the cliff.

Naturally, I hesitated a bit before my first step out into the open, as it was essential that this meeting went well. He didn't see me until I was almost next to the bench.

"Good day," I said plainly.

Though clearly slightly startled, he didn't answer. The only sound was the persistent whisper of the wind through the Sea Witch's forest.

"My name is Malin . . ." For me, the information was an offer of friendship, one that I hadn't given to anyone since I was quite small.

He remained motionless on the stone bench and made no sign of getting up. Neither of us extended a hand.

Right then, I wouldn't have bet even a single cent that I'd ever be able to get closer to him. He must have thought our meeting was an accident—and on that autumn day, barely three months before the Widow's disappearance, it might as well have been. Of course, I already knew his name, and in some strange way I think he sensed that, though I couldn't say why.

Now—as then—his name struck me as a bit comical, with the two *g*'s in Viggo and the two *s*'s in Larssen. Viggo Larssen, fifty-nine years old, haunted by demons, recently relocated from the center of Copenhagen to this, his apparent final resting place.

I sat down on the bench next to him—but I was perched so precariously on the edge of the cold stone seat that a medium-size puff of wind would have blown me out over the edge of Hell's Deep.

Even though we sat less than two arms' lengths apart, and despite a lack of eye contact, I could still sense the loneliness that had always surrounded him, his eyes filled with a touching sadness that revealed no signs of regret.

A book lay on the bench between us; it was the reason I decided to come out of hiding.

I had watched Viggo Larssen sit there reading before he slowly, carefully set it down on the stone seat, almost as if it might crumble at the slightest touch. It was no larger than my old composition books from school, and it was the first time he'd done anything other than stare up into the sky or straight ahead, or drink a little wine. The cover was green, and up close, I was almost certain that it was made of leather. The binding was beautiful, faded with age and slightly stained, as if it had been protecting the book's contents for a hundred years.

There was no title on the cover.

I fought a violent urge to reach for it. I think he sensed my interest, because he moved his treasure away from me and out of sight. I didn't care; patience was my main virtue, and anyway, I had other methods. Haste would be your last resort if you wanted to get close to a person like Viggo Larssen.

"I'm your new neighbor," I said, despite having spied on him for almost a week. But he would have no idea that a newcomer had arrived. A day, a week, a month—he wouldn't know the difference.

"I live in that red house on the cliff, up in the woods," I said. He didn't respond, but I thought I perceived a slight nod. That would have been a tremendous step forward, but it may have only been my imagination.

Then I made a small but obvious blunder: "That's a beautiful book."

I could have bitten my tongue in two. Naturally, my comment was too forward and came at the absolutely worst moment. The faint light in his eyes—if it had even been there—disappeared, and he folded back into himself.

I remained seated, silent, for a couple minutes more before I rose and said good-bye. Once again, neither of us extended our hands.

At least he didn't actually ask me to leave, which is the most I could have hoped for from our first meeting. He had no reason to invite anyone into his space, neither into the light nor the dark. It was the latter he possessed the most of—something I knew better than anyone.

When I visited him the following week, I mentioned the book again.

It sat between us on the bench once more, almost as if he were teasing me, and this time he didn't move it.

He was wearing faded brown Wranglers and a green windbreaker that stretched to the middle of his thighs, enveloping him like a shield, with only his head protruding from the fur collar.

"It's a really beautiful cover," I said, without looking down.

His left eye, the one closest to me, twitched slightly. His gaze held, unwavering, straight toward the horizon, out across the ocean.

"Where is it from?" My boldest volley yet.

He straightened a bit, for once his back and shoulders no longer resting on the lighthouse's wall. I could see how hard he was struggling to keep his hands, folded on his lap, completely still. He had no way of knowing that I was more familiar than most with these outward signs of a person's inner idiosyncrasies, with all the uncontrollable tics and involuntary movements we carry throughout life. Right then, despite decades of training and all his cleverness, Viggo Larssen was having difficulty hiding them.

Then he shrugged his shoulders and spoke for the first time: "It's just a journal . . . an old journal from the Spanish Civil War." His left eye had blinked significantly at the word *old*, and I realized that his childhood tics had returned, as if they had never gone away.

"It's nothing," he added, stressing the last word slightly.

I turned and looked at him. My curiosity must have crawled out to the tip of my tongue, where it floated into the air as a tall, but unusually insistent, question mark—and nothing else. As a child I had learned that this form of silence, a kind of wordless exclamation, was the best means of opening adults up. The twitching around his left eye became even stronger, traveling down his cheek. I could have cried for him right then, merely because of that detail, but naturally that would have destroyed any advantage I had just gained.

Standing, he abruptly shoved the book inside his jacket, within a hidden pocket that appeared just large enough to hold it. "It's about a time . . . very long ago," he said. It was a remark that could mean everything—and nothing.

I looked out over the ocean. It didn't matter. My patience was boundless. I didn't know why he was fascinated with the green book. I didn't even know who had written it, but it was clear that I shouldn't underestimate its meaning to him—and thus to the problem I had come to the Lighthouse to solve.

I also stood up, then walked back through the woods. I slipped and almost skidded down the long hill, through the Giant's Footprint, before continuing back up the steep, crumbling slope to the Sea Witch's house.

If he wouldn't willingly open the door to his precious treasure, I would have to find another way in; as always, my curiosity would make its way through whatever barriers anyone might set before me.

***

The day the Widow disappeared, three months had passed since our first meeting. I had lived on the cape for half the winter yet had gotten no closer to him.

My house was still standing, and it creaked and groaned as if demonstrating that it still had some life left before its inevitable and final collapse. On a shelf in the living room, I unearthed an old book, bearing the date *1878* in gold-stamped letters, in which a long-dead poet had written about a legend known by everyone on Røsnæs. According to tradition, King Valdemar the Conqueror's son, while on a hunting expedition in the year 1231, was killed by a stray arrow. Afterward, in a fit of uncontrollable rage, the king ordered all the trees on the cape burned down to the ground: not one trunk, or stump, or even the smallest branch or twig should ever cast its shadow on that cursed ground.

> Where once a Royal Child
> In the Cape's Woods, on a Barrow,
> Fell suddenly into Death's trap
> From an Archer's errant Arrow,
> Now shall Denmark's Children
> Safely, freely run,
> Behind Refsnæs' thorns and thickets
> Laughing in the Sun!

It struck me as a bit pompous—plus, I'd never thought of children so clearly laughing because of what adults do. On the contrary. Children laugh for reasons adults don't understand, because they live in a world adults can never see.

I replaced the book on the shelf. When the time came, it would fall into the sea, along with the house.

That night I had the feeling I was being watched by unknown eyes deep inside the woodsy thicket; yet, when I opened the door and listened, I heard only the sound of the wind in the treetops and the surf pounding the coast. Several times since my arrival at the Sea Witch's house, I had seen a fox crouching in the dense thicket, but on a night like tonight, it would certainly rather take cover in its deep hole.

I closed the door to the darkness, but I didn't lock it; no demon was going to prevent me from carrying out the plan that had led me to this house in the woods, to the cape, and to the man in the tower.

I tensed the muscles in my lopsided shoulders and shook away my fear. My task had become no less interesting because of the information streaming out of the radio since early this morning, filling all the news programs.

The strike against the Cave Bear's otherwise invincible clan.

***

Office of the Homicide Boss
Friday, January 2, morning

The Homicide Boss turned toward his Number Two, both men appearing to be listening for unspoken words, which—if interpreted correctly—could possibly solve the mystery that lay before them.

They had temporarily silenced their iPhones. They both knew that once they turned them back on the insistent stream of urgent calls would mean only one thing: they were up to their necks in their most difficult case.

That the country's Grand Old Lady could disappear for as much as an hour was dramatic, two hours was shocking, and more than half a day constituted an all-out sensation.

"Nothing . . . significant."

Number Two shook his head. The evidence technicians had learned nothing from examining the old folder. Not that they had seriously expected to find anything.

And yet.

They had discovered a little yellow slip of paper, glued to the inside cover, with a date written on it—completely commonplace and yet inexplicable. That slip was now lying inside a clear plastic evidence bag on the desk in front of the Homicide Boss.

"Why would anyone . . ." The Homicide Boss stopped and stared at the date on the note.

Number Two could have easily finished the thought but remained quiet.

"So, the will is missing . . . and instead there's a note with the date on it, which—"

"—makes no sense." This time Number Two completed his boss's thought.

"A date that is—"

"—more than four decades old, although analysis shows that . . ."

"—it was written recently . . . with a blue ballpoint pen."

That last observation hung quietly in the air.

The Homicide Boss held the strange discovery up to the light, as if the sun's first rays could provide an answer.

"Why would anyone write down such an old date and place it in her folder?" he said.

He continued in an even more hesitant tone, "There's something *strange* about it . . ."

"Yes, but perhaps all of us are strange," said Number Two, noticing the uncharacteristic hesitation coming from the man he admired so unconditionally. "We're born strange . . . and we die strange."

That was more philosophic than anything the Homicide Boss had ever heard from the otherwise down-to-earth man. He glanced cautiously at him and replied, "If we're all strange, then that would be the norm. Unfortunately, I think—no, I can *sense*—that this case involves something we've never encountered before. That's what I'm feeling. That we don't know the half of it yet. Indeed, maybe we know nothing at all."

His second in command kept silent, and that said it all.

He felt exactly the same way.

***

The Lighthouse on the Cape
Autumn 2014

My little house had obviously been empty for a long time, and the old woman with the curious nickname had let me move in without asking for anything more than four months' rent in advance.

I didn't have to answer any nosy questions, produce any papers, or offer any explanation for my sudden urge to live on top of a cliff with a steep drop to the shore below. She didn't care who I was—or how I had stumbled upon the tiny sign at the end of the gravel road, next to the tourist parking area, that read "House for Rent"—written in an old woman's almost illegible hand.

My new home was only just large enough for two wood elves to have lived there in luxury. The peeling red plaster around the sunken window frames indicated that no one had shown any interest in this place for decades.

Inside, the living room was furnished with an old table and a few chairs of indeterminate wood species. To someone who grew up surrounded by fine antique dressers and bureaus, it might have seemed spartan, but not to me.

My first night in the house, I turned around completely three times, feeling satisfied with the space. I was sitting on the old woman's furniture, sleeping in her bed, drinking water out of a faucet that frequently sputtered and gurgled, with a view between the trees, up toward the hill and the Lighthouse, where the purpose of my journey lay. Sometimes I would spot a red-brown shadow between the craggy branches, indicating that the fox was on the hunt. I recalled a tale from one of my childhood homes about a fox that spoke to a boy about invisibility and friendship—right before my foster mother determinedly threw the book out. She had no use for false dreams that might influence the budding destinies she was protecting against all evil until they could encounter life without any fear of going astray.

The second time I visited the Daily Market in Ulstrup, I asked the manager about my gnarly old landlady, and he said she had inherited the red house when her parents had died. Her parents, who'd built the house, had lived there all their lives. If I wanted to find the Sea Witch, I simply had to walk across the street to the cemetery, where she sat so often that almost no one could remember having visited their parents' graves without bumping into her there.

And sure enough, there sat my landlady, bony and hunched over, dressed totally in black, sitting on a little stone bench right across from two black gravestones. In the late winter sunlight, a red glow fell across her neck and shoulders; in a way, it was a beautiful sight, although it also disturbed me. She sat just as motionless as Viggo had, and I got the same feeling from her presence that I had gotten from his: that she seemed to be waiting for something that she'd hidden scrupulously from the world around her.

Back in my lopsided house, I turned my attention once again to that mystical journal he had been reading—first questioning myself, then firmly making my decision. I realized that there was no other way.

Every afternoon, at the same time, Viggo Larssen left his lonely tower, walked down the crooked stairs to the shore, and wandered along the water toward the cliff. It was a difficult trek, rocky and uneven. He stopped to rest frequently and was often gone for a couple of hours, sometimes even longer.

Before he left, he would place the key to the lighthouse door under a tuft of moss in the front yard, a safe place only if you're naïve. It was a breeze for me to spot his hiding place through the powerful binoculars I had brought with me to the cape (and that I'd had all my life), and to uncover the large rusty key.

The small green leather-bound book was lying on a chair just inside the door.

I opened it with reverence, with anticipation, soon replaced by disappointment.

The journal, as Viggo had called it, contained no author's name, only about fifty handwritten pages written over the course of a few weeks, while the writer—apparently a young Dane—was traveling south to join the International Brigades during the Spanish Civil War. It was decades old.

The first entry was from Esbjerg, dated June 18, 1938, when the young volunteer boarded a ship for Antwerp along with a friend. From there, they traveled by foot through Europe, and I leafed impatiently through descriptions of landscapes, villages, mills, rivers, and hostels. By the end of the journal, the writer had almost made it down to Basque country. None of it struck me as particularly interesting, and I couldn't understand why Viggo read all of it so carefully, again and again.

I sighed and studied the few pieces of furniture in Viggo's living room: a small round table, shoved up against the window, and a black easy chair with rips in its shiny, worn leather. A vintage transistor radio rested on a low coffee table. In its own way it was as dreary and bland as the descriptions in the journal.

On the next to the last handwritten page, the young journal writer finally made it to the front. It was in July 1938, at the Ebro River, where the International Brigades were involved in a large attack on the fascists, but apparently he never managed to fire a shot, as his last lines described nothing but a very strange dream, which I read somewhat impatiently before setting aside the book.

The abrupt ending and the remaining blank white pages might indicate that the soldier had been grabbed by the enemy after his final entry about the dream. Perhaps he had fallen in battle on a remote Spanish hillside.

I found no explanation for how the book had come into Viggo's possession or why he found it so interesting that he had brought it here, to this place near the end of the world, as his only reading material. I just couldn't understand it. Not then.

Of course, I had overlooked one small detail, one that I discovered months later, to my great horror—one which the man in the Lighthouse, my friend Viggo Larssen, son of a long-dead single mother who had been buried one sunny summer day in a cemetery in Søborg, had not.

And that was my first big mistake.

***

Office of the Prime Minister
Friday morning, January 2

The Homicide Boss's call was transferred to Palle Blegman via his permanent undersecretary, a tall, somewhat lanky man who, rumor had it, had been a relatively aggressive, highly ranked socialist in his more youthful days, but who now belonged among the realm's most powerful and loyal men.

If a more recent rumor were true, he was also a member of the Tårbæk Club, an almost- mythical exclusive organization for the highest-ranking government officials—both old and new.

"Did you ever notice if your mother had a piece of yellow material lying around?" The Homicide Boss had cut straight to the chase. "In her house—or at the nursing home?"

There was a pause of several seconds, then the Bear's voice was cautious when he answered in the form of another question: "A piece of yellow material?"

"Plastic," said the Homicide Boss. "Old, torn. With some dark spots on it. From what, we don't know."

The next pause lasted even longer. "No."

"We've found some things, but it's too early to say whether they . . ." The Homicide Boss let the sentence fade into the air.

"What did you say?"

"Nothing." The Homicide Boss could hear that his answer sounded absurd.

Nothing was not a concept found at this level.

***

The Lighthouse on the Cape
late autumn 2014

The second time I snuck into the Lighthouse, I was determined to read the book as thoroughly as possible. There had to be an explanation *somewhere* for Viggo's almost obsessive protection of his treasure. There was something in that book that the rest of the world wasn't supposed to see—after a day's worth of speculation, I was totally convinced of that—I just couldn't figure out what it could be.

Nevertheless, I sensed that it could be of utmost importance to the mission I had come to the cape to carry out, and I had time—lots of time, or so I had naïvely believed. This was two months before the Widow's disappearance.

Once again, he had gone on his solitary walk to the cliff, but to my great irritation, the book was not on the chair. Indeed, I couldn't find it anywhere. A narrow bookcase on the opposite wall had maybe fifty books on it, and I spent a good fifteen minutes skimming their titles. There were several books about journalism and the media; a series of older, vaguely familiar Swedish crime novels; and a cookbook about mussels that must have been here when he arrived. Personally, I never cared for seafood. The Spanish journal was not there.

For a moment I stood there, hesitating, while I stared at the door to the next room; then I let my curiosity push all concerns aside, and I opened the door with a firm push.

To the right, under a small window, was an unmade bed. Half of the comforter was lying on the floor, spilling out of the duvet cover, and I couldn't see a pillow anywhere. I could not fall asleep without a pillow under my crooked skull, which my foster mother had always told me looked shrunken.

To the left, just inside the door, was a wooden shelf, painted blue and fastened to the wall with sturdy brackets: it held a portable electric typewriter, the kind considered modern in the seventies. A piece of paper was hanging halfway out of the roller.

I stepped closer, leaning over a beaten-up desk chair with a frayed gray seat. He had written only five words, at the very top of the page, and they provided just as little meaning as the Spanish journal with its long-winded travel and nature descriptions: *My mother and the canary.*

It was like the beginning of a childhood diary. My only source from that time told me that the man in the Lighthouse had fled the city to take control of his life and to write down everything that had pained and tormented him. She also told me that he bore a mysterious story, one he had never shared with anyone. A secret that could explain his lifelong shyness.

Then I spied a trash bag under the table, in which there were some ten-odd crumpled pieces of typewriter paper. A couple of them had been torn in half—as if in irritation over incomplete thoughts.

I placed the first of the torn pages on the table and smoothed it out. Once again, only two words had been written on it, providing as little meaning as the others: *The tricycle.*

I placed all the pages on the table, but none of his aborted writing attempts offered any insight.

My grandfather appeared on one of them. Once again, only two words.

So I turned toward the bed, which was no more than an arm's width and certainly not intended for visitors or a restless sleeper. I lifted the comforter off the floor, the result of a long-ingrained and now-routine sense of tidiness, which irritated me but which I knew I could never escape.

To my surprise, the move revealed a small three-legged stool that seemed to function as a nightstand. On it lay a single book: a small, very old copy of *The Little Prince*—the tale of the pilot who meets a boy from another planet after they both crash-land in the desert and become friends with a fox.

I opened it with the fingers that had rummaged through countless other hiding places and found what I expected. A handwritten inscription: *To my own boy, Viggo, August 31, 1963.*

Personal yet also quite formal. From his mother.

On one of the first pages, she (or so I assumed) had circled the passage in which the author mourns that his very first childhood drawing—of an elephant being swallowed by a boa constrictor—had never been understood by others.

I understood that better than anyone. The snake had swallowed an elephant, but everyone thought they were looking at the drawing of a hat.

For a moment, it softened my mental image of the woman who had given Viggo the book. Otherwise, my opinion of adults is rarely warm and fuzzy.

As I placed the book back on the stool, some invisible hand—or maybe a sixth sense—nudged the bedroom door back toward the door frame, revealing a small cabinet hanging on the wall behind it. When the door stood open, the cabinet was completely hidden, making it impossible to see from outside the little window over his bed.

Behind the cabinet's glass door were three shelves. A large, thick red book sat on each shelf, each with the same title, leaving no doubt about what I had found: *My Diary*—embossed in gold letters—followed by Viggo's mother's initials.

The book on the uppermost shelf was dated in gold lettering: *1955–1964.*

On shelf number two, the dates read: *1964–1970.*

And on the bottom shelf: *1970–.*

No final year had been engraved on that cover.

That book would remain unfinished, which I knew better than anyone, and I hardly even blinked before grabbing the little brass handle and trying to pry open the door.

It was locked securely.

I searched for almost twenty minutes for a hiding place for the key—a drawer, a box, a crack in the wall. Beneath the lighthouse steps was a blue dresser, but there was only a pair of pants, along with some shirts, tossed inside the drawers. I even went into the lighthouse tower and up the steep spiral staircase, which made me a bit dizzy but no less impatient.

He must have the key on him.

I didn't sleep well that night. And, of course, I went back the next day.

As soon as Viggo had left the house and was nothing more than a tiny spot on the shoreline, I let myself in. That pattern repeated itself throughout the ensuing weeks, while autumn turned to winter. I always left the lighthouse master's small residence in the same condition, so he would never have even the slightest suspicion that he'd had an unexpected visitor. At least that's what I believed at the time. Also, as I said, Viggo Larssen was punctual in a way—even though he had abandoned everything else.

At one point I tried to pry open the glass cabinet with a thin knife, but to no avail.

I left some small scratch marks in the wood around the keyhole, just like the ones my foster mother had found once on a bureau drawer after I rummaged through her belongings, but I didn't think Viggo had her powerful sense of intuition about those things. He'd never notice.

Every day, I sat down in his chair and read the new sentences that showed up on the roller of the old Olympia typewriter, without ever noticing anything of interest. *First day of school. Ove, Adda, Verner, and Teis.*

Names from his past. I knew some of the families in the cul-de-sac, but that was long after the five friends had lived there. They were born several years before me.

It seemed as if he couldn't come up with a single word past that first line, as if as soon as he shoved the roller to the next line, all contact between his hands and the keys was broken and he had to give up.

I leafed through the old copy of *The Little Prince* and took note of the places Viggo's mother had circled in pencil. Maybe she was thinking about Viggo (or maybe only about herself) or (it suddenly occurred to me) maybe about her own mother: the little prince must tame the fox if he wants to play with him.

I understood the reference. There was a fox living on the slope beneath my bedroom window.

My foster mother didn't care for fairy tales. She loved only a few children's songs whose choruses involved straightforward lessons: marching across an abyss while maintaining one's balance—and for God's sake, not looking down.

Her favorite song about elephants caught in a spider's web had countless verses.

On the first of December, the Spanish journal was lying on the chair just inside the door to the lighthouse. My relief was indescribable, because I was beginning to fear that he was taking the mysterious writing with him on his daily walks as a precaution.

I sat next to Viggo's desk, with its peeling blue paint, and read the first twenty pages again, slowly, thoroughly. The young journal writer was traveling with a Danish friend, and among the handwritten entries the two adventurers had placed small pieces of paper, postcards, stamps, and point-of-entry stamps that they must have cajoled out of border guards. They had made a two-day stop in Paris, and next to a line drawing of the Seine there was a long passage about the people they met there.

Along with a German and a Czech, we went for a walk in the
city. In the evening we walked up to Montmartre, where we
met all our friends from the hostel: Americans, Australians,

*Danes, Swiss, Germans, Frenchmen, my friend Kalle from
Helsingborg.*

I studied the meaningless passages for at least another half hour,
then put the book back exactly as I had found it, long before Viggo's
frail figure would appear on the horizon on his walk home.

Despite the daily break-ins—and my renewed reading—I still
didn't understand what was so terribly important to him about the
little book. The eager volunteer for Spain wrote about his final dream,
which read more like a delirium he'd had just before the battle by the
Ebro River, where it was also thought that the young writer Gustaf
Munch-Petersen had fallen. As did many other Danes.

The description of the vision filled the last half page before the
writing stopped inexplicably: *It is the most frightening and ominous sight
I have ever experienced,* he wrote in the last line. I wasn't surprised that
the soldier had nightmares about confronting the Devil himself in the
figure of the Generalissimo, who had wiped out all that era's young
heroes in his dark crusade.

In the middle of the book was a lined piece of paper with a slightly
clumsy rhyming poem handwritten in pencil, but since it wasn't written
in the young man's handwriting, I put it back impatiently. I left the book
on the chair once and for all. I simply couldn't figure out its importance.

***

*Office of the Homicide Boss
Friday, January 2, around noon*

By the second day of the Widow's disappearance, bloggers and tweeters
and anyone else with an opinion—including news commentators and
editorial columnists—had already questioned the quality of the police's
investigation. Wasn't it going much too slowly?

Wasn't there any news they could elaborate, exaggerate, or otherwise comment on?

And was Homicide really the right venue for such a delicate case? They needed to establish a task force; indeed, that very word had a calming effect.

The Widow with the famous Blegman name, the head of that dynasty, was gone. That was the only thing that mattered.

None of the media outlets were pulling any punches. None of the media displayed any empathy for the police; they all demanded action and immediate results. Exclamation points riddled all of the press's calls and accusations; journalists rattled the doors to the police chief's office. Every single editor let their criminal reporters crack the whip over the Homicide Boss's head. In this case they were all, regardless of political affiliation, on the side of the Blegman dynasty. It had a unifying effect on the nation.

There was no sign of anything at all abnormal in the Widow's apartment at Solbygaard Nursing Home, wrote the news agency Ritzau, making a point about the poor police work by adding: *or so say the police.*

The two lead investigators didn't counter the accusation.

Seen superficially, it was indeed true. At first everything appeared completely normal. And yet it wasn't.

The prime minister and the minister of justice found their mother's two rooms gapingly empty and sounded the alarm with all the efficiency and discretion that define the Blegman dynasty's two renowned sons, wrote the bureau, in something resembling royal reverence.

She vanished into thin air, wrote the daily *Berlingske Tidende* quite simply.

No clues in the case, proclaimed three of the leading national newspapers, all owned by the same publisher. Of course, that wasn't true. The two officers were at their wits' ends by the thirtieth time they'd examined the three slightly peculiar clues they did have, none of which seemed to provide any insight. The two yellow pieces of plastic, the (almost) empty folder in which there should have been a will, the slip of paper with a date they didn't understand: these three small things, which individually seemed meaningless, taken together made them uneasy. There was no reason to believe that the public could do any better—and if the odd findings really held any meaning, public disclosure might harm the investigation and their hunt for the beast (the Homicide Boss refused to use a milder term).

Only one person also knew about their strange findings—and that was whoever was there when the Widow disappeared.

On the desk between the two policemen lay a brochure, created by a management firm north of Copenhagen, with the title *Solbygaard—Life at Its Best*. The Homicide Boss shook his head irritably. As if anyone in the twilight of their life would be thinking about sunshine in such a lifeless place, which in no way reminded him of the farm where he had grown up, in eastern Jutland.

According to the nursing home manager's statement, she'd hired a professional branding and management consultant to update all of the home's "internal and external workflow to better benefit the elderly," all of which was outlined in the brochure. The Homicide Boss had seen evidence of this from the first time he walked the area. The lawn between the nursing home's tall gray buildings had been filled with bars and hoops and chalk lines, evidence of a new training program that promised to bring "pep to both the staff and the elderly," as the manager put it. More likely to tire the oldest residents to death, thought the Homicide Boss, but no surprise for a municipal facility like the home. When forming their government, the Blegman brothers had promised a thorough cleanup of bureaucracy at both the state and municipal levels, but inexplicably, the cleanup only led to a slew of new agencies and functions just as burdensome as those already in place.

That the two conservative front-runners had won governmental power in 2011, at the head of an otherwise deeply ailing party, had come as a gigantic surprise. It happened only because the two largest parties on both the right and the left had lost the threads tying together a government, and so the vote went to the Blegman dynasty, with its almost mythical status.

The Homicide Boss took another look at the nursing home's brochure and repressed a snort, a sound not usually heard in his office.

Then he looked back at the brown folder and the little yellow piece of paper with the date on it, which the police had failed to get any information from, and which no one could explain.

There was no will, which was alarming given the nursing home's careful record-keeping. Plus, the Widow had mentioned the existence of a will several times, and her lawyer revealed that it had been delivered from his office in the summer of 2014 because she wanted to make a new one.

The lawyer hadn't seen it since.

She could have written a new one and placed it in her dresser drawer—that was the only plausible theory given the title on the empty folder—but if so, what happened to it?

And, as Number Two remarked, why hadn't she locked the drawer?

In the Homicide Boss's preferred words these days, it was all very strange.

CHAPTER 2

The Lighthouse on the Cape
Friday, January 2, early afternoon

The five typewritten lines looked like black strokes running across the white paper. He had never written so many words in a row before once again tearing the paper out of the typewriter and crumpling it up.

This was the day after the Widow's disappearance and the subsequent hysteria.

I picked up the paper and smoothed it out; it looked like the beginning of a letter:

> *Dear friend,*
> *It has been a long time. I think the current events in Copenhagen (regarding the Widow Blegman's disappearance) made me think of you. You probably remember her, and we both certainly remember her two sons. For a long time I have been trying to tell a story so strange*

that I haven't known exactly how to begin. That's why
I am asking you for advice. My story is about Death.
It began in Søborg when we were children. Right after
Arrow's death.

It seemed as if the second appearance of the word *death* had been too much for the man in the Lighthouse, since he then abandoned the letter.

I looked around. No other pieces of paper were lying about. I had no way of knowing if he had finished the next version or if he had given up on the endeavor entirely.

I couldn't understand the connection between the Widow's disappearance and a long-ago death, yet there was no further explanation. *My story is about Death. It began in Søborg when we were children. Right after Arrow's death.*

Once I had read those lines for the third time, I finally understood that Viggo had changed tactics—if you could refer to his numerous crumpled-up pieces of paper as a strategy—and abandoned his time-consuming attempts at depicting an obviously important childhood event. The letter form showed that Viggo Larssen had decided to share his thoughts with someone he trusted, and naturally that was not going to be me.

I replaced the paper where he'd tossed it. I felt like I knew the lines by heart.

As usual, before I left the Lighthouse, I gave my routine tug on the handle of the glass cabinet door guarding the three red books that bore his mother's initials. And as usual, it didn't move an inch.

Once home, I turned on the radio. On this Friday afternoon the nation was still momentarily obsessed with the Widow Blegman's disappearance into thin air, as if she had ascended into heaven—which many thought was the wrong direction in the afterlife for any member of the Blegman dynasty (although they wouldn't dare say so out loud).

Restless, I listened to the news reports, then a little later I left the Sea Witch's house and half ran, half slid down the wet, rocky hillside, through the crooked branches, down to the hollow where nothing remained except the half-white birch trunk. From there it was only a short way up to the topmost shrubbery, where I could watch the Lighthouse unseen by its resident and make sure that he was home and not doing anything that I ought to know about.

I suddenly had a premonition that I couldn't explain, and naturally it had something to do with the most recent lines he had typewritten.

Maybe I could sneak a little closer at dusk and venture a peek in the window. I had to know if he was continuing to write that mysterious letter.

Just then, the lighthouse door opened. I froze, and then slowly slunk back into my hiding place. The little I knew about my shy neighbor as an adult I'd heard secondhand or read on the Internet. He had been a journalist for a grassroots magazine and later for the Danish Broadcasting Corporation. He'd had a nervous breakdown—what the journalists in his social circle called *burnout syndrome* (many of them had quietly burned themselves out)—yet he had continued working, caught in a deadly blend of pills and booze and unfinished work, until he collapsed and was placed on disability.

It struck me yet again that I had never seen the strange man on the bench with any texts other than the old book from the Spanish Civil War. And he had never left the Lighthouse twice in the same day.

Now, he was walking my way, carrying a medium-size envelope. I barely managed to sink behind a broom bush as he walked by, heading in the direction of the woods and the road leading to Ulstrup.

I pulled my binoculars out of their worn case, which was always hanging from my belt, and studied him.

Through the strong lenses I could make out both a stamp and the fuzzy form of a handwritten name and address.

There had been an uncharacteristic sense of purpose in his stride down the gravel path, then past me into the woods; his expression also struck me as different than usual. In the previous days and weeks, he had held the world at bay by staring across the ocean with that distant look and those half-closed eyes. Now they were wide open and fixed on the path that led through the dense woods, toward Ulstrup and, I assumed, toward the mailbox hanging on the wall of the market.

I almost felt an absurd attack of unadulterated jealousy at the sight of the envelope. He wended his way through the woods and headed east. And I was right behind him.

The entire trip took almost an hour and fifteen minutes, with me constantly trying to avoid being seen should he suddenly stop and turn around. He didn't.

He stood motionless for a moment at the mailbox, then he mailed the letter, turned on his heel, and walked back toward the Lighthouse.

I stood there for a long time; I even considered finding a tool strong enough to break open the mailbox. It wasn't misplaced ethics or other nerves that held me back. In some way I sensed that the letter should continue on its journey, which evoked in me a feeling so strong that it overcame my curiosity.

Although I couldn't explain my reaction, I had no more doubts. The letter should be read by whomever Viggo Larssen was thinking about when he wrote it.

***

Back at the Lighthouse, the man sat on the bench and rested his back against the wall. He looked like he'd returned home after a long day's work, exhausted but satisfied with his effort. He fetched a bottle of wine and poured himself a glass, then stayed seated, completely still. As I watched him through my binoculars, it occurred to me that I had never seen him like this before.

Toward evening he got up, walked back into the small house, and closed the door behind him. I wanted to warn him of my sense of impending disaster, but that would have been in bad taste.

I turned on my flashlight and wandered back to my wobbly haunted house, which would undoubtedly fall into the deep during the next big storm. That night I could hear the breakers on the reef and the wind in the treetops, and I could almost sense the fox's watchful eye from the hollow the Sea Witch's forest hid so well.

Maybe that's the real meaning of life—that the world's oddballs must find each other. That's what my only true friend (long since dead) had once said to me.

People like us have no language, we have no room where we can share our hard-won experiences, and so we meet in silence—nowhere.

She'd always laughed so hard that her crooked limbs would dangle over the armrests on her rusted wheelchair. She often spoke in riddles. Still, what she said made sense to even the loneliest child—which I should well know.

That evening, I should have sensed what was to come of the tale that Viggo had carried to the mailbox in Ulstrup. Only later did I easily count fifty years since Viggo Larssen had first had the dream that he called *the Omen*, an eternity over the course of a human life.

Actually, as I realized later, there was only one odd thing about his decision to wait so long to share his revelation with the world, a revelation he must have believed had the power to shake a society down to its very foundation: Why was Teis, the awkward, fat boy who also foundered late in life, the one Viggo Larssen had chosen to share the first glimpse into the world he had hidden for so long?

***

Teis from Søborg
Saturday, January 3, at noon

Teis Hanson leaned back and closed his eyes. His arthritis was always worse when something was bothering him, especially in the arm that had been partially paralyzed since high school.

In another lifetime, on such a mild winter day, he might be enjoying lunch at home with his wife and young children, basking in the light of yet another award for his research—maybe even a Nobel Prize.

It shouldn't have seemed like such a far-fetched idea.

The wide antique armchair had been placed precisely between the floor lamp and the north-facing window. He'd lived in that third-floor condominium since he began his medical studies at the University of Copenhagen in the mid-1970s. Below lay Gothersgade, its far eastern end boring directly into the square known as Kongens Nytorv, the heart of the city.

His parents, both schoolteachers, had bought the apartment for him because they wanted their son to concentrate fully on his academic endeavors. They intended for him to be the first in their family to win prestigious awards, renown, fame—maybe even a Nobel Prize. Back then, with a little good will, such dreams could be fostered in children, even in the dining room of a schoolteacher's modest row house. And though little Teis had been shy and a tad eccentric, he was a budding genius, or so his parents believed. And his parents had supported his choices with a tenacity that refused to leave their son's happiness to chance.

Now they were dead, and nothing seemed as it once did.

Still, he had pursued his life's greatest academic challenge: the exploration of human heredity and the double helix of DNA, with its marvelous codes for all living things on earth, which had turned into human genome research and a teeming host of miraculous new medical advancements.

If any path could lead straight to science's holy grail, he believed that was it.

Today, Teis would call his choice the gold rush of science. All kinds of social climbers and self-promoters had overrun the field; also, his department funding had lessened as the years passed, until the new conservative government cut his research unit—then finally the entire department. The Blegman government had slain him with one fell stroke of the pen. Today, the founders of modern genetics, like Watson and Crick, were nothing but shadows in his faded dreams of greatness. He had been sent packing. The strange and rare illnesses he had researched were filed in binders and folders and packed into boxes, to be stored in a university basement, where a stray spider—or another eccentric scientist—might one day discover them.

Fortunately, his parents had died by the time his lifelong dreams had been extinguished, and since he only believed in matter and molecules, he figured that he wasn't being observed (or reproached) from above.

In his forty-fourth year, Teis Hanson became single when his girlfriend since college vanished without warning or any word of farewell. She hadn't taken anything with her when she disappeared, other than the clothes on her back. The police had said there wasn't anything unusual about vanishing that way. If people become unbearably tired of their life partners, some of them prefer to simply leave everything behind. They erase themselves, so to speak.

They refused to even search for her.

He ransacked the apartment, looking for a good-bye letter, but he had never found so much as a torn piece of paper in all those dozen-plus years since she left. Sometimes the impulse would return, and he'd spend an entire Saturday afternoon searching, but with less and less enthusiasm as each year passed. He thought that time would eventually soften his loss, as would the microbiological mechanisms he had researched in his glory days.

They'd never had children, and now he was sitting in his massive easy chair and staring at a mysterious letter with no return address. He wrinkled his eyebrows, which were pronounced and steel gray, as befitted any Nobel laureate.

The letter seemed almost surreal. His name was on the front, *Teis Hanson*, and both the name and address were written in cursive that was neither attractive nor particularly consistent.

He didn't know anyone who would send him a private letter. Still, it must be someone who knew him well, because most people still made the mistake of spelling it *Hansen* with an *e*—as if the *o* were a spelling error, or the remnant of some long-lost Swedish ancestor.

That had always irritated him.

He turned the letter over, checking for any clue the sender might have left, then split it open with the fine whalebone knife from Greenland his girlfriend had given him their last Christmas together, right before the millennium. He had no idea that she had any interest in Greenland.

The first page was dated yesterday, January 2, and he read the beginning, perplexed.

> *My dear friend. It has been a long time. I'm writing to you because something strange has happened. The events in Copenhagen—the disappearance of Widow Blegman—and my discoveries as a fifteen-year-old and in the years that followed—are somehow connected. I don't fully understand the connection, but I am certain it must exist. Something happened that I never told anyone about . . .*

Teis hesitated and then turned the page over before he continued reading.

Søborg . . .

This was not just a letter from a distant friend—it was a message that would remind him of a past he didn't always want to remember.

Viggo Larssen . . .

. . . standing at the end of the road, by the hawthorn bush, with his jug ears and weird tics on either side of his face; at times they tugged at his eyes or pulled an entire eyebrow out of shape.

A strange boy, the grown-ups would say.

Teis Hanson returned to the first few lines, scanning the text skeptically with scrutinizing slowness.

Once again he wrinkled his gray eyebrows, his high forehead furrowing. What in the world had his old friend from the neighborhood been thinking with this peculiar story?

He would like to have shown someone else the letter, especially his mother, but Alice Hanson was long since dead (no genetic miracle had been able to prevent her lung cancer), and there was no one else he could ask. His old colleagues had turned their backs on him when the media tagged him "the leading conspiracy theorist" for defending the theory that the American government had been involved in the terror attack of September 11—the real reason the Twin Towers had collapsed into rubble. The nickname had erected an invisible but impregnable wall around him. No one understood how a once-renowned genetic researcher could support a theory ascribing responsibility for 9/11 to the former American president. It was as if the scientist, at the end of his career, had used the supernatural and the inexplicable as some childish response to all of his career disappointments. No Nobel Prize, only mysterious theses about crumbling towers and flying saucers. His colleagues had thought that perhaps an incipient senility had made him turn to the unknown.

Of course, even for a scientist raised on chemistry, biology, and physics, it was true that sudden revelations could turn out to be correct. Just look at Einstein's theory of relativity, which had upended everything. Even so, Teis Hanson felt almost physically ill while reading the bizarre three-page letter, in which his childhood friend set forth a single (horrible) thesis, resting on a foundation that the aging scientist barely understood.

The theory was truly unpleasant, and no one would want it to be true; it would alter people's lives forever.

For some reason Teis Hanson blushed a faintly disturbing hue, like a piece of clothing that has been washed on the wrong setting.

He could see his friend, small and a bit hunched over, because shyness often made him collapse into a defensive position, as if longing for invisibility.

Maybe it was his attachment to the peculiar grandparents whom Viggo and his mother had lived with that had caused that effect.

Or maybe it was the death he had been exposed to early in life, far too early. Teis recalled glimpses of events that had changed life in the neighborhood and that he never wanted to experience again, or even remember.

He had seen Viggo Larssen's strange fall onto the stone steps, his blood on the white flagstone, adults kneeling by his side.

He had also seen little Arrow in his torn raincoat before they carried him away. He had seen the red stains on the asphalt and heard Mrs. Blegman screaming by the open gate.

The third catastrophe occurred without warning—not even the creaking sound of a gate's hinges could have warned Viggo Larssen of Destiny's blow. He was simply struck down.

Understandably, he hadn't gone outside for three weeks afterward. No one had ever experienced anything even remotely similar, and no one (except maybe Palle and his equally malevolent little brother) would wish it on anyone. Those three brutal events had undoubtedly made the lonely boy a bit crazy.

And now, the densely written page Teis Hanson was holding in his hand seemed to prove it.

He could see Viggo Larssen before him once again. Those blue, blue eyes that betrayed everyone and everything, not maliciously, but because they had to hide the peculiarities jostling around in what the adults would call his soul.

Teis Hanson read the letter for the third time and then set it aside.

Somehow, a strange child must attract strange happenings. That assertion was totally unscientific, as was the theory about the Twin Towers. Yet, he thought, that's the way it was in both cases.

He closed his eyes, and his mind drifted back to memories of his childhood . . .

It's not God who determines where we grow up. No, God simply plants three blocks of red row houses and lets mortals move in.

Viggo and Verner. He could picture them.

Ove and Agnes. Who lived today in luxury up near Dyrehaven. God and Satan under the same roof. He almost laughed out loud, which he hadn't done in a long time.

Everyone grows up with peculiarities they fear someone will see. But his life had never forced him to the extreme, into life's darkest corners.

Very few get to avoid that, so maybe he had been lucky after all.

***

Office of the Homicide Boss
Saturday, January 3, a little after noon

Yet another day had begun badly for the Homicide Boss. It was day three following the Widow's sudden and absurd disappearance from the upscale nursing home in Gentofte.

The telephones had been ringing off the hook all morning for his industrious band of detectives and their assistants, yet not a single piece of information had led to anything other than frustration.

Looking at his deputy, Number Two, he felt momentary relief that he shared his office with this man who rarely said anything—and almost nothing unsolicited unless it was of the utmost importance.

So when he did speak, the Homicide Boss listened intently.

"This is a story in two acts. Each with its own headline." Two unsolicited sentences in a row, an almost superhuman amount coming from Number Two. Then he added a third: "And we've only gotten the first act—at the crime scene—so we're still waiting on the second."

The Homicide Boss started to tilt his head to the side but stopped himself. He didn't want to look like a character in a bad novel—or even worse: a police boss in some TV drama. "You mean—the discovery of—?"

Number Two nodded. Yes, the discovery of the *Widow*.

First thing that morning, the two detectives had gotten a message from their two bosses that the investigation was entering a new and necessary, but also sensitive, phase. They had been told to examine the Widow's closest family members and their pasts—discreetly—and come back with the information before the end of the weekend.

"Both brothers also . . . *those* two," the youngest investigator had whispered at the morning meeting, staring at the other cops like a hamster in a cage.

"The two Blegman brothers—yes. And it must be stressed that this course of action is completely normal. We can't avoid a normal investigation because of the victim's closest relatives . . . but naturally it should happen discreetly."

The Homicide Boss had no doubts about taking the utmost care. This part of the investigation could irritate the country's most powerful pair of brothers beyond belief. No one wanted to see the Bear standing on his back legs, growling senselessly at police headquarters and the inner city, while threatening everyone involved with immediate termination without pension—threats that the powerful prime minister and his equally domineering little brother would happily execute.

And everybody in the room knew it.

"They were born in Søborg but grew up on Smakkegårdsvej in Gentofte, in a nicer middle-class home. Their father was a so-called éminence grise, a kind of ideologue in the Conservative Party during the seventies and eighties, an executive committee member, lawyer for the Supreme Court, filthy rich . . ." The Homicide Boss stopped himself and then added: "The mother stayed home."

"Mrs. Blegman," Number Two clarified.

"Yes."

The youngest of the detectives had cleared his throat, despite his cautious appearance and nervous mien. "But they didn't move to the upscale neighborhood until the father was allowed to practice before the Supreme Court—several years after the accident that befell them."

The Homicide Boss nodded. That was true. And it was a problem.

The accident was one detail in the Blegman dynasty's past that had to be looked into—and then skirted around—and that could be quite difficult as it was undoubtedly a lifelong sore point for the two powerful brothers. In newspaper features on the family and the two brothers' past, they'd never wanted to talk about that time—or what had happened.

"They had a younger brother who was killed in an accident." Once again, it was the young detective who, despite his nervousness, doggedly kept talking. "There wasn't any . . . crime, but naturally it left a certain . . . sorrow. It's difficult to see what the relevance might be today."

No one could argue with the youngest man's somewhat self-contradictory conclusion.

"They've created a lot of enemies on their way to the top, haven't they?" The question, phrased more like a statement of fact, came from Number Two.

Created was an especially imprecise word in this case, thought the Homicide Boss. One doesn't create enemies the way one creates a painting or a deep poem. Enemies are generated by brutality and a lust for power. Nevertheless, the two brothers had to be investigated.

"Yes, the past can always mean something," the Homicide Boss said.

"You mean there could be something in their past . . . a motive for revenge?" Number Two pronounced *revenge* in a slightly singsong accent, reflecting his upbringing in the northern Fyn coastal town of Kerteminde.

The Homicide Boss nodded. "Yes, but it's a huge history to tackle, and—"

"—they'll be furious."

Anyone in that room could have finished that sentence.

Now that the two men were alone, the Homicide Boss repeated that again and then said to his second in command, "Our only hope is to show them that the investigation will help solve the mystery and save the Widow, wherever she is . . . if she's still alive. They can't possible say no to that . . ."

That statement should have resulted in nothing more than a nod from Number Two; however, he delivered his fourth unsolicited sentence that afternoon, this time a short but no less ominous prediction: "We'll definitely find her . . . but we'll find her *dead*."

It was impossible to argue with him.

Not after the void that had followed the Widow's disappearance. No tips, no whispers in the city's underworld, not the least sign of any abduction.

There was only one sinister conclusion: that she no longer existed.

PART II

VIGGO LARSSEN

CHAPTER 3

Søborg, near Copenhagen
1955–1960

Viggo Larssen did not seem like a normal child, yet that is *exactly* what he was. Which is something I only realized much later.

Maybe I understood all his quirks—his tics, his strange behavior and odd sounds, his urge to explore the darkest corridors of a mind not made for that sort of thing—because I recognized him deep inside myself. I had grown up with the same tendency to distort everything that should remain beautiful and, in others' lives, would seem totally normal, the terrible fear of laying yourself bare, mixed with a child's intense need to feel invisible, especially when everything surrounding you has crumbled and oddness flows from every pore.

It's just genetics, Teis would have said. Defective mechanisms, bad biological compounds, garlands of genes strung in some misplaced strand of DNA.

But Teis, maybe we're made of more than you suspect. All children grow up with secrets, secrets hidden by the Devil and God and Science.

So maybe your explanations are merely some bizarre comfort demanded by your ever-present and all-controlling sense of reason. A hat placed on top of reality, so that we never see the terrible snake that has swallowed the elephant—or something even worse.

Viggo Larssen was born in Copenhagen to a single mother, and long before his birth, his father had renounced any responsibility or paternity and moved home to Sweden. "Beyond all mountains," as they used to say in the Copenhagen Council for Unwed Mothers and Their Children, at a time when thousands of unfaithful fathers left their children every year, often before they were even born.

This time, however, the saying rang true, at least in terms of geography: Viggo Larssen's biological father had fled all the way to Kebnekaise Mountain in Lapland, where the Swedish authorities found him. Following a blood test tying him to the unwanted seed he'd left in Denmark, he was forced to send monthly child support checks. And that was all Viggo Larssen knew of his father.

Viggo's mother was a small, solidly built woman, darkly beautiful in her own way; her hair was almost black, even though there were (supposedly) only fair Jutland genes beneath her skin. She had attempted suicide with sleeping pills when Viggo's father left her, fleeing in the direction of Sweden's highest peaks.

One time she read aloud for Viggo from *The Wonderful Adventures of Nils*, but she slammed the book shut when she realized where the lead goose Akka—with Nils on her back—was planning to land.

Back then, single mothers bent their heads in shame over having what was called an illegitimate child; maybe that's also why, in the fullness of time, his mother gave Viggo the book about the boy who had neither father nor mother and yet ruled his own planet: *The Little Prince*.

Dear God, the little *fool*, people thought as her stomach grew. Her father had said it aloud, only without the unnecessary modifier, so that the word *fool* could haunt and condemn her. A more Danish and devastating epithet didn't exist back then, and the shame was unbearable for a man like him.

When the hardships of single motherhood became too great, Viggo's maternal grandparents decided to leave the fjord town of Vejle, where they had moved after recently retiring, and relocated to Copenhagen. Viggo's grandfather already had two brothers living there, which became the official explanation for their new life. They bought a row house in Søborg, so that their daughter and grandson could move in with them.

The suburban neighborhood of row houses was considered a vanguard in the early welfare state of the sixties. They built kindergartens, grade schools, riding schools, sports clubs, high-rises, television stations—even a huge open-air swimming pool where some years later, on sunny summer Sundays, you could watch the day's freakiest rock group, Savage Rose, sunning themselves on the lawn right across from the ten-meter diving board, which no one dared use.

In Viggo's neighborhood, adults spent their weekends working in the garden, cutting the grass, laying flagstones, cultivating tulips, raking rose beds, planting crocuses, pruning rhododendrons, and arranging rows of potatoes and parsley that were flanked by red currants, strawberries, and black currants, as well as apple, pear, and plum trees. Anything could survive the new garden owners' slightly untrained fingers, with the help of some solid doses of DDT and artificial fertilizer, as this was before the time when environmentalists cared about that sort of thing. In general, an immense array of plants could be squeezed into a very long, narrow garden of flowers, trees, and bushes—and pesticides—where neighbors peeked discreetly over the low, newly planted hedges at the glory of the competing plant kingdom.

"The grass should be really green this year," said Viggo's grandfather. But you could tell that he didn't really think so, because he was born skeptical—some might even bluntly say grumpy. In the neighborhood of row homes, he was known as a very moody man, a man who occasionally nodded but rarely spoke.

Until his third or fourth year, Viggo Larssen seemed like a relatively normal boy. Nothing hinted at the defects that would later manifest themselves. Yes, as a three-year-old he was still drinking milk with his lips against the cup's upper rim—he had a small silver mug with his initials engraved on the handle—and naturally the contents landed in his lap. On the other hand, it looked so comical that the hearty laughter of everyone around him hid what was probably concern. Sometimes I think that it was the accident on the tricycle that resulted in something serious—that, in any case, revealed a side of him that no one knew before.

I think that all people live both a real and a fairy-tale version of their lives. The first is visible, while the other is invisible, at least at first. On the outside, Viggo struggled to be like everyone else, to appear normal, but deep down, strange and unspeakable thoughts and ideas were rattling about, coming and going as they pleased. Knowing instinctively that he mustn't put them into words, he forced them back into his body, into a dark bottomless pit (what the faithful would call a soul), from where the strange visions and dreams could not return.

But they could—and naturally, they did.

For Viggo Larssen, they surfaced as strange tics in his face, an involuntary toss of the head or a lengthy crick in his neck, a bewildered blink of an eye, first one and then the other, and finally as a snorting sound that came from deep in his throat, a sound that made people turn around.

Often he would sit motionless, staring at his wrists, and no adult could figure out why. In kindergarten he had heard a mother talking about a boy who died of a sudden case of blood poisoning after getting a tiny, almost invisible scratch on his hand. As a result, Viggo was struck with fear over even the smallest cuts and scratches, a fear of dying, which none of the adults around him realized. He had no doubt about it: one day he would see a red streak shooting up across his wrist and traveling up his arm, running toward his shoulder and his chest, while the poison aimed straight for his heart.

If people had asked, "Is something wrong?" they wouldn't have gotten an answer. Children refuse to grant adults access to a world that grown-ups cannot understand. Children know instinctively that doing so will only lead to their downfall, with adults first showing amazement, then irritation—and finally anger.

Therefore, countless children just like Viggo grow up with thoughts and quirks they never reveal. On the surface, they seem so innocent, so childlike. Beneath the surface, they're stunted seeds that sprout in the dark and have visions that can never be shared. We carry those thoughts with us throughout life, children and adults, the old and dying alike. All people possess that knowledge, just like the picture of the hat that hides a snake. Or maybe, in reality, it's an elephant.

My foster mother would have chosen the latter transformation.

***

Viggo's story is not, therefore, easy to tell. I simply don't know all the nooks and crannies where he stored his secrets; and even though I've always had a certain knack for observing boys like him—peering into their dungeons—he was something special.

If he reminded me of anyone, it was myself. Not that I'd ever tell anyone else that.

My own story is not important. I grew up an orphan and came of age very late—as people would say back then—when I left the orphanage in Skodsborg, north of Copenhagen, where I had lived my entire childhood and youth as foster daughter to the woman who ran the home.

Viggo Larssen had been there the first few months of his life, too, but that was several years before my time.

I first met him in the cemetery in Søborg when he was fifteen, right after his life capsized—at least that's the way I see it. My foster mother towered over me among the gravestones. In her eyes, what Viggo went through that day was not all that devastating. People die, and the only important thing is that amends are made on earth.

After my foster mother died, I finally left the nest (as those fortunate enough to be raised at home call this not-so-simple feat). I wrote my name on one of the baptismal forms my foster mother always had lying around and took work as a night watch at a nursing home in the city's nicest suburb. I was the best night watch they'd ever had. Caring for the elderly is like taking care of babies, and for years I lived discreetly, almost unseen, in a small basement apartment beneath the nursing home. When I first moved to the cape, the light and the wind and the vast ocean nearly knocked me over.

Although I hadn't seen Viggo Larssen in decades, barely a week or month passed that I didn't think of him. Maybe because he reminded me of my own past—or maybe because we shared the same sensibility. Whenever the world's troubles became overwhelming, I'd leave planet Earth and set up headquarters on a small, obscure planet where, from a safe distance, I could observe the people down there in their beautiful gardens.

One day when he was three years old, Viggo Larssen was standing at the top of the stone steps that led from his front door down to the garden, his round shoulders hunching slightly forward, as if he were vigilantly waiting for a sudden blow or a shove from some invisible opponent whirling down from the sky.

I recognized his watchful stare; I saw his gaze floating in front of him, around the corner, past the low row house hedges, in and out of garden gates and behind parked cars. Was someone lying in wait, someone watching him?

No, but on that spring day, a tricycle was sitting by his front door. He was three and a half years old, and I've often thought that if he hadn't noticed the tricycle just then—hadn't gotten on it with that look in his eyes that I knew so well—that everything that followed would have remained a cruel but unexecuted glint in some devil's eyes.

Even before the crash, the tricycle already bore signs of what was then called a healthy boy's usage, to put it mildly, with scratches in the paint, bent handlebars, and a frayed seat. Bloodred, the bike was equipped with a small basket, which that morning held a Donald Duck comic with one of his favorite stories in it.

Maybe he heard a voice in his head taunting, *You don't have the guts to do it!* Or maybe it really was Agnes who yelled the cruel challenge from her spot behind the neighbor's hedge. As Teis later contended, "She wanted his Donald Duck comic, the one about the duck family's trip to the Land before Time in search of square eggs from Peru."

Teis was standing out on the road when it happened, and he heard a voice challenging Viggo—a girl's voice. In all those years since, he's still willing to swear to it.

A second later, when Viggo Larssen rode those few inches toward the edge of the high staircase's top step, his decision was firmer than the cement beneath his wheels. He wouldn't stop—he wouldn't stop for anything in the world. This spite, mixed with a kind of defiance, often frightened other children. Viggo narrowed one eye and measured the distance to the flagstones at the foot of the stairs, while keeping the other eye closed—as if aiming down the barrel of a rifle. Then he pushed off with his small, naked legs in his shorts, and the cycle with the boy on it tipped forward and rattled down, down, down . . . and everyone closed their eyes . . . then opened them again, as children do, to see what happened after such a precipitous fall.

The Donald Duck comic, miraculously, was still lying in the basket, trapped in a crease of bent iron. Viggo had clearly struck his head, because he was lying motionless on the flagstones at the foot of the stairs, with both eyes open. If not for his tears, everyone would have thought he was dead. The mangled tricycle was upside down, one pedal bent crooked and the small white basket pushed halfway up toward the seat. It sat there at a grotesque angle, looking like a leg or a bone jerked loose from a human body.

Just then, she stepped out of the shadows. Agnes, the only girl he occasionally played with, had been standing a short distance from him, on the other side of the neighbor's hedge.

As a child she was teased because her last name was Persen instead of Pedersen or Petersen, like everybody else. When she started at Søborg School, you would often hear the shouts in the schoolyard: "Little Persen! Little Persen! Little Persen!" It was mortifying to her.

Viggo Larssen was lying on his back, unmoving. He closed his eyes briefly, and when he opened them again, she was gone. As was his Donald Duck comic book.

The front door at the top of the steps flew open, and his grandmother and grandfather came rushing toward the half-conscious boy. There were red stains on the flagstones, and Viggo's grandmother dabbed the back of his head with a wet washcloth. From far away, the ambulance siren could be heard with its ominous sound of death and terror. The families on the street stood bathed in its blinking blue light in the front yards of their low connected houses. They had never seen an ambulance in the neighborhood before then.

Later, after they came home from the hospital and put Viggo in bed (a chalk-white bandage wrapped around his head), the three adult members of his family sat in the living room and discussed the strange episode.

Clearly, no one had shoved their boy; his cycle must have rolled forward because he'd made a mistake and gone too close to the edge. It was simply impossible that he had intentionally done something so strange.

His mother's eyes were brimming with concern. She and Viggo had two rooms on the second floor of the little row house. She slept on a pullout couch, and Viggo had his own room with a bookcase, desk, and bed—and a view of the Yellow House on Maglegårds Allé at the end of the backyard, the house where a family with three young sons had recently moved in.

Viggo's mother had a somewhat nervous disposition; she was often preoccupied with problems at the office where she worked as a secretary. As usual, when trying to comfort her son, she turned to fairy tales; that night, she kissed him on his white bandage and read aloud to him before she turned off the light. She especially loved the story "The Ugly Duckling." In the light from the bedside lamp, she didn't notice that her boy was squinting, as if he wanted to shut out the happy images of the bird's wonderful transformation (I think Viggo knew instinctively that change like that never happens in real life—and that the picture of the proud young swan swimming behind his new family on the book's last page was, therefore, something adults had come up with).

"Why did that happen to him?" asked Viggo's grandmother later that night in the living room; he could hear her voice in the dark, coming up through the floor, because the older they got, the louder his grandparents became.

"It's because he's a *fool*," said his grandfather, who had been district manager of the Danish Heath Society and who had trod vast stretches of heather-covered hillsides and meadows in his high rubber boots when west Jutland was still barren and uncultivated.

His wife of fifty years stared at him without answering. Perhaps deep down, she accepted his judgment as the only possible explanation—as well as an excuse for her husband's heartlessness. That's how adults judge and absolve each other.

They already knew he had done it on purpose.

I'd seen it often before: how adults avoid a topic regarding something violent—and strange—something that might ultimately reflect poorly on them. Once I'd gained insight into Viggo's story, I should have told him that this kind of adult heartlessness affects more children than anyone could imagine. And I should have also told him that children carry that pain with them throughout their lives, so that when they have their own children one day, they can use it against them. But naturally I didn't say anything, and anyway, it was too late.

In the weeks following his fall, the first strange visions came to him after his mother turned off the light.

When he closed his eyes, his mind was illuminated by suns, stars, and glimmering comets with blue and red tails that shone like fire. He mentioned it to his mother, who took him back to the doctor. It was the first and only time he told anyone about his fear of blindness and the dark. The doctor had patted him on the head (the bandage had already been removed) and reassured his mother and grandmother. The boy had simply experienced something akin to snow blindness from the bedside lamp, he said, and the adults had nodded knowingly, seriously, to each other.

He could hear his grandmother's voice rising from the living room, where he knew they were having their afternoon coffee: "So, fortunately we don't have to worry about anything . . ."

He stared up into the darkness, into the fiery beams, where one brightly colored comet was being replaced with the next. They had left him alone with his fear.

He had told them that it had gone away, just as the doctor said it would. He lay in the dark and tried to sleep, but he knew that at any moment he might wake up blind, a terror he could not escape. He opened his eyes, searching for the outline of the light from the window to make sure he could still see. His eyes eventually turned red from not sleeping enough, and his mother scolded him and laid a black piece of fabric over his face. He didn't say anything.

But he found a slit in the fabric and peered out; over the course of those months, the outline of the window was his only point of reference. I don't believe he changed drastically from striking his head, or that something had shaken loose in his skull that day on the steps, but rather I think he learned that he shouldn't talk about anything out of the ordinary. Instead, he would blink feverishly, first with the left eye and then with the right, and snort as if he were laughing. His mother would get a dark, blank look in her eyes.

Down in the living room, his grandmother took a deep breath and held it for fifteen to twenty seconds before she exhaled. The silence undoubtedly allowed her to send up a silent prayer to Our Lord.

Meanwhile, his grandfather let out a pent-up roar: "What the hell is the matter with that boy now?!"

Everyone understood. In the real world, the weirdest and the ugliest never escape their destiny. That only happens in fairy tales.

Maybe that's why adults read those stories aloud, again and again.

**

Office of the Prime Minister
Sunday, January 4, morning

The Bear grasped his head. It felt like it'd been hit with sledgehammers on both sides.

His massive head felt swollen with equal parts powerlessness and uncontrollable rage; someone had *taken* his mother—*away* from him—away from his brother.

Someone had challenged the Blegman dynasty's absolute supremacy. No one had ever had such audacity before.

He jumped up out of his chair and pointed at his little brother, the minister of justice, and yelled, "You have to find the motive for the kidnapping. What the fuck is the motive?!"

The prime minister's brother stared at the outstretched finger and replied with resignation, "If there even *is* a motive—at least one that has any rhyme or reason."

"There *is* . . . I can feel it. Someone has thought . . . *for a long time* . . . about this. Our mother sure as hell didn't think of it herself . . . somebody has taken her—*somebody* . . ." Stopping in the middle of his tirade, he lowered his outstretched arm and stood there with clenched fists, staring at the other person in the room, his permanent undersecretary.

He was a tall blond man who reportedly had a past as a thug in the suburb of Hørsholm and used to wear his hair down to the middle of his back, before he became a member of a revolutionary party; that part of his past was long gone, however, and now the brothers were venting their frustration to him.

The Bear's outburst clearly indicated that the last few months hadn't made him feel any more tender toward the vanished widow—but his brother already knew that, and kept that fact to himself.

"What do *you* think?"

The permanent undersecretary, standing in front of the desk in his impeccable charcoal-gray suit (they say he used to wear a green military jacket with bullet holes from the Vietnam War), let the question briefly hang in the air before answering.

"I've gotten a tip from—well, it doesn't really matter where it's from—that the Homicide Boss has told his people to start digging into . . ."

"Digging into *what* . . . into *what* . . . into *what* for *Christ's sake?*" The Bear, about to sit down, was now back on his feet in full-blown attack mode.

"Into Widow Blegman's closest family. And . . . yes . . . as far back as possible. *Everything* . . ."

He seemed to be almost smiling as he spoke, yet that would be unimaginable, even for a man who had once demonstrated against the junta in Chile and had been a member of the Left Socialists' executive committee.

The two brothers looked at each other. Now, the minister of justice was also standing; though half a head shorter than his older brother, he was a formidable figure. Until now, the police had mostly been interested in their youth in the Gentofte neighborhood, searching their pasts for any motive for revenge. They both knew that, and neither had made any attempt to interfere with the investigation. It was routine procedure, and any obstruction—so close to a national election—could prove devastating.

But the years of their early childhood were another matter, and naturally the two brothers were thinking the same thing. About the yellow villa in Søborg, when they were just two overgrown boys with a penchant for bullying the bourgeois children who lived in the red row houses across the way.

They thought about their little brother, who was no longer living—and about everything that happened after his death. About their father, the tyrant, about the yellow raincoat their mother had taken off her dead youngest son. And about the anger. About the things no one could know—or would know, unless some very clever investigator one day got lucky.

If so, they'd never be reelected.

Their problems were already bad enough. Their mother had disappeared at the worst possible time, right before the rapprochement she had invited them to at the nursing home.

Both men were thinking about the same thing—and it wasn't their mother. Not at all.

It was what they had expected she would be holding in her hand when they arrived at Solbygaard on New Year's Day: a folder that they knew only too well. It had been their father's.

The Blegman Family Will. Their mother's last will and testament.

They thought that meeting was going to solve all their problems.

CHAPTER 4

Søborg, near Copenhagen
1960–1961

The row house neighborhood known as Lauggårds Vænge was named after a nobleman who had ruled his farmers and servants with a brutal hand. At that time, what is now Søborg had consisted of nothing but fields, swamps, and ditches.

"So why did they name our street after him?" Viggo once asked at the dinner table.

"Because he was a great man."

That was Viggo's grandfather's response. He, too, had been a great man.

Viggo's grandfather, also named Viggo, had spent most of his life cultivating the heath-covered hillsides in Jutland. Pictures of a bright green countryside with undulating gold cornfields hung above both the sofa and the bureau in the living room; the retired couple had left their beloved Jutland to support their daughter when she gave birth. Their move couldn't be undone.

Also living in the low-ceilinged rooms was a canary that Viggo's mother had christened Piphans. In time the bird learned to sing at the top of its voice when the mood struck—and to stay quiet when the old heath farmer's mood veered dangerously close to the breaking point. Which was often. It wasn't only in the mines that the golden bird sensed danger long before everyone else; Piphans also shut up when the old man gave off signals that Viggo intercepted, too. All sound in the row house disappeared then, and silence pervaded the home. None of them dared make their presence known.

Viggo's mother left for work at six in the morning, then was gone until six at night. Back then, a single mother could only regain the respect of others slowly—very slowly—by working steadfastly and doggedly, without complaining, silent and self-sacrificing, year after year. That's how it had always been in that windblown, heather-nourished country with its wide expanse of fields and lakes and its hardworking people.

Søborg's newly built blocks of row houses illustrated the fruit of generations of hard work. Even the police, the clerks, and the shipyard workers—with wives working outside the home—could have their own plot of land here and enjoy sunny summer Sundays with beer and aquavit on the patio.

All the long, narrow backyards emptied into the heavily trafficked street called Maglegårds Allé. The responsible family men safeguarded their children from the cars by installing heavy gates between solid posts, equipped with stainless steel hinges, to which were added sturdy padlocks, just in case curious fingers became too strong or inquisitive. Every family had heard about accidents in which children managed to slip out into the dangerous world beyond their fences, out onto the road that connected newly built Bellahøj—and the country's first skyscrapers—with Søborg.

Cars came barreling around the curve by the grocery store at break-neck speed before they sped to the intersection, where many finally came to a screeching halt at the very last moment. The wide roadway, the hilly terrain, and the long, sharp curve by the grocery seemed to attract all kinds of speed demons. Even professional truckers and taxi drivers drove too fast there. One of the fathers in the neighborhood had nicknamed the road Death's Highway, and all the neighborhood boys from their vantage points behind the hedges and gates now called it that, too.

"But it's not a highway," said Teis, the son of two no-nonsense schoolteachers. "It's a street." Even then, he focused on precision, evidence, and scientific integrity.

Little Ove, who would later become renowned throughout Denmark as a creative consultant for the largest and finest firms in the country, stared at stocky Teis and said, "A street can easily become a highway—if you just make the effort."

Naturally.

As usual, Agnes was standing in the shadows behind the gate to Number 10 and watching the boys. In a closed plywood box up in her room was a small, rolled-up, dirty Donald Duck comic that was opened up to the place—Teis believed—where Huey, Dewey, and Louie were trying to blow big, pink, square bubble gum bubbles in the Land before Time in Peru. Agnes had undoubtedly tried to achieve the same feat, but with no success. Very few had mastered the technique.

You could see her standing there by the road, slightly knock-kneed (yet already pretty in an unusual way) and puffing and puffing and puffing her gum, until it went pop!—and her fine face, which Viggo already thought was the most beautiful face in the world, was half covered with sticky bubble gum from Dandy. They had collected all the world's flags from the small yellow packs of Dandy gum, most of them in doubles. Zambia was number 106.

Agnes was called Little Adda by her parents. When the boys heard them shout "Adda" with the accent on the second syllable, followed by a far too drawn-out *a*, because she had to go home to eat dinner, she would blush. But eventually everyone called her Adda—until she became a teenager and blossomed into a beauty who reclaimed Agnes as her name. The name was Gothic, old, and quintessentially Danish—the very symbol of the Denmark everyone loved. But even today, so many years later, in a moment of distraction (or was it nostalgia?), she might suddenly write *Adda* below her monthly pastor's message in the Søllerød church bulletin.

In time she became more confident, and some found her ruthless about things she really wanted to achieve in life.

One time Viggo popped a wart on the knuckle just below his middle finger, and the fluid struck him in the eye.

"Now you'll get warts in your eye!" screamed Agnes—budding minister and future shepherd of souls—with something akin to sheer malice in her voice.

She danced around the terrified boy. "You're going to look like Quasimodo!" she yelled, because she had just read an Illustrated Classic about the Hunchback of Notre Dame, who was worse than any monster. She seemed to sense the shafts that led straight down to Viggo's innermost fears. He ran inside to his grandmother, who spent the rest of the day rinsing his eye out with a boric acid solution, trying to calm him down (while breaking her own deep-breathing record, several times holding her breath for almost half a minute).

For three days, Viggo dared not look in the mirror for fear of finding even the smallest protuberance or deformity in his otherwise handsome face.

Then he was out there again, calling for Adda across the low hedge. A keen observer would have sensed the longing in his eyes. That Agnes later found a calling that was so innocent and demanded such compassion must have amazed even God, who inexplicably let it happen anyway.

Viggo's grandmother and grandfather smoked cheroots in the low-ceilinged rooms, even when he was quite small. He had initially coughed but then stopped, as children often do when they realize that the powers that be are too great. His grandparents didn't give a thought to the strain on his little lungs; they never even noticed him cough, unless the sound drowned out the *Radio News* or struck the nerves that spurred his grandfather's migraine.

Viggo Larssen had jug ears—he'd had them since birth. They stood straight out from his head and became brilliant red after other children had tugged on them for an entire day, comparing him to Dumbo, who flew around making an ass of himself in *Donald Duck*—"the world's funniest magazine," as some called it.

Even little Teis, who generally seemed gentle and shy to both adults and children alike, displayed a boldness never before seen when the herd began teasing Viggo and pulling on his ears. No one pulled harder than Teis did. Only Ove, Viggo's closest friend at that time, refused to participate in the teasing. After Ove slowly acquired power over the herd, because his sharp tongue could divide and paralyze them, he started to defend Viggo—and the worst of the abuse subsided. Ove always spoke bluntly. He made a virtue of the honesty that later completely vanished. The only one he had trouble reaching with his words was Teis, who found a way out of his loneliness by persecuting Viggo. Perhaps this was when Ove first revealed the ruthlessness that would become his proud trademark as adviser, spin doctor, and communications consultant in a much harsher world.

One afternoon, when Teis had once again gotten a good grip on both of Viggo's ears, Ove screamed at him—using the meanest choice of words any child had ever heard in the neighborhood:

"You fat little dwarf, Teis! Teis, Teis, Teis, round like a soccer ball and always whining about nothing, while you scratch your ass and look like a toilet that's so fucking full of shit that everyone has to hold their nose, because you stink and waddle on your fat little legs, which make you look like a crippled duck!"

It was linguistically unassailable—a sign of Ove's future greatness.

On that day a sudden silence seemed to permeate the entire neighborhood; even the workmen and the half-deaf retirees paused, all eyes open wide, staring directly at Teis. Everyone understood that they had witnessed an execution, the target felled with words he could never escape and had no hope of combatting.

Then all those voices started to laugh, creating a gigantic echo between the row house gables and the garage walls, while Teis stood there, frozen like a deer in the headlights, before he finally turned and ran and ran and ran, until no one could see him anymore—as children do.

After that day, Teis turned inward; he didn't go near the other boys until an entire summer, a whole autumn, and a long winter had passed. During those months, Teis may have developed the introspection and concentration that, in time, made him a brilliant geneticist, one of the few Danes following in Watson and Crick's marvelous footsteps in pursuit of the genome, the very origin of humanity.

***

Office of the Homicide Boss
Sunday, January 4, afternoon

Two yellow pieces of plastic lay on the rosewood desk between them.

Number Two had taken them out of the bags the technicians used to preserve their findings.

"An old *raincoat*?"

The Homicide Boss looked at his deputy, who had uttered his question incredulously.

Number Two repeated himself: *"A . . . raincoat?"*

"Yes, that's what analysis shows. These two small pieces are probably a few decades old . . . maybe even more. And the small stains are blood."

"But why?"

The Homicide Boss shook his head and leaned forward. He touched one of the pieces with a long index finger—almost as if he were prompting a response from the plastic.

"One of the social workers thinks she's seen it before—in one of the Widow's drawers—but she's not sure," said Number Two. "They're very busy. And the elderly need to become self-sufficient."

The Homicide Boss understood that buzzword all too well. "Do they think it was something that belonged to her," he asked, "or did someone leave it there like this—and what in the world would it mean, in either case?"

Number Two changed the subject; the two men didn't need any more acknowledgment of their impotence regarding the two pieces of yellow plastic. "The technicians are still examining"—now he was the one hesitating—"samples from the other item."

They both knew what he was talking about.

"But there's no easy explanation, is there?"

It didn't require an answer. Deciphering a yellowed piece of paper with an old date on it was no simple task.

"Naturally, the brothers are furious over our lack of progress," added Number Two. "And our press department is being inundated with—"

"Yes, you don't have to be a psychic to know that." It was rare for the Homicide Boss to cut off his second in command in that tone of voice. "But do we know more about that explanation they've given us—if there was any special reason they were visiting the Widow at exactly that point in time?"

"No. They insist that it was a typical New Year's visit. There's nothing alarming or unusual about that."

"But . . . ?" The Homicide Boss could easily read the hesitation in his right-hand man.

"But . . . the pastor—Agnes something or other—confirms that they were invited. But . . ." Number Two hesitated.

"Yes . . . ?"

"She also says that it wasn't normal. They weren't there very often, and the Widow had never invited them before."

The Homicide Boss dropped the little piece of plastic on the table and sat back in his chair. "I see."

Number Two said nothing. Almost a minute passed. Neither of them knew whether the pastor's information held any meaning.

"Is there any news about the investigations into their past? Or into the Widow's? Anything?" Number Two silently shook his head. They both knew the answer.

They had nothing to go on.

***

Søborg, near Copenhagen
1961–1962

In his own sober, Jutland way, Viggo's grandfather was a tyrannical man. In addition to tilling the heathlands, he had also been a resistance fighter in the East Jutland Regional Command. The damned Germans had trampled all over his ancestors' ground with its newly cultivated meadows, drained ditches, blossoming heather, and light green forests—and as a result, he wanted to shoot all of them. Many would have called him a hard man, but as always even the hardest exterior can belie a tender interior, one that is often rather uncomfortably so and therefore completely hidden: a disturbingly soft core that few ever discover.

Viggo sensed that—probably because he had become expert in that kind of anger—yet he was still afraid of his grandfather. One time, the old man threw his cane at Viggo's friend Ove simply because he jumped through the perennial garden in search of a blue ball. The thick cane had whizzed right past the boy's face and landed in a hedge behind him, causing two medium-size branches to fall to the ground.

Another time he held his grandson out over the curb on Maglegårds Allé—the stretch they called Death's Highway—at arm's length while a truck towing a trailer came thundering up, heading directly toward the boy, whom the aging man pulled to safety at the last second.

His grandmother had seen the whole thing from the patio and, appalled, came running between the bushes of red and black currants, down toward the gate, before catching her husband's facial expression and stopping midway between the strawberry patch and the new potatoes.

He was just doing his duty.

"He needs to learn the dangers of not staying on the sidewalk!" yelled the old heath wanderer. "Later in life the lesson will do him some good."

They should have heard Destiny laughing. The old codger failed to notice the real source of danger.

Whereas Viggo's grandmother seemed kindhearted and tender toward Viggo, even fond of her grandson when his weird, dark side wasn't showing, his grandfather spent his days in the easy chair in silence, a grouch in the sourest sense of the term. His lower lip was always sticking out, as if almost touching his nose (at least to the eyes of a frightened child). When he finally spoke, he would complain about his headaches, which turned into migraines as the years passed, probably further twisting his social skills and sense of consideration in the process.

In those few memorable moments when his grandfather exuded a kind of joy, almost a satisfaction with life, he would suddenly call his grandson *Master Viggo*. The nickname made Viggo bend his head and stare down at the tiles, so no one could see how much it meant to him. His grandfather would have been embarrassed.

Viggo's grandmother took care of her difficult husband and tried to protect her grandchild from the old man's increasing petulance. In her softness, however, she forgot—as have countless mothers and grandmothers since then—her duty to ward off the tyrant's rumblings in the all-too-small and dusky rooms. There was a short reprieve from his moods at around three in the afternoon, when Viggo's grandmother served coffee (orangeade for little Viggo) in the living room and suggested a game of cards during this flash of coziness, which even the elder Viggo managed to reward with a grunt.

As they played Hearts, they would let the old man win by a lot, and then the usual discontented grumbling would cease. Then there would be a triumphant noise as he gleefully smacked the dreaded ten of hearts down in the final blow to his grandson, thus stealing from him any chance of winning. By an elegant sleight of hand, the two women always saw to it that the old wretch got the trump card—the ten of hearts—with which he could crush his hopeless opponents.

Another brief appeasement occurred after dinner, during dessert, when the old man challenged the other three to count their prune pits. They almost always had stewed prunes, because they were incredibly inexpensive. The old man used to place all his pits on the edge of the plate, one by one, until they reached all the way around. That way no one could doubt who had amassed the most prune pits. Viggo and his grandmother would cleverly hide a few pits in their laps, so that the family harmony would remain intact until the bowl was empty. Viggo hated stewed prunes with all his heart.

He even learned to bestow each year's most coveted prize on his grandfather, a prize won by the person who found the one gigantic almond in the bowl of rice pudding on Christmas Eve. The almond could be exchanged for a plump marzipan pig that always spent all December sitting on the windowsill, wrapped in cellophane, with a red ribbon around its neck.

In the kitchen he and his grandmother would place the almond into the bowl at a discreetly marked spot, smiling knowingly to each other. As it was served, she would deftly turn the fine crystal bowl so that her miserable ogre of a husband couldn't possibly miss getting it. He would hide it for a long time in his cheek, far behind his dentures, joyful that no one knew his secret.

Finally, when Viggo and the two women leaned back, bloated from eating, he'd spit it onto the plate—with a triumphant plunk—and collect the pig with the red bow. It would then sit uneaten on the little glass table next to his wing chair through Christmas and the days leading up to New Year's, becoming quite dried out, until Viggo's grandmother finally threw it into the trash can on New Year's Day. Where it landed with a plunk.

These types of rituals can be beautiful and seem like small learning experiences in caring and sensitivity—and maybe sometimes they actually *are*. In Viggo's case, though, I think they gave him a warped sense of having to constantly maneuver across dangerous and terribly unpredictable terrain. At any given moment, his foundation could collapse beneath him, sending him tumbling into a maelstrom of his grandfather's bile and capriciousness, reducing the house to silence for days at a time.

I think it was in this spirit that he begged God to watch over the whole family when he said his evening prayers by his bed, kneeling with his grandmother at his side: *Now I close my eyes, Dear Father up on high, In your care please keep, For daddy oversleeps . . .*

It wasn't until he was an adult that he corrected the last line to: *From danger and the deep*—a change perhaps more symbolic than anyone could imagine.

. . . My angel, keep me safe, So great my foot today. Amen.

That, too, was wrong.

That guides my foot today. He corrected himself much later, but by then it was too late.

Every night after prayers, Viggo Larssen searched for the angel, but she was never sitting on the edge of the bed or in the window facing Maglegårds Allé, both of which would have been natural places for her to be. And after his grandmother had gone downstairs to clean up, he would silently pray even more. Viggo Larssen feared any kind of separation, because he believed that one day something would explode—and everything would change. He prayed, because he must have sensed that he needed a higher ally, some covert heavenly alliance, to thwart the threat of earthly dangers.

That vulnerable feeling that the walls and ceilings and floors could crack and split in two probably pursued him until the day that all three adults were dead. When he was older and his evening prayers with his grandmother ceased, he still prayed silently—even in daylight while walking round the schoolyard or sitting in the number 68 bus on his way home.

He would go around reciting long silent monologues in which he pleaded with the powers above, clustered under the name of Our Lord, to preserve everything just as it had always been . . . to never disappear . . . not fall apart . . . never change . . .

> *Dear Lord, please help protect my mother and my grandmother and my grandfather and me from all misfortunes, from anything evil or nasty or tragic, bad or irritating or strange or weird or terrible. Please see to it that seven or eight decades pass before I die; five or six decades before my mother dies; and four or maybe five decades before my grandmother and grandfather die—I ask you this—eternally yours! Amen.*

In that way Viggo maintained an especially good relationship with God—one even a pastor would have envied—although at the same time, he was terrified that others might discover his unique connection and the content of the prayers he sent heavenward.

Most odd people understand fully that someone discovering everything they hide could result in unbearable embarrassment, even if their weirdness had become totally normal to them—as normal as brushing their teeth or using the toilet (although these, too, are strange behaviors).

Back then, no one knew anything specific, but his mother sensed Viggo's strange connection to God, which sometimes seemed to manifest as a slight twitch at the corners of his mouth, a trait bordering on absolute subservience—and it frightened her. She had no idea what was going on inside his mind. She hid her fear, along with so much else that went unsaid between them, and mentioned it only in the diary with the inscription *1955–1964*, which I had seen in the glass cabinet one of the first times I broke into the Lighthouse.

***

For months I had studied the solid lock that I didn't dare break for fear of being discovered. And then suddenly the aforementioned diary showed up on his nightstand on the fourth day after the Widow's disappearance.

Almost as if the dramatic events in Copenhagen had compelled him to delve into his past.

I was about to pick the comforter up off the floor, as the ladies in my foster home by the sea had taught me, when I spotted it. Leaving the comforter where it was, I picked up the book instead, quite carefully, as if it were a tiny newborn (and, really, it almost was). I then lay down on his bed, my head flat on the sheets, right where he rested his, without any pillow, just as he did. It was Sunday, and I figured I had enough time to read the first half of the thick book, even if the almost sixty-year-old, slightly faded handwriting would undoubtedly give me some difficulty.

To my boy, Viggo, b. 1955, she had written on the first of the square pages, its paper thick, as was a common custom back then, probably so that a fountain pen wouldn't bleed through.

Viggo's mother couldn't afford a fountain pen, which I could plainly see, but her handwriting was like slender spider threads, with many lovely curves on the first letter of each sentence: *This diary was bought five weeks after the birth of my son. Here, I will write the thoughts I cannot share with anyone. Everything is different now . . .*

I turned the page. They had moved in together in Søborg.

. . . I'm going to live here in the house with Viggo for many years, as has been arranged for us. Fortunately, my father and mother have welcomed us; they haven't asked for this ordeal I've put them through, and we two have to make it right again . . .

She was already including her son in the appeasement effort.

. . . they deserve a good life, a quiet old age, with a daughter and grandson who show them respect and love . . .

I glanced up at the ceiling, which turned out to make sense since Viggo's mother concluded her first entry with a fervent prayer.

. . . I thank God for taking care of us. I have asked Viggo to remember our gratitude every night when he kneels by his bed to say his evening prayers with his grandmother.

***

When I see Viggo sitting on that bench in front of the Lighthouse, I know that his silent monologue has never ceased.

Often he sits there with his hands folded, as if speaking to someone or something deep inside; I'm well trained at seeing that kind of thing.

Maybe it has occurred to him that God had no intention of keeping his promise when it came to the first three people in his prayer. They're gone, and he's the only one left. Or maybe he doesn't care; some people don't once they finally find themselves alone.

Really, I didn't know what Viggo was living for; he knew no one and did nothing. Perhaps that's the only mystery that really needs solving.

***

When I finally got the chance to read his mother's notes, I discovered a more direct connection between the small family in the red row house and the rich man's children in the yellow house across the way. Those three brothers.

That day in the Lighthouse, I got almost halfway through the first diary before I didn't dare read any longer.

I got up from the bed, smoothed out the sheets, and replaced the book on the stool.

Then I rushed through the shrubbery, across the Giant's Footprint, and up to the Sea Witch's house, where I sat a bit out of breath by the kitchen window, looking out at Hell's Deep.

Most fascinating to me had been her description of their home, which I remembered from my earliest childhood, because my foster mother knew Viggo's mother. He had spent the first part of his life very briefly at the orphanage in Skodsborg, because his mother was deeply depressed and even more deeply dependent on her father, who wasn't so sure he wanted to live under the same roof as an illegitimate child. Supposedly, he acquiesced only after Viggo's grandmother threatened to divorce him, which in those years would have been an even bigger scandal for such a stout and stubborn heath wanderer.

That's why her entries didn't start until the fifth week after Viggo's birth. Even though she later described bright and cheerful memories about her son and his closest playmates playing hopscotch and soccer on the road running through the row houses, a shadow fell across her narrative when she moved from the kitchen into the low-ceilinged living room. There, she stopped and observed the man in the blue high-backed wing chair with the faded armrests or focused on the old woman sitting on the sofa, a cigar in her hand, trying to lift the mood in their little family with coffee and cake and a game of Hearts, all the while pulling God closer and closer as a kind of coconspirator in her unfulfilled life.

The bird in the cage—the canary—may have symbolized Viggo's grandmother's duality. She'd had canaries all her life, and for some strange reason they all met an untimely death, long before they should have expired naturally. This strange tradition continued unabated in the row house.

The first Piphans in Viggo Larssen's young life was sunshine yellow, beautiful, and perfectly formed (like one a Spanish conquistador would have discovered on the Canary Islands in the fifteenth century). It died of severe asphyxiation when his grandmother mistakenly gave the bird a frozen piece of lettuce.

Its little golden stomach could not handle it. It shook on the perch where it usually slept, and Viggo sat and watched it until it released its toe-clenching grasp and tumbled directly onto the bottom of the cage. Its wings flickered like the wings of a blowfly caught in a web, and then its eyes closed and it let out a strange sound, as if the two small canary lungs had exploded from within and shot out its open beak. Viggo watched the horrifying spectacle without being able to intervene, while his grandmother sat by his side and wept.

For a moment the poor creature stared up at its perch. Viggo saw death come crawling, first as a series of convulsions, and then as a still weaker tremor across the yellow breast, and finally as a shadow in its eyes, a shadow that grew and grew until it finally burst, making his grandmother let out a little scream.

Piphans was lying on its back in the sand, a shapeless clump of feathers.

Just then, they heard a noise behind them, sounding almost like a satisfied grunt. Viggo looked up from the little pile of feathers, turning to meet his grandfather's strange gaze—as if the bird's plunge from its carefree perch was the fulfillment of a grim prediction only he had known.

They buried the dead bird in the long, narrow backyard in a white shoebox that almost looked like an actual coffin; they said a prayer to Our Lord, patted the earth, and stood for a moment in silence.

Suddenly, Viggo spotted the three boys who lived in the Yellow House across Maglegårds Allé. Gathered on the sidewalk just outside their gate, they had been following the ceremony with wide grins on their faces.

There stood broad-shouldered Palle, the oldest brother, and right beside him Poul, a year or two younger, and finally little Benjamin, whom everyone called Arrow because he ran so fast and ducked from reaching arms so cleverly that no one—not even the bigger boys—could catch him. Some of the adults in the neighborhood discussed his capacity for speed, and how maybe the accident that happened later was caused by such a flaw. His parents should never have let their smallest run around so freely.

The two older brothers were known for a malice that was either innate or beaten into them by their violent patriarch. Sometimes, on a warm summer evening when the villa's second-floor windows stood open, you could hear the father's bedtime ritual of loud slaps and pleas for forgiveness, often followed by a completely unintelligible snarl, coming possibly from a person but sounding more like a saber-toothed tiger, the kind the boys in the row houses read about in their comic books. Obviously, there was no watchful God or guardian angels in those bedrooms, and Viggo's grandmother would fearfully shut his window until the sounds subsided.

Now, the three brothers were standing there, observing the ceremony with dead little Piphans. Palle, who was as broad as a bear, even lifted up his youngest brother, so that his eyes and the top of his nose were above the gate.

Before Viggo could avert his gaze, trying to ignore the three boys, Palle yelled his gruff greeting to the grieving family and to the dead little creature in the cardboard box.

"Bird, bird, dead little bird, damned in hell's blackest dirt!"

A strange rhyme—probably invented on the spot for the sake of provocation.

Naturally, it worked as intended. Viggo's grandmother blanched beneath her rouge-covered cheeks. At those rare times when Viggo cursed, she would take him up to the bathroom on the second floor and make him repeat the swear words into the toilet, after which she pulled the chain, and all was forgotten. But Viggo had never really been in the vicinity of such ugly words as those that left Palle's sneering mouth, with his playful tongue behind those candy-yellow teeth. *A bear with the mouth of a rattlesnake,* thought Viggo—terrified that the two largest brothers might lunge across the gate and clobber him.

Now, Poul supplemented his big brother's greeting with equal, hateful volume, though its poetic power didn't quite reach his brother's: "Dead, dead, dead bird—Now you're just a turd!"

Viggo's grandmother spun on her heels, abandoning the failed ceremony. Viggo ran after her. Behind him he could hear the two oldest brothers' loud, mocking laughter.

The very next day his grandmother bought a new little Piphans—Piphans the Second—at the pet store on Søborg Hovedgade. This one was even yellower than its predecessor, and his grandmother, closing it contentedly into the cage, filled its bowls with water and birdseed. So simple to replace an extinguished life with a new one, if you could manage to forget yesterday's tribulations—and Viggo's grandmother excelled at that. Otherwise, she would never have been able to live more than fifty years with the miserable man in his high-backed chair.

That night, Viggo had an unsettling dream, the type that, as an adult, he associated with descriptions from both his mother's diary and the writings of other long-dead people whose portents he was still saving when I made contact with him in the old lighthouse.

The first time, the dream consisted only of the faint outline of a person; he thought he could see a pair of thin outstretched hands, reaching toward him out of a grayish golden mist, as if she wanted to grab him and carry him away.

He thrashed about in his sleep—awakening with a scream that no one in the house could hear.

CHAPTER 5

The Lighthouse on the Cape
Monday, February 5, a little past noon

Through my powerful old binoculars, I studied the man in the Lighthouse while I crouched in the thicket directly across from the Giant's Footprint.

The Giant's mighty toes stretched like four trenches beneath the gnarly, torn branches, toward the slope leading up to my little house. A heavenly observer with an eagle eye might be able to spot the small shadow painstakingly crawling and sliding across the branches and trunks encircling the border of the heel just beneath the slope to the lighthouse, occasionally pausing, especially when it rained and the water turned the morass at the bottom of the Giant's heel into a sloshy joy.

Early in my stay on the cape, I viewed my spying on Viggo Larssen as a necessary part of my task to describe him, evaluate him, and make contact with him with a view to one day telling him what needed to be told.

Yet, as the days passed, I increasingly felt a kind of affection for him—I can't think of another word—as if something in his behavior or his stature had changed.

Naturally, I feared the unusual feeling might develop into a form of pity, because I detest that misguided longing for others' hardships. Pity is like a cloak one solemnly wears—an expression like that on a bishop caught in the middle of a hymn, a cloak you wrap around both yourself and your chosen to ensure eternal sovereignty, one that can never be removed. Pity is both demarcation and humiliation. Compassion is something entirely different, even though it has the same religious undertones. Affection is their more earthly cousin, a naïve and yet dangerous feeling that can seem like real love. I didn't know where my growing understanding for the man on the bench was leading me.

It was the fifth day of the Widow's disappearance. I had barely reached my usual place in the soaking wet thicket before I saw him put the key under the little tuft of moss in the lighthouse garden and then head up the path that led into the woods. He would pass me only a few arms' lengths away; his goal must be the same as it was three days earlier, when he mailed that letter in Ulstrup. Instinctively, I connected his secret letter with the vanished Blegman matriarch; of course there was a connection—from the past—one that I knew all too well.

He was out and about earlier than usual; clearly, he had once again canceled his walk along the beach because of more pressing matters. I couldn't see any letter, but in the pouring rain, it would be soaked through in less than a minute. Also, the pockets in his long green windbreaker were large enough to hold the contents of a quarter of a mailbox.

He disappeared into the woods, and of course I followed. It was only a twenty-minute trek to the open landscape, where forest turned into fields and dirt road into asphalt. A rainbow shot up over the valley, stretching from the bluffs in the north to Bavnebjerg's Cliff in the south. It was a singular sight, which the inhabitants on the cape could have talked about for hours, but my wanderer simply continued his purposeful walk along the road toward Ulstrup. Large white flocks of seagulls circled above, and just before we came to the farms in the valley, two birds of prey completed their dive toward the shrubbery. My only ornithological expertise was in domesticated birds that sat on a perch in a small cage, but I had heard that on lucky days you could see the red kite, reed bunting, and white wagtail, which accounted for the marvelous number of bird-watchers who populated the area in the summer.

Viggo Larssen didn't stop on his way to the little village. When he reached the mailbox at the Daily Market, I caught a glimpse of white in his hand. Then the letter was mailed, and I could only congratulate him. And myself. Any answer to his letter would probably tell me much more about him than the few details I'd pieced together so far.

Curiously, he kept standing there, and I was startled. He stood as if he was confused about what to do next, which seemed strange to me. I stepped back behind the cemetery wall, so he wouldn't see me if he suddenly turned around.

Then he stuck his hand in his jacket's other large pocket, this time almost in slow motion, and retrieved another white envelope. He stood for a moment with it in his hand—a few seconds more, and the handwriting would wash off in the rain—then mailed this letter almost impatiently.

Before I could react, he disappeared in the direction of the woods and the Lighthouse. There was no reason to follow him back. In a few days he had mailed three letters—to three different addresses, I was sure—and that meant everything. I was almost certain who was receiving them. Viggo Larssen had sent messages, so to speak, back to his childhood, to the few loyal friends who had been named in his mother's diary.

Teis, Verner, Ove, and Agnes.

Suddenly I heard a slight rustling behind the stone wall, and though I never frighten easily—not even in the dark—I could hear my heart beat faster for a moment.

I stepped forward and stared over the wall into the cemetery. I could see the little bench that the Daily Market had pointed out to me. The Sea Witch's spot.

She was sitting there again. Across from the two gravestones whose inscriptions I could now read. I could just make out her face beneath that large hat, turning toward me, as if she wanted to say, *Where are you going?*

Nowhere.

Maybe I even said it aloud.

In Viggo's book, the snake told the boy he could take him farther than any ship. The boy hadn't answered.

I stepped back into the shadows. I tend to avoid old women sitting in cemeteries, waiting around for death with their ghostly relatives.

The snake had coiled itself in the sand by the boy's feet and issued a warning that by merely touching someone it could send that person back to the earth they came from.

I turned around and headed back toward the woods and the Sea Witch's house.

***

Later that evening, as the moon rose like a silver disc through the deep purple clouds, I visited Viggo Larssen on his bench, following a somewhat neck-breaking journey through the thickets, with my foster mother's old flashlight swinging in my hand.

He sat as he often did, staring intently up into the sky and the moonlight.

There would have been something eerie about it if he hadn't done it so often; I'd gotten used to it as the days and nights passed. I wasn't superstitious, at least not when it came to the heavenly bodies' influence on human bodies and souls. Viggo Larssen never shifted shape—not even on nights of the full moon; he showed no sign of wolf ears or pointy teeth, no predisposition to dark hair growing up over the collar of his jacket, no startlingly bushy eyebrows. *He isn't really that strange,* I thought, before reminding myself that his physical appearance had nothing whatsoever to do with me; people like us have always been ugly, and as all people born without beauty know, even God can't fix that. Avoiding fur and yellow eyes is the best we can hope for; silently sitting next to someone without touching is often as far as we can get.

Still, in the light of the moon, I thought that Viggo was handsome, though I'd never tell him that or even indicate as much; that was a sign of weakness that should not be cultivated, as experience had shown me.

He offered me a glass of red wine from his bottle. It was an old Siglo Rioja, wrapped in light brown burlap. I'd never seen him fetch a second bottle, and he never got drunk, but he couldn't be totally unaffected. I knew instinctively that he was comforting himself, and I had a good idea why. Naturally, I wanted to ask him about it—it was one of my most important questions—but up until then we had only talked about the moon and the sea and storms and shipwrecks on the rocky coast below. Apparently he knew that part of the cape's history quite well, though I have no idea why.

At midnight he stood and poured the last few drops from his wineglass onto the ground. Then he took the empty bottle, nodded to me, and shut the lighthouse door behind him.

I could picture his movements inside the house—I certainly knew its rooms, maybe even better than he did. He would close the door to the little bedroom, then he would stand for a moment in front of the glass cabinet with his mother's diaries and . . .

I stopped my train of thought there, because I would never want to see him undress. I would never want to see myself standing right behind him, like some phantom reflected in the cabinet's glass door. Children who are born ugly and crooked don't forget it—even if one day they actually change, because they'll never see it for themselves. They don't suddenly leave their assigned place to start a new life like the ugly duckling in Viggo's fairy tale. It's a ridiculous thought. Destiny doesn't ignore that kind of arrogance.

In the darkness, where my friend now was lying alone, all of his tics and twitches, his shimmering and flickering visions, were gone. That's why he had come to the cape. I was convinced of it.

I sat by his front door and watched over him for another quarter of an hour.

That night I didn't sleep at all; I simply lay there in the darkness, listening to the sounds coming from the cliff and the creaking of the walls. Maybe I also heard the fox, or maybe it was just my own voice, saying, as in the book, *I can't play with you . . . I'm not tamed.*

***

Søborg, near Copenhagen
1961–1962

In her own way, Viggo's mother was a beautiful woman, although over the years her sedentary life as a secretary working for a British oil company in Copenhagen made her a bit rounder.

She went to work in the high heels that were popular at that time, though they weren't nearly as high as they are today and definitely not as pointy. A single mother had to be careful about not encouraging the married men she found herself surrounded by in any way that could be misconstrued. Personally, I've never worn anything but rain boots or sneakers (as a child I had serious problems with my feet)—and I'm not fond of changing habits or appearing vain in any way.

When Viggo was smaller, every year his mother would send him to a summer camp near the beach in Odsherred, probably so she could just be herself for a couple of weeks out of the year.

Viggo hated being away, and he dreaded the holiday camp with an intensity no one around him understood, since most children would love to spend a few weeks at the beach. Yet his mother seemed to thrive in his absence. She had her fillings replaced by a dentist (she saved up all year and always cried when the bill came); without her usual daily chores, she had time to listen to her Mozart, Beethoven, and Bach records and to sleep late in the mornings. Sometimes an admirer would even take her to Dyrehaven Park, but she never brought any of them home. One Saturday evening she let a younger clerk from the office who didn't seem to look down on single mothers invite her to the movies—but she said good-bye after one post-film drink.

She was an honest woman.

On the day he left for camp, she would follow her son to Emdrup Square, where the children were picked up by two large buses and driven north toward the promised forests and the chalk-white beach that was the stuff of suburban dreams.

The young women on the bus got the children singing, tunes like "On Your Way! Be Brave and True!" and "The Early Bird Gets the Worm," while they rounded the forests of Hareskov and rolled ever faster northwest. Viggo sat in the very back seat next to Agnes and clutched his little Mickey troll doll with the stiff, tangled red hair that he loved so much. His fingers were swollen and his joints sore from grabbing the railing on the steps in front of the row house in one last vain attempt at preventing his own departure.

It took all three adults to pry his twisted fingers loose from the railing; finally, his grandfather pulled his fingers backward, one by one, so that his grandmother could get a good grip and remove his hand from the bars.

His mother cried while he struggled, but she knew that it was all for the boy's best; that's what the young chaperones said, and their words seemed wise at the time. Woods and fields and beaches were a healthy break from a single mother's safe but somewhat suffocating embrace.

Still, Viggo screamed right up to the last minute, crying, "No, no, no . . . !"

And he heard his grandfather hiss, "Such a little *fool!*"

Then they lifted him up onto his bicycle seat, where he collapsed, powerless, so that his mother had to hold on to his jacket for the entire ride to Emdrup Square.

Viggo hated the red vacation cabins at Ellinge Lyng with a force that only a little boy's heart can muster (a kind of hatred that never fades or weakens and even fifty years later can still be triggered by even a whiff of freshly cut grass or the sound of the wind rustling in the spruce trees). The six wooden cabins that housed about a hundred lucky children from Copenhagen were near Sejerø Bay. Miss Salomonsen and Miss Thorsager almost danced around in the light green grass while they unlocked the doors to the cabins, opened the windows, and aired out the rooms. They made lemonade and cooked hot dogs, which they placed onto long wobbly tables, while the children swung on old car tires and tried out the seesaws, beaming under the butter-yellow midday sun.

Viggo hated it, and the chaperones hated the little jug-eared boy's obvious sorrow and his careworn face. He hated the taste of freshly made lemonade and burnt hot dogs; the chaperones hated the way he picked at their welcome meal before turning away, wandering off in the direction of the fields and the woods. I really don't think that these young women, in the goodness of their hearts, ever realized that he wasn't really even present, and that his longing came from a world other than the one they knew. They were thinking only of their own good intentions, with their lemonade, hot dogs, sing-alongs, and walks on the beach—such activities were the stuff of life, goodness, and health—that no child should ever refuse.

Viggo stood alone at the border separating the campground from the forest and stared into the spruce trees. Each day passed with eternal slowness while they arranged hikes and sing-alongs—he especially hated "Row, Row, Row Your Boat," with its embarrassing rounds and built-in traps—and served chocolate and marshmallows in the afternoons, and newly scorched hot dogs for dinner.

The sun set in a bloodbath behind the spruce trees. Viggo hated the sinking red ball in the sky with all his heart . . . the silence as it sank and sank, finally disappearing.

Later that summer, on a dark night when everyone was staying indoors because a storm was rolling in over Sejerø Bay, the chaperones suddenly discovered that Viggo was gone—and that he had taken Agnes (who went by Adda back then) with him. They knew that Viggo and Adda were friends from the same neighborhood.

The chaperones tried to hide their panic while, shoulder to shoulder, two by two, they set out with long flashlights into the darkness, calling loudly. They struggled forward on the narrow forest paths, down toward the beach, while their anger grew; they hated Viggo (and to some extent Adda) with young women's hearts, which can become icy cold and stone hard under pressure. If they prayed to anyone that night, out there in the darkness, it wasn't to God but to Satan, whom they asked to take Viggo—and keep him for all eternity—but to simply bring him back first, so their good-hearted devotion to their small flock wouldn't suffer an irreparable catastrophe, or a terrible scandal.

They found the two refugees lying completely naked beneath an upside-down boat on the beach just below the woods; their clothes were lying out in the rain, which had started at midnight. They wanted to go in the water, they explained, shivering and hiccupping, then the downpour had suddenly started. The explanation made the senior kindergarten chaperon, Miss Salomonsen, even more furious, and the two small figures' nakedness was enough to make her lift her hand to strike them. She had to be led away by her second in command to a rear barrack, where she sat for two hours afterward, shaking with a feverlike rage. Thinking about Viggo and Adda—their separation occurred only a few years later—I envy them that night, naked, together in each other's arms. Even if they were too young to get any real pleasure out of the experience (and it was way too dark for them to really see each other).

At his third summer at camp—which was the last one—Viggo locked himself in a toilet stall in the bathing cabin, and they had to break down the door with an ax from the stack of firewood to get him out. As punishment, they took his Mickey troll doll from him and put him to bed without any supper. They already thought it was totally unnatural for a healthy boy to have such a close relationship with a foul-smelling plastic doll. They no longer wanted him to have anything to do with it.

The next morning they found him still sleeping in his bed long after the other children had gotten up. They tore the comforter off him— which they should not have done. Miss Salomonsen's scream could be heard all over the campground (apparently she had never screamed so loudly before, not from fear, terror, surprise, or joy)—and everyone reared back, stunned, at the sight before them. Next to the boy lay the treasure he must have found while his playmates were eating dinner: a dead blackbird, its wings spread open wide and its head twisted at an impossible angle on a broken neck.

It lay there with its beak open, as if it were singing, or as if it were just as shocked as the young women standing there with their white fingers splayed in front of their faces.

The first thing the women did was keep their discovery quiet. They seemed to sense something that they didn't dare speak of; they just sent the boy in to breakfast and removed the sheet with the black feathers before anyone could see what had happened. The bird was eased down into a red toy bucket from the sandbox, which Miss Thorsager then covered with a rag and carried out to the closest thicket. The children got no explanation for the mysterious scream they'd heard. Fearing the answer, the chaperones dared not ask each other the obvious question: Had the bird been dead or alive before it was placed beneath the warm comforter?

That afternoon, they saw the strange boy sitting in the swing and staring, just as he usually did, intently toward the southeast. That was the direction the buses drove when the campground's residents finally headed home.

Maybe he was sitting there, swinging lightly in the breeze in that car tire, and thinking about the little blackbird he had found on the ground on his way back from brushing his teeth last night. It had been easy to put it in a towel and smuggle it into the dormitory, where he had hoped that a good night of warmth would make it open its eyes again. He would set it free at sunrise, right before the others woke up, and watch it fly up into the sky, over the woods and out over the bay. He had tried to stay awake, and even managed to do so for an hour or two, but finally he fell asleep, and as he sat there on the swing, he knew that his sleeping had cost the little bird its life . . .

The oldest chaperone ripped him out of his thoughts, angrily yanking him off the swing and tossing him to the ground.

The little sprig of heather he was holding flew up over their heads, landing behind them.

Little Viggo Larssen reacted abruptly with a ferocity that no one present, child or adult, had ever seen before; it came from somewhere unearthly. Everyone on the playground remembered that seemingly eternal moment when the boy stood over the aging woman, bent over, his fingers like claws as he grabbed her neck and squeezed. Only the sheer number of chaperones who came running saved the gasping woman from the boy's furious grip.

The other children stood at a short distance away, dumbfounded, motionless, watching the battle like a regiment of tin soldiers—almost as if they understood that this boy was not the enemy.

That was the last time Viggo Larssen saw Ellinge Lyng. He was driven home that same night.

For some reason, no one ever mentioned the incident.

And Viggo Larssen started school a month later.

***

Verner from Søborg
Tuesday, January 6, afternoon

If Verner Jensen had been able to bend down just a tiny bit toward the right—which he couldn't thanks to a recent operation on his damn hip—he could have opened the lowest drawer in the rosewood desk and taken out his notes from his youth in Lauggårds Vænge.

Not that there were that many pages or that anyone was particularly interested—they were merely the ramblings of a teenager who loved to write.

Some had been written for the high school magazine, right before forces stronger than he shut it down, and others dealt with everyday life in the neighborhood.

Even in the early grades, Verner was a lanky brown-eyed boy loved by all the girls: the sweet ones, the shy ones, the pushy ones, and even the truly beautiful ones. His family moved from a two-room apartment near Buddinge Station to the neighborhood of row houses in the development after his father got a raise as a janitor at Søborg School. Verner had long since accepted Viggo Larssen's shyness, as children sometimes do, and that's how they became lifelong friends—the bright, outgoing, popular boy and the dark, slightly hunched-over boy who, over the course of high school, had some of his shyness beaten out of him. Their friendship didn't last a lifetime, sadly, but it got Viggo Larssen through his teen years, a time that could otherwise have been the toughest for him.

Later, Verner realized that in reality very few people would want to return to that period of their lives, to their earliest youth, with all its defeats, terrifying visions, fiascos, mistakes, and anxiety attacks.

Now, in the far more sophisticated world of his career in the Danish Broadcasting Corporation, he would never use that expression: lifelong friends.

It was far too sentimental; also, they hadn't seen each other in years—until recently, right before Viggo moved to the cape. Verner had met up with Viggo at a bar on Sankt Hans Torv in Copenhagen. They toasted their reunion with a couple of beers, a little awkwardly, as men do in that situation. Viggo Larssen was still living in the same place he had been the last time they'd seen each other; as Verner could have said (though he didn't), Viggo was at the end of his rope. Living alone in his one-room apartment by the lakes, with no work, surviving on half disability after two nervous breakdowns.

That was the spring of 2014.

A few weeks later Viggo went to the Lighthouse on the cape where Verner's family was from.

The night before he left, Verner suggested to his old friend that he write some kind of life story out there on the cape.

Maybe that was overly sentimental. Still, Verner knew that his friend had certain thoughts that he kept hidden deep inside, only occasionally made manifest in certain sudden movements—so he had given him a place and a challenge he couldn't refuse.

Write about your dreams, write about your nightmares, if that's what you need. Send your writing to me when you're done. Finished or unfinished. Either way.

Verner made the offer for old time's sake, and he hadn't received so much as a line of writing or any sign of life in return. Until now.

At first, he thought the letter from Viggo might contain an explanation. It was far too thin to hold a completed manuscript.

He placed the white envelope on the table in the high-ceilinged kitchen that his fourth wife (there's a word he hated) had insisted on updating, for six figures, right before their divorce. The tall barstool was apparently designed by a Parisian craftsman whose family business went back several hundred years. He leaned forward carefully (that movement caused a lot of pain in his damn hip) and shoved aside the day's newspapers, which were full of reports about the Blegman dynasty's woes.

He had personally directed news coverage of the story at the DBC for the last two days (almost without any sleep) because of that damned family and its even more damned tragedy. As national news chief, everything he said and did had to appear professional. Yet no one knew what he knew. Nor should they.

But then he had known the two brothers for a long time, longer and far better than anyone could imagine, and he also knew the Widow.

Everyone did in Denmark, but he had met her personally as a child. As had Viggo. He knew what she was made of. He knew her sons and some of the family's deepest secrets. Still, despite two sleepless nights, he couldn't see how they had any connection to her disappearance—and he couldn't come up with any ways to direct his investigative reporters toward the strange occurrences that had happened in Søborg in the distant past.

He maintained his strong, objective facade. Meanwhile, his reporters worked on the case in ever-greater frustration because it had been unusually difficult to get the least bit of information out of the aging Homicide Boss. Now, a letter from the one person with whom he would have discussed the mysterious event in some long-forgotten time was lying on his previous wife's high-tech kitchen table.

Viggo and he had become journalists at almost the same time. Then, in the mid-eighties, they started a somewhat successful grassroots publication, before Viggo Larssen suddenly began to fall apart and lose self-control (as indeed a number of young idealists did back then—many of them without any warning).

Some of them crashed on beer, some on tranquilizers, others in one last dramatic gesture—like their advertising salesman Jørgen, who in an attack of paranoia jumped onto the train tracks at Nørreport Station. They belonged to the generation that grew up in the wake of the sixties' youth movement but didn't become teenagers until the seventies. So they were caught at the crossroads between their predecessors' brash and unfocused sense of rebellion and their own ideals of working tirelessly as grassroots activists for a better world—in exactly the way they'd been prompted by their predecessors.

After the sixties, almost all of the decade's most ardent radicals bought expensive houses or apartments as soon as they got the chance. They took university and research jobs, while their successors—an entire generation—were left with their idols' useless, faded slogans. It was a veritable bloodbath. Verner recalled train platforms and rooftops as the most frequent choices among those who suddenly crashed and burned—but also trees, bridges, and cellars. Those who survived patiently buried all those shattered lives, each time with fewer and fewer mourners in attendance. The strong ones finally abandoned the illusions left behind by the sixties radicals.

Viggo wasn't cast in the mold of many of his peers; he didn't want to die. He withdrew into himself and avoided all his friends, including Verner.

Verner Jensen now sat on the high barstool, opened the letter, and read the words that were the first sign of life from Viggo since he'd gone to the cape in the spring of 2014. As he read, all the questions that should have been answered many years ago suddenly resurfaced. What had really happened to Viggo Larssen, and how had the catastrophes he had been exposed to affected a boy of his age?

Why had Viggo, his colleague at the grassroots magazine—and some years afterward also at the DBC—had such a sudden breakdown when he had an interesting job with good colleagues and a salary and pension?

Even Verner's knowledge of Viggo's innate eccentricities provided no clear explanation. Maybe it was the result of one last strange impulse—like some massive tic that struck from above, knocking him totally off course and away from the real world forever—but Verner really didn't know him that well, despite everything.

Now, three pages of Viggo's story were lying on the beautiful kitchen table, slightly crumpled, as if the news editor's fingers had shaken while reading them.

Verner closed his eyes, and for once, no internal headline appeared in his editorial mind's eye.

What had happened to his friend? The story he told couldn't possibly be true . . .

Maybe his staying in the Lighthouse was his final plunge into the sea of madness he still felt within—and it was Verner who had made the offer. Without thinking.

Closing his eyes, he could see himself on that very first day of school, next to Viggo Larssen. They were standing at the water fountain. Two small schoolboys in blue blazers and knickerbockers, their small knapsacks on their backs, like soldiers in a fairy tale. He opened his eyes. He wasn't used to thinking so despondently about anything or anyone. That's why he had to break free from the idealists' insufferable kamikaze project, though the Saints of the Final Rebellion still reproached him for both his betrayal and his bourgeois lifestyle working for the country's largest media outlet. That small band of his contemporaries was still hanging on, with their poorly printed pamphlets and their declarations of support for the rain forest, their aid to refugees, and their painstaking calls to stunted demonstrations against issues that no one with any ambition could relate to.

He closed and opened his eyes repeatedly, quickly, as if he, too, had acquired tics in his old age. The letter still lay there.

What a bizarre tale . . . if it's true . . .

For a moment he imagined the possibility, this time with his eyes closed. It couldn't possibly be true.

Journalists were always toasting the *truth*, their ultimate goal, but no one could handle the truth anymore. The large truths were so rife with catastrophes, war, terror, and abuses of power that even TV editors almost fell off their costly adjustable office chairs from utter despair. That was one of the reasons why the Widow's disappearance had its own slightly odd, exhilarating effect on both the media and the general population: finally, something different had happened, something mysterious, like an old-fashioned adventure, captivating no matter how it ended. And only one single life was at stake—not everyone's. All within a relatively understandable framework.

Viggo mentioned the Widow's disappearance at the beginning of the letter. As if there were some connection between that event and what he really wanted to discuss. If that connection did exist, it was beyond Verner's comprehension as he sat there on the barstool in his villa in Frederiksberg. Although the police might find it interesting. A bizarre man with a previously unheard-of form of paranoia, who had known the Widow . . .

He even mentioned the episode that no one in their old neighborhood could have forgotten. The death of her youngest son.

No one should see that letter. Viggo Larssen's theory was insane—as were so many of the theories he developed while he was a journalist, until no one wanted to listen to him anymore. Not even Verner.

Unless it was *true*.

Viggo Larssen could be seductive on those rare occasions when he surfaced, his imagination making him such a promising journalist. You almost believed him, even when he would fabricate, blink, clear his throat, and toss his head, exuding all the weirdness any being in the universe could possibly muster. He did so whenever he spun his yarns, whether back in high school or working on their shipwrecked grassroots magazine, where he fought for the strangest ideas and was the real reason they both lost the battle and floated with the rest of the capsized seventies generation down various tributaries.

Verner had chosen the right route and moored safely on the other side. Viggo was still floating, but only just barely—if that's how you could describe a stay at the edge of Hell's Deep.

CHAPTER 6

Søborg, near Copenhagen
1962–1963

After Viggo returned home from his decidedly final summer camp, he looked almost like an old man; he had red eyes and red protruding ears, gray skin, and slightly droopy shoulders. Later, his mother heard some rumors circulating among other children's parents about the attack on Miss Salomonsen—but she simply couldn't believe it.

The only thing Viggo told her was that the others were teasing him about his flappy ears, as always, and calling him Dumbo. He missed home, and the chaperones just didn't care.

His mother listened, then put him to bed. He could hear her playing classical music the rest of the night, turning up the volume in the belief he was sleeping. Or maybe just to let herself be swept away by the music.

A few days later, Dr. Fagerlund heard a description of the camp incident from Viggo's grandmother, who was nervous about both her grandson's appearance and the rumors she was hearing. If Viggo was having violent outbursts like that—outbursts directed at elderly ladies—it had to be rectified.

Dr. Fagerlund lived right across from Søborg School, where Viggo was about to start first grade. With a Freudian wrinkle of the brow, he said the boy's bizarre behavior could be due to a repressed inferiority complex—and what could be a more obvious reason than those two gigantic ears? The boy basically deserved the nickname "Dumbo." Smiling, he shook his head as if picturing the little elephant who flew; but indeed it was quite serious if the boy were to start school with such a deformity.

The following week Viggo was admitted to the Military Hospital on Tagensvej in Copenhagen, where there were some of the only doctors who could perform the somewhat complicated operation of bending the cartilage in both ears and then sewing them closer to his head, after which a tight gauze held them in place for several weeks.

He started school a week late, his head crowned in a dome of white gauze that made him look like an astronaut or a being from some distant and hostile planet.

But Ove, Verner, and Adda—and even Teis—formed a ring around him to protect him from the worst teasing. That's something children occasionally do. If you really want to deal with the hostility and strife found in the adult world, start with four hopelessly outnumbered friends who, in an instinctive act of community, turn the rest of their class into better people.

***

On the outside he seemed almost normal.

Inside—especially in private—he wandered around in a strange, impassable landscape that only he could see.

During the ear surgery, the doctors sedated him with a strong dose of ether. I've heard that a tiny residue of ether (like other consciousness-altering agents) can remain, invisible, imperceptible—even the most skillful neurologist can't find it—and never disappear.

He was struck by various plagues that didn't affect normal boys and girls.

In his early school years, it was a mix of obsessive thoughts and physical reactions, strange little movements and sounds that made his classmates wonder, and fantasies about sickness, poisoning, and violent death.

All of these small, self-made terrors came to him like demons from a parallel world; they marched straight through his defenses and tortured him at home, at school, with friends, anywhere, anytime—but mostly at night.

At first it had been the cascades of fire and flashes of light in the darkness, which the doctor had called a form of snow blindness; later, he dared not close his eyes for fear of not awakening.

He would worry that if he didn't close his eyes before the light was turned off, he'd never open them again. Often he would flick the light on and off twenty or thirty times before he was satisfied with the way he had closed his eyes.

If anyone down in the living room caught flashes of the blinking lamp, they never said so.

In the winter of 1962, his worry that night and sleep also brought death strengthened. He would lie with his eyes open in the dark, staring at the ceiling, and imagine that his chances for survival were significantly greater the shorter he slept. With a little luck, Death (which surely had enough else to do around the globe) wouldn't be able to find him. He just needed to slip back to being awake in the course of a couple hours, three at the most.

That same thought prompted him to snap two matches in half and place them between his eyelids to keep them open. During the night, though, the matches would fall out and he would awaken with burning eyelids, as if the sulfured end that held the upper eyelid in place had ignited itself.

He would find the two match ends in his bed, the sulfur having turned black, with the room smelling faintly burnt. In the bathroom mirror, his eyelashes seemed a little sooty, but no adults ever commented on it.

While that phase lasted, you rarely saw the whites of his eyes, as you would in other healthy and well-rested children, back when the welfare state made almost every home a little better and a little healthier. He showed up at school with red, swollen eyes, but if any of his teachers wondered about it, they never said anything. At that time a little neglect didn't bring down a home; it almost had to crumble from within before anyone reacted.

None of his friends, not Adda, Ove, Verner, or Teis, showed any sign of detecting any disorder. Sometimes the others in class called him Crybaby-Viggo, but the nickname didn't stick. He sat next to a boy who was even smaller and shyer, who sometimes took Viggo's hand under the table, though only for a second. His name was Uffe.

In the evenings, Viggo's mother rinsed her son's eyes with that era's miracle eye mixture, a solution of boric acid. For years she used that remedy to combat all of her son's nightly visions, delusions, and nightmares. She never lost faith that his red eyes couldn't possibly have any emotional cause.

Naturally, Viggo learned to hide all his peculiarities and not look for any comfort from her.

Once he tried to tell her about his fear of poisonous mushrooms— the ones growing between the bushes at the kindergarten playground— and she gave him a worried look and said, "Well, don't touch them."

He didn't reply.

That was the problem. What if he still happened to touch one, stepped on one, had one thrown at him when the other boys were playing and throwing sticks and cones? The possibilities were endless—he'd heard the other children telling stories about someone who sucked on a finger after barely brushing a mushroom with the arm of their jacket and died of convulsions only a few minutes later. He looked down at his wrists, and it seemed that the red telltale lines were already running up his forearm, past his elbow, and toward his shoulder and chest.

From time to time, his panic over a mushroom or a scratch or a viper would manifest itself as snorts or hiccups. The other children must have heard them, but they chose to ignore him. Although children can be merciless, I think they hold back when they face things that are inexplicable, as in Viggo's case.

Ove was the only one who dared to walk right up to him. One time he put both hands on Viggo's shoulders and said, "Listen—there are *no vipers* in Utterslev Bog." Strictly speaking, he didn't know that. The bog was big, and the snakes were so small that they could be there. But he said it anyway.

Strangely enough, in his early years, Ove Nilsen seemed like a vastly different, milder version of his adult self.

Throughout his childhood he tried to earn money to cover his relatively high consumption of candy and Donald Duck comics by selling things to adults; to put it mildly, most of these products lacked both the quality and the effect Ove had promised. During such sales drives, he got all the children from the neighborhood together and had them push ants and flies through garlic presses; squash beetles, worms, and wood lice in parsley grinders; and crush earwigs and ladybugs into jelly with flat stones. Then he would add a little saliva and maybe a dash of whipping cream to the entire insect mush and sell it under the name Ove Nilsen's Elixir of Life (he learned that term from a Captain Mickey magazine). Customers simply had to dip eucalyptus candy in the indecipherable mix and let all the heavenly glory melt on the tongue—with eternal health and an extended life as the certain reward.

He garnered respect. That kind of initiative thrilled the adults on the street. This was in the early sixties, and children's work ethic said something about both themselves and the country they would grow up to help build. Had Ove jumped on the current craze for wonder pills and dietary supplements, no one can say what might have happened.

Only Viggo's grandmother flatly refused to buy the little bottle with the strange fluid in it when the boys rang her doorbell; instead, she glanced nervously at Viggo, who had borrowed her garlic press the day before. She had cleaned it herself and was positive she had found something in the bottom that looked like a fly's wings—maybe even a leg—and in one of the holes a small eye staring blankly up at her.

Even though Ove already loved to give orders back then—he instructed all of his friends to keep the recipe for his Elixir of Life a strict secret, so no one could steal it—he always kept an eye out for his closest friends, a personality trait that has long since vanished. Like something out of a simplistic and overly sentimental film, the calculating, fast-talking consultant had once been a curious boy who supported and comforted children like Viggo, Adda, and Verner, apparently without wanting anything in return.

Teis was the first to see Ove's other side, what they'd call his "real" side today, though none of the five friends knew it yet.

They used to run through the bog together, four boys and a girl, and by the end of first grade, Adda was already in bloom. She brought her feet together, so that her knock-knees disappeared, she straightened her back, her hair got lighter, and her face freckled softly. She would look at her friends with those blue eyes, and her smile made them want to hold her, the way you hold a beautiful flower.

During one friendly tussle in the bog, Viggo managed to pin her on her back; he sat astride her and held her wrists firmly against the grass, his face as close to hers as possible, their breathing and laughter the only sounds in the world.

Afterward, he remembered the strange feeling he'd had, right before she twisted loose, slightly frightened: the feeling of his crotch against her stomach, pushing her lightly against the ground, the warmth from her body and their breathing, her eyes open and her lips apart. For months he longed to do it again, but he never got the chance, and one day it was too late. And maybe that's the way it is in everyone's life: destiny rarely provides a second chance for what should have, and maybe even could have, been.

A rather banal thought.

***

Had Viggo Larssen written an essay about his nocturnal visions and desperate obsessions and delivered it to Miss Iversen at Søborg School, she could have read it aloud for everyone in class; then they could hear that the strangeness that blooms in everyone is a common condition—something I believe everyone knows in one way or another. But that was, of course, unthinkable. Viggo dared not share his peculiarities with anyone. He buried his terrifying childhood visions deep inside, in a dark place he never wanted to give anyone access to. If his spiritual disruption had been an earthquake, it would have measured at least eight on the Richter scale—and it would have been designated *severe, intensive, destructive, indicating internal collapse.* But no one saw what was happening.

More accurately: if anyone had seen it, they would have immediately sensed that he would have considered any interference so embarrassing and terrible that it would have destroyed him.

As long as his weirdness stayed invisible, he could get up in the morning, eat his breakfast, ride to school on a scratched-up blue bicycle, and look exactly like all the other children growing up in Søborg at that time.

Children like Viggo—I think there are more of them than anyone suspects—carry their secrets with them all their lives. Perhaps as life goes on, some of their distorted worries are replaced by new visions and even stranger obsessions, by totally new tics and secret imaginings, longings, anger, and involuntary movements. Yet it is all part of the same thing: a dark substance that remains intact deep within the human body. What believers, for lack of a better term, call the Soul.

And which no one can see or prove exists.

For people as conscientious as Viggo Larssen, their entire being develops over the years into an underground network of tunnels and hallways that only extremely observant adults would sense were there—though they'd never gain access.

One day his friend Verner asked a question, quietly so no one else could hear.

"Sometimes you seem a little . . . sad?"

That was a heavy and difficult word for an eight-year-old to voice.
But Viggo never answered.

***

Office of the Prime Minister
Thursday, January 6, afternoon

The fifth day after the Widow's disappearance, the two brothers received
a visit from their two undersecretaries, who marched into the office with
a pair of trusted advisers, both so-called spin doctors.

So there were six tremendously powerful men gathered in the prime
minister's office, sitting in fine antique chairs. And all but one of those
men were asking themselves how they could fade into the wallpaper, in
the hope that someone else would be the one to be struck senseless by
the Bear's opening assault.

That included Palle Blegman's own second in command, who was
currently sitting closest to him; his high-ranking status didn't help him in
the least right now, however. The Bear's demented rage affected everyone
in his path. If his gold wristwatch hadn't been an Omega Speedmaster
'57, it would have stopped on the spot—that's how violent the atmo-
spheric pressure was inside that room. Time seemed to stand still inside
the office with the spectacular views of the city's rooftops and spires.

"It's been *six* days!" he roared at his permanent undersecretary.

No one would dare to correct the realm's top official: *Barely five,
actually.* The Widow's disappearance had been discovered by the two
brothers at 5:57 p.m., on the first day of the year. After which, everything
had gone to hell. At least that's what Palle was thinking, that the whole
thing was like one giant absurd joke, the work of some out-of-control
demon with only one aim in mind: to wipe out the Blegman family.

"I want the *entire* police force in this damn *shithole* working on the
case!" His voice maintained its thundering volume.

Both undersecretaries stiffened involuntarily. *Shithole* could refer either to the country's capital or to the entire kingdom over which the Bear ruled. Such an uncivilized term for the country, with its rolling landscape and broad beech trees.

Technically the request was impossible. The Bear's top government official opened his mouth to point out the total absence of logic in that request.

Then he lost his nerve and shut up.

He knew other department heads who dared contradict their superiors. They discussed it at the Tårbæk Club, the nation's most legendary and exclusive network, which usually met on the first Tuesday of every month. That discussion topic always made him noticeably silent among the other officials who sometimes criticized their bosses. Palle Blegman was a difficult and unpredictable opponent.

The prime minister's brother saved him at the last moment: "Palle, we can't just . . ." He stopped. He was about to make the same objection.

If the moment hadn't been so serious, someone might have started to laugh. But no one dared do that.

"I want her found now! Alive or . . . in whatever state!" The Bear slammed his mammoth paw on his desk, and the pretty copper lamp with the floral, hand-sewn shade fell to the floor with a bang.

The minister of justice's personal adviser, sitting nearby, looked as if he were about to pick it up but decided against it; any sudden movement might detonate the next explosion. The antique desk had absorbed the impact of the prime minister's anger, but there was no certainty it would do so again.

"The only thing we hear from the Homicide Boss is that the police are searching and searching and that *no news* must be viewed as *good news* . . . but that's utter nonsense! If someone has taken her and is sitting around waiting for . . . something . . . is that good?"

The five members of his audience shook their heads no in unison.

"The Danish Broadcasting Corporation . . . ," said Palle Blegman, staring directly at his own spin doctor, a narrow-shouldered man with pale skin and a pointy nose who used to be the DBC's TV news editor. As a trusted adviser, he was clever enough to sense the question mark following the minister's remark—and strangely brave enough to reply.

"The DBC has started to dig into . . . well, everything about you . . . your family . . . your past . . ." His courage only lasted so long before his voice trailed off.

"*Verner Jensen!*" The prime minister exploded again.

Now the Ministry of Justice's undersecretary gave it a go. "Yes, Verner Jensen is the news chief. He must have followed in the police's . . . in our people's footsteps. Maybe there's a leak . . ."

"You better *fucking* believe there's a leak!" The Bear flew out of his chair, and everyone momentarily thought he would knock the other man to the floor. "I want them stopped. I want . . . *Verner Jensen* is a vicious, poisonous . . . *shit turd!*"

Shit turd, the prime minister's top official thought, was totally redundant and oddly old-fashioned.

"A *snake!*" The prime minister had found a more current term.

But no one could respond to his accusations.

No one could solve the huge problem at hand. Namely, where had the Widow Blegman gone? Nobody—least of all some senior citizen in a Danish nursing home—could simply vanish into thin air. Silence descended upon them, eventually filling the entire room.

That was just a little under one full day before they found her.

***

The Lighthouse on the Cape
Tuesday, January 6, evening

I could already hear the sound of the six o'clock news as I clambered up the slope toward the Lighthouse, flashlight in hand, the scratchy voice sounding slightly dramatic, as if the terrible state of the entire kingdom was being documented right then.

Nothing unusual about that. Viggo Larssen often sat on the bench, the door to his living room slightly ajar, listening to the evening news—but I had never heard his old transistor radio turned up so loud before.

He didn't so much as glance at me as I sat down on the bench beside him.

For at least the twentieth time, the news anchor had questioned someone at police headquarters in Copenhagen, and the voices of both the anchor and the police sounded urgent. Something had to happen—someone needed to find the Widow.

Other reporters were literally swarming around the government buildings on Slotsholmen, and two national newspapers and three television stations had supplemented their on-the-ground forces with helicopters; the danger of a collision loomed large if someone didn't separate them soon. Also, no one really understood the point of filming from the rooftops.

Only that it was an unusually *good story*, as they used to say: the mother of the prime minister and minister of justice had been kidnapped, was perhaps lying alone in some unknown location where every second counted toward finding her alive (like in some American movie). Everyone had seen films about people being buried alive, and as the days passed without any news, there was plenty of time to discuss such nauseating scenarios.

Early that afternoon the minister of justice—shielded from reporters by a veritable phalanx of government officials, bodyguards, and security personnel—was escorted to the prime minister's office.

A shiver had run through the newshounds in front of Parliament. The Danish press corps perceived that unmistakable blend of excitement and schadenfreude that struck the wealthy and the nobility in these situations. Despite all their castles and towers and gilded halls, they suddenly found themselves at wit's end. Even in that land of fairy tales, no one would confess to such a reaction in front of the camera, and no reporter could put it into words. Instead, they would conjure up common themes everyone could relate to.

Did they find any clues indicating a kidnapping? Had someone demanded a ransom? Had the police been secretly contacted by the kidnappers?

Was she lying dead somewhere?

I sat down on the bench and glanced at Viggo Larssen, but I couldn't discern any reaction. Nor had I expected one.

I had already considered the connection between the Widow's disappearance and his somewhat frantic behavior over the past few days—especially the dispatch of those three letters. I had a clear idea who the recipients were, even if their contents remained a mystery.

After all, there were not so many possibilities to choose from in a lonely man's existence.

Viggo Larssen had no idea how much I knew about his past, and he wasn't going to find out, unless he caught me in the act, lying in the bed next to the three-legged stool and reading his mother's first diary. Anyway, he had to know that the police at some time or other would find him and ask the questions any skilled investigator would ask once they reached the obvious point—which they naturally were going to reach. They would ask about the accident that bound his life inextricably to the Blegman clan, and they would search for a possible explanation for the strange coincidence they'd discover. A second's hesitation—and everything would change.

Some months before my arrival on the cape, I'd written an anonymous letter to him that I hadn't found, despite searching all his drawers and between the books in the bookcase. He must have burned it or thrown it away, and in a way I could understand why. It had been a hasty, ill-conceived thing to do. I had told him about the family in the Yellow House, not in detail, but enough that he could figure out the rest; in my naïveté, I'd been convinced it was the right thing to do. Yet it was singularly stupid and, to a certain extent, the reason I was here now.

He had definitely visited the Widow, which I—in my foolish role as anonymous adviser—had suggested; but the stubborn and unyielding old woman had maintained her decades-long silence (I should have foreseen that), and he had gone back to the cape without any reply. Which had only made matters worse.

I thought I could free him of his guilt, though I should have known better.

The problem was that he believed only one person responsible: himself. The boy who had neglected to be by his mother's side at the moment when, in a perfect world, he should have been there.

**

Søborg, near Copenhagen
1963

To everyone who knew her, his grandmother was what people in the early sixties called a warmhearted person.

Whenever she went to the bakery (her miserable husband on her arm), she smiled gently at the small children playing hopscotch on the street. She stopped at garden gates and chatted with the young housewives about their recipes and flowers. She bent down and patted Miss Bachmann's white poodle—even though everyone knew that that dog barked at night and left small droppings behind the garages during the day. You'd see her out on the patio, whistling heavenward at the birds or on the lookout for a wayward hedgehog or chasing feral cats away from the small birds by the birdfeeder on the patio, which she filled with sunflower seeds and millet.

Strangely enough, her concern for all the creatures in the bushes and trees ended far too often in tragedy.

One sunny afternoon she found a blackbird with a broken leg in the garden; she wound gauze around the break and laid it on a bed of straw in an old cigar box. During festive occasions, Viggo's grandfather liked to smoke cigars, and his grandmother would save the boxes for buttons, needles, and thread—and blackbirds. This one died during the night, probably choking on the lingering smell of old cigars in the cramped box.

The next day she found its fledglings—its mate had apparently flown away—and fed them boiled potatoes, which she thought cured everything. They died one after the other, and she cried for hours, sitting on a lawn chair, just as she'd cried when a sparrow flew into the recently cleaned living room window.

One day a black cat showed up on the patio beneath the living room window, its claws wrapped around a little bullfinch, all torn and bloody. It felt like an omen.

The next Sunday the patio door suddenly stood open, and Piphans the Second took off from the top of his cage, flew triumphantly through the living room, out the open door, into freedom, arching high into the sky and landing in a birch tree, just high enough so that no one could reach him.

Viggo's grandmother stood beneath the tree and called repeatedly, whistling the two-toned melody she had taught all her canaries to sing.

It didn't help, of course. The bird simply sat there as the sun began to set, and she finally stopped calling, tears streaming down her cheeks. Viggo's grandfather never got up from his garden chair, where he sat, occasionally dozing, under a blue umbrella. He was the one who had left the patio door open.

He simply sat there, unmoving, watching the already doomed creature.

At that moment, a shadow came rushing down from above, the sun at its back, almost like Battler Britton in his Spitfire in Viggo's war comics. A black raven swooped down on the little yellow quarry, the black almost swallowing the yellow—the way a tarantula would devour a small, fat caterpillar.

Viggo's grandfather let out a grunt, drowned out by his grandmother's scream; then the doomed bird crashed to the ground in a flash of red, landing in a clump on the edge of the strawberry patch.

Viggo and his grandmother ran over. Piphans the Second lay completely crumpled up, his head half hacked off and both eyes dark and glazed; they had burst at exactly the moment when freedom and defiance met with horror and death. High above their heads, the raven let out a triumphant cry. Viggo looked up at the bird, then toward the patio where his grandfather was still sitting.

The old man's face was in shadow beneath the blue umbrella, but it seemed to Viggo as if he had glanced up at the raven and winked. It must have been his imagination.

His grandmother gently wrapped Piphans the Second in the dark purple cloth they usually covered his cage with in the evenings and then laid him to rest next to his predecessor. This time the Blegman brothers were not in attendance.

The next day she crossed Maglegårds Allé and rang the doorbell at the Yellow House. She'd never done so before. Then, curiously enough, she and the Blegman brothers' mother went to the pet store, where they each bought a canary.

Mrs. Blegman also bought the largest cage in the store.

The cage and the bird were for little Arrow, who always ran so fast that the adults feared he would one day run right out into the street before anyone saw him.

"He needs something more peaceful to deal with," Viggo's grandmother had said to the Blegman brothers' mother, as she had several times before whenever they would meet at the fish market or the corner butcher's.

Everyone in the neighborhood knew that the boy had received too little oxygen during birth and may have therefore been a bit mentally deficient. He was only interested in running, and he ran after the sparrows and the blackbirds in the garden and tried to catch the great tits on the birdfeeder. Over time, his father and brothers became more irritated with him. Arrow was blond, blue eyed, loving, and dreamy—the complete opposite of his two brothers, who tyrannized the neighborhood children and whose clenched fists and menacing scowls sent even the larger boys fleeing. Obviously, they were more than a little jealous of their younger brother, probably because of the way their mother protected him, seduced by his joyous, playful madness. Finally her husband floated the idea of placing the boy in a calmer environment outside the home, but little Arrow's mother knew instinctively that then she'd never get him back. Instead, she would try to steer him out of the tyrant's sight, and she decided that a calm, indoor interest might offer a solution.

No one knows how the Patriarch in the Yellow House on Maglegårds Allé took to the little yellow songbird. But those first few weeks, Arrow spent almost all his time taming the bird, getting it to whistle, and teaching it to sit on his shoulder and nip at his earlobe. In line at the grocer's, Mrs. Blegman apprised Viggo's grandmother of the promising developments. Little Arrow had christened his new friend Buster, after the crazy clown in *Cirkus Buster*, which all children loved and could buy a recording of, if they had the money and owned a record player.

Despite the older brothers' blatant contempt for the yellow songbird, everything would have remained idyllic—it was April, and the springtime sun had made all the buds bloom on the bushes and trees throughout the suburban neighborhood—if the Patriarch hadn't blown up three small kittens in the garage.

As leading member of the Conservative People's Party, he had built up a vast network of influential pillars of society, whom he feted on special occasions at the family's abandoned farm in Sweden. Reportedly, not only party members and prominent business folks showed up at Blegman's Swedish house, but also prominent and powerful Social Democrats (among them several ministers), who discussed the nation's problems with people they otherwise would never allow themselves to be seen with.

Yet everyone knew about Peter Blegman's temper and his often-brutal behavior, though no one dared say it out loud. And when the Supreme Court lawyer set a goal for himself, his stubbornness was legendary. So, naturally, the three little kittens he had found behind a bush in his garden in Søborg, left by a feral cat, didn't stand a chance.

The blast from the old rifle he'd inherited from his father could be heard from blocks away. He had lured the three doomed kittens into the garage with a bowlful of cream and then loaded the old weapon with black powder and bullets. At such close range it sounded more like a bomb exploding than a rifle shot.

Two of the kittens splattered all over the back wall, where they were found in bloody piles when Mrs. Blegman and her three sons came rushing into the garage.

The Patriarch had just reloaded his weapon, so that they managed to see the third and last of his unwelcome guests pulverized in a cloud of red droplets and incinerated clumps of scorched cat fur. The family's reactions were wildly divergent.

The middle brother, Poul, caught his father's satisfied, almost delighted expression and immediately broke out in high-pitched laughter. If there was anything redeeming about the oldest brother Palle's response, perhaps it was the initial shocked look in his blue eyes at the sight of the three kittens. Perhaps it would've been a stretch to call it compassion, but a feeling seemed to hover in the air—up through the gun smoke, up to the ceiling of the garage—as if he knew that a course had just been mapped out for him, a course no one could ever change.

And then, of course, he laughed even louder than Poul.

Mrs. Blegman covered her mouth with her hands and screamed into them. You would think that her youngest son, that naïve little dreamer, Arrow, would have followed her example, but no. To her horror, his mother heard him laugh even louder than the others, clapping his small hands together and yelling, "One more time! One more time! One more time!" But there were no more kittens to massacre, and instead Peter Blegman placed his smoking weapon in a corner and left the battlefield, followed by his three sons.

Maybe the episode didn't significantly change anything between the three boys and their mother.

On the other hand, Mrs. Blegman must have seen the writing on the wall—writing she had long feared yet always anticipated. No higher power, let alone her own earthly efforts, could stave off her husband's influence on their three boys.

Hopelessly, she had watched Palle and Poul each turning into a spitting image of their father, and now she saw that little Arrow was willing to follow them.

After that day she must have given up trying to keep him safe in their warm living room, sitting in front of the canary's cage, far from his brothers and father. Little Arrow ran back and forth in the garden, while he sang and called to the birds, as if crazy. And maybe he was.

Viggo's grandmother stood at her living room window, shaking her head at the boy's haphazard, demented movements on the garden tiles across the way.

"That won't end well," she whispered to Piphans the Third, who was sitting on her shoulder.

He had tucked his little beak behind her earlobe.

Naturally.

***

It was August 23, 1963, only a month before Viggo Larssen's eighth birthday. None of the families in the neighborhood near Maglegårds Allé would ever forget that day.

A few days earlier, Viggo's grandfather had borrowed his brother's car after driving him and his wife to the airport to catch a flight to Palma de Mallorca.

His younger brother had both the time and the money for such luxuries, thanks to a generous pension from FLSmidth, where he had recently ended a run as vice president with a very high salary.

He had also been given the company car, a beautiful blue Opel Kapitän, which Viggo's grandfather could only dream of owning—and borrow on rare occasions.

His grandfather had to run errands in the city that day—which he rarely did—but Viggo could see his grandfather's eyes beaming when he set out that afternoon in the shiny car. He really wanted to go with his grandfather; he tugged at his sleeve and begged his grandfather to let him come, but his grandmother called from the living room and told him to do his homework.

Later, they pieced together his route—the police had mapped it out quite thoroughly: Viggo's grandfather had driven down Frederiksborgvej into the city center, past Tivoli, back toward the Danish Broadcasting studios on Rosenørns Allé, right onto H. C. Ørsteds Vej, and then left onto Åboulevard on his way home. He passed the row houses at Bellahøj and minutes later turned onto Horsebakken before reaching the fatal stretch of Maglegårds Allé known as Death's Highway.

It had drizzled a bit earlier that day, and perhaps the road was a little slippery, although you couldn't tell; afterward, no one could blame the old man for anything.

Viggo's grandfather sped up slightly as the road began to rise, right before the curve with the small grocery and the neighborhood of row houses to the right and the large villas to the left, but according to later measurements, at no more than the speed limit.

A short distance beyond the curve, just across from Viggo Larssen's backyard, was the Yellow House where the three Blegman brothers lived with their parents. Anyone standing on the sidewalk at the moment the car approached might have heard a front door slam and seen a flash of movement in the garden in front of the Yellow House.

An observant soul would have noticed that the gate to the little front yard was open—which was unusual. Any passerby who considered childhood safety would have shut it. But there wasn't a soul on the street.

The boy they called Arrow must have started running as soon as he jumped off the steps to the front door. He ran out the open garden gate at great speed, his little blue ball dancing on the moss-green rubber boots that were found on the road almost a block away.

It was impossible for the driver of the blue Opel to stop—as the police later ascertained. His speed was appropriate and visibility satisfactory, but there was no way to account for the little boy chasing the ball out past the curb.

Right at that moment, Viggo was putting water in the little birdbath that Piphans the First and Second used to giddily splash around in.

He heard the screeching brakes, and then he heard something that sounded like a muffled slam and a scream—or maybe it was the plaintive sound of locked wheels and tires on the asphalt.

He heard his grandmother let out a cry—and then order him to go stay in the living room. But his curiosity was too great. He tore open the garden door and ran down the path toward the road and the Yellow House.

He remembered the first thing he saw. It reminded him of the raven and the canary.

A long shadow was standing over a small yellow pile on the road, the darkness almost swallowing the yellow, which suddenly turned another color that no one could ever wash away. Viggo knew immediately that it was blood. His grandmother, frozen on the sidewalk, was staring at the child and the car, which had been turned halfway onto the sidewalk in a vain attempt to avoid what had happened. The boy in the yellow raincoat was lying half under the front bumper.

That sight changed Viggo's life. The contours of the dead boy's body never disappeared from his mind's eye. The yellow, the black, the shine, the asphalt, the hood of the car—steam rising up in the air—the blood oozing out, slowly engulfing the yellow, the boy's oddly peaceful eyes, as if the pain had never reached them.

Then he heard the scream from the car and thought he recognized the sound, though it couldn't be possible.

He reached his grandmother and pulled her back onto the sidewalk in front of the Yellow House. To his horror, he saw the car door open and his grandfather almost tumble onto the road. He saw him crawl on his hands and knees over to the car's front end, pull the little yellow clump free from the bumper, and lift it up in his arms.

His grandfather was sitting there with a little boy in his arms.

A loud cry came from the front yard of the Yellow House, and then the sound of the front door opening wide, slamming into the handrail with a metallic clang. A large man came running out of the gate, and right behind him the two almost equally large bullies who were his sons. Like their father, Palle and Poul flung themselves at Viggo's grandfather as their father brutally kicked the old man, wrenching the small yellow body from him.

His grandfather sat in the gutter with his head in his hands. The still-youthful Palle and Poul stood there, bodies a little lower and narrower than their adult selves, but already with wide backs and fists like bear paws. It was a wonder they didn't touch the old man again.

His grandfather never stated the obvious: *It wasn't my fault—the boy ran out right in front of the car.* He never said it that day on Maglegårds Allé or any time later.

Not even to the police.

Just the opposite, in fact.

"It was my fault . . . oh, it was my fault . . . I should have been able to stop . . ."

His voice faded into deep despair as the police tried to calm him down; it pained Viggo to hear it. He had never seen his grandfather so miserable before, had never seen him cower before anyone or anything.

Even many years later, Viggo still recalled his own reaction, more intense than anything he had ever experienced.

It was an anger that built inside of him until it exploded in his head, turning into a strange, milky mist that blinded him for almost a minute.

He didn't come to until his grandmother touched his arm and pulled him back into their own garden. To safety.

***

The police later figured out what had happened.

It wasn't difficult.

At the scene of the accident, one of the police officers had the presence of mind to hit the nail on the head regarding the question of guilt: Was the gate open?

Several neighbors answered with certainty. Yes . . . Though usually it wasn't.

The policeman nodded. The sidewalk was about an arm's width across. If the little boy had opened the gate first, passed through it, then stepped out onto the road, there would have been plenty of time for the driver to see him and stop, despite the wet asphalt—as long as he was going the speed limit.

Measurements of the skid marks indicated that Viggo's grandfather had indeed been doing so.

In court he said, "The boy came running . . ." Still, despite the truth of this statement, he reiterated what would become his refrain: "It was my fault . . . I should have seen him in time!"

Both boys and their father denied that the gate was open—and no one thought of putting Mrs. Blegman on the witness stand; she was too distraught and out of touch with reality during those weeks following the accident, on strong sedatives and sleeping pills.

The question of guilt was settled in a classic manner. Doubt worked to the accused's advantage. According to the police investigation, Viggo's grandfather had followed all the rules, and everything indicated that the gate was open. Irresponsibly so. Negligently so.

When he was found innocent, Viggo's grandfather cried again, though there was no relief in his tears.

***

Two days after the accident, he had crossed Maglegårds Allé, the road that had lived up to its terrible nickname, which strangely enough no one ever mentioned again. He carried a bouquet of freesia (it was his daughter's favorite flower), and he walked through the garden gate, up the steps to the front door of the Yellow House, and rang the bell. No one had ever seen anything so brave, so foolhardy—or so stupid. Viggo's grandfather simply didn't understand what was in the hearts and minds of those in that house.

The door flew open and a dark shadow towered over him. No one could hear what was said, but Viggo's grandfather stepped back, aghast, then continued backing down the steps, several times almost falling before he backed all the way to the garden gate that he had carefully closed behind him only seconds earlier.

Either the flowers were knocked out of his hands or he dropped them when he realized there was no atonement for his sin. They lay strewn on the garden path.

Arrow was buried some days later, and Viggo walked with his grandmother and grandfather down to Søborg Church.

It was a Wednesday afternoon, and his mother was at work. Viggo sensed that neither she nor his grandmother had any desire to participate in this last ceremony for the little boy, but his grandfather couldn't turn his back on what he thought was his obligation. It was his car that had crushed the little boy to death in the road.

I'd read two pages in Viggo's mother's diary about that afternoon in the cemetery, and it was not a pleasant read. The Blegman family had wanted to bury their son the day before, on his fourth birthday, but the body wasn't released in time. Instead, the ceremony fell on the same day that Jens Otto Krag set his second government, with new ministers, into motion. The problems apparently began when Viggo and his grandparents stepped into the church. I guess his mother got the details from Viggo's grandmother later that day.

The small coffin was up on the altar, and they sat at the very back of the church. Nevertheless, their arrival did not go unnoticed.

A whisper ran through the church until it reached the front rows, where the dead boy's family sat shoulder to shoulder in dark suits and black dresses. Heads turned, and little Arrow's father—the mighty patriarch—started to rise from his seat but was pulled back down onto the pew by an invisible hand. Everyone could feel the anger, like a cold blast of air from an abruptly opened door, as if the Devil had slipped into the flower-bedecked church and was standing in the shadows, grinning behind the baptismal font.

Frightened, Viggo's grandmother turned toward her husband, but he seemed oblivious to the Blegman family's reaction.

Following the short service, Viggo and his grandparents stood up, like all the others, as the flower-covered casket was carried past them on its way out of the church. The two brothers were in font, the Patriarch at the back, to the right. None of them looked around, and none of them were crying. They didn't want anyone to see their grief.

Outside the church, Arrow's mourners had gathered behind the hearse, and although Viggo's grandfather also tried to stop—which would have been a total catastrophe—his grandmother managed to regain control of her miserable husband. They walked closely, arm in arm, and Viggo did something he had never done before: he took his grandfather's hand—and the old man let him.

All three of them stopped briefly when they reached the cemetery gate, while his grandmother struggled with the heavy wrought iron handle. But before she could open it, her husband suddenly turned around, let go of Viggo's hand, and stepped away from his wife and grandson. The hearse had stopped a little ways away, and they could see Mrs. Blegman standing with both hands resting on her son's coffin. She had black gloves on, and little Arrow's coffin was only shoved halfway into the dark, shining car. It was as if his mother were trying to stop that final part of his journey and, with one final, futile gesture, pull him back to life, to his family, and to the sidewalk in front of the Yellow House. Back before the moment that never should have happened.

Viggo looked up at his grandfather and discovered, to his horror, that he was standing with his face turned toward the church and crying. The man who had never cried for anyone. Not for himself, not for his wife, not for his daughter, and never for Viggo—yet he was crying for the boy in the coffin. Viggo hunched over and ran; he kicked the half-open gate to the side (it struck the cemetery wall with a loud bang), and he could hear his grandmother's frightened cry behind him.

But he didn't stop, not before he reached Marienborg Allé, a good distance away. And he didn't come home till much later.

In the following days, they would see Mrs. Blegman standing at her window in the Yellow House, staring down at the spot where her son had departed this life.

They could hear her giving commands to the two remaining sons. Yet her voice was flat, toneless. They saw her in the garden with her husband, as he lifted the gate off its hinges, laid it on the grass, and mounted a bracket with a strong steel spring that would ensure that it shut automatically after it was opened.

But it was too late, of course, which you could sense from Mrs. Blegman's immovable presence during the two hours it took to do the repairs.

It's a strange fact—one that both Viggo Larssen and I understood only much later—that Mrs. Blegman had been the one who had opened the garden gate on the day Arrow died. There was no reason to worry about Palle or Poul doing anything as foolish or clumsy as their reckless little brother. They would calculate every step in life without any admonishments, steel springs, or advice from the mother who had protected their little brother against everything he couldn't understand. Arrow had literally run out of life.

On the third day, she set Buster free, and it was undoubtedly the most bizarre of her few, though violent, reactions to Arrow's death.

She came out the door with a little yellow clump of feathers in her hands, and Viggo's grandmother, who had been dozing in the late summer sun, rose halfway out of her garden chair.

With a swift motion, Mrs. Blegman loosened her grip around the bird. It looked like a little yellow streak shooting straight up, high above the villa's roof and up above the houses on Maglegårds Allé, disappearing into the sky. Viggo's grandmother was relieved that Buster had at least had the presence of mind not to seek refuge in the nearest tree. No blackbird came tearing out of anywhere to knock it to the ground in a cloud of yellow and red.

She turned and walked over to her husband, who was sitting beneath the umbrella. She called for Viggo and put water on for coffee. They would play Hearts, and they would let Viggo's grandfather win, as always. The only difference was that he no longer made that triumphant click with his tongue when he crushed his grandson with the ten of hearts.

Later, Viggo's grandmother heard from friends that the Blegman family matriarch had kept little Buster's cage, leaving it standing on the living room windowsill of the Yellow House.

***

After Arrow's burial, Viggo's mother came home with a little package.

She handed it to her son and said, "I know it's been a tough day . . . so I've bought you a gift."

He was hoping it was a box full of small cars—or maybe a game— but to his surprise it was a book, and on the cover was a small boy being pulled into the sky by a flock of large birds. He was holding on to the birds by a bunch of long cords, his face turned up toward the stars.

Viggo's mother had never given him a book before, and for a moment he thought it was a comic book, because both the boy and the clear yellow stars around him were drawn with a thin outline, as Viggo would have drawn them. The boy's hair was as yellow as the stars and in an odd way reminded him of Arrow, except that he was *flying*—not running. The boy was gazing up at the birds pulling him, with a slightly surprised, almost sad expression on his face.

Right below the birds were three large words in delicate green letters: *The Little Prince.*

His mother took the book and pointed at the cover with its picture of the small boy being carried away by a flock of birds. Then she placed the book on the table by his bed. "It's a book I read when I was young, a book for both children and adults."

Viggo nodded. He just hoped it wasn't boring. Many years later his grandmother told him that Arrow's mother used to read it aloud to her son.

As Viggo lay in bed, after the funeral, still thinking about his grandfather crying for the little boy in the coffin, his mother read him the first chapter of the new book and smiled at her son to cheer him up. He could hear how happy she was—as grown-ups often are when they read aloud—when she came to the first drawing of a hat lying on top of an elephant that had swallowed a snake . . .

. . . or was it the other way around?

Viggo could tell that his mother understood, and he smiled at her.

That evening she played classical music so long that he finally fell asleep.

***

The next day Viggo asked, "Where is the prince's mother?"

He thought that the prince didn't have a mother since he'd landed all alone in the desert.

His mother said, "All children have a mother—but his is far away."

She smiled again when the prince became incredibly happy about a box with three holes because he thought there was a sheep inside.

Viggo had thought about Arrow then, because the boy in the book was just as odd and maybe also even a little retarded; that was the word his grandmother had used to describe the boy in the Yellow House.

"They should take better care of him," she had said. But they didn't.

In the book the little prince saw the snake that had swallowed the elephant, which none of the adults had seen: snakes can be quite dangerous. His mother lowered her voice a little when reading that part.

That night Viggo had the strange dream he'd had before, about a woman waving to him, calling him to her. This time the dream was clearer—the fog had lifted—and it returned frequently throughout the fall and winter. It never lasted very long, and there was only one person present, his mother, and she never moved. She stood in the desert—or maybe it was the ocean (everything was an endless, shimmering white)—and she looked at him without coming closer. The odd thing was that she was reaching her hands toward him, as if she wanted to say something or call him to her; he had the clear sense that she wanted him to come closer, that she wanted to take him somewhere. He woke up in the darkness with both arms folded over his blue-striped pajama top and his fists clenched so tightly that his fingers hurt.

He had never awakened like that before.

He lay there for a while, staring into the darkness, remembering the bizarre vision. His mother had been wearing a long black suit, or maybe it was a dress; her legs appeared to be bare, but he couldn't see her feet.

He never said anything to her about his peculiar dream, because he felt it would ruin her joy in reading the book.

She read the whole story about the strange prince in a little over three weeks—one chapter every night—and then placed it back on his table, where he left it. With all his heart, he felt that the boy in the desert was irritating, much too confused, and way too selfish. He didn't ask for repairs for his good friend's airplane, even though the pilot (who made an emergency landing, as Battler Britton would have done) only had enough water for seven days and risked dying before his engine started.

Finally, the prince was bitten by a snake and fell over dead in the sand. Viggo thought long about that: the snake and the boy. He really didn't care about either of them.

His mother thought that one passage was especially beautiful, and she repeated it, again and again: in it, the Little Prince said he would be living in one of the stars and that you could hear him laughing in the stars at night.

That's what the little boy said before he died.

Viggo hated those words.

When he opened his window, he didn't see any stars, only the Yellow House, whose outline told him he wasn't blind.

He closed his eyes and tried to imagine a boy who looked like him, standing in the desert with a flock of blue birds on strings. It looked totally wrong.

Much later, on the bench by the lighthouse residence, I understood why he kept that book his mother used to read to him. Even though the boy irritated him, his mother had loved it, and he knew why. Perhaps she saw her own boy in the little prince, a boy so good that he would give up his life for a sheep, or a flower, or a sunset.

Yet, Viggo knew that he was nothing like that. He was the dark side of everything light and fragile. The little prince was ethereal, innocent, brave, and wise; Viggo was shy, mistrustful, strange, and afraid—afraid of almost everything.

But he hid it in the darkness. He closed his eyes and hid it.

CHAPTER 7

Office of the Homicide Boss
Wednesday, January 7, late morning

"Why?"

Through all their years together, Number Two had never seen his friend, colleague, and boss so close to exploding—or even raising his voice. Normally, as everyone at headquarters knew, the Homicide Boss faced the most critical moments with a low-key calm.

But this was no normal crisis. Clearly.

As the Homicide Boss placed the photo they had just received from Forensics in front of him, his hands had—quite uncharacteristically—trembled a bit.

To any outsider, the photo would seem innocuous, peaceful—almost typically Danish.

Still, the Homicide Boss shook his head in wonder, as did Number Two, because what they found in the Widow's apartment, what the officers had photographed, made no sense at all.

They saw the cage with the canary in it, just as they'd seen it the first night after the Widow had disappeared, sitting on the windowsill where they'd found one of the plastic pieces, the bird a bit frightened.

"So why is she telling us this now?" The Homicide Boss stopped, at a loss for words.

Number Two had just gotten back from Solbygaard after receiving the call, then rushing over to question the nursing home manager for almost two hours.

"Because she was placed on sick leave by the crisis counselors," Number Two said. "So she couldn't meet us at Solbygaard until today, and that's when—"

"—she discovered something was wrong."

Number Two nodded.

"Totally wrong . . . ?"

"Yes."

"It shouldn't have been there?"

"No."

"And she's certain of that?"

Number Two nodded. They'd all been certain: the nursing home manager, who was placed on sick leave yet again following the interrogation, and the health care assistants, who were questioned about the same thing—the bird in the cage.

They'd all confirmed it.

"And not one of them thought it might be important?"

"Not the assistants," said Number Two, sounding almost apologetic on their behalf. "They'd given it some seeds, a piece of poppy seed bread, and some water . . ."

"A piece of poppy seed bread?"

The Homicide Boss dropped his head, exhaling deeply.

Seeds, a piece of poppy seed bread, and water. You could almost hear him silently repeating the words to himself, enraged.

"They didn't think it meant anything," said Number Two. For some reason, he was defending the young workers, who had seemed as frightened as the bird. "It wasn't until their manager came to work that she realized we needed to know about it." He placed an index finger on Forensics' magnified picture of the birdcage with the little yellow creature inside.

"So the Widow brought the birdcage with her when she moved into the nursing home, but there had *never* been a bird in it?" The Homicide Boss asked the question almost offhandedly to himself.

Number Two confirmed that with a shrug. No, there had never been any bird.

"So where did it come from?"

"She brought the cage with her as a reminder of her son who died. It had been his cage. But you're not allowed to have pets at Solbygaard."

They were both thinking the same thing, at the same time, without needing to say it out loud.

They had to keep the bizarre discovery of the bird in the cage a secret for now. It shouldn't have been there, and they had absolutely no idea what it meant.

By all accounts, someone had left a living bird in the old cage at the same time the Widow disappeared.

It was such a strange occurrence that neither of the two police officers had any hunch about a possible motive.

"They couldn't have gone there very often." Number Two was stating the obvious. The Blegman brothers must have seen the cage with the bird on the windowsill when they'd arrived to find the room empty and their mother gone—yet they hadn't mentioned it.

The Homicide Boss lifted his gaze from the picture of the birdcage, which the technicians were examining at that moment.

The two investigators looked at each other. They wouldn't be going home anytime soon. If the press, and thus the brothers, heard about their strange discovery before they'd come up with any theory at all, they'd be thrown off the case.

They would have to spend the night at the office to survive the coming days.

Number Two had no problem reading his boss's questioning look. There had to be something in the case—something—that could move them further along in the investigation, which was currently threatening to unravel.

Following a tip from a retired policeman, the new deputy on the team had found the only possible lead, a note from an old police report, attached to a several-decades-old newspaper clipping from the *Søborg News*, dated Friday, August 24, 1963.

Fatal Accident: Boy Killed on Dangerous Road.

The article continued: *The boy killed yesterday was the son of the Conservative Party's board member, Supreme Court lawyer Peter Blegman.*

The father of both the country's current prime minister and the minister of justice.

"Glorious work," said the Homicide Boss, though Number Two couldn't tell if he was being sarcastic. Obviously, the note offered no great revelation; it was just one small newspaper account of the accident the press had already briefly mentioned as a dark chapter in the family's life.

"We *did* say no clue is too small. But there's no correlation. How does their little brother's death—five decades ago—have any connection to their mother's disappearance today? It doesn't make any sense."

Number Two nodded in agreement.

He may have even sighed, though no one could have heard it. As a skilled detective, he had learned how to sigh without anyone noticing.

They couldn't decipher any more in those clues that morning, even with the collective powers of their investigative experience.

***

Ove from Søborg
Wednesday, January 7, afternoon

Ove Nilsen's title appeared at the top of his business card: *Strategic Planner*. Then just below: *Business Development and Personal Management*.

He had inspired a whole new zeitgeist in the country's public and private workplaces, an entirely new worldview with innovative milestones for development and management; he had reinvigorated perceptions about business structures and employee relations, and he had opened the market to all types of tools for development and progress—many created in an almost euphoric mix of his own ideas and swiped foreign management concepts.

Countless employees at both small and large companies had drunk his elixir, which bore no semblance to the earthier mixture he'd sold as a child in his neighborhood (though it seemed just as exotic, complex, and irresistible).

Because no one knew exactly what he was selling, everyone believed in its efficacy. Naturally, they had to tell others about it, or they would seem naïve and gullible to have swallowed it in the first place. First the neighbors on his block—and then half a nation, ultimately communicating with each other in business code: *benchmark, facilitate*, and *think outside the box*. All of them dressed in black and white and yellow hats—it was completely marvelous, as the old fairy tale writers would have observed.

And all of them struck by a group psychosis in which no one dared refuse for fear of judgment by their colleagues. *You're behind the times. If you don't hire a business consultant, your company will die.*

It was a totally updated version of "The Emperor's New Clothes."

No one could vomit such powerful and irresistible half-Danish, half-English slogans in their customers' faces like Ove could. It had to do with *presentation* of the right *concept* for every occasion and every *opportunity*.

The incantations exploded like fireworks on their way up, but on the way down, had the same effect—none, except for alienating large numbers of employees who acknowledged (in secret, fearful of being fired) that their bosses were complete idiots. Companies had slowly begun to grasp the truth in 2011 and 2012, when the rhetoric from all the management consultants had proven useless for solving the global crisis or even keeping the Chinese and all the new competitors at bay.

So Ove Nilsen had a problem: his business was starting to fade.

He had just completed an unpleasant four-hour workday, most of those hours spent counseling Solbygaard Nursing Home's management during its acute crisis following the Widow's sudden disappearance.

They'd be receiving a hefty bill—but still it was a setback for his plan to use the Widow's disappearance to promote the concept that would save his ailing business (not to mention saving the beautiful home in the Dyrehaven woods that both he and Adda loved so much).

He sat in his softest easy chair, which he had covered with a gigantic polar bear skin, complete with razor-sharp claws and an enormous snarling head dangling toward the floor. From here he could enjoy the view of the garden and the woods; the panoramic window filled most of the western wall in the living room. He poured himself a generous glass of Rémy Martin.

Despite his current challenges, he was feeling quite satisfied.

For almost seven years, he had managed to ride out the global crisis as if it were nothing but a drop in the bucket—as adviser, chief consultant, director, and sole proprietor of Blue Light Communications. Companies, municipalities, and ministries knew his company's name as simply BLC.

"Call Ove at BLC," the country's top executives would say when things began to heat up.

The number of inquiries fell, however. At the last minute, Ove Nilsen hit on the solution he should have seen ages ago: developing a business plan for what had become the country's great problem, the rising number of aging citizens, which, if handled properly, could be a gold mine, a dance on all those waiting graves.

He had stumbled upon a huge overlooked market. All those Danes on their way out who had saved up and wouldn't be afraid to spend part of their fortunes on a warmhearted consultant's tempting offer: to bring a little light and joy to the darkness of their physical decay, loneliness, fear of dying, and tremendous boredom.

Ove viewed the latter as a particularly significant factor for the inmates at nursing homes like Solbygaard. Accordingly, he had presented his proposal to a number of municipalities, a plan for the physical and mental training of the elderly, listing all the advantages he could guarantee that would result in a win-win situation for all involved parties: community taxpayers, the elderly, their caregivers, and—in all modesty—Blue Light Communications. A mix of ingredients that no one had seen before, yet one that still promised a miracle. Ove had been the first to recognize the market potential of the aging; of course it required a certain cynicism—he knew that. No one else had connected expansive, effective consulting with the elderly and ailing.

Initially, it looked like a serious loser of a project. A flock of unmotivated, worn-out, world-weary people, frightened by sickness and death, gathered at the door to the unknown.

Ove smiled at the thought.

It was that last part—death itself—that had given him the idea for a way out of the global crisis, that was the crucial concept in his "New Eden Strategy."

What to his colleagues looked like a huge waste of time and money—and a really cynical one, for that matter—was, in Ove's mind, about to become an immensely profitable business.

He rested his legs on the little footstool and took a sip from his generous glass of cognac through a thin green straw.

Every day at 3:00 p.m., the sole proprietor of Blue Light Communications began his afternoon ritual, consisting of a good dram of either cognac or highlands whisky. So he wouldn't be unnecessarily tipsy before dinner, he had discovered "the straw principle," which he only used in private. First of all, it was cozy to sip through a straw, reminding him of his childhood spent sipping Orange Crush, and second, every indulgent sip became smaller, making it that much more tasty.

The straw was barely functional, bent in the middle and wrecked. Yet even though he earned much more than most people, he couldn't stand wasting straws; surely a neurotic trait, but then everyone is neurotic, as Ove Nilsen knew better than anyone. He had spent half his life living off people's neuroses.

Poke at your customers' neuroses to make them weak in the knees. Not even the top business leaders or most powerful politicians would reveal what truly plagued them in life—not even to their own wives or husbands, and certainly not to their parents and never to their children. It was always the same thing just beneath those shiny surfaces: uncertainty, fear, strange visions, obsessions, and longing. A longing that can't be put into words, so they can never fulfill it. It knows no social class, no phase of existence—not childhood, youth, or old age—no specific worldview, no difference in experience or intelligence.

Poke them, and they fall on their asses, every time.

Sipping lightly through the green straw, he could feel the liquid oozing down his throat, crisp and warm. He opened the folder he had sent a year earlier to Gentofte municipality and Solbygaard Nursing Home. He had readily given it to the police when the detectives had asked about it. Although the Widow had barely participated in any of his life-enhancing activities, the folder still provided insight into her daily existence at the home.

In the center of the folder sat the glossy brochure, which the conservative Gentofte politicians had found irresistible. He had miraculously offered to prolong life—and at the same time increase its quality—for all of the nursing home's 173 residents, and it wouldn't cost the municipality or the nursing home more than the price of the initial operating equipment. The residents would contribute their own money to the project as soon as they realized its advantages; they would buy shares in

Ove's promise to improve and above all prolong life—a life that, thanks to Ove's brilliant concept, would last forever, in a way.

He smiled above his straw as he stared out at the garden and the woods. The old, luxuriously modernized cabin in Dyrehaven had been a real find. Even Agnes, who renounced extravagance as a natural consequence of her vocation, allowed herself to be tempted by a real estate agent who looked like a wood elf. They bought the place in 2007, one year before the start of the global crisis, for sixteen million crowns.

Ove Nilsen had carefully chosen Solbygaard as the first target for his new concept.

The clientele there consisted of relatively wealthy and predominantly single seniors and, until the other day, even the leader of the Blegman dynasty. That fact had not affected his choice negatively.

He developed the concept at his office on Amaliegade, just a few steps from the royal palace—which always made him chuckle. If anyone had created a gigantic castle-in-the-air, it was the Royal Danish House of Glücksburg. For twenty years, Ove had provided services that met society's need for making things faster and more effective, responding to the country's seemingly limitless desire for self-improvement and change. Over time, when darkness fell and things collapsed, those desires turned into admiration for the least effective, most change-resistant sort of fairy tale: gold carriages and straight-backed tin soldiers standing like eternal monoliths in their sentry boxes on the palace square.

Naturally, people had fallen madly in love with this crazy storybook image—although republicans critical of the royal house had tried to snap them out of that illusion.

It wouldn't work.

After an hour of Ove presenting his visionary ideas at city hall, the mayor and all his followers had tears in their eyes—even the stenographer had to blow her nose—while they all shook their heads, spellbound. He had called his idea a *groundbreaking, innovative method*; in a moment of divine inspiration, he had christened the whole concept:

Gerontio-Management—a proposal for management of your own life in the final stage. By the time work on Solbygaard had begun, enthusiastic reporters had made the brand nationally known.

Even the Widow Blegman wanted to participate actively.

There were pictures of craftsmen building the new training center and gym, and interviews with the psychologists Ove had hired for his clients' mental training; TV news hosts presented them excitedly in a stream of positive stories about the welfare nation's care for the downtrodden elderly who had been left far too long in the cold hands of unfeeling systems.

It was a spectacular and beautiful story, but the conceptual wizard behind all of it hadn't yet told them about the deeper levels of his plan, Eden's New Garden, which in those days was still awaiting final financing.

Death had always fascinated Ove Nilsen, and you'd have to be blind not to see that Death was flourishing throughout the vaulted halls of the nursing home. Barely any sun made it through the tiny beveled windows, and the social workers and part-time help nursed their dissatisfaction with poor staffing by sitting in the break room for long periods of time in a state of depressed absentmindedness.

Privately—and at home in his beautiful cabin in the woods—Ove Nilsen got goose bumps thinking about the building that housed almost two hundred seniors who would die in that four-story oversize coffin, without much contact with life, except for the purely practical and unavoidable.

No one spoke seriously to them, no one had the time to cheer them up—or even just to relax a bit with them. It provided fodder for the fantasy he was selling, because nothing could be worse than the status quo in 2015. He felt that he might as well distract the shut-ins while they waited for the inevitable, and earn a little money for the house in the woods at the same time.

He shook his head, closed one eye, and followed the straw's descent into the last bit of cognac.

Despite its architect-designed luxury, everyone knew that Solbygaard was no different than most of the country's nursing homes.

Behind those walls, loneliness crept from room to room, like a small, dark, vibrating insect, through the heavy locked doors—because the senile and demented, whom no one had time to care for, wandered aimlessly through the halls.

In the great room, the elderly sat rocking back and forth over their manufactured meals, and when they responded with a lack of interest, they were immediately fed or restrained.

Afterward, their still-full plates would be removed.

Ove had felt the icy breath of the thousands who had already expired—and would expire—in those rooms. He had heard their voices echo up and down the halls, and he shivered at the sound: *Don't leave us . . . don't leave us . . . don't leave us!*

But everyone did, without exception.

A health care assistant named Pia was the last to have seen the Widow, after lunch on the first of January. As usual Pia had been carrying the still-full plates back to the kitchen, and in a stretch of hallway, she saw the Widow chugging along, as she put it, nodding enthusiastically.

"Chugging along?" a young policeman had asked, and Pia had blushed a bit.

"No one understands how it could have happened," said the nursing home manager to a slightly older detective (right before she fell apart).

Ove knew quite well how it could have happened. Often there were no staff to check on areas; halls could remain deserted for hours at a time, especially in the afternoons, when the old were supposed to be resting in their little apartments.

His mind shut off the depressing images of the sunless terminus for wealthy seniors. Instead, he looked down again at the envelope he was holding in his hand.

He set his drink aside and took out the letter yet again, while shaking his head.

Why in the world would anyone write on a typewriter nowadays, except as a stage prop for some dusty play about the good old days. He could clearly see the imprint of the letters on the paper, and in a way it was beautiful—*authentic*, he would have called it in a sales pitch—but it was also totally hopeless.

Of course he remembered the name—*Viggo Larssen*—from childhood. A boy who (though he tried to hide it) was so terrified of everything that by eight years old he should have been admitted to a psychiatric clinic.

The problem was that he never told anyone about it but rather—with a determination Ove couldn't help but admire—shoved it down into the deepest recesses of his soul.

He should have gotten help. Not least of all after the experience with the boy in the Yellow House, whom Viggo's grandfather had run down one misty afternoon a long time ago. It had been an unusually bloody affair, and Viggo had had a front row seat. Even then Ove caught himself envying someone who'd first experienced something truly sensational: death. Death had literally hopped down right in front of the shy boy, who already saw visions and used to snort in horror when he thought no one could hear it. But at the last minute, Death had chosen someone else.

Arrow.

It was difficult to imagine how Viggo had survived his visions over the next few weeks.

Ove still remembered Viggo sitting under a tree in Utterslev Bog, his eyes covered as if he could still see the dead boy. Ove had silently crawled closer, hunched over like an Indian in an episode of Davy Crockett. From behind the tree, he could hear Viggo crying, and he understood that the strange boy's problems felt greater—more isolating—than his own. He'd always had a sense for that sort of thing.

Although they never discussed it, Ove had always known. Viggo's thoughts were different than those of the neighborhood children when they dramatically predicted death and destruction if you stepped on a crack on the way home from school. Those were obsessive childish thoughts, a kind of game, and would disappear eventually. Viggo's thoughts came from another world.

He had received Viggo's letter the day before, and he'd read it at least five times. It had upset all sense of calm in his forest retreat.

He had no intention of responding. The letter was a complete farce. Ove smiled joylessly. Maybe he should simply hire Viggo Larssen as a kind of advanced communications manager for BLC. Actually, his old friend did have the potential to make even the most absurd message seem rational and logical. He had to give him that . . .

He'd surfed around the web, looking for info on Viggo. His childhood friend had apparently taken a rather erratic course since they parted ways after high school. He had been hospitalized a few times, which he'd heard about from Verner, whom he saw now and then since they ran in the same communications and media circles. Basically Viggo had been bonkers. Or at least close to it. He'd done some freelance work for the Danish Broadcasting Corporation, which Verner must have procured for him, but except for the news from Verner, neither Ove nor Agnes had heard anything about him in all those years.

Even though the letter was one big fantasy—and no one knew fantasy better than Ove Nilsen—certain passages still startled him.

The last page was particularly disturbing.

The typewritten words seemed a bit darker and deeper there, as if his fingers had pounded on the keys when he came to his final and totally insane conclusion.

Ove poured a third tiny glass of cognac and read the letter yet again. He noticed a growing irritation about its mysterious, fascinating power, almost a kind of professional jealousy, even though it was nonsense.

It had to be nonsense.

Ove stared at the cherry tree and shook off his irritation. He bent forward and tucked the letter under the polar bear skin's enormous paws resting on the carpet.

Maybe he'd take a look at it again tomorrow.

He couldn't explain why he didn't just throw it out. He couldn't explain why he didn't show it to Agnes, with whom he shared almost everything. He loved her. He had brought her with him when they fled all the horror that had happened. She had known Viggo as long as he had. Just then, he heard her opening and closing the front door.

He took a final sip from his straw and stood up. She didn't even ask about the letter when she saw him open it yesterday. That's how she was. God—and all his creations—would speak when the time came. And not before. She sat motionless by his side while he read it.

"Adda," he said, and all the phantoms—and all thoughts of death—left him. "Is that you?"

She answered softly, as she always did. "Yes." He could feel her presence. She was a shadow slipping closer, embracing him, and easing all his sorrow and fear. He loved her.

The world outside was completely insane—Ove knew that better than anyone—but peace pervaded their forest home as if in a pact with God, which Ove thought was the result of the world's greatest and most effective fantasy, even greater than the Royal Danish House: belief in a higher purpose.

Eternal life.

As if living beings could ever really revive themselves.

***

Søborg, near Copenhagen
1963–1965

The weather was beautiful in the weeks following little Arrow's death. Viggo's grandmother and grandfather sat in the shadow of the blue umbrella; Viggo had learned that older people could sit like that for hours, without speaking, and that there was nothing strange about it.

Sometimes an entire afternoon would pass without a word being said.

And so life went on in the row house—as it had always done—despite the silence that seemed to grow with each passing week. Viggo knew it was his grandfather's only defense against the guilt that he (just like Viggo) was feeling.

One Sunday afternoon, two years after Arrow's funeral, Viggo was hiding behind the gate, watching the Yellow House. He wanted to get a glimpse of the parents who had lost their child; he wanted to see them walk down the steps and open the gate, and pass the place where Arrow had died without looking down, without casting a glance up toward the patio where his grandfather and grandmother were sitting.

Instead, Palle appeared. He opened the gate and stood for a moment on the sidewalk, where his little brother had taken his all-too-quick steps for the last time. His face revealed no emotion; his blue eyes were merely fixed on the spot where the blood had run into the gutter.

Just then, he saw Adda. She was walking down the sidewalk on the same side where Viggo sat hiding behind the gate. She was holding a lollipop in the shape of a car, the bluish-green candy sticking out from her thin lips. Suddenly she saw the boy from the Yellow House and stopped in her tracks.

That was the absolute wrong reaction, which she must have realized immediately, as it seemed to make the large and frightening boy react instinctively in an oddly bestial manner.

With just a few leaps, he crossed the road right behind his terrified prey. He was upon her in one fluid movement; he turned her around and laid her down on the concrete with an expression on his face that—to Viggo's horror—was both gentle and utterly ruthless. Adda had obviously abandoned any form of resistance; her gaze was fixed on the sky, the little lollipop still sitting between her teeth with its long stick poking out the side of her mouth. The moment Palle squatted on top of her slender body, Viggo should have reacted heroically—like all his heroes in the comics: Kid Colt, Captain Mickey, Akim, and Davy Crockett.

Instead he simply sat there, paralyzed with fear at the thought of the large boy discovering him so close by.

There were only a few yards and a garden gate between them, and he could hear the Bear's heavy breathing, almost like a growl. He could also hear Adda whimpering through the candy spit oozing out the corners of her mouth.

Then Palle did something strange. He bent down over her face and carefully clamped the lollipop stick between his teeth. His own thick, brutish lips were a breath away from hers, and Viggo wanted to jump up and scream in wild fury, but his body wouldn't move and his voice didn't make a sound.

Still biting on the stick, Palle leaned back from his victim and slowly pulled the lollipop out of her mouth. The candy escaped her mouth with a pop that sounded strangely intimate (or so Viggo thought many years later), before Palle stood, turned the lollipop around between his thick lips, and started to suck on it, all the time holding the girl on the ground with his gaze.

At that moment, Palle's mother opened a kitchen window and shouted across the street, repeating his name in a tone Viggo couldn't quite discern: angry, fearful, reproachful, or maybe something else.

A second later the Bear had crossed the road and disappeared into the dense garden surrounding the Yellow House. Adda lay crying on the sidewalk; the blue lollipop was lying on her chest, where the Bear had spit it out when he heard his mother calling.

Viggo wanted to get up, but once again his body failed him, its heavy mass trapped by gravity, nailing him to the ground behind the garden gate.

Later, he thought maybe everything might have been different if he'd had the courage to get up, open the gate, chase away all her demons, and hold her till she was safe.

By the time he'd lifted his head again, she was gone. The sidewalk was empty.

Some weeks later he turned ten. It was a Saturday, and everyone on the block was supposed to come over for birthday cake, which his grandmother had bought at the bakery on Gladsaxevej.

That morning a single story on the *Radio News* had struck the whole nation with fear. Four young police officers had been shot and killed by a burglar on the island of Amager.

Viggo saw his grandmother crying in the kitchen with the same despair as when President Kennedy was shot in America—or that afternoon when they watched *Captains Courageous* on television, and the old sailor slipped down the deck and into the deep with a final gesture to his friend, without hope.

Viggo locked himself in his room and refused to open the door for anyone.

The party was canceled. His mother had to go door to door and apologize for her son's behavior. He didn't even know any of the dead.

Viggo sat alone in his room for the rest of the day and all that evening, and she had no idea why.

***

In fourth grade Viggo Larssen was old enough to help his mother with her daily chores, just like the boys in his children's song: turn on the lights, fetch the milk, run errands.

He would get up fifteen minutes before her alarm clock rang, put on his clothes, and go down to the kitchen, where he'd place a glass, a knife, and butter on the table and put a teaspoon of instant coffee in her favorite cup.

Once he heard her footsteps on the stairs, he'd let the hot water run for a few seconds and then fill her cup from the faucet.

No boy could offer his mother a greater declaration of love. On the other hand, she had to drink the lukewarm, not completely dissolved instant coffee—yet she never once complained in all those years. She simply drank the tepid solution till the cup was empty. That was the love they shared.

On Saturdays and Sundays, weather permitting, the whole family ate breakfast on the patio, and his grandmother served soft-boiled eggs that were neither too hard nor too soft, but just the way his grandfather liked them. The old man got two eggs, Viggo only one. With a swift swing of his butter knife, he would lop off their "hats." Viggo would instead carefully use his teaspoon to crack the top and then remove the shell, piece by piece, placing them in the bottom of the eggcup, beneath the warm egg.

His grandfather viewed this convoluted process with blatant disdain, but Viggo didn't dare try to replicate his grandfather's feat. A single failed attempt would trigger even greater contempt, and he knew it.

That morning his grandfather swung his butter knife so that the "hat" flew off the egg in a perfect arc—but to everyone's shock it also pulled a strip of watery egg white out with it. On that particular morning—it was September and the blackbird was still singing in the birch tree at the end of the garden—his grandmother had not cooked the egg quite long enough, a mistake she'd never made before. At that moment, Viggo's grandfather also cracked right before their eyes, just like the top of Viggo's egg beneath his teaspoon.

Viggo saw his grandfather blink and then blink again, as if confused, suddenly lifting his hands toward the sky.

Sensing the impending catastrophe, his grandmother stood up beneath the umbrella.

The old man blinked again, as tears ran down his furrowed cheeks in large drops, onto the plate and the half-cooked egg. He then put his hands over his eyes, as his shoulders shook.

When he saw his grandmother throw her arms around her husband, Viggo stood up and ran into the house, out the front door, down the road, and around the corner by the garages. He didn't stop until he had reached the bog. Staring down into the creek, he couldn't stop wondering whether it was his fault that his grandfather suffered so terribly. The old man's feelings for the dead boy were stronger and deeper than anything Viggo had ever seen.

He knew only too well what his own role had been in the catastrophe. Right before his grandfather got into the car he'd borrowed from his brother, Viggo had run over and pulled on his coat sleeve in hopes of coming along—or at least so his grandfather would honk the horn as he rode out of the neighborhood, as the other boys' fathers did every morning. That small gesture, that result of sheer selfishness—he wanted to show the others that *his* family also had a car—had changed everything. If not for that tiny delay, everything would have been different. That's all it takes to change the world and knock all the planets off course. That second of hesitation had been enough to cause disaster two hours later on Death's Highway. That single second let Arrow reach the road before his grandfather's car had passed; that one second, which never should have happened, closed the gap between the boy and the car . . .

To another child, or a thoughtful adult, a single act several hours before the accident would not be enough to raise the specter of regret, let alone guilt; but for Viggo, it was the beginning of a chain of events that *could* have been moved in time, just a tiny bit back or forth, if only he had acted slightly differently.

He stared at his reflection in the stream. A flickering, blurry outline of a face in the green water. Viggo Larssen knew that every one of his actions had a meaning—he just didn't know what they were before it was too late to turn things around. Either God was merciful—which he was most of the time—or else he suddenly let a minor detail result in terrible consequences. Every afternoon, when his grandfather perused that day's accidents in the evening paper, Viggo could sense the common cry of the suffering: *Oh no, it shouldn't have happened!*

But it did.

Viggo sat under the large oak with his eyes closed. He thought about his grandfather, sitting in the gutter with the dead boy in his arms. That's how the little boy and the old man lived for years after the accident, but no one really saw it. And maybe it would have been unbearable for them to know, because what could they do? Besides, adult sorrow always seems larger and more important, because a child's problems appear lighter and more fleeting; normally, they can be erased with a smile—or some comforting words. Maybe that was why Viggo's mother loved *The Little Prince*. She comforted her son with it (or so she thought), without ever discovering that the boy in bed hated the little planet-born child. Ultimately, he chooses death when he lets himself be bitten by the snake.

One night Viggo woke with a horrifying feeling.

Yet he hadn't been dreaming, and he hadn't seen the strange vision of his mother, standing in a black dress and reaching toward him.

He turned on his bedside lamp and lay there for a moment, letting his eyes become accustomed to the light, then pushed the comforter to the side and threw it down on the floor; he lifted his arms and looked at his hands. Something was wrong with his fingers; they seemed longer and thinner than usual. He rolled his pajama sleeves up and looked at his arms. On his right arm, just below his elbow, he was missing the birthmark he'd always had.

On his left arm he was missing a scar that had run across his wrist since he burned himself on a sparkler in kindergarten. He took short deep breaths. Had he awakened in another body? Did it happen while he was sleeping? He shut his eyes tight and sat for a long time rocking back and forth in bed, his heart pounding. It wasn't possible. It couldn't have happened. God would *never* let him travel into another child's body, but still he couldn't escape the thought. At some point he must have fallen asleep, because when he woke up the next morning, everything was back to normal. The marks and the scars were back where they were supposed to be, and there was no sign of the changes in the night.

His mother must have turned off the light, or maybe he had dreamed the whole thing.

A few nights later, he woke up with the same uncomfortable feeling and again turned on the light. His body was normal, his hands and fingers his own, but the room around him was suddenly different. The furniture wasn't his. A green upholstered easy chair had replaced his little red stool; by the window was a large bureau where his desk had been.

In the morning, the light had been turned off again and everything seemed normal.

The following nights he was afraid to go to bed. Somehow, he was starting to disappear. Either his body—or the world around him—was disappearing. Someone wanted him, but he didn't know where or for what reason. He lay on his back, his hands folded on his chest, moving his lips while he spoke about the visions he was having.

Dear God, can't you protect me . . . even though I don't deserve it . . . dear God . . .

He prayed to make God, his mother, and grandmother love him again. He had to make himself worthy to remain in the world he knew; he didn't want to live somewhere else, in another person's body, yet he had no power over that decision.

Dear God. I'm sure angels exist. I've heard their wings in the dark. I think they're blue, not white, because then I could see them in the dark. Won't you let your angels watch over me tonight? They can sit at the foot of my bed.

Bending his knees, he pulled the comforter up a bit to make room for the angels. It might have seemed absurd—especially to an adult— but in the dark of the night in a boy's room, it was all completely logical.

During the same time period, he dreamed about his mother's death. His grandfather was sitting in his easy chair and reading the evening newspaper; suddenly, the paper slipped out of his hand and fell onto the carpet, where Viggo picked it up. His mother, lying in a pool of blood, was on the front page, her picture appearing below two words that made Viggo awaken with a start: *Woman Murdered.*

In those first terrifying seconds back in the darkness of his room, he knew what had happened: God had refused to protect them. God was punishing them for his grandfather's carelessness that day.

Why don't you honk?!

It no longer mattered.

***

Office of the Prime Minister
Wednesday, January 7, afternoon

The prime minister sat motionless behind his enormous teak desk.

He looked like a man who'd just awakened from an unusually bad dream, and his eyes were red and bloodshot beneath his shiny granite-like forehead.

The easily frightened officials who manned the front office had heard a strange sound behind the minister's almost soundproof door; it sounded like sobbing or moaning—but that couldn't be right.

Their gruff and irascible boss would never have such an embarrassing breakdown over something that was, despite everything, quite private. No prime minister would behave like that. None of them had ever cried there—except maybe tears of joy when something went terribly wrong for one of their political opponents.

Poul Blegman had arrived at the prime minister's office an hour earlier. Summoned by a voice he barely recognized as his brother's, he had raced over with three out-of-breath bodyguards and his private secretary at his heels. None of his entourage was granted access into the kingdom's finest office.

Palle Blegman was sitting hunched over his desk. It looked as if he were praying.

His younger brother knew how far-fetched that notion was: the clan's patriarch had never prayed to anyone or anything. His white knuckles only revealed the anger that at any moment would become a roar, a curse more than any kind of prayer.

The bear stood up before the minister of justice could take cover and shouted, "The Homicide Boss—and his *asshole* of a deputy—want to meet with us! He wants to speak with us about . . . our *past* . . . Gentofte . . . high school." The last two words landed in the space between the two brothers.

Poul Blegman just let that hang in the air, as he did when they were younger.

"Our *past*." The prime minister's voice suddenly lowered to a whisper as he sat down again. His sudden quiet didn't make the situation any less threatening. Quite the contrary.

The minister of justice remained standing. Even as a child, he had never been physically afraid of his brother, but there are many other kinds of fear. Just then, the two brothers felt the same shaky, dreamlike sense as the time their father massacred those three kittens in the garage—the time Poul heard himself laughing because he knew that any other reaction would lead straight to damnation.

He recalled the rest of the meeting at the prime minister's office in the same hazy way. As voices and movements that seemed real yet couldn't be. His brother had pushed a button, and the Homicide Boss had been brought in by the Bear's permanent undersecretary.

Only three men were present: the two brothers and that nuisance the rest of the country viewed as its closest ally.

The policeman had asked ten or twelve—maybe even more—questions about their years in Gentofte. Was there *anything* in the past that might shed some light . . .

. . . maybe someone who held a grudge, someone who had always hated the two ministers . . .

. . . or their father . . .

. . . or even the Widow . . .

. . . someone who wanted to harm the Blegman family . . .

. . . a political opponent, maybe a spurned businessman . . .

. . . or . . . ?

The last unspoken question simply hung in the air like a dark cloud above their heads.

As everyone knew, the Blegman brothers had no reputation for being soft on anyone or anything, in any context, neither women nor men nor . . .

. . . their own mother.

"We've found no evidence of a kidnapping, no ransom, no terrorist activity, no financial gain. *Maybe* it's something personal."

Maybe was the Homicide Boss's most-used word that afternoon in the prime minister's office; he almost barricaded himself behind it, though he was in no way a timid man.

"Unless she just wandered off and you"—the prime minister stood up and leaned over his desk—"*you twerps, you idiots* . . . simply haven't found her—*yet!*"

The word *twerps* sounded just as strange in the kingdom's highest office as the word *asshole*, and the minister of justice still felt he had been given a strange role to play in a crazy dream no one could control.

"She hasn't just wandered off," said the Homicide Boss. "She wasn't the least bit senile. And all the doors were locked."

"And yet she *has*. She *has* left—unless she made herself invisible." The Bear's sarcasm filled the entire room. Outside the tall windows lay the city with its spires and red-tile roofs. Just then, the fairy tale land seemed more real than what was happening in front of the minister of justice's eyes.

The Homicide Boss stood his ground. "Yes, that's exactly what we don't understand. That's the mystery. There has to be an explanation." But he had none.

"One that needs to be searched *forty to fifty years ago*?" The Bear's sarcasm had taken on a sound so threatening that his younger brother became a bit faint; in their father's time, sarcasm was always a precursor to some catastrophe that couldn't be averted. Like being struck with a stick the old man had found in the garden.

"People can bear a grudge . . ." The Homicide Boss spoke with all the courage of a military commander facing an unbelievably dim-witted tyrant.

"We're the ones who should be bearing a grudge." For some reason Palle lowered his voice and bowed his head.

The Homicide Boss took his cue: "Yes . . . if you're thinking about your *little brother* . . ." The words shot through the room like lightning.

Palle Blegman stood up. "What in the world does Arrow's death have to do with any of this?!" It wasn't a question; it was a protest. For Arrow's sake.

"I don't know," said the man standing across from them. He said nothing else before being escorted out of the Bear's office by the adviser. Out into freedom. Both brothers had to admit—though neither of them would have said it aloud—that their opponent had been wiser and more formidable than they had imagined.

When the adviser had closed the door and the two brothers were alone again, the real world seemed to reemerge for Poul Blegman. The towers outside began to fade, and the city's rooftops lost some of their charm.

"But *maybe* it is . . ." He stopped.

The prime minister looked at him for a long time before answering, but this time his words came in neither a whisper nor a shout: "Maybe you *forget* . . ."

It was probably best that his sentence wasn't finished. No sense formulating hypotheses that even the Homicide Boss hadn't stumbled upon, even in a soundproof office.

Instead, the kingdom's highest-ranking official sank deep down into his leather chair, both bear paws resting, somewhat limply, on the armrests.

They were both remembering the same night, from when they'd been in high school.

A summer night from another world . . .

***

A good hunter hunts at his own pace, in his own rhythm, based on his own observations.

The Homicide Boss was incredibly clever.

Poul Blegman thought about what would happen if their mother really were dead. He knew that death would loosen its grip on the secrets the two men were keeping, and no one could know just where that trail might end.

Someone had torn apart the two inseparable brothers. And that should never have happened.

CHAPTER 8

The Lighthouse on the Cape
Wednesday, January 7, afternoon

Viggo Larssen left earlier than usual. I watched the mail truck drive down the gravel road on its way to the Lighthouse, and then I rushed over.

Thanks to his unwavering sense of routine, I knew I had at least an hour and a half before Viggo returned.

A lone letter was in the unlocked mailbox attached to the wall. I picked it up and turned it over to see who the sender was. It didn't surprise me. He had sent his letter to his old friends, and Teis was the first one who had answered. I briefly considered stealing the letter and taking it back to the Sea Witch's house—my need to pry was stronger than ever—but I didn't need it. Anyway, that would be too dangerous; if he asked about it at the post office in town, he would become suspicious.

In all the months we had spent together, he couldn't have possibly overlooked my curiosity; indeed, that was probably what had made me even slightly interesting to him. Also, I had no doubts about what the very thin envelope contained: an invitation—and nothing else.

Viggo was going to travel. He would leave to meet with the four people in the world in whom he dared to confide.

And I was going with him.

I left the letter in the mailbox, stepped across the threshold, and sat in his chair next to the blue desk. He had written only three words on the page in the old typewriter: *Near-Death Experiences.*

It made sense that he would be preoccupied with that.

The idea rested on the notion of a borderland between God and Science.

I didn't believe in that sort of thing. Only the very naïve could believe that the soul, once it broke free, would ever dream of returning to its earthly home. In the descriptions I had read, the soul flew around like a remote-controlled drone, filming the death scene below, complete with doctors and crying family members. Once it regained composure, the soul would open its parachute and land effortlessly back in the body it had left.

It was completely absurd.

I couldn't understand how any of it held interest for a man who had always been fascinated by real death—the kind of death that didn't give and take but only took and never looked back. In one of his closets, I'd found stacks of death announcements, some so old they had yellowed with age; all of them were the type in which authorities were searching for living family members of a deceased person.

One day, randomly leafing through a stack of the announcements, I found several telephone numbers scrawled on the backs. When I looked them up, it became clear that he was contacting secondhand dealers and estate buyers.

For some unknown reason, he had also called cemetery offices; he probably told them that he was a distant relative and only wanted to know who had cleaned out the deceased's last residence. He was clearly looking for something in them.

That thought made me uneasy.

I noticed that my patience was turning into something resembling anger—as it had back when I ransacked my foster mother's papers, trying to discover her secrets. She never anticipated such patient, searching fingers—least of all from a child. The woman who cared for the nation's smallest and most vulnerable citizens until they could find a home and a family had never believed that her own child was made of far stranger and ungrateful stuff.

I let myself out of the Lighthouse, carefully locking the door behind me, then stared out at Bavnebjerg's Cliff.

I could see him far out there, a tiny dark spot against all that white.

He'd never be able to see me.

As far as I could tell, the man in the Lighthouse had only two interests in life: death and what I would call restrained drinking.

He always got up late in the morning but, on the other hand, a light stayed on in his two small rooms until late at night.

I had never dared sneak over to the Lighthouse window when he was in there (although God knows I'd had an uncontrollable urge to do so)—so I didn't really know just what he was doing. I only knew that it would be a catastrophe if he discovered my intense spying, and there was no way I was going to risk it.

Before the Widow had disappeared, I'd grown accustomed to being by his side on the bench, just letting time pass. I'd almost forgotten why I was there, but that was no longer possible. The Widow Blegman was now gone, and he had written three letters to the world, a world he had otherwise abandoned.

***

I wandered back across the Giant's Footprint in the early twilight and up to the Sea Witch's house. I sat down by the window and stared out at Hell's Deep, and I thought about all those souls no one really cared about once Destiny had arranged their final shipwreck.

I thought about Viggo and turned on the radio.

My heart almost stopped—though usually it was made of a material no normal circumstances could shake, least of all those from the land of the living.

A news reporter—in breathless and dramatic tones—was updating the nation about the latest surprising developments in the Blegman case.

In a totally unexpected turn of events, a large number of police, with the two lead investigators at the helm, had dashed out of police headquarters early that afternoon. With sirens blazing, they had sped over to Solbygaard Nursing Home, which was now swarming with police. No one knew what was happening. Barricades had been set up at all entrances, and all outsiders—including the press corps—were being kept at a distance.

Everything indicated that the police had found *something* behind the thick red walls that necessitated the presence of both the Homicide Boss and his second in command, including the fact that they cordoned off the entire area.

In front of the tall building where the Widow had her little apartment was a broad lawn with tall trees. A long row of police cars was parked there now, explained the reporter, apologizing because *unfortunately* he was unable to get the least bit of information about the reason for the commotion out of the irritable and easily disturbed detectives.

Every question had been met with complete silence, he lamented, then continued with a voice that had basically lapsed into a sob. The silence from the police was so overwhelming that you almost expected the worst—although no one could figure out what the police could have found. *Everyone* thought that any attempt at finding possible clues at the nursing home had been abandoned long ago.

So what had happened?

I turned off the radio. I had no doubts. I understood what had happened.

I had lost my only connection to Røsnæs. Viggo was all that remained. I had lost the ally who had enabled me to check out the cape and move into the Sea Witch's house. It was a problem I couldn't ignore.

I could manage—at least for a few days. The Widow had paid my rent to the end of January. After that, I was on my own.

I had three weeks and maybe a couple of days left. And that was all.

PART III

Death

CHAPTER 9

Søborg, near Copenhagen
1965–1968

He was haunted by yellow. At least that's how Viggo felt sometimes.

First, the dead canaries, then the dead boy in the torn raincoat, and shortly thereafter the dream about his mother, murdered and on the front page of the afternoon paper. Even though newspapers didn't print color photos at that time, he recognized the yellow dress his mother had bought with her last savings before an anniversary party at the oil company where she worked.

At the beginning of fourth grade, Viggo found a new obsession, one that (just like all the others) had to be kept hidden from the rest of the world. He had no idea where it came from, and he wondered if other children—or at least boys—had tried the same thing. Of course he'd never dare ask them. When he sat close to a girl, either in class or on the bus, he had to touch her hair. His fingers would start to tremble—knowing what was about to happen—but the chosen ones must never realize it. Fortunately, he only needed to touch a few hairs, even with just one finger, and that was enough to satisfy his strange new compulsion. With one intentionally accidental movement, he could slide forward on his bus seat and move his hand all the way over to his target. Once he touched the tip of the girl's hair, he felt enormous relief. It couldn't compare to the satisfaction that grown men felt, but the feeling of having conquered—and won—something unobtainable always satisfied him.

Sometimes, if the bus suddenly lurched, the touch became too obvious and his hand got too close; then the girl would turn and glare at him. But he would act as if nothing had happened and stare out the window, leaving her with the strange sense that it was only her imagination. After all, no normal boy would do such a thing, and Viggo Larssen certainly didn't seem like a boy who would attempt anything so bold.

When he came home from school, he was often sent to the butcher or the grocery store—and sometimes over to the mailbox on Lauggårds Allé. His grandparents wrote letters by hand, as people did back then, even several times a week. His grandfather sat at his writing desk with his back to the family, bent over the green desk pad and his fine lined stationery. Viggo could hear the fountain pen scratching across the pages, sometimes vanishing to a whisper and sometimes stopping completely; a single letter could take a whole day to finish.

Right before he reached the mailbox, Viggo would stop beneath the glow of the streetlamp, take the envelope out of his coat, and carefully work the flap open, resealing the envelope after he read the letter.

His grandfather wrote frequently to his younger brother, the owner of that fateful Opel, and at other times to his two sisters on the island of Falster. The letters never included anything personal, just irritable observations about the wind and the weather, sickness and other trials—with long, painstaking descriptions of everyday trivialities. The next family birthday gathering; how the days passed since they held the last birthday; the small, unexpected troubles the aging faced in life.

My heart can't take the cold, wrote Viggo's grandfather to one sister. That winter he had all but stopped talking at the dinner table, and when they played Hearts, he was often left holding the ten of hearts.

My springtime arthritis has arrived—and it won't go away before Easter, he wrote in early spring.

Summer was no better: *We old people can't even soak up a little sunshine outdoors without still feeling some cold breeze that almost cuts to the marrow. I can barely stand it.*

After Arrow's death, Viggo's grandfather seemed to lose interest in everything other than the weather and his body's decline. Maybe it was his way of scaling an impenetrable wilderness—like when I worked my way over the Giant's crooked branches onto the cape—a kind of tenacity I couldn't help but admire. He pushed forward, even though someone had shouted *Halt!* a long time ago.

During the Christmas of 1965, his headaches got worse: *My memory is shot once the headaches kick in,* read Viggo on his way to the mailbox—before once again sealing the envelope with yellow fish glue. You could see the deterioration in the scratchy writing from the fountain pen and feel the despair rising through the words, as the old man inched toward the shadows.

Now a grown man, Viggo sat on the bench outside the Lighthouse and stared into space. He had lived in a home in which people longed for summer in the winter—and winter as soon as summer returned—in rooms in which every change in the weather manifested itself as aches, lumbago, and arthritis. He noticed the increasing number of adults who ignored him as if he were no longer part of their future. Death, which was both in front of them and behind them, rested between the lines in every letter he read and within the silence in the house. His mother tried to drown it all out in her small room, behind a closed door, with Beethoven's Fifth, Mozart, Haydn, and Handel.

Viggo Larssen felt that something was about to happen. All his experiences thus far—especially after the tragedy with Arrow and his grandfather—had made it clear to Viggo that invisible forces affected every movement and all of time, and so, too, life and death.

If he woke up just a minute too late—or too early—it might trigger a fatal accident. If he made his mother late by only a few seconds, she might roll out onto Gladsaxevej on her black bicycle right as a large truck swerved to the right, crushing her. A second earlier—or a second later—and it never would have happened. And he had no idea just where that decisive second lay: in a moment's delay or a moment's haste. It was an absolutely unbearable worry he lived with in those years; he knew some horrible force was out there—but it was invisible . . .

He set his alarm to 6:15 a.m. and turned off the light, thinking about the coffee he always served his mother in the morning. Then he turned the light back on and set the clock a few minutes back, because he sensed that timing might be catastrophic. Lying with his eyes closed, he imagined how these minute shifts in seconds, even the most infinitesimal fractions thereof, would affect the coming day, the coming weeks, or the rest of his life. Especially for the adults around him who had no idea what was happening.

If he failed to make the right choice, he would be guilty of all the world's accidents.

His teachers cautiously asked his mother why he was tired so often and why his eyes were usually red, but she just shrugged it off. She knew her boy was completely normal. Still, for a few days after, she would turn down the Beethoven, so that the overture wouldn't wake Viggo.

CHAPTER 10

Office of the Prime Minister
Wednesday, January 7, evening

The prime minister stood motionless by the window, his back to his two guests. He could have done without both of them (to put it mildly), and they observed him with some fear (and not without reason).

Slightly hunched over, he turned and walked slowly back to the desk, one arm behind his back. It was an unbearable moment, and the Danish prime minister's eyes were bloodshot from a lack of sleep.

"You're saying that she . . . ?" The country's head of state only made it halfway through the question.

". . . has been found dead, yes." His brother, the minister of justice, finished the sentence.

"Yes," confirmed the Homicide Boss.

"She . . . ?"

The answer remained the same, delivered in unison.

"Yes."

"In a basement . . ."

"Yes."

The prime minister stood up straight, looking more than ever like the wounded bear in the comic books that even the Homicide Boss had read as a boy.

Slightly stunned, his brother, the minister of justice, sank down into a chair, where he began ruminating about the world—which until recently had contained a certain degree of normalcy.

True, the day had begun with a terror attack in Paris. A couple of fanatical Muslims had attacked the editorial offices of a satirical weekly magazine, and at least ten were dead. Both brothers had expressed their sympathy for the French people. Behind closed doors, however, they couldn't get that worked up about a shooting in a country they had both come to despise for its weakness and snobbery. Their father had a special saying about timid political opponents: "They're behaving like the French!" His judgment had been merciless. The country that had been headed by that pompous ass Napoleon had also—at least as he saw it—caved to the Nazis in 1940. Its leaders had never been able to defend themselves. After the war, it was Germany that had displayed an iron will that was admirable, which continued even today, with a woman as Palle's fellow head of state. France was, historically, a nation that cowered at the least provocation—and Palle Blegman's mother's fate far overshadowed the crazed work of two French madmen.

"But . . . that's absurd," he said. He stared long and suspiciously at the Homicide Boss, who didn't react. Then he pointed at the office's beautiful though extremely uncomfortable Hans Wegner chair (the policeman was familiar with it from previous visits). The prime minister sat on the office's largest piece of furniture, a solid Børge Mogensen sofa that, despite four massive teakwood legs, creaked loudly under his weight.

"No," said the Homicide Boss tentatively. "They don't have a handle on things . . . at the nursing home." He knew that he was dodging—or trying to dodge—the issue.

"Have a *handle* on . . . well, that's a nice way to . . . and neither do you *for Christ's sake*! You've been searching for seven days—and then you suddenly find her right *there*, a few steps away from where she first disappeared!" The prime minister's fury was apparent.

The Homicide Boss bowed his head, a rare gesture on his part, but he couldn't deny the accusation. A cleaning woman of Middle Eastern origin, like half the employees at Solbygaard Nursing Home, had made the discovery and raised the alarm. He hadn't shared that piece of information; the two brothers were on the brink of an election, and someone in their camp might demand a momentary halt in hiring refugees and immigrants in the health care sector.

While trying to find a bucket for the afternoon cleaning, the woman had opened a locked cellar door only a few floors below the Widow's apartment. And then she screamed.

The realm's most searched-for woman was sitting in an old lawn chair in the middle of the floor.

Stone-cold dead.

The mystery of her whereabouts had finally been solved. But the rest of the mystery was like a giant question mark that no one could erase. There were no visible signs of violence, no signs of a struggle, only the smell of death due to natural causes. She had been sitting in that rusty and dilapidated old lawn chair for several days. Her facial expression was almost peaceful. As if she had just given up, without fear, without anger.

The door could only be locked by slamming it. It was an old emergency shelter left over from the Cold War, and as soon as the door locked, it sealed the room completely. But why would the Widow even go into a dark cellar—and then slam the door behind her?

The door could also be closed and then locked from the outside with the help of the key, which was still sitting in the lock. Yet why would anyone take the old woman to a dark room and then simply leave her there?

Still, that must have been what happened. It was the most plausible explanation.

Someone had locked her in and then left her sitting in the middle of the floor. She hadn't been bound and she hadn't been beaten—as far as anyone could see. The room was small and quite isolated, and the air was heavy and low in oxygen; the old woman with her weak lungs would not have lasted long under such conditions. Back when this was a shelter, there would have been enough ventilation, oxygen reserves, and emergency rations to last a long time—but all of that was long gone.

In the minutes following the gruesome discovery, the police had cordoned off the area. The entire nursing home—especially the basement—was swarming with detectives and forensic experts. The neighborhood echoed with sirens, and all three national news helicopters came barreling down from above, hovering over the spot where the Widow had been found.

"Who has done *this* . . . *to her*?" roared the realm's highest official from his place on the sofa. He had almost said "to mom," but it would have exposed an almost childlike vulnerability unfitting for a prime minister.

The Homicide Boss shifted his weight, ever so slightly, from his right to his left leg, and briefly seemed to sway a little on the uncomfortable chair. It was a sign of discomfort, one that Number Two would have noticed immediately if he hadn't been leading the investigation at the nursing home.

"It's not . . . ," said the Homicide Boss, choosing his words carefully. "We don't know if anyone has done anything . . . not yet. It's *possible* that Mrs. Blegman wound up there by mistake and then died from a lack of oxygen. The nursing home was recently renovated, but the basement rooms are remote. The lowest floor was originally designed as an emergency shelter, back during the Cold War, and the air ducts haven't worked in decades. So when the door slammed—" He didn't get any further before the Bear got up from the sofa, which creaked loudly again, and stood erect, furious, at his full height.

"Just shut up . . . shut up, you little shit . . . you fucking idiot. She sure as hell didn't go down there by herself—alone!" A purple color spread across the prime minister's thick, strong neck. Slumping back onto the heavy teak sofa, he pounded his right fist on the table where secretaries normally served coffee to the country's finest visitors. The huge paw would have shattered an even slightly less well-built piece of furniture.

The Homicide Boss squinted faintly. "Well, we don't know that for sure," he said, with a slight air of caution that Number Two would also have felt was quite uncharacteristic. "Solbygaard is not noted for a high degree of employee presence during daily chores." So that it didn't sound like he was criticizing the two powerful brothers for putting the clan's crown jewel in such a dreadful place, he quickly added: "That's certainly a part of the nursing home's new approach. They've hired a business consultant who has developed a whole new, ultramodern concept of care."

"Yes, that's the damn reason why my . . . is so happy about it . . . and that's why we've chosen it for her!"

He spoke as if she were still living. A second later when he realized his mistake, instead of his usually hard, blue glare, there was a tiny glimmer of something else.

The Homicide Boss squelched his own irritation and kept to the matter at hand—while deciding to overlook the fact that Ove Nilsen hadn't chosen the nursing home until *after* the Widow had moved in. "Yes, and that's why she *might* have gone down to the basement without anyone realizing it."

"And what the hell was she doing in the basement . . . what *in fucking hell* was she doing there!" The Bear had jumped up again.

"We don't know. She may have been led down there, but she could have gone there on her own."

"Yes, I *understand* that. But what the *hell* would she be *doing* in some fucking *basement*?!" The Bear was emphasizing almost every other word. It was like being lashed by a whip.

The Homicide Boss nodded as if he were acknowledging the question, then shrugged. "We're still in the middle of the investigation. She might have died of shock—possibly of shock at being imprisoned—or over something else. More than likely she died of a combination of things . . . a weak heart, a lack of oxygen in that small room . . ."

The flaming purple color shot up over the Bear's neck and cheeks. He opened his mouth to utter the fabled roar feared by everyone in his presence, but it never came. It was a gesture of impotence that no one had ever seen before in this man.

Maybe that's the reason why the aging head of homicide—who in his youth had chased down armed criminals through countless alleys in inner Copenhagen—looked away for a moment and stared out the window, out over the city's towers, glimmering green and gold in the glow of an early risen half-moon.

"Where . . . were . . . the police?" It was the policeman's top boss—the minister of justice, Poul Blegman—who filled his brother's silence.

The Homicide Boss turned his gaze from the window. "As . . . you . . . know . . ." He was imperceptibly copying his superiors' odd staccato speaking style. ". . . as . . . you know . . . the nursing home isn't famous for . . . well, the home is about to implement a new form of active management in which the old . . . the elderly . . . must increasingly manage on their own and become self-sufficient." For a moment, he sounded as if he were reading from the glossy brochure prepared by Blue Light Communications, from its descriptions of physical rehabilitation and mental training modules to the purchase of robots that would help replace time- and money-hungry caregivers.

"Yes . . . we *know* that . . ." The minister of justice seemed disoriented, sitting next to the usurped bear and mostly resembling a sick dog, thought the Homicide Boss.

"So you simply overlooked that room in the basement?"

"We didn't overlook the room. We asked the head of the nursing home whether they had searched the home thoroughly, all floors, every room, and they did. Of course they did."

His assertion was weak—and he knew it. It wasn't worthy of such an experienced investigator.

The police should never have taken any of the nursing home's assertions at face value. They'd seen how the tired, preoccupied eyes missed old people reaching out for help, how the simplest routines fell apart at even the slightest absence of manpower. To credit the practitioners of modern elderly care—especially as practiced at Solbygaard—with such a high level of conscientiousness was simply poor police work.

"But they didn't—did they?" The minister of justice stuck his needle-sharp sword right through the Homicide Boss's paper-thin defense.

"Apparently not." It was a gross understatement. The two experienced investigators and their small army of detectives had not investigated anything other than the common rooms and the old people's private residences. Even if the Widow had tried to call for someone through the hermetic door in the basement, no one would have heard her.

Still, that was not the most important item on the agenda, and the Homicide Boss again shifted his weight uncomfortably to his left leg.

They'd found something else in the room in the basement, something quite disturbing. A little book was lying next to the Widow's feet. As if it had fallen out of her hands when she collapsed and died.

After their initial inspection of the basement room, Number Two had called the Homicide Boss, his voice shaking ever so slightly. Although that was unusual, the discovery in the basement was outright bizarre.

It was a very unique book.

He didn't want to share that piece of information with the two shocked men in this office—not now, and not in a couple hours. Not before he was totally certain what they were dealing with.

First, they'd discovered the small pieces of old yellow plastic in the Widow's apartment. Then came the empty folder that should have contained a will. Next, the third discovery, the bird in the cage. That defied any logical explanation. It was like someone was trying to tell them something, something very precise, that they just couldn't decipher.

And now this fourth strange discovery: the book that was lying by the Widow's feet. The investigators had fished it up off the floor with infinite care, as if a single wrong move might alter its contents.

He couldn't let anyone—least of all the realm's top officials—know the details that, according to police logic, he needed to keep under wraps.

Instead, he said, "When we went through your mother's apartment—the day she disappeared—we found this in a bureau drawer." He handed the two men a transparent plastic bag with the small piece of yellowed paper in it. He had carefully avoided mentioning the brown leather folder.

The prime minister leaned forward and read "June 23, 1971." He looked up at the Homicide Boss.

"Do the two of you recognize this date?"

The two powerful men shook their heads simultaneously.

Had their joint response come too quickly? The Homicide Boss wished that Number Two were there. Even though the realm's two top officials were not suspected of killing their own mother, they could still be hiding important information. Their paths to the nation's highest offices had been anything but smooth.

The Bear's face was expressionless. It was impossible to see whether the question had actually shocked him or was simply another unsolved mystery.

"It looks like it was written recently and—we assume—by the Widow herself."

"Where did you find it?" asked the prime minister.

"Well, in a slightly odd place. In a brown leather folder in the top bureau drawer."

"My father's old bureau, surely his folder. He used to—" The prime minister stopped abruptly.

The Homicide Boss leaned forward. "Yes. It said 'Will' on the front of the leather folder. But there wasn't any will inside. Just this piece of paper with a date on it."

The two men sat like mannequins. Completely motionless. For some strange reason, though, the Børge Mogensen sofa seemed to move a bit and creak, but quite faintly.

"The family lawyer doesn't have any will," said Palle Blegman. "We've been interrogated about it. It's even been reported in the news. We don't need any will"—he hesitated for a brief moment—"so when all this . . . *commotion* . . . subsides, we'll receive our inheritance. Naturally."

The Homicide Boss nodded. Commotion. That was an odd word to describe a murder investigation. With the utmost discretion, he and Number Two had gathered information about the two men's private lives—mostly from an old colleague now employed at Police Intelligence—and neither of them had mentioned it to anyone, not even their subordinates. If the media discovered they were looking so deeply into the brothers' private lives, it would explode into an inferno of *breaking news* (the older detective hated that term) and the brothers' fury would know no bounds. *The Police Suspect the Prime Minister!* That would be a fantastic story. And a very short one.

The two lead investigators would undoubtedly be fired on the spot. And they wouldn't get any help from anyone. The whole country would stand by the brothers.

True, certain reporters, possibly due to the lack of new angles on the case, had started taking a closer look at the Blegman dynasty's background—and at the two powerful men's pasts. But nothing had materialized that would shine a light on the Widow's disappearance. Most of the information from that time seemed like pure gossip. Several anonymous sources described the two brothers' tyrannical teenage behavior at Gladsaxe High School. No one had found any descriptions of their early childhood in the Yellow House on Maglegårds Allé, which the Homicide Boss was relieved about, given the current highly sensitive situation.

But it could happen.

Old high school friends had referred to the prime minister as a bully in the worst possible sense of the word—a grim counterpoint to the far more folksy and somewhat warm impression evoked by the nickname of "the Bear"—a quality that everyone around him knew he had never possessed.

One of Copenhagen's largest newspapers, which sympathized with the opposition, had revealed that the prime minister had been accused of several serious assaults on boys his own age. In his junior year, he had kicked a younger boy down in the schoolyard.

The same reporter hinted at rumors of an even greater scandal the following year, a scandal that once again involved the older Blegman brother, but he didn't go into details. Either the rumors necessitated more evidence than the journalist could procure, or they involved something that, from a distance of several years, would seem like a gross violation of the nation's sitting prime minister.

With the discovery of the old woman in the basement, the rumblings about the family would probably subside, thought the Homicide Boss. All sympathy would turn back toward the two men. Even in politics, a little human understanding can sneak in; but if you understand that that type of compassion never lasts very long, you can exploit it while it lasts.

The police were still in the media's watchful eye. Their work was painstaking: detectives were going door to door to find people who had known the Blegman family, not only during high school and at the family's address in Gentofte but also much further back, in the far less upscale neighborhood near Maglegårds Allé in Søborg. There was something hesitant about the reactions the door-hopping detectives encountered, something they almost unanimously described as very cautious. Perhaps it was the time that had passed, a discomfort of talking about small, seemingly inconsequential details from so long ago—and about a family that was not inconsequential in current-day Denmark.

Besides, what would small, uncomfortable stories from the past have to do with a recent murder?

The Homicide Boss took a deep breath and looked directly at the head of state. "Did anything happen on that date—June 23, 1971—while you were living in Gentofte?"

Only much later would he realize his mistake: that his question was formulated all wrong—and that the answer, therefore, was also totally useless.

"No," said the two men, strangely enough in unison, a humming sound that followed him out of the plush office, only to hover over the roofs of Slotsholmen before finally vanishing into the sky.

***

The Lighthouse on the Cape
Wednesday, January 7, late evening

I'm the type of person who can't picture myself—pretty or ugly—a fact that probably stems from my first years at my old foster home by the water.

While the other children found loving adoptive families, I soon realized that I would be left behind. I'd been sickly since birth, with a crooked back and deformed limbs. As time went on, the headmistress could see that no one wanted me, so she adopted me as her foster daughter. She laughed heartily at my slightly waddling gait and said that my dark, silent smallness reminded her of a shriveled old man. She probably intended the comparison as a kind of comfort—that was her way; other people were often thrown off base by her unbridled optimism and spontaneous goodness.

For me, the darkness gradually brightened and my body slowly straightened out as the years passed, thanks to the wind and the sun on the sound. At one point, my foster mother cheerfully pronounced to some guests, "I do believe that this ugly duckling is about to turn into a swan."

Her well-meaning statement, which made those visiting smile kindly at me, was actually a compliment to herself about her own lifetime of effort. In her presence, crooked and forsaken creatures straightened out and found their place in the universe. At her forge, lives were cheerfully bent and hammered into place—and ultimately released into the blue, out into freedom.

Surely she must have sensed my skepticism about a fairy tale turning into reality. No one ever changes like that. Darkness and ugliness persist, despite the maudlin dreams invented by adults.

I shared this skepticism with the man in the Lighthouse.

Night after night, throughout his boyhood, he tried to escape the darkness because he knew the visions that accompanied it. But it never worked. He hadn't been spared—not on one single night did any of the demons from the depths ever release their hold on him. Only as an adult did he finally learn to live somewhat amicably with his pursuers.

Over the years he'd learned to control the strangest of his obsessions and to succumb to his physical tics only when he was alone. He knew there must be others like him, but he also knew that they would be hiding their peculiarities in the same variety of ways. He'd learned how to stuff his wildest thoughts and involuntary movements deep inside, invisible to the outer world, and almost invisible to himself. This seemed to have been successful by the time I arrived at the cape. He was almost safe from his pursuers, sitting there slightly frozen, his back against the wall, yet despite everything rather calm, finally liberated from his visions. Until the Widow's disappearance released the worst vision of all . . . death.

The manager of the Daily Market in Ulstrup told me that Viggo Larssen earned some money writing songs and poems for local families for wedding anniversaries and birthdays (his advertisement was hanging on the bulletin board at the store's entrance), but that couldn't have brought in much.

A couple of newspaper articles I found online referred quite discreetly to the end of his career as a journalist in Copenhagen following a nervous breakdown. He was probably on some kind of public assistance, although life in the Lighthouse must have required only a modicum of income. His only luxury was the six-pack of burlap-wrapped bottles of Rioja that he had delivered from the Daily Market a couple times a week.

When the weather was nice, we'd sit on the bench, the bottle between us, and he'd offer me a glass—but never more than one. Sometimes we'd sit together watching the sun go down over Hell's Deep, and I'd make my one glass of wine last for an hour. He'd fetch a couple of blankets for us to throw around ourselves. The bottle stood there between us; right from the start, I understood its purpose to ward off any intimacy. It created a small but safe barrier between us, even though I knew he had given up on that kind of intimacy a long time ago.

When they found the Widow, I walked to the Lighthouse. We sat for a while, as we usually did. I had no idea what he thought about the whole thing—his only reaction had been: "I've heard." I dared not ask anything else for fear of revealing my knowledge about his much deeper relationship to the Widow.

And so we sat in silence, a state that made both of us comfortable.

Suddenly he turned to me and said, "Malin . . . that's a very special name. Where does it come from?"

It was the first personal question he had ever asked, and I was shocked, not because of his rather banal curiosity—but because he spoke directly to me at all. Naturally, there was only one possible reaction.

I said nothing.

I was hoping he'd think that the wind had sucked the question from his mouth, lifted it up, and then blown it out over the deep before it ever reached me.

Maybe the Widow's death had made him start to think about the past; anyway, the wine had had its effect, and he again asked, "Where have you lived before?"

I decided to answer him, but as vaguely as possible. No one had mastered that art better than I. "I come from a place just like this, a house by the sea." I may have slightly emphasized the word "sea," as if it were the beginning of a fairy tale, though not necessarily one with a happy ending.

Apparently he didn't notice and abruptly changed the subject. "How did you find that house out there in the woods?"

"There's an old woman from Ulstrup who dresses all in black. They call her the Sea Witch. I rented it from her."

"The witch in black," said Viggo a little cryptically; I could tell he'd seen her before.

"Yes—she must be at least a hundred years old."

"The Sea Witch . . ." He studied the words rising into the air. Then he said, "Yes, I've seen her in the cemetery. She sits by her parents' graves."

I nodded, but he didn't say anything else. I didn't dare break the silence. I needed all the trust I could get, especially now.

For more than three months, I'd stayed patient.

But suddenly it had all become meaningless. The Widow's death had torn my plan into a thousand pieces.

***

Ove from Søborg
Thursday, January 8, afternoon

Ove Nilsen was annoyed. The nursing home was teeming with police, who were denying him access to most departments.

It was impossible to get any serious work done on the training programs he had planned for his clients. Even a centenarian could sense that something was wrong. Some of the elderly sat around crying, others went to bed in the middle of the day, and staff used the state of emergency as a much-needed break from their monotonous daily routines and duties.

In other words, it seemed as if time had stopped. Ove knew better than anyone that time—especially wasted time—costs money, and the police's manic rummaging in the basement felt like an intrusion on his own private domain. He feared that something unforeseen and terrible would tarnish his reputation, doing his brand irreparable harm. After the discovery of the Widow, a single cynical person could expose all his efforts at the nursing home as nothing more than a gigantic fantasy. The idea of making the old self-sufficient, thereby developing a better and happier old age, had suddenly ended in death and complete failure—as personified by the country's most famous matriarch.

In more ways than one, it was a catastrophe.

To complete the absurdity, two newbie detectives had called him in for questioning in the nursing home's management office. Although they hadn't referred to it as an interrogation, they asked questions that seemed to include him in the host of possible suspects.

"Surely you must be familiar with all the work procedures at the nursing home—can you explain why no one noticed that the Blegman widow had disappeared from her room?"

He had stared at them for a long time before saying, "No."

"Didn't you know about the room in the basement—before the Widow was found there?"

That question was a direct insult. Almost an accusation.

Of course the police had read the newspapers, in which rumors about the Blegman brothers' wild youth had now been publicized. They'd run an entire high school, just as they now ran the country, feared by their critics and political opponents. As several of the newspapers reported, that terror had culminated in an attack on a young woman after a high school party, and it was more than implied that the brothers had been involved.

The police must have known that the unnamed young woman in the article was Agnes, his wife. In their twisted reasoning, they must have thought that it gave him a motive to take revenge on the Blegman clan, despite it having happened forty years prior.

Now, the entire nation was demanding that the case be solved immediately, and the police were under enormous pressure to do so. He hated the Blegman brothers and everything they stood for . . . Palle more than anyone. He'd thrilled at the prospect of ordering around their doddering old mother, and he'd had even greater plans for her.

Those plans had possibly capsized—it was impossible to say at this point. The last twenty-four hours had shaken even Ove Nilsen. His dream of building his paradise on earth, Eden's New Garden, had depended on the Widow's final will. She wanted to add him to her will, so that at her death his project would finally take off. That had been the plan, anyway.

According to the press, however, no one had found any will— which meant that the two brothers would inherit everything.

Now, one of the officers asked him about the Blegman family, and he answered in very vague terms. Yes, he went to high school with the brothers, and yes, Palle had been active in the Young Conservatives. Later, Poul also joined the youth movement at the insistence of his father and big brother. He wasn't as domineering as his older brother, and old man Blegman clearly viewed him as wishy-washy—he was just like all those socialist whiners back then, with their riots, campus occupations,

Woodstock, and posters of Che Guevara and Rosa Luxemburg on their bedroom walls. The Blegman dynasty had fought all of it, and the two boys had spearheaded the battle against it in high school—using the very methods still employed by the family.

"But what did any of this have to do with their mother's death?"

Ove's counterquestion made the police abandon that subject.

They hadn't asked a thing about the years before high school, and maybe that made sense. If they were searching for a deeply hidden revenge motive, it probably wouldn't involve small children playing on the narrow streets of Søborg a long time ago.

He hadn't mentioned Viggo, Teis, or Verner—although the police might have found their stories interesting—and he said absolutely nothing about Agnes. He would do anything to keep her away from the memories the old scandal might trigger. He spent years removing the dark shadow from her face, though at times he thought it had never really gone away.

He went straight home after the interrogation. Although much too early in the day, he had poured himself a large cognac and was now sitting in his cozy chair with the snarling polar bear skin, the green straw in his mouth, pondering his next move.

Outside, the sun was shining on the cherry tree. Behind it lay the woods, where they took long walks in the spring, enjoying the smell of lilac and elder. Agnes, who had taken the day off, was kneeling in the rose bed, a pair of small silver scissors in her hand, probably on the hunt for some sign of spring in these climatically disastrous times. She was always kneeling in the garden, searching for small sprouts. He found something eternal in that vision, and he loved her for it. She still looked the same as when they'd first met. He smiled above his straw: she could never grow old, never really die. That was an impossible thought. Little Adda in her small green galoshes on a rainy day, always standing behind the neighborhood hedge—wearing that sou'wester that covered those blonde curls, a mysterious smile in her blue eyes.

He thought about Viggo's letter again and, irritated, set aside his glass. He bent down and pulled the letter out from beneath the polar bear's enormous claws.

For the eighth or ninth time, he read the three pages as he sipped from his straw, and then he made a decision. He would give the letter to the detectives at the nursing home. Let them make the final evaluation. Since Viggo had sent it right after the Widow's disappearance, it was definitely too much of a coincidence to be ignored—not in such an important case—and not when Viggo had mentioned people who had known the Widow from a long time ago.

One of them even had an obvious motive. The writer himself.

If the letter helped draw attention away from himself and Agnes, well, that was an added bonus. The sooner the police left Solbygaard, the better. He couldn't let a prolonged police investigation get in the way of his largest project ever. No one had devised such important plans in the last seven years—and the Widow's nursing home was the very portal to a world where everything would change.

He poured himself another cognac and sucked a modest mouthful up through the green straw.

As Ove knew, when people age, they become like children again. The day should never end. Darkness should never be allowed to swallow up the happy hours—the darkness should have to wait. Forever. Sooner or later, that fear of darkness struck everyone, both rich and poor. Ove did his homework thoroughly. In small circles and diagrams, he charted people's fear of declining, all of which he enumerated in bullet points.

All culminating in death. The knowledge that everything ends, that breathing suddenly stops and it's not humanly possible to hold your breath for more minutes than the Heavenly Creator has doled out.

He had played with the thought of trying to avoid death—of just living on while the years passed. His company's slogan was "Everything Is Possible." Why should that be limited only to business? Both personally and in her ministry, Agnes believed in Eternal Life—but why should that life be relegated solely to the Hereafter?

Ove had never understood that.

Of course it was a pipe dream. But he had an idea. Through his research, he noticed one central fear: *oblivion*. More than anything, all God's children hated the thought of being forgotten.

Being *remembered* is the only thing that somewhat challenges death. Not merely being remembered in five or ten or fifty years—by your closest friends and family (if they have the time)—but to be remembered at all times, for eternity, by all people, everywhere. That was the vision.

No one had ever realized the potential. To Ove, that was a revelation.

He decided to develop his concept in a large nursing home in the nation's capital.

He knew that it would have to be a nursing home with inhabitants who were relatively affluent and had both the will and the resources to invest money in his groundbreaking idea. Solbygaard housed a plethora of wealthy seniors, most of whom moved there from large houses they could no longer manage on their own. Transitioning to a traditional nursing home environment must have been a shock for most of them. To their surprise, suddenly they could no longer do anything with their wealth; instead, they were stowed away in small rooms and apartments, guided by basic routines from morning till night. They had the money to buy luxury and comfort, they had dreams of a far better old age (maybe even of delaying that last breath), but no one had offered them any alternatives. Not the politicians, not the health care sector. Everyone perceived these places as storage areas, warehouses for worn-out furniture. Not even their families offered more, having absolutely no interest in eroding their future inheritance. The rent at a nursing home like this one was already sky-high.

Ove watched the sun set over the edge of the woods. He wanted to alleviate the worst consequences of aging's decay, provide the elderly with a far more beautiful twilight—and make money doing it.

The municipality of Gentofte had purchased the entire package, with a combination of public and private financing. The investors were the taxpayers, a number of charitable foundations, and, naturally, the elderly.

Ove's project had been given a three-year run. That was enough time.

On the first day, he had arranged the elderly on the lawn in front of the nursing home and divided them into three groups: the visually impaired, those with mobility problems, and the wheelchair-bound. He'd directed them into three rows, after which he taught a select group of health care staff the exercises the elderly would need to learn.

They had to turn their heads from side to side for five minutes, then bend and stretch their arms and legs for fifteen minutes, and finally wander, arm in arm, around the oak tree in the middle of the lawn for twenty minutes. Although that exercise was not easy for those in wheelchairs, it added an extra challenge to their training. Ove had impressed upon the staff that physical development was indispensable as preparation for the mental training he would provide.

The exercises on the lawn would bring the residents together, he said, creating invisible bonds among them and releasing all of the body's hidden tensions.

Afterward, he stood on the second floor of the nursing home, looking down on the soccer field, where three assistant caregivers were commandeering their teams.

One of the seniors sat down on the grass, as if she suddenly decided to stop being part of such a bizarre circus. Another started to cry, a natural reaction to the fact that something new and surprising had finally happened in their stagnant lives.

Then, the mental training, in which residents had to think of synonyms, talk about their favorite color, and memorize hymn verses and then sing them in unison.

Ove sent an enthusiastic progress report to the nursing home's management after the first week. Because it offered documented proof that the money had been well spent, the report was accepted without reservations and passed on to the municipality. Evaluations were always positive—a shared secret among consultants and spin doctors. Afterward, none of their customers could call the purchased products fiascos.

At no point had Agnes ever commented on his new idea. She was affiliated with the nursing home as a chaplain—and had been since they'd moved to Søllerød as newlyweds. She had been visiting the Widow for several months, and he knew exactly what kind of grief was involved: the kind that never disappears. Still, he had the feeling that Agnes hadn't told him everything, since she piously took her ministerial obligation of confidentiality quite seriously.

When the Widow disappeared, she had only participated once in any training. But that was all right—the picture of old Mrs. Blegman walking arm in arm with another resident had appeared in all the magazines, and as a result, Ove had received around twenty applications from other interested municipalities and nursing homes.

The problem was that he hadn't gotten into the concept's final and most important phase before the police stormed in—and that was the part of the project that really meant something, the very core of his idea. He hadn't even revealed its contents to anyone other than his wife and the Widow.

He couldn't help but think that the two training programs, those two first phases, were only window dressing. It never ceased to amaze him that intelligent adults could become so excited about totally banal exercises.

Once the police finally left the home, he would continue with the final part, the part that involved the really big money. Authorized to develop individual counseling for each of the elderly, he naturally started with the Widow. He made her an offer she couldn't refuse; then over the next few days, he launched his master plan, which was, of course, dependent on financing.

He could tell that she understood the idea and that he had struck the very nerve he had intended. Everything had seemed more promising than he dared hope, when she suddenly disappeared.

Her kindness made her death that much more frustrating.

After deciding to give Viggo's letter to the police, he called Agnes over and showed it to her.

She read it in silence, and he watched the dark shadows return to her eyes.

"You can tell he's a little . . . special. No?"

She didn't answer.

"Actually, I've always been a little afraid of him . . . I *really* think he struck his head that time you pushed him down the steps on his tricycle—"

"I didn't push him." There was a tone in Agnes's voice that sounded like anger, which was not the reaction he had expected.

Anger was not a reaction people associated with Agnes Persen.

"Okay, fine. But you did take the Donald Duck comic he had in the bike's basket, according to Teis. The one about the square eggs from Peru."

Agnes blushed. "It wasn't the square eggs . . . it was . . ." She stopped.

As an adult, Agnes had mastered a truly solid blush from the roots of her hair all the way down to the middle of her neck. She thanked her Maker for the ministerial ruff that hid the evidence of her uncertainty, evidence that must be God-given and have a purpose (even though it had plagued her throughout her childhood and early adolescence).

"Well, I've always been a little afraid of him. And the police *will* get this."

Ove took the letter out of his wife's hand.

She didn't react, and no more was said in the old cabin in the woods.

CHAPTER 11

Office of the Prime Minister
Thursday, January 8, afternoon

The head of state placed his powerful paw on the folder that the Homicide Boss had sent to the prime minister's office: it contained a brief but accurate summary of the case's latest developments.

They were going to start digging into her economic situation. Their little police hands would dig into the Blegman family's innermost secrets. They would find the papers that both Palle and Poul knew had to exist—and that would change the focus of their investigation.

Attention would turn toward the two of them. The existing evidence would make it obvious: an upcoming election, an impending bankruptcy, and the possibility of an inheritance that would save them from everything. Like something right out of an Agatha Christie novel.

"The will." Poul pronounce the words in a muffled, nondescript tone.

His brother reacted with the expression that had never lost its ferocity—not in the yellow villa, not in elementary school or in high school—and certainly not now.

If you have something to say that you don't want anyone to hear, then choose silence. Poul knew his brother's answer without even hearing it.

After Arrow died, he had become the youngest child, and his mother had turned her attention toward him. When he started high school, he was on the verge of something like a rebellion, but of course it never materialized. Instead, Palle committed his mortal sin at the end of his senior year, and everyone in the Yellow House circled the wagons around him.

Their father, the Patriarch—the despot—had died in 1988, and since she'd become a widow, their mother had jealously guarded the family fortune. Occasionally, she'd toss symbolic crumbs at the two sons in a world where fending for themselves and making it on their own were never up for discussion. Only naïve little Arrow, who ran so fast that he finally ran away from life—after passing through the open gate like a yellow streak in the air—had ever had her love.

Poul's expression matched his brother's; of course they agreed on the necessary caution triggered by their mother's death. They'd sometimes feared she might bequeath the family's considerable fortune to the Cat Defense Fund or some other nonsense (Poul often thought about the kittens spattered all over the garage wall), but that was just exaggerated worrying.

Over the years, both brothers had asked their mother to support both small and large entrepreneurial projects—and in hard times for much-needed emergency funds. Their private lives had not been made of the same humble stuff as their father's. Both sons had bought villas in Trørød, supplemented with a boat in Vedbæk Harbor—and there was a renovated antique Bentley in Palle's garage. Symbols, naturally, of the dynasty's power and influence, far beyond the reach of typical government wages and moderate stock returns.

The financial crisis had taken a toll on their latest investments, and they'd both felt moments of panic, even Palle, who only feared one person in the world: the Widow, his own mother.

But their financial requests were almost always denied. She had refused to help them when their finely polished upper-class veneer began to crack.

They got loans from both banks and friends, and within a few months their financial positions become even more precarious and promises of quid pro quos became ever more encompassing. Behind closed doors, their kingdom was eroding in a vast web of favors that many would have called corruption. They were supposed to keep their private households above water and outside of the press's and the public's spotlights. Especially now, the slightest ripple in the brothers' finances would result in irreparable embarrassment over the fact that a prime minister might be insolvent and even bankrupt. No one would ever reappoint him to the realm's highest position—and the election was only a few months away.

Had either of the two brothers been inclined to show weakness, they might—here in the privacy of the prime minister's office—have confided in each other about their fears. But that would never happen; for the Blegman family, fear could only result in contempt.

"She had written a new one." Poul Blegman still couldn't use the actual word. The family's lawyer had delivered the old will to the Widow because she wanted to make important changes.

The two men had no doubts about what they were; she had told them in no uncertain terms. The visit on New Year's Day was supposed to be the rapprochement that never happened. They had no doubts about that, either. A rapprochement with a hefty bottom line.

The family fortune was worth at least a half billion Danish crowns, which their father had invested solidly in stocks (and a smattering of bonds). The fortune that had been waiting for them for decades, or more accurately, waiting till their mother's long-prophesied death.

"But it hasn't been found." Palle Blegman stated the obvious.

There was no will.

In the end, they might have to thank their invisible enemy—their mother's murderer—for both their personal and political survival. And that would be Destiny's own twisted little irony.

***

Søborg, near Copenhagen
1969–1971

Viggo's father was Swedish. That's why there were two *s*'s in *Larssen*, his mother explained, showing him a black-and-white photo of a man with his hair parted perfectly straight on the side, a fixed gaze, and a relatively large and square chin. The small photograph resembled a miniature picture of Clark Kent, taken at the exact moment when he realized he was Superman.

Viggo had stared into the mirror and tried to make the same facial expression—clenching his chin—without much success.

"Where is he, Mom?" He immediately regretted asking the question.

His mother didn't answer, and he never asked again.

In his early teens, Viggo also grew slower than most of the other boys—and some of the girls, too. So, he took some new milk cartons, stomped them flat, and shoved them down into his shoes, beneath the insoles. Although his heels hurt like hell, he felt as if he'd moved a bit closer to the other boys' heights. His gait became so odd, however, that his classmates sometimes made bewildered comments. Eventually, he was walking on so many blisters that he tore the flattened cartons out of his shoes.

Ove, Verner, Teis, and Adda helped him celebrate his birthday by going out to the park at Dyrehaven. His eyes followed Adda, who wasn't so little anymore, as she ran among the trees, disappearing into the shadows, then coming back into view, again and again. If she were out of sight a little longer than usual, he would hold his breath and pray she would reappear. The thought that she might stay hidden, swallowed by the darkness between the tree trunks, was unbearable—and to a boy like Viggo, it was also possible. If you made yourself invisible to others, you might suddenly become part of the invisible world, even if you'd thought it was only a game. The girl in the woods was toying with Destiny. She would cover herself up in withered leaves and lay motionless for long periods of time. Then she'd purse her lips and whistle just to provoke Fate: *Now you see me—now you don't—I'm here—I'm not here* . . . Yet he feared that only too late would she discover that her teasing game had turned serious. She would want them to run around looking for her, the four boys, her four friends, and she'd call to them and whistle and yell, *Look at me . . . look at me . . . I'm over here!* But then they'd no longer be able to see her nor hear her—and she would become lost to the visible world forever.

The thought terrified him. His friends laughed while he stood hunched over a little ways off, his knees bent as if he were having stomach pains.

Viggo Larssen prayed directly to the God his grandmother had told him about, in the way she had taught him. His prayers gathered like rockets above his head, fired off their thrusters, and shot directly toward heaven.

Dear God, I'm sorry I'm not down on my knees (which he always was when he prayed with his grandmother)—*but won't you help me find Adda again anyway?*

Whenever his prayer worked, he would pause a little distance from the others, bend slightly down on his knees, and pray again: *Dear God, Thank you for helping me get Adda back.*

Boys like Verner, Ove, and Teis would never understand anything so strange. If they knew that Viggo prayed every day to God—on the street, at school, while playing soccer near the bog—it would have been too weird, even for them. But as long as he didn't move his lips or fold his hands, they couldn't see that he was establishing contact with a higher guardian.

The year before, Viggo's entire class had attended confirmation preparation with Pastor Bendtsen at Søborg Church; no one dreamed of backing out.

At that time, all young people were confirmed, whether they were religious or not; the most godless of them justified their sudden conversion with the prospect of gifts, parties, and a day off on Monday.

Adda sat next to Ove and Teis in the last row and giggled; if anyone had suggested back then that she would become a minister one day, the merry triumvirate would have died of laughter.

Pastor Bendtsen glowed with a good-hearted, liberal nature that no one, living or dead, could extinguish. With his full black beard, the pastor resembled a combination of Abraham Lincoln and the Danish hymn writer Grundtvig. One time, he wore a "No Nukes" sign around his neck while he knelt in church asking Jesus for world peace. Even though Gladsaxe at that time was considered an especially progressive suburb with an exuberant, visionary mayor at the helm, several local residents left the church in protest. The subsequent uproar—including coverage in the *Søborg News*—had nearly cost the pastor both his earthly and divine office.

Tall and slightly bent over, he stood in front of the green blackboard that had been placed beneath the crucifix and talked about the gospel of love to the confirmation class.

Judge not, that ye be not judged. For with what judgment ye judge, ye shall be judged: and with what measure ye mete, it shall be measured to you again.

"The New Testament—Matthew, chapter seven."

For some reason he had an affinity for Bible texts that seemed much older and more caustic than his modern and progressive political leanings.

Right in the middle of a sentence, he suddenly pointed at Viggo with a piece of chalk between his two skinny fingers: "With your background, Viggo, you must be into free love."

Two classes of adolescents were gathered in the parish classroom, yet at that moment, you could have heard a pastor's chalk-white ruff floating onto the dark-stained floorboards. Intuitively, they all knew that they were witnessing something that should have remained unseen and unspoken.

Viggo sat frozen in the center of that silence; only a deep blush revealed that the pastor had struck his mark. Verner had stiffened in shock to his right. To his left sat Uffe, and Viggo could almost physically feel his pity.

He had never believed anyone would say that out loud—certainly not in God's house. He'd always felt his mother's shame; children sense those kinds of things. It had wandered around their rooms ever since he was born. She was the only unmarried mother on the block; he was the only fatherless child in the whole neighborhood. He had never seen his vanished father—and he never would. He felt a stinging in his eyes. He was far too old to cry, and he knew it was too late for him to respond.

The pastor walked over to him—as if he were about to perform a laying on of hands. "But Viggo, haven't you spoken with your mother about it? It's nothing to be ashamed of. There's no sin in having illegitimate children. That's just bourgeois hypocrisy!" But the pastor persisted—as all sinners do in the middle of their sin. "You're a true love child, Viggo!"

For a moment, everyone in the room thought he was going to reach out and anoint the boy by touching his hair. Then he stopped and stood up straight, as if he'd had a long pitchfork shoved into his shoulder blades. Some impulse had stopped his tirade, but the sound of his message still resonated for a few seconds. The long, bearded face with the round glasses had glowed with the innocence that makes Our Lord's select few capable of preserving a pure mind throughout life—despite what they may say or do.

At that moment the Devil—dressed in Pastor Bendtsen's vestments and ruff—raced through the confirmation classroom and danced a happy jig around Viggo. Everyone in the congregation bowed their heads in shame—on their own behalf, on the pastor's, and on Viggo's.

Perhaps Jesus twisted with anger on his cross up there on the classroom wall—but even the Son of Man, despite his exalted status, was unable to conjure a miracle to save Viggo Larssen. That was the revelation God showed Viggo there in the confirmation classroom: that the son must atone for his mother's (and his father's) sins, and that parents everywhere let the guilt pass to the next generation.

Pastor Bendtsen got his tongue back, leaned forward, and looked at his victim. "We can talk about it later, Viggo—with your mother, too."

Then he straightened back up to his full height. "Let us sing 'On Your Way! Be Brave and True!' while we think about the meek—for they shall inherit the earth."

Viggo Larssen could recite the three short verses by heart, but despite Verner's hand on his shoulder, he was unable to sing along. He never sang that hymn again—he hated it with all his heart—all of its nauseating messages about alleged willpower, reconciliation with death, and celebration of hope.

The night of his confirmation party, in the fall of 1969, he had the strange dream again: his mother was standing in the middle of a golden mist, which might have been a desert—or more likely an ocean—and reaching both hands out toward him. Her legs were still bare, and she was wearing the black dress again (though she had never actually owned a black dress). As always, he couldn't see her feet, and he thought they must have been covered by water or sand. He sensed a faint movement right behind her. The sky was always golden and shimmering, and there was something calm about her stillness and outstretched hands—hands that he sensed one day he'd have to grab.

He was almost fourteen when Neil Armstrong stepped out of his earthly vessel and took a walk on the moon. Something about the conquering of the yellow celestial body had made Viggo uncomfortable, almost as if it involved him personally. A few days later he developed a faint rash all over his face. The doctor thought it was a form of shingles but of a type he'd never seen before in any patient.

And Viggo Larssen was no normal patient.

A couple of days later, he was standing at the blackboard in Søborg School and telling the class about the moon landing. It was supposed to be a typical summation of newspaper stories, but Viggo spoke only reluctantly in front of so many people—and his rash wasn't helping his shyness. His ears were buzzing, and he thought he was going to faint, when suddenly something strange happened. In the middle of a sentence, all sound disappeared and he could no longer hear his voice. He tried to keep speaking as if nothing had happened, as if his classmates could still hear him. Oddly enough, they didn't react. They just stared at him as if he were still talking. And then he shut up. In some bizarre way, he found himself in a parallel world, as if there was one world where he was speaking and another where he wasn't.

Bewildered, he looked down at Adda, his safest point of reference in the world. Then he looked over at Teis and Verner, and he realized that he had crossed an invisible border.

He turned his gaze toward Ove, but his good friend was sitting, motionless, at the farthest table and squinting at him.

At that moment his teacher, Miss Iversen, walked up to him and—as if a magician or a hypnotist had snapped his fingers—the sound returned.

"Hey, say something, Pierrot!" To his surprise the voice belonged to Adda. Everyone in class was laughing along with her. Sometimes she left her normal body, spread her black wings, and abandoned her role as the soft earthly being everyone in class loved. At those moments the delicate halo that usually hovered above her blonde curls sharpened into a sword that she wielded without effort or warning, slicing through the air before anyone could react . . .

And every time she did, a head rolled.

Over the next few days, the strange deafness returned, again and again. When he spoke to people, the sound would disappear as abruptly as when his grandmother turned off the radio—even though he was still talking and his lips were moving and people kept listening. If he suddenly shut his lips, he could see the confusion in people's eyes. Right then, the sound would come back—with a roar—and he'd startle. He could see that his friends thought it was a very strange reaction in the middle of a conversation.

After some weeks, his rash disappeared, as did the strange hearing disorder that he couldn't explain and would never dream of revealing to any living being.

That fall he began to masturbate with a pillow between his legs and terror in his body at the thought that his grandmother might open the door and see what he was doing. Closing his eyes, he suddenly experienced a feeling of weightlessness, as if he were floating through the room, out the window, over the city, almost like Peter Pan, but alone and with no control over speed and direction. Down in the beautiful gardens sat everyone he knew—or had known—talking to each other. From far above their heads, he could observe them and he felt joy in their happiness . . . his mother and grandmother and grandfather sitting on the patio, and Miss Iversen speaking to the class . . . his friends running and calling to each other. Meanwhile he hovered half hidden behind a cloud, a shadow of the person he thought he was. Eventually he started to feel sorry for himself and fell asleep, awakening with a wonderful feeling in his stomach.

He could feel the strange tingling rising in his thighs, up through his diaphragm, up through his entire body; then came the orgasm and the moisture and his heart pounding beneath the comforter. It happened again a week later, and he knew what it was and made it a habit (every afternoon) to go up to his room to experience his body in this new way, detached from his soul and his surroundings.

He dared not think about how long he would have to stand there cursing into the toilet—let alone what he should yell—if his grandmother discovered his strange new infirmity. No words would be good enough to atone for such stupidity; his curses would have to be so loud and clear that everyone in his neighborhood—every single family—would know what he was trying to hide. He would blush so strongly that he'd outshine even Adda Persen—a blush that would never disappear.

***

Some children change more than others when, in the middle of puberty, they step into the adult world. They seem to take their newfound calling a little more seriously than their peers do—perhaps exuding a certain contempt for the innocence they are about to abandon even while still clinging to it. In rare cases their whole character is erased, or at least hidden so deep in their soul that it never emerges again. Generosity becomes stinginess, insouciance turns to anxiety, and empathy into mistrust.

In the months leading up to high school, Ove Nilsen changed more than most.

His eyes became sharper—they narrowed, some would have said—like when Kid Colt and Hopalong Cassidy took aim, their fingers on the triggers.

A marksman focusing on his target is entitled to that calculating expression—and Ove started choosing his targets almost as if he were in training for the future.

His father, an officer in the merchant marines, was rarely home. For the most part, Ove's mother left him to manage for himself, as she looked after his little sister, who was thin and pale and had been ill since birth.

Ove never responded to his sister's crying; he would just walk past her without saying a word and head out the back door, ignoring her high-pitched, incessant whine.

No one can explain why certain children develop a hardness that becomes so ingrained that you can see it in their eyes and hear it in their voices—even when they're standing around and laughing with their friends on a sunny summer day.

I really don't think Ove understood in those early teen years how much he was about to change. I wonder if some people, as adults, look back and think: *How did I get this way? How did I become so hard toward people? How did I become this indifferent toward others?*

There are questions people never ask each other, let alone themselves.

To confide in someone about something so secret, at that age, would be as unthinkable for Ove as it would be for Viggo to tell someone about his nocturnal visions and strange wanderings in and out of parallel worlds—or about his pact with God to spare his mother and grandparents as long as he remembered to say his prayers.

For some reason Ove had never really teased Viggo, even though he saw through his friend's desperate and sometimes even comic defenses. He always hesitated, stopped by a discomfort that Agnes would have undoubtedly called sympathy, or even empathy—two concepts that made Ove nauseous as an adult, and got him to cock the hammer on the largest management revolver his arsenal could muster.

Souls—and companies—that ignored the globalized world's undeniable demands were hopelessly lost.

Recent times required a much harder constitution than even God would recognize. Survival depended on a cynicism that, yes, could have its good sides (like his new Gerontio-concept), but the cynicism must always come first.

Softness was like mold in a neglected wall: it grew, unseen, and then suddenly one day the walls, floors, and ceilings became dark and stained, eaten from the inside.

Even as a child, Ove had always been good at speaking. He directed all their neighborhood games, telling the other children softly but firmly what they needed to do if they really wanted to have fun. He always said what he thought, but in such a way that it didn't offend anyone.

Although that childlike tone of complete honesty never left him, in early puberty his thoughts became far more calculating. As his voice deepened, a certain coarseness and darkness wormed their way into his mind. He began speaking "honestly"—bluntly—no matter how it affected others. And he lied.

At first he didn't direct his newfound gaze at Viggo. He found a different victim instead, a target that one might compare to a plywood figure at a shooting range, a target that didn't stand a chance.

"Teis," said Ove, "you have the fattest legs of anyone in school— you really ought to do something about that."

Frightened, Teis looked down at himself. It was true, of course, that Teis had grown fatter as his boyhood passed. He'd even gotten a double chin, a rare sight among boys that age. With guileless eyes, Ove took him by the shoulders, pushed his head back gently, almost lovingly, and said: "*Teis, Teis, Teis*—with the chin, chin, chins!"

Everyone around them roared with laughter. Ove let go of Teis and repeated the curse: "*Teis, Teis, Teis*—with the chin, chin, chins!" It was wonderfully alliterative, and even as an adult, Ove could still taste the sweetness of it on his tongue. Sometimes he'd still mouth the words, though he wouldn't say them aloud; he knew that Agnes didn't approve of scorn and derision, although she, too, had laughed back then, admiring Ove's fine sense of language and his skillful destruction.

No one can resist when someone expresses insults in such a treacherously concerned tone.

And that's just what made the trap so perfect.

Teis couldn't escape the humiliation, delivered in such a tone of genuine worry, tinged with just a little irritation. As was only natural between friends.

When the other boys repeated the curse, it took on the same friendly tone, as if it were meant affectionately. Teis suffered as only humiliated teenagers can suffer. Ove knew full well what his witticisms and humiliations did to people. A boy like Teis would never forgive him—he'd only tolerate him (out of fear)—but that didn't bother Ove in the least.

Viggo couldn't understand why Ove hated Teis so much. He was just happy it wasn't directed at him. Besides himself, the only one spared Ove's constant teasing was Adda—whom Ove later started dating.

Viggo knew he didn't stand a chance with Adda and that he couldn't compete with Ove for her affections. Still, he sensed some sort of connection.

One Friday evening early in June, when they were fourteen, they were standing around, drinking beer under the oak tree near the bog, and Verner, Ove, and Teis went down to the creek to take a piss. Viggo and Agnes were toasting, when her bottle of Wiibroe Gold suddenly slipped out of her hand. They bent down to pick it up at the same time, and when they stood up, they were holding hands. The next moment he had done what he thought he would never dare to do. He had touched her hair—and she had suddenly kissed him on the mouth. How long does a kiss last? Viggo would have said a billion years in that one second. He heard a sound and opened his eyes. Behind some trees stood Palle, slightly hunched over, as if ready to pounce.

Just then, they heard Ove and Verner approaching, and the boy from the Yellow House vanished into the shadows.

Adda had finished her beer, but something had changed, and she wanted to go home.

They watched her walking over the bridge without turning around, without waving good-bye to her three admirers.

The next day Viggo heard about the attack. She had confided in Verner. Halfway up Kirstens Allé, Palle had suddenly stepped out from behind a hedge. Adda sprinted the last bit to the row houses; he had only been able to grab her hair before he fell on the asphalt and abandoned his pursuit. No one dared imagine what the brute would have done to her if he had caught her. Adda refused to talk about it, and none of the adults were supposed to know. Many years later Viggo thought back to those days when everything could have been different. If only he had understood the signals being sent.

On Midsummer's Eve, his mother asked if he wanted to go to the bonfire at the old orphanage in Skodsborg. She was going to ride over when she left work.

He shook his head without explaining why.

Adda was going to be home alone that night, and if he got up his nerve, he planned to ring the doorbell and ask, *Can I come in? We can just sit and talk for a while.*

In a strange way, the kiss and the attack—the beautiful and the ugly—had opened a door he never thought he could enter.

And as it turned out—he couldn't.

***

They got the news from two uniformed policemen.

The doorbell rang in the middle of the night, and he heard his grandmother get out of bed, put on her robe, and go down the stairs.

Viggo could feel the terror; he knew something was wrong.

He had come home early, and only sleep could save him from the self-recrimination that had followed him under the covers, deep into the darkness where we hide our most unbearable stupidity. His visit with Agnes had been a catastrophe. He'd thought she would still want to kiss him. Sitting on the sofa, they were sharing a beer when he leaned over and reached for her hair. Just as he had done near the bog. It was a mistake. In that second, they parted ways forever.

Many years later he remembered his thoughts at that moment, thoughts he couldn't reconcile: the irresistible urge to protect her and simply hold her, and the conflicting desire that he knew had been Palle's when he'd tried to capture his prey. Viggo had felt the same desire, that feeling of power that shouldn't have been there.

She must have seen both urges in his eyes, and then, it was too late. "You'd better just go home. I'm going to bed, anyway."

At home, and now awake, he snuck downstairs and saw two uniformed policemen when his grandmother opened the front door.

She must have sensed something, because she quickly turned and shoved Viggo into the kitchen, closing the door behind him.

He stood in the darkness by the stove, not knowing what to do. Images of Adda swirled in the air before being replaced by his mother; he knew that everything had changed and that nothing would ever be the same again.

Hearing his grandmother's cry, he opened the door to the hallway.

She was sitting on the bottom step of the staircase, holding her hands in front of her face. The policemen were gone.

His grandfather was nowhere to be found—maybe he didn't hear the doorbell.

"Your . . ." His grandmother couldn't say anything else; she just sat there, a white embroidered handkerchief crumpled up in her hands.

He had never seen her look so distraught. She cried often, usually when she was touched by films like *Captains Courageous* on television, or when one of her old girlfriends phoned with yet more disheartening news about illness and death.

"Your grandfather . . . get your grandfather."

Viggo turned and ran up the stairs. The word *dead* had never been mentioned. Not then or ever since.

He found his grandfather just behind their bedroom door. He must have heard his wife's cry a long time ago.

Viggo wondered why he hadn't reacted.

He couldn't remember the rest of the night. Only what he was told later—and that hadn't been much. His mother was cycling home from the orphanage in Skodsborg around eleven that night, and they found her and her bicycle a half hour later on Hellerupvej.

She had been hit by a car. The driver had vanished. The police questioned witnesses and visited mechanics and auto repair shops, because the hit-and-run driver's car must have suffered serious damage. Viggo's mother's bike was completely mangled.

Nothing came of it.

His mother was buried the last day of June at Søborg Church. All of Viggo's friends had gone to Roskilde for the music festival, which they had been looking forward to for weeks.

Only Verner stayed behind with him in Søborg and stood with him when the coffin was carried out. Next to him was the headmistress from Skodsborg—dressed all in black—and at her side a little girl about ten years old.

His grandmother pulled her fur collar up around her shoulders because it was a cold day—but there was something other than cold in the air: a strong breeze from the east, as if both the higher and lower powers had decided to breathe down on the little group.

If he hadn't chosen being with Adda, he would have been by his mother's side that Midsummer's Eve, and the accident wouldn't have happened.

He remembered something else. In his infatuation and longing to see Adda, he had waved good-bye to his mother on her bicycle but had forgotten to ask Our Lord to take care of her. Which he always did. And in his frustration over Adda's rejection, he had forgotten the most important thing of all: asking God to bring his mother home safe again.

He had fallen asleep without ensuring that an angel would be watching over her.

His grandfather stood slightly hunched over in the cemetery, looking like a broken reed in the wind. His wife had cried for six straight days while he'd sat in his wing chair and said nothing.

He just stared straight ahead, not even turning on the marine forecast or the evening news.

The rest of Viggo's childhood departed along with his mother that day; it jumped up into the hearse and rode west with her—as he had already seen in his dreams.

In the following weeks, the police searched for the perpetrator, but they never found a single clue.

At dinner, Viggo's grandparents sat in silence; they turned on the television without watching it, and they went to bed as soon as it got dark. His grandmother kneeled by Viggo's bed, but she didn't pray; she just folded her hands and sat silently.

From then on—when his grandparents should have been making every effort to save their boy—life seeped out of the two old people like water in a cracked tub. Viggo Larssen sat alone in his room; he was on summer vacation, and soon he would start high school. Most of his friends were away on holiday.

One day in the middle of July, he got up out of his chair and walked into his mother's room. Everything was just as she'd left it.

He stared at her small stack of Mozart, Bach, and Beethoven records lying on the coffee table and suddenly kicked all of them onto the floor.

Bending down, he pulled out all the drawers in her blue dresser; then he opened the two cabinet drawers in her writing desk with a key—he knew where it was hidden—and found what he was looking for: three journals he had often seen her writing in, her only activity other than playing Beethoven's Fifth and soaking his eyes in boric water.

In the first of her journals, he read: *Now they've found him on Kebnekaise.* "Him" was his vanished father.

In the second she wrote at one point: *What role does the past play when you find the person you really like and want to spend your whole life with?*

She had never found that person.

Instead, she had recorded details about every holiday, birthday, and Christmas—who had attended, and what gifts they'd brought. There were numerous entries about all of Viggo's gifts as a child: *toy bus, conductor set, traffic cop,* Palle Alone in the World, *flashlight, modeling wax,*

Märklin, tiddlywinks, Monopoly, globe with light, paint box, Legos, When the Robbers Came to Cardamom Town, Cirkus Buster, Twist and Shout, *Jørgen Clevin's playbook, magnet, stamps, fort with Indians, military car with tank, microscope, Fred Flintstone costume, gun and holster, Chinese checkers, magic set,* Year's Best Soccer Matches, Five Go to Smuggler's Top, *telephone set, stop watch, The Visible Man, labyrinth ball game . . .*

He couldn't imagine the boredom that must have produced such banal detail, and he sensed the irritation that it all led nowhere. Nowhere. Not a single meaningful trace of her life with him could be found, nothing of their days together, almost as if they had never existed together.

He threw the first two journals on top of the records on the floor and opened the last one.

He knew immediately that it would be different. The first few pages continued where the two previous journals had stopped—but then it began to approach the day of her death.

Sitting down in her easy chair, he leafed carefully forward. Later, he often thought that he should have listened to the alarms ringing loudly and clearly in his head, like the bells during his mother's funeral, and taken the journals and thrown them far, far away. His grandfather could have burned them in the backyard; it would have given him something to do.

Instead he found something he had never imagined.

He couldn't believe what he was reading. His mother's very last words.

He closed the book, looked carefully around his mother's room, and then opened it again. Nothing had changed. The words were still there.

She had written her final lines early her last morning, a few minutes before she came down to the kitchen for her lukewarm Nescafé and asked if he wanted to go with her to Skodsborg and light the bonfire in the evening, to celebrate Midsummer's Eve with her.

He read the final lines for the third time. There was no doubt.

And there was no possible explanation.

***

Ove from Søborg
Thursday, January 8, evening

Ove couldn't stop thinking about Viggo Larssen's strange letter (which was now in police custody). He could still clearly remember Viggo's mother's death more than forty years earlier, even though it really hadn't affected him. They'd never found the driver, and Viggo's mother had apparently been scraped off the road in very bad shape.

In his boyish mind—at that time he was just starting to harden from a lanky boy into a man—he'd thought it was the payback Viggo's family deserved. Viggo's grandfather had run down an innocent boy, and eight years later his own daughter had been cut down in the exact same way.

Viggo sat alone crying at the bog without knowing he was being watched. Ove and Teis were lying on their stomachs, stretched out among the reeds. Ove knew instinctively that he could never really be friends with a boy as distraught and inconsolable as Viggo. Afterward, Teis had cried like a snotty child, and his three much-maligned chins had shaken with sympathy beneath his soft face. Ove's anger almost made him want to kick the sobbing boy. That day at the bog, he knew that he was different—that he had changed much more than his friends.

Getting up from his easy chair, he stared out at the cherry tree and its still-naked branches. He and Agnes had found their dream home in the middle of the woods they'd visited in their childhood on those beautiful sunny summer Sundays, the woods they'd then gone through, shitfaced, at midnight following their first teenage excursions to the park at Bakken: four boys, with Agnes weaving in and out between them like a moth trying not to get too close to the flame.

He knew full well that Viggo had been in love with little Adda for at least as long as he had been; he saw them kissing each other that evening near the bog, right before Palle attacked her on the way home.

The other day he said to Agnes, "Look at Viggo . . . he's become a complete zero. He's living in a lighthouse on the outskirts of Denmark."

She didn't answer.

Now, Ove placed a green folder on the table next to his glass of cognac.

It contained his concept for Solbygaard—and for all subsequent eldercare homes in Denmark. He had crafted an offer that no senior, sick or dying, could refuse: a dignified end of life, starting with some mental and moderate physical training, a colorful final farewell with specially designed death announcements, and an elaborate display in the church or chapel where they were laid to rest.

The resounding finale was a new, ground-breaking design for the deceased's final resting place, located as far as possible from the usual deadly gray, mathematically precise gravesites of cemeteries. It would be in an Edenic spot in the very image that even God himself must have first imagined. The place where Eternal Life (in Ove's version) could begin.

Eden's New Garden.

Ove had yet to name the final phase for his business partners. First he had to be sure that the technology was in place, which the IT folks had promised would happen within a few months.

Afterward he would have the patent authorized before anyone else seized his genius idea and tried to copy it.

And then there was the financing, of course, for the first land purchase and the specially designed gravestones.

He outlined his ideas for Agnes, who sat frowning in her polka-dotted chair in the corner before saying, "Ove, I would *never* try to keep myself alive artificially in this world. We're all called to Eternal Life."

He could feel his irritation as he grabbed her slender shoulders a little more forcefully than usual. "It's not artificial life—it's people's life stories . . ." He'd almost added, *What the hell is more artificial than religion's absurd belief that the dead rush off to heaven to dance the cancan with holy virgins and ascended angels with outspread wings.* But he said nothing, naturally.

He rarely set foot in his wife's church. In Ove's eyes, her Christian God was cut from the same cloth as her fanatical communist father. Both preached utopias whose endgame was powerlessness and guilt.

The only difference was that her father had gone to heaven without first asking anyone about the inconvenience of nailing his limbs to a cross.

Every hour of the day, Adda lived by the gospel of love. It surfaced in even the smallest of deeds: while picking his socks up off the floor, when she washed his clothes, changed the bed linens, and served venison with mushroom sauce and lingonberry jelly. He never managed to catch her in a single unpremeditated move; he'd never seen the corners of her mouth quiver with rage or heard her curse anyone. Since he had taken inspiration from the first Creation, it would only be logical that God thought he deserved a little commission in this earthly life.

Ove had realized how globalization fostered insecurity, especially for the elderly. He'd sensed the growing fear—how visions of an increasingly ungovernable world resulted in an enormous need to turn inward, pull down the blinds, and focus on your own little manageable world. The body, the soul, family, and the good life. The more troubled the world became, the more the wealthy focused on their own vulnerabilities, on the body's decay and their lack of control. Death was therefore the ultimate betrayal from above. An injustice that simply didn't harmonize with popular conventional wisdom: that people were strong, invulnerable, and that they could have everything they wanted.

Then—*suddenly*—darkness.

What the hell was the point? How could that be the reward?

He could see it in the fitness centers of the many firms he visited as a consultant: terrified and desperate people exercising on strange equipment in neon-lit gyms, trying to find some security, some shelter, trying to postpone the inevitable, loosen the grip of those cold skeletal fingers . . .

He could see it in their faces, their fugitive eyes, and in the sweat on their foreheads, sweat caused by more than their workouts.

This entire health craze had resulted in an overall mass psychosis about running that affected all of Ove's acquaintances, nationwide. They ran as if they were possessed, morning, noon, and night; they ran at work, they ran in their private lives, they ran like hamsters caught on one gigantic treadmill, always in motion, in perpetual motion. They were running for their lives. As if the body's health meant anything at all when Fate said your number was up, shoving its circular saw in the wheel of your careening chariot—as in Ove's favorite childhood film, *Ben-Hur*.

As a joke he'd once suggested producing a light, cheap, and durable plastic helmet that protected its wearer from head injuries as a consequence of falling in wet or slippery areas. Everyone noticed that it was raining harder and that the wind was blowing stronger than ever in Denmark thanks to climate change. Even in the best of health, you could drop dead if you didn't take the proper precautions. Even the most advanced societies had developed strict, half-crazy solutions—like suggesting a ban on outdoor smoking while letting cars, busses, and trucks whizz around in ever greater numbers or letting chemically treated, contaminated foods fill every refrigerator. Symbolic acts—not real ones—that were supposed to save lives and consciences.

So, his concept was a sure bet. Of course the elderly and dying would pay for any promise of utopia, a newfound Fountain of Youth, like the one in the Donald Duck comics he and Adda had loved as children. Like, they wanted to believe that a magic water existed that everyone could bathe in, that would make them all young again.

He realized that most of his clients would die before him. Squawking and defiant, but they'd still die. So he teamed up with an architectural firm that would design these new cemeteries that Ove's people would place in the most beautiful surroundings, all called Eden's New Garden. To the wealthiest of families, Ove would offer the purchase of a forest area, a meadowland, a hilltop, maybe even a glade with a small idyllic stream running through it, locations that could house a family's deceased members for time immemorial. Exactly what he had offered the Widow and little Arrow.

For a one-time fee, managed by an irrevocable fund, families would be able to secure future memories of themselves and their families for all eternity. They could purchase their own immortality in sound, pictures, and words produced by professional documentary filmmakers and storytellers. All thoughts of oblivion would vanish. Their life stories would be heard and seen throughout Eden's New Garden—the true genius of his concept.

The Real Eden Foundation would ensure perpetual maintenance of all gravesites and histories, along with the beauty of these areas. There would be rabbits, foxes, and grazing deer—great tits, thrushes, and diving sparrow hawks—and all this beauty would calm souls even before they were laid to rest, chasing away any dark thoughts about actual death. Forever.

CHAPTER 12

Office of the Homicide Boss
Friday, January 9, morning

The Homicide Boss had started the ninth day of the Blegman affair with a very strong cup of coffee—and Number Two had followed his lead.

They had slept for maybe six hours combined. The Homicide Boss had turned on all four lamps on the large rosewood desk they shared: it was so early in the morning that the sun was only beginning to stir below the horizon. They had about an hour, maybe less, to talk quietly before all hell would break loose in a series of hectic calls from their bosses, the two central ministers, and swarms of both national and international reporters.

"Let's recap how she was found." The Homicide Boss signaled for Number Two to take over.

"She was sitting in the chair facing the door. There were no immediate signs of violence—the entire scene was almost peaceful—her heart had . . . just stopped beating."

"Yes, that *is* what happens when people die . . ." The Homicide Boss's sarcastic tone was uncharacteristic. No one knew better than his deputy that it was a clear sign of the pressure they were both under.

"She simply gave up the ghost after being in the room for a short time. It stands to reason. Fatigue combined with a shortage of air. Ventilation hasn't worked in there for decades. Whoever did this definitely knew she wouldn't last long down there and that no one would hear her—even if she'd had the strength to scream—" Number Two suddenly interrupted himself.

That was the painful fact they both had to live with: they were too trusting of the nursing home's management. They had trusted that everything had been meticulously and conscientiously examined—all three times the nursing home management claimed it had done so. They had overlooked the fact that the health care assistants had probably only shaken the locked doors to the old basement room that no one used any longer—if they had done anything at all.

That left a scenario that, at worst, made the two police chiefs jointly responsible for her death. A thorough search of the entire nursing home area could have bought her time, once they'd realized she was missing. Right then they should have insisted that everything was gone over again— with the assistance of the police, dogs, flashlights, and years of experience.

The locked doors had seemed to rule out the Widow's disappearance as the result of a sudden onset of senility, thereby hinting at the far more dramatic scenario of a kidnapping—and that had sent the police on a wild goose chase outside the walls of the nursing home. So they had contacted all the residents in the neighborhood around the nursing home, searching for witnesses who might have observed suspicious-looking people or vehicles.

The Homicide Boss interrupted his own gloomy thoughts with a question he already knew the answer to. "The book . . . lying by her feet . . . on the basement floor . . . were there any fingerprints on it other than the Widow's?"

"No." Number Two would have already said so had that been the case. "Strange."

"The staff has confirmed that it was hers. From her bookshelf. She read it often."

"It's an unusual title, isn't it?"

"*The Little Prince* . . . yes." If Number Two thought that was an odd question, he didn't show it. Apparently his boss had never heard the title before.

The Homicide Boss quickly changed the subject. "The Gentofte trail—it hasn't led anywhere, has it?" He was referring to their recent efforts to map out the brothers' past. They had investigated the date on the piece of paper found in the brown leather folder in the Widow's top bureau drawer: *June 23, 1971.*

Both brothers were in high school that year, and the two chiefs of police had felt that might be important without being able to explain why.

They had no idea if the note had been written by the Widow or by someone else. A few numbers and letters didn't provide much evidence for graphologists to analyze. Though the brothers had said they didn't recognize the date, there had been something in their answer . . . a slight hesitation, a hint of discomfort . . . a fraction of a second that shouldn't have been there.

Despite the uncertainty, they had intensified their investigation into the brothers' early youth.

Number Two was relieved to turn attention away from their initial blunders. "The only thing we know is that the press is also on the trail . . . and that yes, they really were a pair of bullies already in high school, which comes as no surprise to anyone."

"And the two friends—the ones who might have a motive for"— the Homicide Boss hesitated—"for such hostility?"

"Teis Hanson, yes. The Bear attacked him in high school, and it was quite serious. He's unemployed today. The conservative new government shut down his institute—and with it his research into rare genetic diseases. So now he spends most of his time on . . ." The rest of the sentence hung in the air.

"On what?"

It was unusual for Number Two to find it difficult to complete a candid assessment.

"He spends his time writing theories on the Internet about . . . well, rather far-fetched theories about the Twin Towers in New York."

"The Twin Towers?"

"Yes. A theory that President Bush initiated the terror attack on New York in 2001. You could say he's a little crazy now, but he used to be a highly regarded geneticist. From sublime science to conspiracy theories."

"He needs to be further investigated." The Homicide Boss didn't wait for affirmation. "And then there's Ove Nilsen."

"Yes," said Number Two. "That episode . . . when Palle was a senior and Agnes was only sixteen . . . would certainly give her current husband a powerful motive. But why wait until now? Why take revenge now, after all these years, unless she . . ."

". . . has just started having problems?"

The Homicide Boss nodded.

They sat in silence for more minutes than they really had to spare. The sun had risen over the green and golden spires of the nation's capital. Other than a few incomprehensible *effects*, as the Homicide Boss preferred calling them, they had no leads.

They changed topics.

"*The bird* . . ." It sounded almost like a curse.

"And *the cage* . . . from Søborg."

Hoping to figure it out on their own, they had concealed from everyone else the most important clue in the Widow's apartment. They had to—only the perpetrator would have the same knowledge.

"But we've certainly tried . . . their little brother's death just can't . . . it . . . just isn't possible . . ." Number Two stopped talking.

Once again, the Homicide Boss's reaction was a shade out of step with his normally calm approach to the world. "I don't give a shit about that little brother!"

It was easy to see what was coming.

"It's a feeling. That birdcage, that book in the basement room . . ." Number Two uttered the words so that no one outside the office could hear them. ". . . it gives me . . . there's something . . . far, far in the past. Can you . . . ?"

The Homicide Boss had the same thought. The unspoken question was crystal clear.

"Yes," said Number Two, even though he knew what his agreement meant.

Once again, the large flock of detectives they had deployed would have to move their area of operations slightly southward and—not least of all—a number of years back in time.

To Søborg and the brothers' childhood. As a much more intensive investigation.

It was still a long shot—but a logical one.

Something about what they'd found—and in their shared sense— compelled them to make their decision.

They had to dig in that direction. Even deeper into the morass where the brothers' reign of terror first began. If there was something to find, they'd find it there.

***

The Lighthouse on the Cape
Friday, January 9, shortly after noon

There weren't any mirrors in the lighthouse. I'd noticed that during my first visit.

It hadn't come as any surprise.

Just the opposite.

To view himself in a mirror would cause a panic he couldn't control.

He would see himself reflected in his own eyes—and that would make him react quite strangely. At least by most people's standards. But not mine.

He would run around screaming in the small rooms while beating his face with his fists, in a desperate attempt to escape from his own image and the devastating thought: *Who am I . . . ? Who am I . . . ?* I knew that better than anyone.

The fear of being trapped inside the mirror and thereby trapped inside himself. Since I had left my childhood home, I hadn't owned a mirror, and I never will.

Closing the door to the Sea Witch's house, I felt the porch rock a little as I stepped down; its few planks had long since rotted out.

Suddenly I sensed movement to my right, a shadow among the craggy branches that seemed to stick straight up out of the forest floor. I stood still, then slowly turned my head. Once I'd spotted it, the fox froze in time and space, caught between some branches and a half-toppled-over pine trunk. I could have sworn that we made eye contact, for at least half a minute, while we both considered our next move. Maybe the fox sensed that I was different from the usual disturbers of the peace who passed through the Witch's woods; it had probably observed me often without my noticing it (and that in itself was an achievement). As a child I had a little elephant on wheels that I would pull through the home's dark corridors on a rusty chain, much to my foster mother's great irritation. I used to tie it to the chair beside my bed when I slept. Maybe she could hear our whispers in the dark, without comprehending what a child could possibly be confiding to an elephant. The elephant in the book had been swallowed by a snake—and no adult had ever been able to see it. Then the fox appeared to the boy and told him that to be his friend the boy would have to tame him.

I could hear the words so clearly, up there on that cliff, that it made me jump.

The fox was gone in the same instant.

I was certain I wasn't the one speaking aloud. I looked among the branches, but the fox wasn't there anymore. For a moment I thought of calling out—but that would have been absurd. And I was no longer a child.

***

Søborg, near Copenhagen
1971–1972

When Viggo Larssen's mother died, I think he felt a strange form of guilt for letting her die while he remained alive; but since this was long before crisis counseling, no one thought about it.

Walking around his house, he felt a deep sense of responsibility that his grandparents never sensed: *I could have prevented it. It never should have happened.*

The car could have passed the bicycle as if it had never even existed.

I also had a mother who died—several, in a way—and death is never beautiful, even though good people try to create that illusion.

If it had to happen, it's just as well that she died peacefully, the well-meaning would say.

But Viggo's mother hadn't died peacefully. On the contrary, she was scraped off the road near Hellerupvej and placed on a bloody stretcher beneath a plastic tarp.

Whenever I sat on the bench outside the lighthouse with him, I knew that a picture of his dead mother was always in his head. Perhaps it had changed slightly; it might have lost a little of its intensity, but I wasn't sure.

In the months following his mother's death, he perused her three journals thoroughly, finding almost nothing but notes about weekdays, holidays, family birthdays, and classical music.

She discussed her son in short, mundane observations and reflections:

Viggo has learned to eat his oatmeal by himself. When he was three.

Viggo has had his ears tucked. When he was seven.

Viggo received "Excellent" in Danish. He's proud.

Nothing interesting showed up till the end, and he turned back to those last lines repeatedly. He'd read them several hundred times, but he'd come nowhere near any understanding of their meaning. They described a dream—her last—and the description was strangely similar to the dream he'd had as a small child (and again after Arrow's death). In her version, the dream ended far more disturbingly. These were the last words his mother ever wrote.

Viggo tried to ignore it. As best he could.

For more than a year, his mother's room stayed just as she left it. After finding the three journals, he hadn't gone in there again, and he was certain that his grandmother hadn't either. Nothing should have been moved or changed.

Maybe, when Viggo wasn't home, his grandmother would open her daughter's door and stand there, staring at everything, before shutting it again.

His grandfather sat in the living room and read the evening paper. Silence trudged around like the hands on the clock, which struck on the hour, causing the old man to look up—as if every single chime came as a surprise.

Viggo wandered around the bog alone. Often for hours. He was avoiding the silence in his room and the sight of his grandparents, incapable of combatting their grief. He would have been destroyed if Verner hadn't stepped in. His father, a janitor at Søborg School, suddenly invited Viggo along on the family's annual camping trip to Italy.

They drove down in the middle of July and didn't come back until the beginning of August. Viggo sat between Verner and his little sister in the backseat of their red Ford Taunus. The farther they got from Søborg, the better he felt.

He started high school in August with his four friends from Søborg School.

Over the following months, he began to grow miraculously; he bought a green military jacket and let his dark hair grow down to his shoulders. Looking back on that time period—the early 1970s—you would think that people's weirdness had become a virtue, weirdness we've had to hide in all other eras of human history.

Suddenly it became normal to go around in bare feet and wear thick Icelandic sweaters even in the middle of summer. Any strange behavior was viewed as a sign of rebellion, and with people like Janis Joplin and Jim Morrison giving the finger to everyone and everything, almost anything could be justified. Greasy hair became a badge of courage; bizarre grimaces and incontrollable behavior were merely warnings to the rest of the world. I think the entire era, which the next generation called the age of rebellion, camouflaged Viggo's far more sophisticated parade of hidden peculiarities. Though he felt that his growing popularity at high school was all just a lie—I have no doubts about it—there was no reason to rectify that lie for the few years it lasted.

At that time Poul and Palle Blegman were in their sophomore and junior years, respectively, and the oldest brother's grip on Gladsaxe High School was already well established. Holding court during free periods, he surrounded himself exclusively with those like-minded—the children of executives, lawyers, and government officials from the more affluent neighborhoods. He led political discussions about the decline of the times and the need for a stronger, more conservative grasp on the entire nation. At the slightest opportunity, he'd make derisive remarks about the high school's more freaky members, the misguided and misfits who supported the era's most irresponsible events.

The circle around the two Blegman brothers exuded an insistent contempt for what they summed up in one fear-inducing word: socialism. Even relatively apolitical types like Ove, Viggo, and Teis became an anathema to them simply because the trim on their pants or the peace signs on their army jackets might indicate they were one of the troublemakers who worshipped Chairman Mao, fought the capitalists in the World Bank, or were demonstrating against the Vietnam War.

One benighted member of Denmark's Communist Youth showed up in school with a picture of Che Guevara sewn on his shirt pocket and declared his support for the ideas behind the Red Army Fraction's latest terrorist attack in West Germany.

When Palle Blegman heard that remark, a deep shade of red spread from his neck all the way up to his already-impressive forehead. He tore his way through the circles of supporters and walked directly over to the speaker, who never saw what was coming. With one powerful punch in the back, the Bear dropped the young communist, who collapsed on the asphalt as if he'd been hit by a thunderbolt. For a second it looked as if the oldest Blegman brother would finish the attack with a well-directed kick to the head of the half-conscious boy.

Then something happened that no one has ever understood or been able to explain since.

Teis Hanson, the otherwise quiet, timid sophomore, materialized out of nowhere and stood between the fallen figure and Palle Blegman, the largest and most feared boy in the entire high school—maybe in the entire town. His intention was clear, though I don't think Teis understood that his provocation could have consequences. If the heir to the throne didn't react—immediately and devastatingly—Teis would have embarrassed him.

The punch struck Teis Hanson right in the middle of his chest. It was a terrible blow—and not one of the many witnesses in the school yard had any doubts about its paralyzing effect. Teis fell unconscious next to the groaning boy he had tried to defend. At the same moment, Poul Blegman put his arms around his older brother and dragged him away, terrified at the sight of the passed-out sophomore (who might well be dead).

The ambulance arrived seven minutes later, and no one knew whether he was still breathing.

Finally, at the very end of the day, the students heard over the loud-speaker that everything was just fine: Teis was fully conscious, he had "broken a few ribs" but would soon be fresh as a daisy. The principal's voice sounded strangely relieved. Not on the victim's behalf but on his own. A worse outcome would have provoked a devastating conflict with the Blegman family patriarch.

"He started it." Palle Blegman's allegation was promptly—and repeatedly—asserted to his loyal followers, to the administration, and to the policemen who chose to view the entire episode as a trivial school-yard skirmish with a slightly unfortunate outcome, not least of all because several of the older students confirmed their classmate's version with almost identical descriptions: totally unprovoked, the sophomore boy had lunged at the unsuspecting junior, who had reacted instinctively in self-defense.

Teis Hanson came back to school three weeks later, his stiff right arm hanging awkwardly from his shoulder. Everyone thought it would heal in time, but the paralysis never went away. He couldn't really grab anything; he could no longer turn the throttle on his Puch scooter (Verner bought it from him), and after a few months, he learned to write with his left hand.

Palle had inflicted a permanently disabling injury on Teis, who never overcame it. Nor did he overcome what followed—what nothing can ever change.

***

I believe that episode gave Verner the idea to start a high school maga-zine, which he called *Signal* (it sounded like something from an old Western, probably on purpose). Maybe he had already developed the naïve notion that a critical and independent press can change the tide of battle.

Remarkably enough, Poul Blegman—the country's future minister of justice—joined the editorial staff the very day after the principal announced there would be a new high school magazine with Verner as chief editor.

To this day I think Poul was acting as the Blegman family's emissary. That way, the Bear could secure control of the magazine's contents from day one—from a position quite close to the editor. Not because Verner had ever been the type you'd have problems with; he almost never quarreled with anyone, never raised his voice, and hid any critical thoughts behind his dark smiling eyes in that handsome face, still browned by the sun on Lake Garda. He rode the big Puch he'd bought from Teis and painted white, and he wore corduroy pants and V-neck knit shirts, just like his janitor father. He let his dark, curly hair grow an inch or so over his ears—no more, no less—and it never changed. Verner moved effortlessly among the school's warring factions: the wealthy kids at one end and the freakier crowd at the other. The girls felt safe around him, while the boys sensed his innate kindness—which would never make him any serious competition in any dispute about a girl.

Poul and Palle were in for a surprise, however, as were all the others. And even though the battle was short and brutal, ending in the magazine's death and Verner's ultimate defeat, none of them would ever forget it.

Many years later, you could symbolically describe this start of the three boys' enmity as a showdown between the free press and a powerful political monopoly. Verner wrote his first article about the fight in the school yard, where his friend Teis had been struck down; he found witnesses—anonymous, of course—who described what had really happened that day.

Palle flatly refused to comment. When his father got wind of the article, he became furious. The high school principal, a member of the Conservative Party, gave Verner a serious ten-minute warning in his office, but Verner shrugged it off. The pen had become—as the most grandiose of journalism's pioneers would have phrased it—his weapon. The new editor seemed to change character when he let the words on the page speak for him. That Poul stayed on staff as Verner's assistant editor after that first sensational issue says something about the fix the two Blegman brothers had found themselves in. They didn't know the range of Verner's new weapon; they didn't know the fury that can develop beneath even the most phlegmatic temperament.

During those months in early spring of 1972, everyone was involved in increasingly heated discussions about countries and regimes and conflicts and civil wars all over the globe. The battle between good and evil had become the battle between the rebellious and the established. Both sides viewed the enemy as treacherously subversive at home, brutally murderous out in the world, where East and West were fighting each other on a higher plane, in absolute intransigence.

Palle continued to rule the school yard and maliciously squelched any sign of rebellion.

On Tuesday, March 14, Sterling Airways Flight 296—on its way from Colombo in Ceylon to Copenhagen—flew into a mountainside near Dubai. Everyone on board was killed. You wouldn't think such an event would become part of a political school yard brawl, but as Fate would have it, Adda's paternal grandparents had been on board.

Both Adda's father and her grandfather worked as welders at Burmeister & Wain and were members of what was then Denmark's Communist Party. Although that wasn't something sixteen-year-old Adda advertised, she had started wearing afghan coats and listening to The Doors, Bob Dylan, and Janis Joplin. Every fourth week she would write an article for Verner's magazine about repressed people in Indochina, Bolivia, or El Salvador.

You'd often hear her openly contradicting the Blegman brothers in the school yard. Because she was so attractive—I think all the boys (including the two brothers) wanted a little piece of her—it was especially difficult for the wealthier boys, even the older ones, to argue with the annoying little whippersnapper. Poul was still blushing in that gawky, helpless way boys do when they can't find the right words, whereas his brother turned just as red as he did before the attack on Teis.

Of course Palle couldn't simply swing his oversize paw and knock the pompous little socialist into a corner of the school yard. For the first time, he sensed his own impotence, as well as something even deeper and more suffocating: that the girls in his circle secretly admired Agnes's courage.

He could see it in their eyes and hear it in their silences—and that realization more than anything else resulted in the event that no one at Gladsaxe High School had ever forgotten—right after the terrible news about the plane crash in Dubai, which shook all of Denmark.

Two weeks earlier, in *Signal*'s March issue, Adda had written an enthusiastic article about her grandparents' trip to Ceylon, which had suffered under capitalist colonial rule and was, therefore, of great interest to true communists, like her grandparents, who wanted to study imperialism's basic tyrannical nature as closely as possible.

But now they had been killed on their way home, and Adda wasn't seen at school for the rest of that week.

Monday morning the other students carefully watched her from a distance. There must have been very few who weren't also thinking about their own grandparents—and parents—and about the grief they, too, would have been feeling. All of Denmark was talking about the catastrophe that had killed sixty-eight Danes, mostly vacationers, and crying with the bereaved.

How could anyone have felt differently that morning in the school yard? And yet everyone standing beneath the elm tree between classes suddenly heard Palle's voice rise up from his circle of devoted followers.

His words were unmistakable, and the provocation in them crystal clear. "Well, at least there are two less communists in the world!"

A couple of his friends snickered briefly. And then there was silence. All talking in the school yard came to a screeching halt.

Normally, young idealists like Adda and Verner would have contended that *all* people, *regardless* of their background or heredity, are born *equal*, without evil, with the same capacity for compassion. That the basic, kind human state can only be destroyed by external influences, by the external world, by evil conditions inflicted by others—but I think even they had their doubts when Palle gave full voice to his thoughts.

Adda had been quietly sitting on a bench with Verner, Viggo, Teis, and Ove; they didn't need to talk since they'd already spoken to her over the weekend. She'd told them about the last letter they'd received from her grandfather: indictments of the poverty and repression that had ravaged the island country and how the world had abandoned it. They had agreed to print the entire letter in the next issue of the high school magazine.

Adda got up from the bench before her four friends could stop her and walked across the school yard. Palle's supporters retreated, and she didn't stop until she was right in front of the Bear, who was standing there with his legs apart and his arms akimbo. Her voice was low yet clear. "Palle Blegman—you're a pig!"

Nothing more.

Maybe the use of his name made the difference. His arms fell down by his sides, and his characteristic flush shot up over both sides of his wide neck and farther up to his cheeks and forehead, from temple to temple. Alarmed about the Bear's sudden and visible rage, both Viggo and Verner rose from the bench, but they didn't get any farther before he spoke again. "Agnes *Persen*." He pronounced her last name with all the derision the son of a rich man could muster against a lower-ranking individual. "When you finally come to your senses—and it may just happen someday—you'll see I'm totally right. The world becomes a better place *every single time* a communist dies."

The comment was so brutal that those standing nearby let out a collective gasp.

Adda stood motionless, and some probably thought she was about to strike the huge tyrant standing there grinning, legs apart, in front of her. What followed was, in its own way, more dramatic than any blow or slap, which the Bear might have even welcomed. Violence was his language, and a slap would merely prove him right.

It looked as if she were trying to find the right response—the one that would embarrass Palle more than any other. Suddenly she turned halfway around, as if she were leaving. Then her legs gave way, and she collapsed without a sound onto the school yard.

Adda Persen—who had just started being called Agnes—had fainted.

***

Her fainting exposed something that Agnes wasn't proud of. She knew it even then. She had been weak right when it had really mattered.

No one could mistake the blank, vigilant look in her eyes over the next few days: it was the look of guilt or shame. Yet, her feeling of shame had nothing to do with Palle Blegman's insult. On the contrary, she could have easily turned that against him with the kind of power her grandfather would have admired—if only she hadn't reacted with weakness at that crucial moment.

I don't think she ever forgave herself. In a strange way, the silence that surrounded her in the following weeks became part of the woman who a few years later started dating Ove.

In the high school magazine's April issue, Verner described her showdown with Palle Blegman, without actually printing the remark everyone remembered (since no one dared to repeat it). That omission made the Blegman brothers laugh, only confirming their contempt for the socialist scum.

Viggo may have been the one who was best at escaping their provocations. It was a talent his unusual upbringing had provided. Whenever they tried to approach him, he would fold into himself, engulfed in a silence that seemed neither cowardly nor hostile. He lacked the trait that most people develop early in life as a defense against the unknown, the threatening, and the inexplicable: *condemnation*. And since the Blegman brothers couldn't discern any instinctive disdain from Viggo, they became confused, perhaps even insecure. Maybe they even felt that Viggo saw them more clearly than anyone else—but without the usual reaction.

It was, indisputably, the most remarkable thing about him: he simply lacked any sense of condemnation. If you lack that trait, you become exposed to the outside world and, therefore, are quite vulnerable.

Since childhood, I've been able to see through others' facades, to sense what was happening deep in their souls, while keeping my own thoughts and deeds secret. Weird children often develop this ability. You have to know enough about the deep recesses of your mind so you can haggle with your subconscious for a little consideration: don't interrupt (at vulnerable times); don't make any (unnecessary) noises; don't reveal to the world what's really going on. I knew all that well.

The subconscious would then, for its part, negotiate a peaceful coexistence with the conscience, which would then reach its own settlement with the even deeper urges, those that ultimately involve original sin (children's liability for the sins of their mothers and fathers). Although no one has, as of yet, managed to get any real two-way communication started on that front.

The thought of original sin ruled Viggo's life: his absolute certainty of the responsibility he could never escape—and the absence of any rage or condemnation to protect against it.

He couldn't even see his own enemies.

***

The Lighthouse on the Cape
Friday, January 9, early afternoon

We were sitting in silence and watching the birds above Hell's Deep when Viggo suddenly stood up and walked into the lighthouse residence.

He returned with a small black book I'd never seen before and handed it to me.

Ship's log—"Mycenae" 1872.

"I found it on New Year's Eve. It was hidden in the Lighthouse."

Leafing through it, I glanced down at one of the first pages:

Saturday, May 4th. 45th day at sea. Over the last three weeks, we have sailed 3,600 nm, whereas the first 20 days at sea we only sailed 600 nm. That's how it is when you have to depend on wind and weather. You can easily sail for a while when you have good wind. No washing day, much to do, comfortable climate, your back full of gout. Me and Schmidt agreed tonight that we need a little feminine attention, otherwise we get too salty.

"I asked about it in Ulstrup . . . it was a ship that sank out in Hell's Deep, a Faeroese ship, and legend has it that some locals had lured it onto the reef. Beach robbers. The old lighthouse keeper must have been in on it. Maybe he couldn't get himself to part with the dead shipmate's final words—which in itself would be a curse—so he kept it. And I found it."

I leafed through the book. It contained not only positions and practical information but also small, almost philosophical observations:

Friday, May 10th. 51st day at sea. Most people sleep, waste, or loaf away—if I may so express myself—most of their short life. But the opposite is true for sailors, who have ca. 8 hours free every nautical day which they can use to sleep, mend and wash clothes, and for spiritual development. During the other hours of a nautical day, they have to at least stay awake, even if only at work. People are creatures of habit, so you can get used to it, but it takes time. Everything goes according to command, so it is no wonder that seafarers have fun on land after their travels end.

And a few days later:

Monday, May 13th. 54th day at sea: There is a little storm coming today. It is something that affects your mood, and we are all freezing, as we were at the North Pole. Still, we have had stockfish and burnt gaff-topsail gruel for a change. So, we are scrubbing the deck, since you have to sing for your supper.

"Those are the last words . . . the last words that mean anything."

Terrified was the only word to describe the expression in Viggo Larssen's eyes. The book had clearly touched him deeply with its voice from the past: *Don't forget what you discovered as a child—don't run from it—it exists . . .*

Nervous, almost without moving, I paged through to the end—I already knew what I would find.

Last night I hit the hay at 12 o'clock. I fell asleep immediately and dreamt something I have never seen before. I thrashed around like someone who was possessed and began groaning and calling for the capt. who heard me . . . and then I woke up.

Then he described his dream.

The ship went down only twelve hours later.

***

Søborg, near Copenhagen
1972–1974

Viggo watched Adda from a distance, though a distance only in his eyes, since they were often together within their small circle of friends.

He had kissed her once—which was still more than most had done—but that was almost a year ago, and they had been alone together only one time since. It seemed as if they had both lost interest in that part of life that might have been. Agnes, whom her friends from the neighborhood still called Adda, had become a blonde beauty, but she rejected all advances at high school. And there were plenty of them.

During that first winter, she sauntered disinterestedly through two high school parties. She wouldn't even dance with any of her admirers. The boys in Palle and Poul's circle started calling her the Ice Queen; now and then you'd hear the contemptuous epithet coming from their corner of the school yard.

Although the name was contemptuously meant, it also signaled a lofty, unapproachable beauty that all other girls at the high school must have envied. Maybe that's why Adda never had any close girlfriends.

Viggo, who had loved her ever since that morning he let himself tumble down the steps on his red tricycle, searched out other girls at parties. At the high school Christmas party, he sat in the half dark on the back steps and shared a beer with a blurry figure leaning against him. Right before she kissed him, he noticed her cold sore; she caught his eye and smiled at him, and the message was loud and clear: *If you kiss me anyway, there's no telling what you might get.*

He kissed her—and what he got was a rash, which then turned into a sore that covered half of his upper lip for almost three weeks. It didn't really bother him, though. The little disfigurement became almost a badge of honor—proof that he'd kissed someone. Maybe even more.

Toward the end of that night, Agnes was sitting with Ove and Verner on a bench in the school yard. She rarely left her two guardians' sides when the other boys were drinking. Ove, who hadn't spoken a word as he sat there in the cold night air, was freezing in his frayed denim jacket. Maybe he envied boys like Verner who dared to show up in some old-fashioned green parka, or maybe he already sensed that their rebellious ideals and ragged appearances were merely a blip in time. Agnes's parents had reluctantly let her buy a used afghan coat that, when it got wet in the pouring rain, hung heavily all the way down to her sandals. She often smelled like a wet camel, even from a distance, but that only made her seem even more exotic and unobtainable.

She was convinced that a better world lay ahead, just beyond the horizon—that all it took were a few sticks of incense and a hit on a chillum (she never took more than one). And maybe a guitar solo from *Electric Ladyland*. No one could have guessed that only a few years later she would replace such lofty visions with faith in a demanding and punishing God. In the Bible, people left the Garden of Eden calmly, their heads bent, so that maybe one day they could return, righteous, compassionate, and eternally saved. In reality, we took over the establishment, chased away all the wardens, and instituted the ultimate hunt for validation: careers and material wealth.

For Adda, that first year of high school went about as expected: every other boy at school was in love with her and their collective love surrounded her, lifting her up to float like a goddess through the doors of the old school. Even Palle squinted his slightly bulging light blue eyes at her, like a reptile pondering an attack—that's how he looked to Verner, anyway.

All of the seniors were studying for their exams: Danish novels by Henrik Pontoppidan, poems by Jørgen Gustava Brandt, German novels by Heinrich Böll, poems by Byron and Coleridge, *The Iliad*, integral equations, the inverse square.

The weekend before finals, the school held its annual spring party— on the twenty-eighth anniversary of the liberation of Denmark. That evening, all the book-weary students set aside their texts and arrived on mopeds, on bicycles, and by foot, or they were driven to school by somewhat nervous parents. The richer the parents, the more admonishments you heard coming from the half-open car doors. But darkness finally fell, and the party began.

It was a little past midnight when the teachers herded the students out. No one ever knew why Agnes rode out alone on her red Puch Maxi. And no one knew why she turned in the wrong direction and at some point stopped along the way.

Maybe nausea from the three beers she could normally handle in one night made her stop halfway home, leave her moped resting on its kickstand, and take two, three, four steps into the bushes that then completely enclosed her. As far as she could recall, it was close to the bridge over the creek at Utterslev Bog.

No one will ever know how she could have been found in that exact spot. She was bending over, among the branches, leaning forward; she had stuck two fingers down her throat when she was suddenly knocked out from behind.

She was raped with a fury no one could imagine, yet it left no physical trace beyond some scratches on her face; no bruising or scars, only an anger toward an invisible face, because she wasn't able to turn around during the eternity that it lasted . . .

She woke up the next day in her own bed. Somehow she had gotten home.

Her father, who had lost his parents in the plane crash, was sitting by her side.

"I was attacked." That was all she dared to say. Because of the scratches and tears she couldn't hide, she had to answer him.

"Attacked?" Her father was leaning over her bed. She had curled up in a fetal position, not because of any childlike embarrassment, but because his smell of beer and his being a man reminded her of what had happened.

He sat silently for a long time; then he got up without having asked the logical question: *Who attacked you?*

Instead she had confided in Verner. Actually, he was the only one of her friends who had dared to ask, "What happened?"

When she didn't answer, he said, "Did something happen to you yesterday?"

She told him about the shadow in the bushes: how she knew who it was, even though she had never managed to turn around . . .

If she'd only heard the footsteps in time, maybe everything would have been different. It's an age-old truth, for those who believe it, that if they dare to turn around and confront the demon pursuing them, look it squarely in the eyes, it can no longer harm them.

Verner went straight to her father and told him the name. It came as no surprise.

But something broke in his eyes.

After three days, he got up out of his chair and left the house. The courage he had mustered, a blend of rage and unbridled humiliation, would withstand even the strongest resistance. He crossed Maglegårds Allé and walked through the same gate where Arrow, almost nine years earlier, had passed on the way to his own death. He walked right into the Patriarch's cave and said his name—I'm *Persen*—before collapsing like a punctured soccer ball. Just as Adda would have predicted.

The working man from the neighborhood—the one who should have stood steadfast, demanding justice for his daughter and all daughters to come—left the Blegmans' parlor a humiliated, frightened man, his head bent in shame. He failed his daughter, himself, his comrades at the shipyard, his fallen parents in the plane crash—and every dream of righteousness he'd ever had. Curled up like an insect caught in the middle of some enormous web.

The Patriarch didn't even bother to devour him. He just followed him down to the garden gate and impatiently shoved him out of his life.

Watching her father walk back across the road, Adda knew that they would never again discuss what had happened. The family in the Yellow House had already taken her—and now they'd taken her father, too.

Palle Blegman's mother had categorically denied that her son could have had anything to do with such a heinous act.

Also, he'd been home in his bed when it'd happened—and she'd attest to that fact at any time. She'd seen him in bed herself.

Facing such forceful rebuttals, Adda's father had fallen apart right there in the parlor. His world would now be filled with shame around the event: scandals, police reports, rumors of promiscuity, unsubstantiated accusations against an innocent boy, articles in the newspaper, gossip at the shipyard—all spiraling dishonorably toward another catastrophe for his already-shattered family.

Verner gathered information for an article in *Signal*. The more he researched into it, the more certain he became. Witnesses piled up, and they all confirmed Palle and the Blegman family's story: Palle had certainly never raped her, as the rumors, and she, claimed.

And if it really had happened, why had she never reported him? Why didn't she let a doctor examine her? Who's to say that she didn't secretly desire and admire Palle—like so many of the older girls in school—so she fabricated a dark and malicious accusation out of sheer jealousy?

Still, Verner had no doubts—he could hear something else in their voices. He believed Adda; he could see the truth in her eyes. No one in the Blegman family would speak to him, though. The high school principal categorically forbade him from printing such unsubstantiated speculations—he threatened to shut down the magazine and deny him his diploma—not to mention reporting him to the police.

Even Verner felt as if he were running out of options.

But one Sunday morning, Adda rang his doorbell and they walked down to the bog, where they had gone so often. Walking over the bridge, she pointed calmly at a cluster of bushes on the other side of the stream. "It was there."

He took a few steps forward but she held him back. "Even my father . . . ," she started to say, but then she stopped, squatting down on the ground.

She seemed so fragile that Verner, bending down on one knee, put his hands around her shoulders. "Your father . . . what?"

"This morning . . . when he woke me up. He woke me up and said that I had destroyed everything. As if . . . I think he wanted to say that I invented the whole thing—just for attention . . ." She sobbed into his red pullover.

Monday morning Verner gave his story to a junior staff member for proofreading.

He read it and then stared, horrified, at his editor. "You can't . . . write . . . this is a lie."

"Yes, it's a lie. That's because it's fiction—it's a short story. It's a tale, titled 'The Rape.' Similarities to any living persons or events are accidental, not intentional."

"But everyone will recognize Palle Blegman."

"Yes, but no name appears anywhere."

The scandal spread throughout Søborg and into large parts of Gladsaxe, but it was fiction, after all, a short story with no connection to reality—and the principal's legal friends had advised him against pursuing the matter.

The Patriarch took the same attitude: summer vacation was about to begin, and in a few weeks everyone would forget all about it.

The first day after vacation ended, the principal told his students the news: unfortunately, the high school magazine would have to stop publishing. Over the summer someone had done extensive damage to the editorial office, destroying all the equipment, including the type-writers, and pouring large quantities of varnish on everything.

At the end of August, the Blegmans moved from the yellow villa on Maglegårds Allé to a much larger and more expensive mansion in Gentofte. Palle Blegman started college to study law, and his little brother transferred to Øregård High School in Hellerup.

As summer came to a close, the evil events seemed like part of a nightmare that no one wanted to remember.

***

That autumn Viggo's grandparents set their sights on the end, a jour-ney they had never tried to stop—not for their own sake, not for each other's, and certainly not for Viggo's.

Their daughter's death had been the final blow, and all three of the silent travelers in the low-ceilinged rooms knew it.

Viggo's grandfather looked up at the old Bornholmer clock but could no longer recall what the numbers meant. He stared out the window and couldn't tell whether it was summer or winter. "I can't see the weather anymore," he said, his voice filled with despair.

He cried while listening to the news on the radio, because he could no longer recognize place names—he didn't understand what West Germany was when they talked about the anniversary of the killing of Israeli athletes at the Olympic Games in Munich.

Shortly thereafter, he was admitted to Glostrup County Hospital, more popularly known as the Loony Bin.

Viggo had visited him only once. The calcified old man didn't recognize him but leaned forward, and in a voice breaking with tears, said, "Have you come back? Have you finally come back?"

Then he cried so hard that the tears ran down his cheeks, down onto his white hospital gown in an endless stream. Although the name was never spoken, Viggo knew, without any doubt, that the dying man had finally met Arrow again.

Viggo Larssen, who bore the weight of his family's accumulated eccentricities—and plenty of his own—knew that he shouldn't correct the mistake. Deep in his soul, he knew that he was the real reason why the boy in the Yellow House had died that day. A life for a life. So simple. One lost second for another.

After the old man's death in the winter of 1973, Viggo went up to his grandparents' bedroom and opened the drawer in his grandfather's nightstand.

He didn't know why.

He waited until early one morning, right after his grandmother left to meet with the funeral director at the hospital. He had no idea what he might find.

On the bottom shelf was a strange-looking book that he'd never seen before.

Lifting the book up into the light, Viggo thought that it didn't look like any book he'd ever come across; it was bound in green leather, and the binding had light and dark splotches on it, probably from age.

He opened it to a random spot, where there were pictures of two young men in knee-length pants standing in a landscape that looked more Mediterranean than Danish. *Tage and Halfdan.* On their way to Spain in the spring of 1938.

***

He'd found a journal written by a young man on his journey to fight in the catastrophic war against the fascists, back when fighting fascism was reserved for the bravest and most farsighted—the pure and true, as those praising their deeds had called them.

He couldn't imagine how such a journal ended up with his grandfather, an uncompromising man with his boots planted firmly in the soil of western Jutland.

Maybe it was a childhood friend.

Although Viggo sensed how all of it would end, he leafed through to the last page anyway.

Sitting on the edge of his grandfather's bed, he read the lines that would change his life forever.

After reading them, he sat for a while, rocking back and forth. Whether from doubt or shock—or something entirely different—it was impossible to say.

It couldn't be true.

In a trance, Viggo Larssen walked out of his grandparents' bedroom. Holding the Spanish diary in one hand, he locked the door to his room before opening the top desk drawer, taking out his mother's journal, and placing it next to the Spanish one.

He turned to the end of both books and read both texts carefully.

The two books were almost identical in size, although more than thirty years had passed between their last entries. Once again Viggo felt as if he were in a dream—a dream that was stranger than anything he'd ever encountered.

He couldn't understand what he was looking at. And he couldn't imagine any logical explanation.

These two people—his mother and the soldier heading for Spain—had never known each other. They had died in their own eras with thousands of miles between them. Yet, both had described a dream they'd had on the last night of their lives.

The descriptions of what they saw were almost identical.

And it had made such an impression on both of them that they had written it down on the last days of their lives.

***

The Lighthouse on the Cape
Saturday, January 10, early afternoon

It was the mildest and the grayest winter anyone could remember.

A pair of large dark birds soared over Hell's Deep as I sat down on the lighthouse bench to plan my next move.

The Widow's death had affected Viggo Larssen deeply; we shared that shock, and it connected us in a way he still didn't fully understand.

First there was her mysterious disappearance—and then she shows up inexplicably in a basement. Dead.

He had grown up facing her yard, and he knew her sons, unfortunately. For better or worse, the Blegman family was woven into a past he shared with his few friends. Yet his letters to them had gone unanswered, except for a response from Teis—as far as I knew—which must have bothered him. Still, I sensed that his restlessness would result in some kind of action.

I could see him far out there, wandering along the shoreline to Bavnebjerg's Cliff, a small black line in the middle of all that white. He'd left a half-finished letter in his typewriter, which naturally I'd read, turning the roller as I did so and then turning it back again so no one could tell it had been touched. The short text was unfinished, he'd stopped midsentence, and the letter had no heading. Maybe Viggo Larssen hadn't decided yet on a recipient.

Or if it should even be sent.

Which didn't really surprise me. As I saw it, just these few lines could result in a serious psychiatric diagnosis, and I shuddered involuntarily. Either he'd gone a bit crazy—which wouldn't be so strange—or the lanky kid had stumbled upon something truly mysterious, something he could not forget. It started with his mother's journal and continued with the travelogue from the Danish volunteer going to Spain.

The half-finished letter in the old Olympia typewriter read, *I found the book next to my grandfather's bed. It must have meant something very special to him, though I never discovered what.*

Following the old man's death, his grandmother had begun to fall apart. The country had experienced an oil crisis, a landslide victory, rising unemployment, and a general malaise. For the last few months, his grandmother sat at her desk writing letters to her childhood friend who'd been nicknamed Aunt Jenny.

Only a month later she felt a pain in her side; then the pain spread to her lower back and pelvis, until her entire body started leaning to the left, both when she stood and when she walked, and finally also when she was sitting. Afterward, she became bedridden.

Dr. Fagerlund delivered the verdict: Cancer throughout her entire body. It couldn't be worse. She looked at her grandson, and Viggo remembered her words as her final message, perhaps meant as a kind of comfort.

"In a way I'm thankful. It's your grandfather calling for me—he has heard my prayers. And now we'll finally meet again. He needs me, and I need him."

The day before Christmas Eve, she received a Christmas card from her friend, Aunt Jenny, and that same night Viggo answered a telephone call from Jenny's younger brother. Jenny had died peacefully, right after she sent the letter to his grandmother.

The next morning Viggo's grandmother followed in her friend's foot-steps. As the peace of Christmas descended on the neighborhood, she was still lying on her bed. Viggo decided to let Doctor Fagerlund—and every-one else—enjoy their Christmas Eve; he didn't call until well into Christmas Day, when his grandmother had been dead for over twenty-four hours. She was still lying on her back, on her side of the double bed, her left arm stretched out toward the middle, where her husband had lain a year earlier.

Afterward, Viggo—almost by reflex—took the last letter from Aunt Jenny out of the nightstand and read it.

Perhaps it was some sixth sense, because normally he wouldn't care about some old women's correspondence about their dead husbands and lost years. But she had closed her final letter with a description of a dream. Her last.

Viggo froze. All time seemed to stand still. He couldn't believe what he was reading. He had no idea how long he'd been sitting on his dead grandmother's bed. Maybe an hour. Maybe two. Maybe a day and a night. Maybe more.

Now, I saw that the old letter was lying next to the typewriter in the Lighthouse.

I picked it up and read it. Naturally, there was something in the long-dead woman's words I recognized . . .

. . . I, who was built on a solid foundation of stubbornness and impatient patience, who never forgets a face or a detail.

I sat on the bench and waited for his return from the cliff.

I had reached the end of this part of my relationship with the man in the Lighthouse. At least that's how it felt. It was like sealing a deal, shaking hands on something that had been in the works for a long time—something that we both had felt.

I had knowledge he needed, and he knew something that I, with ever-greater certainty, viewed as important and possibly even dangerous.

CHAPTER 13

Office of the Homicide Boss
Saturday, January 10, afternoon

"I don't get it. Just what . . ."

". . . will he gain?" Number Two finished his boss's question.

"Yes, what will Ove Nilsen—management guru and lifelong spin doctor—gain by sending a letter like this to us?"

"And why cast suspicion on an old friend?" Number Two added yet another question, to their shared amazement.

"Maybe we overlooked something important." Not a pleasant thought, since they had no definite suspect, no theories, and everyone around them was demanding action and answers, conclusions—even the most tenuous theory about what might have happened.

"The letter he's attached . . ." Now it was Number Two's turn to hesitate, though his thought was easy to finish.

"Yes, it's a little . . . *creepy*." A word the Homicide Boss seldom used.

"But just because someone is a little crazy doesn't mean he's kidnapped anyone—or killed them. And what if it was Ove himself . . . and he's just trying to place suspicion on someone else?"

They'd read Viggo Larssen's letter, which Ove had attached. Even though I didn't know its exact contents (at that time), I could easily imagine their amazement.

"Viggo Larssen mentions the Widow—and then there are these . . . *theories about death . . . omens . . .* or whatever he calls them. It's all a little nuts." The Homicide Boss had returned to using his normal jargon.

The media had opened a new can of worms that same morning, and it hadn't made life any easier at police headquarters. The Blegman brothers stood to inherit a large fortune, and management at the nursing home was insisting that there had been a will. And now it was gone. According to one newspaper, several anonymous sources had seen it lying out in the open on the Widow's table only a few months earlier.

"We're going to have to visit this . . . Viggo Larssen, who apparently has chosen a *lighthouse* for his retirement." You could hear in the Homicide Boss's voice that he had no desire to visit the man—or the place.

"He did know the family. True, it's very long ago, but they went to high school together. At least for one year."

"So did a lot of other people."

"If we don't respond . . . well, you know people like Ove Nilsen . . ." Number Two didn't have to say anything else. If they did nothing, then the spin doctor might leak the story to other sources.

The Homicide Boss nodded. He lifted the receiver on the red telephone—the one that couldn't be traced, his direct line to the nation's highest offices—and called the minister of justice.

He was in a meeting and couldn't be interrupted. The minister's adviser listened to the Homicide Boss's request and decided to run the risk of a tantrum; the younger Blegman brother's temperament was only a tad less violent than the Bear's. He interrupted the meeting.

The Homicide Boss cut right to the chase. "Before you lived on Smakkegårdsvej, you lived for a while in Søborg and went to Gladsaxe High School. A lot has been written about . . . violence"—he could hear the minister of justice breathing deeply into the receiver—"and we need to protect ourselves against . . ."

"Against enemies. Yes, you've said all this before."

"Someone from your . . . past . . . may have a motive to . . . to harm you." It was unlike the Homicide Boss to stutter his way through his requests.

"Then this *someone* has waited pretty damned long, hasn't he?"

The police chief had almost replied, *The damned tend to do that,* but decided against it at the last minute. "Yes, but still . . . someone from that time may be a person of interest." He avoided mentioning that it could also be *something*—something about the brothers themselves—that might be of interest, but the minister could surely figure that out for himself.

"You don't need to be digging up all kinds of . . . *dirt.*"

"We won't be digging into anything irrelevant." Although he delivered his assurance in a neutral tone of voice—not exactly his specialty—he couldn't help but think of the grotesque irony in the minister of justice's admonition. This was the same man who, along with the rest of the current administration, had increased the oversight of ordinary citizens by logging phone calls, monitoring mail, and instituting general camera surveillance. Meanwhile, in his own life he viewed even a gathering of fifty-year-old private information as an attack.

"My brother *isn't* going to like it . . . none of us will." The threat was blatant. As far as Poul Blegman was concerned, the Homicide Boss was not only teetering on the edge of being fired—he was already halfway down the dark abyss from which no enemy of the Blegman dynasty had ever returned.

"One last thing. Is there any news about the will—or have you heard anything about where—"

The minister of justice slammed down the receiver.

***

Søborg, near Copenhagen
1975–1976

Viggo had graduated.

He was nineteen years old and had no close family left in life.

It was the spring of 1975.

The row house was sold, and his grandfather's brother, who had been CEO of FLSmidth, got a three-room apartment for Viggo on Læssøesgade, near the lakes in Copenhagen. He moved in across from Sølund Nursing Home, once one of the city's most notorious orphanages. Hopefully the elderly were being treated a little better than the children had been.

He took some of his grandparents' furniture with him and bought the rest of what he needed in one of the many secondhand shops on Ryesgade.

His ground-floor apartment looked like the museum display of a typical bourgeois home from long ago. He hid his most precious treasures in his grandparents' old desk: the three journals his mother had written, the Spanish journal, and the Christmas letter from Aunt Jenny.

At that time he still wasn't sure what he had discovered.

He only knew that anyone—even those who'd never experienced his tics and peculiarities—would have been frightened. All of it involved death. He had stumbled upon something he shouldn't have. That much was clear. The chance—or the risk—of that kind of thing happening was highly unusual, bordering on the impossible. Yet as he saw it, the signs, or omens, were unmistakable. The descriptions in the three documents—documents from diverse times and locations—were so uniform that he couldn't ignore it.

For a moment he wondered if he'd merely been struck by yet another peculiarity that had nothing to do with the world around him. That maybe it was just him. If what his treasures indicated were true, though, then it must have existed for thousands of generations, must have avoided the eyes of untold family members without ever being noticed.

The pattern he had discovered might have gone unnoticed for centuries, or been viewed as merely a strange occurrence or the result of an overactive imagination. Viggo knew that he had the power to just leave it at that—and maybe that was the most terrifying choice of all. If he came forward too early, it might trigger a catastrophe, yet if he avoided any action whatsoever, it could also be terrible. The situation was exactly the same as when his grandfather had left the house to take the last drive of his life. One second earlier—or later—and everything would have been different.

Viggo had a visit from Verner, who was studying for his entrance exam for the College of Journalism in Århus. Teis had started medical school, and Ove had been accepted at the School of Design in Copenhagen (to study advertising).

"I'm going to combine the imaginative with the commercial," Ove had explained. No one back then had any idea just how true that statement would end up being.

Perhaps Viggo dreamed about Agnes in those months, but she never visited him and he dared not call her. According to Ove and Verner, she had been accepted into the University of Copenhagen to study theology.

Viggo thought about the Blegman brothers, studying law at the same school, although the university was large enough that they would never run into each other.

In the following months, he lived off his inheritance and did little else beyond going for walks in Nørrebro, reading, and watching television.

He read everything he could find about the Spanish Civil War at the Central Library, and he asked the librarians to find any historical and philosophical works about death (not that they brought him any closer to solving his own personal mystery).

The Little Prince, which also ended in death—by his own hand, no less—lay as always on his nightstand. Although he rarely read it, the book's ending had taken on a special meaning, one that he could not help but connect to the papers hidden inside the old writing desk.

Then one afternoon in April of 1975—the day the Vietnam War ended in a mighty chaos of refugees and soldiers—he read the entire book, without knowing why. He sat there staring for a long time at one of the passages his mother had circled. It described a weak and naïve flower who had no way of protecting herself.

He understood it as a reference to her own life and to their home in Søborg.

As if such a half-withered, forlorn rose had ever been allowed to grow in their lush backyard.

So why did his mother express her feelings by worshiping a cartoonish figure with spiky yellow hair and a flock of blue birds on long strings? A boy who wound up committing suicide and running away from everything he held dear.

His grandmother had told him that, in God's eyes, that was the greatest sin of all.

How could there suddenly be any exception?

***

Viggo Larssen was accepted to Denmark's College of Journalism in Århus in the summer of 1976, and Verner called from a pay phone at school to congratulate him. A few days later, leaving the Central Library, he almost bumped right into Agnes.

Afterward, the only thing he remembered about their conversation was one terrible detail: she had moved in with Ove, whom he hadn't seen in a long time.

"We're getting engaged," she'd said jubilantly, as if that expression wasn't antiquated.

A theologian living with an ad man, Viggo had thought; so, the airy dreamer and the calculating materialist had found each other. He immediately became embarrassed by his violent reaction.

Still, he couldn't deny a strong and sudden feeling of great loneliness, as if he had lost something he never thought he'd lose.

He rode home to his apartment, with its view of the nursing home, and spent the rest of the afternoon and most of the evening lying in bed, crying. He was twenty years old; he'd seen more visions than most people and lived through all of them in near silence. And he still performed his rituals when he was alone: turning off the light above his bed in just the right way, avoiding his own reflection in the bathroom mirror in the mornings, and moving the alarm clock back and forth on the nightstand.

He rolled down the blinds and, kneeling down by the bed, prayed to his grandmother's God.

Most people would have thought he was crazy.

***

Ove from Søborg
Saturday, January 10, evening

Ove Nilsen was sitting with his feet on the polar bear's curvy claws, enjoying the view of the garden and the woods on that bright, star-studded evening.

But he was worried.

Over the last few days, Agnes had become increasingly distant; only talking about the dynasty's fallen queen made her focus and actually look at her husband. Though she had reacted with the least charitable response one could imagine coming from a pastor: "Now they've also learned what it means to lose." Her voice rang with a devilish satisfaction, and her eyes shone with a glow whose meaning he couldn't quite discern.

He understood her anger full well. Still, they had never spoken about the attack at the bog that night—not even when the two brothers went into politics, slowly becoming stars among the Conservatives, with seats in Parliament in the eighties, as opposition leaders in the nineties, and with ministerial positions after the millennial elections—then finally sitting on the realm's highest thrones, now with a dead mother, whom no amount of power could bring back.

Ove had no control over her high school demons—nor the attack. Yet he knew that the incident had become embedded in Agnes's very core and would never release its grip. And even though he understood that, he still felt an anger that would be dangerous to reveal. He wanted to yell at her, tell her that her feelings about the attack were standing between them. Why had she never been able to just let it go?

He should have been happy for the silence, as it was a dangerous topic, even after all these years. They'd never had children, and he knew that she blamed it on the episode following the high school party. For more than ten years, they tried to conceive; they even looked up Teis, who'd referred them to a friend who ran a private clinic that had great success with artificial insemination. They'd paid dearly for the services, but Agnes finally abandoned the trials.

She'd never been able to fulfill her dream of children, God's greatest gift to mankind. The very meaning of living. The two brothers had children whom they had carefully shielded from tabloids and the public spotlight. One time, though, a paparazzo managed to catch a glimpse of their carefree offspring playing in one of the massive, posh gardens between Vedbæk and Rungsted.

These days, their conversations were punctuated by long pauses; she seemed to be shrinking, silently becoming narrower and thinner, her very outline fading.

She walked out into the garden and sat on the little wooden bench near the edge of the woods. Her silhouette against the blue sky was erect and bright but, for the most part, motionless. Ove, cognac glass in hand, studied her through the picture window. Maybe she was with God at these moments, in a kind of preliminary meeting before the big one—but he pushed that thought aside. They couldn't die, not now, in the middle of their lives; it was too soon to be thinking about death on a personal level.

Adda once told him about a funeral stalker—a man who looked up random names in newspaper obituaries and then showed up at those people's funerals.

That fascinated Ove. He could understand how powerful and all-encompassing that man's interest in death must have been.

That's why there was so much money in it.

How can death be the purpose of life?

He'd set up a joint-stock company under the name Real Eden Foundation: Center of Unlimited Life, and he had smiled at both the imaginative and commercial aspects of his invention. Those two forces always went hand in hand. Even though he was no tax evader, he had considered locating the company in the Cayman Islands—just so he could advertise: "Death comes to the Cayman Islands!"

Maybe he'd enjoyed a little too much cognac now and then.

Over forty years ago, he'd stood with Viggo in the churchyard by Viggo's mother's grave. Even then, he'd wanted to hear her story, he wanted to hear her speak about her life. He had no idea why (not at that time). They were just two half-grown boys. Maybe because he had seen Viggo's sorrow, back when he and Verner—and sometimes Teis—had spied on Viggo at the bog. Hidden and yet so close.

Maybe because Viggo's mother had died under such mysterious circumstances.

Or maybe simply because he sensed that Viggo would have given anything for the smallest intimation of life—for the possibility of any reunion, for some continued life together.

Many years later his revelation came back to him. Suddenly, he could see the gravestone, so the idea came without warning.

It had been a real godsend, he thought, smiling because the idea had almost come from above. Now Ove was making that utopia possible.

He recalled that Viggo, even as a recent journalism grad, was already fascinated with death. They'd met him one day on Vestergade while Agnes was still studying at the seminary and Ove was about to earn his first million as a copywriter for what was then the most famous and celebrated advertising firm in Copenhagen. Viggo was writing for a grassroots magazine that Agnes sometimes brought home; his articles were easy to find. He had done a series of features on gravediggers at Vestre Kirkegård, he'd interviewed a female mortician in Vesterbro, and he'd spoken to three women whose children had died in their cribs. It bordered on sick.

In 1985 Viggo was about to start a new grassroots magazine along with Verner, and Agnes decided to subscribe, probably for some nostalgic reason, some memories of the kids from the neighborhood.

Once again, it was easy to detect Viggo's influence, as he continued writing various articles dealing with death.

Then in the spring of 1986, Viggo read a sensational article in an American magazine about supernatural occurrences. The article described a woman who saw other people's auras; she claimed that the glow surrounding everyone had its own color, determined by the person's remaining lifespan. In 1984 she had been moving from Paris to New York, and right before her plane was about to take off, she realized that all the passengers' auras were the same color. Understanding immediately what that meant, she tried desperately to warn the flight attendants about the impending catastrophe, that the plane was destined to crash. The flight personnel reacted as one would expect and escorted the panic-stricken woman back to the departure lounge at Charles de Gaulle Airport. The flight took off without her and crashed into the Atlantic Ocean an hour and a half later.

Everyone on board was killed.

Viggo called the airline to confirm the story. The airline then called Verner, the magazine's editor, and complained about harassment and an attempt to incite panic. There had never been any such episode. Viggo tried to find the woman, but apparently she had vanished into thin air. Yet, all of this only confirmed his belief that someone was trying to hide the truth about the fatal event.

This was in the eighties, when people could still be a little batty. Everyone saw conspiracies in everything. People on the Left believed their phones were being tapped or that they were being stalked by the Danish Defense Intelligence Service. Several journalists had been hospitalized with nervous breakdowns or paranoia—it was almost a natural consequence of their lifestyle.

Still, the story about the psychic woman was too much for Verner. He refused to print it.

Later, he told Ove and Adda about Viggo's almost sick obsession with Olof Palme's murder in 1986, when the Swedish prime minister was shot on the street in Stockholm. Viggo was looking for Palme's journal, which he thought was an important secret document that might explain everything. The search had brought him to an almost manic state in which he finally tried to contact the murdered prime minister's widow in Stockholm. He was eventually arrested outside Palme's home in Stockholm and sent back to Copenhagen, where Verner—with some difficulty and good contacts at both police headquarters and the prosecutor's office—finally managed to get him released.

He was then rushed to an emergency room with acute paranoia and spent a long period of time as a psychiatric patient at Sankt Hans Hospital in Roskilde.

After he returned to the magazine in 1988, everything went to hell. He insisted on writing a series of articles about a phenomenon he had researched while hospitalized (he called it the Omen of Death). He wanted to use his own mother's death as an example.

At the last moment, Verner averted the demented idea by establishing a special task force that, based on solid research, would write a highly critical exposé about the Blegman family, who were about to develop into the country's most powerful political faction. Viggo Larssen was the natural choice to write it—and he wasn't about to let that chance slip away from him.

The magazine came out in September of 1988 with the headline: *A Family of Butchers.*

It was an unprecedented, tough showdown with one of the most powerful clans in the entire realm. All the magazine's writers and editors were holding their breath. Would their rebellious grassroots colleagues survive this attack?

A few days later they got their answer. The Blegman family patriarch, Peter Blegman, collapsed in his law office on Bredgade, suffering a stroke. In his hand he was clutching (according to his oldest son) a copy of the grassroots magazine with the devastating article. One blow—and that was it.

Verner and Viggo were suddenly fair game; they had crossed far over the line, both professionally and morally. A few months later the magazine was shut down. The critical article had resulted in a massive campaign against the publication's journalistic tactics, readership fell, sources became frightened—and finally their bank withdrew its support. Their finances collapsed. They were finished.

No one had any doubts about the source of such a violent and effective reaction.

***

The Lighthouse on the Cape
Saturday, January 10, evening

I never found a manuscript or a single article from Viggo's days as a journalist in any of the rooms in the lighthouse. He must have hidden his past in a place that even I couldn't find.

People usually say that humans differ from animals in the power of their thoughts, but as I see it, the greatest difference is something else entirely: the ability to sympathize. Maybe he'd had this ability to a greater extent than other children. And it had been directed particularly at his grandfather, who had cracked early in his life.

He had gotten through high school and those first years as a journalist before he, too, began to crack and suffer from breakdowns. Then he had crawled back into himself.

As the years passed, he had opted out of any kind of social life, instead developing a special relationship with death.

I'd seen the obituaries—with all the names of the dead he was interested in—and I'd seen his books and folders filled with articles about near-death experiences and the pages from his old Olympia typewriter.

I knew a lot more about him than he could guess—or would ever know.

I knew that in the months following the Blegman exposé and the grassroots magazine's sudden death, his friend Verner once again helped him to get back on his feet. Most of the staff wound up unemployed (they didn't have the best résumés to begin with) and several went, as expected, to the dogs, whereas Verner Jensen, thanks to his charisma and good connections, found work as an editorial director for the Danish Broadcasting Corporation—and brought Viggo along with him. Yet maybe Verner shouldn't have helped him. My greatest fear was Verner's involvement, because he had become a very powerful television editor—and that combination of the powerful TV boss and the lonely, shattered man sitting on the lighthouse bench could be detrimental for Viggo.

At that time, Viggo began working with the Montage radio documentary group—surely the strangest office on earth—and the only truly appropriate place for a man with Viggo's languid journalistic approach and wild imaginings. Employees could stumble around for half a year pursuing weird ideas about strange life stories.

He started working on a documentary about children killed in car accidents and then continued with another on the plane crash in Lockerbie, Scotland. He spent the following years wandering around the DBC building in Frederiksberg—unchallenged in his own thoughts.

He read about explorers and conquerors, and apparently he also sought out the more mystical and spiritual beings: Satan, God, Jesus, and Muhammad—and he wrote down long conversations he'd had with them. He started working on montages about the Loch Ness monster and the legend of the Fountain of Youth. None were ever finished. Still, Verner kept protecting him.

He received small advances for new ideas and went on living cheaply in his apartment on Læssøesgade by the lakes, across from Sølund Nursing Home.

During this time, both Palle and Poul Blegman won seats in Parliament, while Teis was working as one of the country's most promising geneticists. Agnes had become a pastor in Søllerød, and Ove was teaching leadership skills and employee management at the country's most notable private and public workplaces.

After the Tamil case, which overthrew the government in 1993, the path opened for the two Blegman brothers to establish their power in the party. Their father had died. It was their turn to take over. The gate stood open; they only needed to run through and look both ways.

CHAPTER 14

Office of the Prime Minister
Sunday, January 11, morning

"There's this . . . thing I have to tell you . . ."

The voice was so low and earnest that the prime minister almost couldn't make out the words; his younger brother rarely seemed so timid—especially in private.

The minister of justice had arrived without warning, and the permanent undersecretary, who shared his left-wing, middle-class past with at least half of his government colleagues, had struggled to hide his irritation. He had just presented a crisis plan that was the result of several weeks of intensive work by the Ministry of Finance (whose department head had once been a rock-throwing anarchist).

It involved nothing less than finding the long but necessary way out of the country's financial crisis without going bankrupt. "We have to . . . compromise," he had said. Of course that might seem somewhat cynical if you factored in the legions of citizens who'd become unemployed to make the numbers add up, but to hell with the unemployed, the Ministry of Finance said—using slightly different wording—most of them will end up there anyway out of their own doing.

Right now governing required a firmer hand, and that hand could only be Palle Blegman's—with a little help from his loyal underlings.

"Leave the salvation and charity to pastors and social workers." The undersecretary had just quoted one of his colleagues when he was abruptly shown the door as the minister of justice arrived.

Poul Blegman plopped down into the chair the undersecretary had just vacated. The seat felt warm in a much-too-personal way.

Palle Blegman stared at him inquisitively and, for a change, remained silent.

"There's this . . . thing . . . I have to tell you," repeated the prime minister's younger brother, bowing his large head.

The prime minister didn't respond. That word irritated him: you don't tell someone a *thing*—you stacked things into piles or threw them out when they were no longer useful. Like political views.

"It's about father."

"Father is dead." The statement of fact, though delivered in hushed tones, came like cannon fire from hell. Ominously, like distant thunder.

"Yes . . . but before he died. He regained consciousness at the hospital—before the end."

"Yes, I know that." Palle Blegman folded together the fingers of his two mighty paws. It was not a good (or pious) sign. His little brother knew that better than anyone.

"Father said something . . . right before he died—something that he had done . . . something terrible. But not intentionally."

You could see the prime minister's fingers turning white. The strength in the powerful man's hands was formidable.

"He didn't want you to know—you had to be protected—so he only told mother and then she told me. I guess she couldn't bear the truth alone. You had just been elected to . . . well, where you are now, so it had to be kept a secret. But now that everything is . . . since mother had died like this . . . it's a whole other matter."

"A whole other matter? What matter?" The Bear loosened his grip on his fingers, and the color returned.

It took Poul Blegman, leaning forward and whispering, less than a minute to explain where things stood. The bear paws turned white again.

Palle Blegman slammed his clenched fists down hard on the desktop and screamed, "But we sure as hell can't repeat that to anyone . . . even if . . . even if it is a motive!"

His brother looked like a scolded child. "He wanted to protect you . . . you had just been elected . . . but he didn't want to go to his grave without confessing his sins."

"Yes—I got that!"

"He didn't want to risk . . ." The minister of justice paused. The conversation was starting to go in circles.

Peter Blegman had been willing to take any risk necessary.

The whiteness of the clenched fingers had now spread up to Palle Blegman's neck, cheeks, and forehead. His secretary would never have believed that his boss's current skin tone was even possible. Generally crises and unforeseen obstacles triggered a furious redness in the Bear, caused by blood boiling and the irrepressible heartbeat of a family of warriors.

"Still, it could mean . . . It could definitely mean that someone might be a suspect . . . ?"

"Yes," Poul said.

"Do you think it's possible that—" The prime minister stopped right before saying the name they were both thinking.

"Yes."

"He was certainly strange . . . really strange . . ." The prime minister shook his head. The movement seemed to bring a little color back to his cheeks and forehead.

"Still, there's another possibility . . ." Poul Blegman looked like a child receiving some form of punishment, yet he forged on.

"Yes?"

"We shut down that magazine when they wrote about us."

"Now listen here . . ." The Bear's color was returning to its usual fiery red, bordering on raging purple. "That was in the *last* century!"

"The police are searching for clues. They're searching for people in Søborg—from back then—because they think there's a possible connection. To the past."

"The past. Fuck the past!"

"They'll find things . . ." He was using that damn word again. "They'll find something about what happened . . . in high school, too. And that would be the worst, because we'd have no control over it."

The Bear loosened his grip on himself, and the blood seemed to gush from his forehead down to his wide fingers, which must have been completely numb after three minutes without any oxygen. He spread his fingers out on the desk in front of him and looked up at his brother. "The worst?"

"Yes." Poul Blegman had returned to one-syllable affirmations.

"*What* is the worst?"

"You violated that girl . . ." As soon as the oddly old-fashioned phrase left his lips, the minister of justice bowed his head, as if ashamed of his own audacity. The prime minister squinted his shining blue eyes and glared at someone he now considered an adversary—a threat. Although his little brother was fully aware that it was the precursor to yet another violent outburst, he had to force the issue.

"They'll find out. They wrote about it in their fucking magazine— and in that damn high school rag. Verner Jensen. He was a pest. He wrote that short story, said that you—"

The prime minister stood up so suddenly that the chair toppled over behind him. "I didn't do a *fucking* thing!"

The minister of justice was silent for a moment. Then he continued, with a stubbornness that may have shocked his older brother as much as what he said. "What's really interesting is that her husband works for the nursing home. Ove Nilsen. You must remember him?"

"Yes." The prime minister had turned his chair upright again. He sat back down.

"These stories are going to come up . . . there's no way to avoid it. But it's going to affect them, too. If any of them has thought about this after so many years, it could be the answer to why mother disappeared and then was found . . ." He let the unspeakable hang in the air between them.

Palle Blegman, whose face had regained its normal color, said, "We can't tell anyone what you just told me. It can never leave this office. For father's sake."

Poul Blegman nodded. "Naturally. For father's sake."

But mostly for their own.

***

Office of the Homicide Boss
Sunday, January 11, morning

Three yellowed newspaper articles about Arrow's death lay spread out before them. Their investigators had uncovered yet another pair of old notices about the tragic accident.

The Homicide Boss stared at his trusted Number Two. "Yes. It's weird."

That word—weird—seemed to sum up everything they'd discovered in the wake of the Widow Blegman's disappearance and unsolved death.

They stared at the newspaper clippings.
Boy Killed in Tragic Car Accident.

Little Boy Killed in Søborg.

And not just any boy, but the Blegman dynasty's youngest heir.

Run down by Viggo Larssen's grandfather, the grandfather of the very man the nursing home's management consultant had just accused of suspicious behavior and an almost pathological obsession with death.

The detectives had laid the clippings next to the old edition of *Signal*, the high school magazine in which Verner Jensen described the attack on Agnes, who was married to Ove Nilsen.

Their desk was littered with strange effects: cages, birds, an old book, yellow pieces of paper, yellow scraps of material, blond hair, a folder that shouldn't have been empty, and a missing will.

"All these pieces of information fit together somehow, but it's difficult to see how . . ." If that was another attempt at consolation, Number Two had failed.

His boss didn't comment on the futile attempt.

"If all this is true, Verner Jensen has had two magazines shut down by the Blegman brothers . . ."

"And the last one with Viggo Larssen."

"Agnes . . . she is here also."

In those hours, the two detectives' world must have seemed as foggy and impenetrable as the cliffside thicket by the Giant's Footprint. Everything was too old, worn out, and tangled together . . .

. . . no one could see where the path led. If there had ever been one.

CHAPTER 15

The Lighthouse on the Cape
Sunday, January 11, afternoon

I passed through the hollow of the Giant's Footprint and arrived at the Lighthouse.

It was midafternoon, and Viggo had just returned from his daily walk out to the cliff. Once again, he reminded me of a hamster on a treadwheel. The beach was the wheel that kept him going, day in and day out. If he stopped, his world would come to a halt.

I'd made my decision. I told him about the nursing home, about me and Agnes and the Widow. I told him about the will that the old lady had changed drastically, which Agnes and I had witnessed.

Viggo Larssen sat motionless, and I had just about abandoned the idea of asking a question, when he turned to me and said, "Why are you here?"

I sat for a long time without speaking, and then I answered with a version of the truth that I hoped would seem plausible, or at least somewhat likely.

"She considered leaving you . . . something . . . some compensation for the way her family had treated you. It certainly wasn't your grandfather's fault."

I could see that he was moved and that maybe he even believed me.

"I also think that in some way you reminded her of Arrow. You two weren't really so different."

I held my breath and avoided looking at him. At least that last part was true.

He didn't say anything.

"She asked me to contact you and . . ."

". . . check to see that I wasn't totally . . ."

". . . crazy." Again, true. I nodded.

"But now it's too late."

I nodded again.

"They say that the will has disappeared."

I think he sensed the missing explanations, but I couldn't say anything else. Yet.

He got up and took our glasses and grabbed the wine bottle.

Viggo then shut the door, and I was alone.

***

Copenhagen
2007

Verner Jensen left all his grassroots ideals in a slightly messy pile in his old office. The last few employees of the capsized magazine met at a bar to drink their farewell beer, and then Verner took a taxi to the DBC building to begin his tortuous climb to the top of the heap. There were managers and middle managers for every conceivable area of responsibility, and Verner—both approachable and efficient—navigated the path quite deftly.

By the end of the 1990s, Verner had become head of those responsible for streamlining the DBC and making the institution world-class. That included outsourcing programs and eliminating entire departments, mostly in radio, in favor of an increased focus on viewership. Right after the millennium, Verner had asked Ove Nilsen to help modernize the Danish Broadcasting Corporation's most outdated departments.

Modernizing was usually just another word for *closing down*. In the competitive global marketplace, with its limitless Internet and TV channels, there was no room for lengthy explorations of peace and contemplation. No room for *quality*. That damn word, thought Verner Jensen, who was responsible for the office cleanup.

Oddly enough, it's people like Verner—people thought to epitomize niceness—who are best at implementing the kind of earth-shattering theories that upend while presenting themselves as a science.

The Documentary Department—including the Montage group— had to attend large seminars about *Product Reengineering*, a term no one had ever heard of but one that made all the bosses' eyes light up. It had something to do with improved work processes—with Ove at the helm.

"Together we're going on a journey to a better future. Together we're going to become world champions."

Even people once considered intelligent repeated these sentences like members of some cult. Although no one understood a syllable of the consultants' words, they could all feel the exciting momentum, as if they'd been invited on a long and exotic journey with friends who only wanted the best for them.

Verner Jensen, who had been standing behind Ove as he presented his findings, clapped.

As a young journalist, Verner had felt empathy for each and every mistreated creature on earth, and that idealism had followed him throughout the eighties and into the nineties. But all that was over now. It was as if he had discovered a deep reservoir in the left side of his brain, one he had never noticed before, hidden behind a dam. And now it had broken free.

In 2007, he signed the papers that shut down the last remains of the doomed Montage group, which was about as profitable as selling empty liquor bottles at an AA meeting.

Three weeks later, Viggo Larssen was once again admitted to a psychiatric hospital. He was hospitalized for over a year. I think Verner Jensen was the only one who ever visited him, his final lifeline to the world they had both left (Viggo Larssen a bit more emphatically).

One afternoon, Viggo was discussing with Verner the last seminar Ove Nilsen and his army of streamlined consultants had held. Instead of talking about bars and graphs, charts and diagrams, however, he talked about a female consultant who, over a glass of wine the previous night, had told him a strange story about her father's death. After they had carried his body away, she found a slip of paper lying under his pillow and written in his handwriting—and he usually never wrote anything.

Viggo told the story while sitting by a hospital window facing Roskilde Fjord. Verner smiled while listening, satisfied that Viggo's memories hadn't released any of the past's demons into the halls of those idyllic surroundings.

The woman's name was Linda. In the note, her father had described a strange dream, something he had dreamed his last night, just a few hours before his death.

"Before I went to bed, she promised to give me a copy of that piece of paper and"—clearly moved, Viggo paused for a moment—"and she did. She kept her promise. That paper . . ." He paused again, sitting there for a long time, not saying anything.

"Well?"

"It was the same . . ." This time the pause was even longer.

"The same . . . the same as what?" At this time, Verner wasn't at all suspicious.

"As the Omen."

"As what?"

"The Omen of Death."

Verner knew that his friend was a little batty. His childhood peculiarities, his lifelong fixation with death—these things had grabbed him by the throat and were squeezing the life right out of him. He convinced the doctors to keep Viggo for another six months.

Several years later, Verner made the decision he probably should have made a long time ago. "My family comes from Røsnæs—we're an old, established family who've lived on the peninsula for centuries," he said to Viggo. "There's an old lighthouse out on the tip of the cape that's sitting empty right now. I've seen to it that you can live there for two years. If you like, you can write down everything you've told me. And everything about yourself, too."

"About myself?"

"Yes. I think you should try to tell the rest of us your thoughts—what none of us understands. It might be good for you."

That was in the spring of 2014.

CHAPTER 16

The Lighthouse on the Cape
Sunday, January 11, evening

"Agnes."

The name came without warning. We were sitting on the bench with Viggo's burlap-wrapped bottle of Rioja between us.

He was still holding his wineglass, staring at Hell's Deep, when he spoke her name. Of course I knew whom he was talking about—and I knew he'd take it even further.

"Adda."

"Yes," I said, as if he were talking to me; I understood the longing in his voice, although I hated it.

"She was never herself again . . . not after the attack . . ."

At the last moment he veered away from the word that would have been more precise but which he couldn't stand the sound of. Not even now, after all these years.

Ten days had passed since the Blegman Widow mystery began, and I wasn't sure he would invoke his childhood love's name in any of these shared reflections. I couldn't reveal how much I actually knew about Agnes. Though it's true I knew very little about her and Viggo's love, which never manifested itself as much more than a shadow.

First she was attacked—to use Viggo's word—and if there had been any chance for them after that terrible night, Ove ran off with it. He was more patient, more calculating, more trained in getting what he wanted, in ways that appeared innocent and without an ulterior motive.

Agnes had chosen Ove, and Viggo reminded me of a boy who still doesn't understand how the darkness works, so he keeps sticking his hand in it, again and again.

Had I been a butterfly, floating above the lighthouse, with my elf wings and golden hair, I would have looked down and seen two people sitting awkwardly apart yet close together. As if they were touching.

Unlike other men, Viggo Larssen was unable to see me as a woman, someone whose body he could conquer. He could only sense that I was similar to him inside.

As he told me, he had met Agnes again right around the time Verner offered him a new life in the Lighthouse. It bordered on symbolic.

It was April of 2014, and they met once again on Købmagergade in Copenhagen. She was with Ove. They all stood there awkwardly, until Viggo finally said he would be living in a lighthouse that Verner had secured for him. They smiled in that way people smile at information they don't totally understand.

Here, he paused for a moment, and then he suddenly turned toward me and said, "All these years . . . I have hated the Blegman family." As if it were the end of a long statement he'd spent months trying to formulate.

It startled me. His remark had come totally without warning.

He poured himself another glass of wine and ignored my empty glass, just as he always did. It didn't matter.

"I moved here because—" He stopped suddenly. Although shyness had stanched the flow of words, I knew them only too well, because they were so banal.

He wanted to escape the thoughts that were haunting him. He wanted to forget the undeniable strangeness of his boyhood—the loneliness, and the terrible omens that had plagued him.

In the Lighthouse, he'd made his new home look as spartan as humanly possible: one small bookcase, a couple of tables, a pair of chairs, and a bed. He was almost at peace.

And then on New Year's Eve, he discovered what he later referred to as "the seventh omen" when he bent down to search for a lens that had fallen out of his glasses. It was hidden behind a stone in the wall, just above the floor.

The stone had worked its way loose over the years, and his innate curiosity compelled him to pry it out of the wall. There, he found the old ship's log, written by the Faeroese sailor, and that was the real cause of his current angst.

I could see it in his eyes.

He'd gone to the Lighthouse to escape, to think, and write, and find some peace. Yet his fear about the omens had preceded him, reminding him of their inevitability right when the Widow disappeared in Copenhagen.

He sat with the old logbook in his hand. The words were the same.

No destiny—or God—should be able to design such a strange world.

And so he'd sent the letters, his last cry for help.

"I've written to my old friends—Ove, Teis, Verner—from Søborg. They're the only ones I dare tell. Only one of them has answered, but he wants to see me."

The last part had been easy to figure out: Teis would never let such a vast conspiracy theory go uninvestigated.

For a moment, Viggo squinted his blue eyes into the wind. Out toward Hell's Deep.

I took advantage of the pause. "Why not also write Agnes?"

He looked at me. "Agnes is living with Ove."

"But then she would have—" I stopped. Ove had probably shown it to her. But she hadn't responded, either.

"I need to see them. I need to talk to them."

I didn't say anything.

He stood up to go in. At the door he turned and said, "I'm thinking of going to see them. It's time now to"—he was nodding as if to reassure himself—"travel."

Travel. It sounded like a foreign word coming from such a timid man.

"I can go with you," I said. Fearlessly.

He stared at me. For maybe ten seconds. Then he shut the door, and I understood that meant something totally different than you'd imagine.

Viggo Larssen had invited me to come with him.

I could feel my heart beating in a way I usually didn't allow. My long wait for the right moment to win even a smidgen of his trust had finally arrived. Slowly. Hesitantly. Finally. Love doesn't always show up as an unexpected guest, as in fairy tales, jumping out of a frog costume in front of a princess, stumbling off to party in mismatched shoes, or lying alone on the world's smallest pea. That's not the way it always happens. For Viggo and me, it was a long, drawn-out affair, much more drawn-out than this strange man knew, because in reality—as in fairy tales—it's the woman who knows the most. That's the only sure bet.

And that's why I knew it wouldn't last.

In my world nothing lasts. Nor does it in the real world. Only the crazy or the seduced would believe in such nonsense.

***

Office of the Homicide Boss
Sunday, January 11, evening

All weekend long, civilian police officers had gone door to door in the neighborhood around Maglegårds Allé where Palle and Poul Blegman spent the early years of their lives—this time slowly and thoroughly.

The strangely old-fashioned and laborious approach reminded the youngest of the investigators of something from their childhood detective novels. When you can't find sufficiently promising clues, even at the crime scene, then ring doorbells in the houses nearby. Except this time they had no crime scene. The investigating officers couldn't point to anything other than an old yellow villa that had once housed what was now the country's most powerful family.

Would anyone remember *anything* that had happened in those years—more than forty years ago?

If they'd even lived in the neighborhood back then.

A number did, actually, because Søborg had turned into a graying neighborhood since Viggo's childhood; the old villas were filled with retired people who tried to remember any unusual episodes from back then—or even just something interesting, some recollection or observation related to the Blegman family.

Five people remembered the car accident that had taken Arrow's life. The police had spoken with three of them previously.

Not everyone could recall the boy's name, but they remembered the sorrow and the rumors—and that the Blegman family's anger was directed at the man who was responsible for the boy's death.

Two old women still living in the row houses remembered more than that: they remembered Viggo's mother—and not least of all how she died.

They had known Viggo's grandmother from their childhood; she was such a kind person who unfortunately had a miserable husband. So sad she would lose her daughter in such a tragic way. That was in the early seventies, one neighbor recalled.

The Homicide Boss was like a boxer trying to shake off a hard punch.

Agitated, he stared down at the printout of the two witness statements and at the newspaper clippings flanking them.

"The date . . ." He shook his head and folded his hands—something he never did. He was not given to prayers or invoking any higher power than himself.

Number Two nodded. "June 23, 1971."

They had read about the accident before, in a newspaper clipping from back then, but it had only said Midsummer Eve.

"Midsummer Eve, shortly before midnight. Woman killed by hit-and-run driver. Daughter of the man who ran down Arrow. Mother of Viggo Larssen . . ."

". . . who knew the brothers as a child."

"That was the date we found in the Widow's folder."

"We connected the date to Gentofte, but back then the Blegman family was still living—"

"—in Søborg." Number Two dutifully finished the sentence.

"We missed it."

Number Two didn't respond.

"And now this." The Homicide Boss tapped on yet another folder lying between them on the desk. It contained a report of the reinvestigations of the most important nursing home witnesses. Agnes Persen was one of them. In her role as chaplain at Solbygaard, she had known the Widow about as well as anyone outside the dynasty could know her.

"She confirms that there was a will . . . she witnessed it herself."

The Homicide Boss stood up, regretted the move, and then sat back down. It indicated, more than anything, just how frustrated and uncomfortable he was. "Why the *hell* didn't anyone ask her . . . sooner . . . about something so simple?!"

"She says that it was signed—by herself and the night watch—in the summer of 2014. She thinks it was the queen's birthday because there were flags on the windowsill and all the seniors got cake."

The Homicide Boss stared at his second in command as if he'd attempted a badly timed joke. "That's probably right. What I really want to know is where the damn will is now—since the chaplain says she has no idea."

"She doesn't know what was in it—she just signed it."

"That could be important. You saw the brothers' mugs"—no one other than the Homicide Boss would dare use such a condescending word, even when the two ministers weren't present—"they have *no idea* what the old lady wrote in that will, but at the same time we know . . ."

The Homicide Boss stopped, as if he feared that the walls might be listening, and Number Two continued: ". . . that they've been living far beyond their means for decades, especially since 2008 when the financial crisis destroyed their fortunes, and they've had to sell everything that wasn't nailed to the floor. They were completely dependent on the Widow. On their mother. On their inheritance . . ."

The Homicide Boss nodded. "The only thing missing is to find the night watch. She worked there for over four years, and she lived in a small one-room basement apartment in the building next door. The super said she gave notice suddenly on the first of September last year and then moved to Røsnæs."

"Something isn't right . . ."

"About her giving notice?"

"No . . . about Røsnæs."

"Røsnæs . . . ?"

"I don't understand . . . that's where . . . yes, that's where Ove's letter came from . . ."

Now the Homicide Boss rose up to his full height—and this time he remained standing. ". . . from Viggo Larssen on Røsnæs."

Number Two stared blankly at his boss. Something was totally wrong. But he still didn't have any answers.

PART IV

THE JOURNEY

CHAPTER 17

Verner from Søborg
Monday, January 12, afternoon

We left on the second Monday in January. Five days after the Widow's body was found.

I never thought he'd ask me to come with him, but he did—and I immediately said yes. To be honest, the offer made me feel more alive than I'd felt in years.

I speculated about my role in the trip there and back, and the only explanation I could come up with was quite simple, though certainly not definitive. For some reason Viggo Larssen needed support before, during, and after the visits he had planned. I thought of us as two strange birds, leaving their nests to fly across the ocean to distant shores, and I smiled at the ridiculous cliché.

***

The house was enormous. Verner Jensen could afford all the square feet he wanted ever since he abandoned his youthful journalistic ethics and said, "Yes, please," to a full-time corporate job.

The villa was in Frederiksberg, on a side street off Gammel Kongevej. Although Verner Jensen was currently single, he had two children from a previous marriage. He greeted us in a red pullover, as if time had stood still since those days in the neighborhood when he was just a friendly, lanky guy. We sat on a giant blue-velvet sofa with a view of the birch trees in the garden.

Before we sat down, he had squeezed my hand and said, "Well, I'm glad Viggo has a . . . glad to meet you." Maybe he didn't know if *friend* was the right word—or if he should have used something more intimate.

Verner Jensen looked at Viggo Larssen and said, "You might have been the last idealist—the very last of all of us. But the politicians wanted cutbacks, outsourcing. Mostly, they wanted to close the whole thing down. At least we avoided that. As you know, the Montage group was the last piece of the pie we gave them."

Viggo Larssen sipped his glass of freshly squeezed, handpicked organic apple juice, wishing instead for his beloved Rioja.

"The Blegman brothers pushed for it. They were obsessed with the idea of hurting us, and unfortunately they had powerful friends on the board. It was a great victory for them when they crushed our finest department—more than you know. Revenge for all the humiliations the right wing thinks the liberal DBC had subjected them to back in the seventies and eighties."

Verner drank his juice, and I followed his example. The sweet juice was lukewarm, and it took some willpower to swallow an entire mouthful.

"But that's not the way journalism works anymore. Spend an entire year on one hour of radio—or a TV documentary? No way. Fortunately."

"Fortunately?" Viggo reacted spontaneously, slightly shocked at his friend's new attitude regarding what might be their profession's biggest problem: that the faster pace of the increasingly competitive newsroom had destroyed any possibility of in-depth journalism—the one thing those in power feared most. The time to dig down and investigate an issue—or even just think about a subject—was the most precious weapon in any editorial arsenal. Yet it had been driven into the ground like the legendary sword in the stone, and no one would ever have the strength to pull it back out again.

Verner set aside his glass on the square blond-wood coffee table. His hands were large and well manicured—almost rosy from ample scrubbing with soap and water—just as they were in his youth. He spoke a bit slower and leaned toward his friend. "Immediacy, Viggo, doing things a little more—impulsively—you can't underestimate it. We just didn't know it back then. To be *first* with the latest news, that can also help keep the powers that be in check. We need to be *first* every single time. It's part of what it means to be—"

"—*world champions.*" Viggo pronounced Ove Nilsen's old buzzwords in a sneering tone. I could see a couple drops of that sickening apple juice on his lower lip.

"Yes . . . Ove. Well, that's a long time ago. I've heard that the police intend to question him about the Widow. He works with the nursing home."

Viggo didn't respond.

Verner took a sip of his apple juice. "Idealism is over. Everything is commercial now. That's just the way it is." He stressed that last sentence. "It's not our fault. It's globalization."

Globalization. Not an area the man from the Lighthouse was well versed in. Viggo Larssen remained silent.

"In a way, you could say we've been wiped out three times as journalists—and each time by the same damn family. *Signal*, the magazine—and finally the Montage group. And it drove you mad."

I stared at Viggo's old friend. Pretty harsh words from a man who had always seemed so friendly, the one who had helped Viggo Larssen.

Despite their shared past, could Verner be feeling a slight but gnawing fear about Viggo's role in the disappearance and death of the Widow? Did he believe that his old friend . . . that somehow . . . ? Irritated, I pushed the thoughts out of my head. Of course, I had a reason for such a strong reaction—a reason that Verner knew nothing about, fortunately; otherwise, he might have pressed his friend even harder.

Instead he said, "But still . . . it was never proven in high school."

"That they trashed the magazine office." Viggo's words were framed as a statement.

"But it was never really *proven* that it was Poul and Palle."

Typical Verner Jensen, I thought. Typical for this man, who'd become someone Viggo could never consider becoming, to shove a slick ethical barrier between himself and his accused. The very aim of all his politeness.

Then he said, "I managed to stop some of the worst ideas Ove came up with. He thought we should create a hard-hitting debate program— a clean break with the social crybaby state, as he called it. *Welfare-pity, self-sentimentality*—he had expressions for everything. Political developments had convinced him that there were more viewers to be had, a lot of viewers, with totally new kinds of programming. He advised us to launch the new debate series with an attack on 'undemocratic voting rights' that gave lifelong slackers, welfare recipients, and unemployed immigrants the same influence on the nation's development as honest, hardworking citizens. That would really create a stir."

Verner smiled.

"I remember one of our interns saying, 'But for native Danes, isn't *equality* one of the most fundamental pillars of society?' Ove exploded. 'Is it *equality* that some uneducated loafer on welfare gets the same political voice as you or me about a society that basically doesn't give a shit about him—and one that he's decided to sponge off of?!' To Ove it was perfectly clear that everyone—including low-wage Danes—would support a proposal that radiated firmness and power, as long as it only affected people on a lower social level than themselves. That's our national soul."

I stared at the three glasses of juice on the huge table—one empty and two almost full.

"It went too far. But that was some years ago. It'll happen. We're there now . . . just wait until the coming election."

He got up and left the room. I could hear him walking up the stairs to the villa's second floor. A few minutes later he returned with the letter in his hand.

"You wrote this letter to me." He placed it on top of Viggo's juice glass.

I recognized the envelope immediately.

Viggo started to reach for the letter and the glass—but then he leaned back in the giant sky-blue sofa.

"Clearly you've been really agitated about this." Verner's voice had changed; that slightly overbearing, friendly tone was gone. It sounded now as if he were reading from one of his well-prepared and exhaustively researched speeches.

"We talk about death all day long at the DBC—we barely talk about anything else. How many deaths appear on any given day in the media—on film and in news broadcasts? Try counting them . . . you'd go crazy."

He paused for effect. In fact, he was responsible for reporting a large part of them as head of news at the DBC.

Viggo Larssen said nothing. I knew why—and I knew where Verner was going with all this.

"But we talk about it in a totally superficial way . . . to keep our distance from what we don't understand. Maybe that's our biggest problem—death has completely taken over our media, our world. It's everywhere you look, in all our entertainment, all the news, in every way of thinking—even when we try to forget it. It's a strange phenomenon. In many ways we've filled our books, our films, our newspapers, all our conversations—with the very thing we fear the most. We're afraid that the smallest unforeseen incident might result in Armageddon—and maybe it could. We see it all the time. New York, Paris, Copenhagen. Terror. Terror everywhere. War in Syria, war in Iraq, refugees drowning by the thousands. Meanwhile, we grill. Buy new clothes. Surround ourselves with luxury items." Verner waved his arm around, disregarding his guests' more modest lifestyles. "That's how we *survive*. But it's *everywhere*."

Viggo Larssen sat motionless throughout the monologue.

Taking a deep breath, Verner said, "Your theory"—he glanced down at the letter lying on the glass in front of Viggo—"is very strange. If it were true . . ." He stopped. He didn't complete his thought but instead immediately changed the subject. "When did all this start?" He sounded like an overworked doctor questioning an obvious hypochondriac.

Viggo Larssen lifted the envelope off the glass, but he made no move to open it. I resisted the urge to do so. "As you know, my grandfather died a couple of years after my mother. I found her final words first—a dream she had the night before she died—and then the same thing in the Spanish journal that I wrote about here." He placed the letter on the table next to the glass. "I'd stumbled upon something that wasn't possible."

"They had both described the same dream, in almost the same way, right before they died. There was no doubt about it, and it shocked me. My grandmother had a friend—Aunt Jenny—and it was the same thing. She sent my grandmother a letter at Christmas, right before dying, and in it she described the same thing. It was *exactly* the same. I came across the dream a few more times then I decided to just forget it. I moved out to the cape. But the other day, I found another example in the Lighthouse . . . the same description in an old logbook from a shipwreck."

Viggo Larssen shook his head, and I understood why. To an outsider, his words sounded like pure nonsense.

"You write that you have . . . seven examples." Verner's voice sounded extremely cautious, like a doctor's right before he reveals that there's nothing wrong with you.

"Yes, on New Year's Eve in the Lighthouse I found the last one. I thought I was done with all of it—and then there was the logbook in the old lighthouse keeper's hiding place. It was the exact same dream, written on the very last page—*the Omen of Death*. And that's why I wrote you."

I could see the news editor in Verner wince at the sound of such melodramatic words. I saw something else, though, a glimmer of interest, because Verner wasn't a doctor. No, he was something totally different, something more powerful. He was a hawker of good stories. At the country's largest media conglomerate, no less. A sense of truth wasn't paramount—not if the content was sensational enough.

"What should I do?" Viggo Larssen's simple question was filled with despair. The room was silent.

I don't think Verner knew how to respond. As a distraction he drank the contents of Viggo's glass. Mine was the only one left.

"Do you have these things with you?"

"No, they're hidden away. In a secure place. In the Lighthouse."

"I need to see them. As soon as I have time, I'll come visit you. After all, it's my ancestors' home . . ." Verner Jensen laughed, and a moment later my glass was empty, too. "It will be good for me to take a little trip to the most backwoods part of this whole backwoods nation!"

***

Office of the Prime Minister
Tuesday, January 13, morning

"I have to ask . . ." The Homicide Boss paused somewhat uncharacteristically. That had happened a number of times in the past few days. It was a sign of hesitation in a situation in which any hesitation could result in an abrupt end to his career and brand him as useless and incompetent.

Then he inaudibly took a deep breath, and said, "I want to know if either of you has ever . . ." He stopped for a second, a wrinkle of irritation spreading above his thick white eyebrows. "There's something about what has happened that . . . looks like revenge."

Neither of the two men sitting across from the Homicide Boss reacted in any way. They were the only people in the prime minister's office.

The Homicide Boss looked at the two Blegman brothers. Three sets of eyes and none of them blinking. Everything might be a lie in this office.

The moment passed without the nation's two most powerful men uttering a word. Both sat in chairs, elevated slightly above the Homicide Boss, who had been relegated to the sofa.

"It doesn't need to take very long, but it is . . . it could be . . . important."

Poul Blegman folded his hands in a gesture that managed to seem both superior and arrogant. "Yes, of course it's important." Subtext: *since you're disturbing the nation's two most important men.*

The policeman sat up straight on the uncomfortable sofa. "I've gotten a tip that could point back to Søborg . . ."

Folding his hands exactly like his brother, the prime minister spoke for the first time. "A tip—as in *tips*—like when the lucky winner of some random drawing gets everything he or she has dreamed of."

The words seemed to come from some dark ravine where they'd spent decades gathering shapeless green moss. Their only purpose was to unleash a little rage from that large body, thereby preventing a direct physical reaction. For a moment it looked as if the chief of police were dodging an imaginary blow from the Bear's massive paws.

"A man the two of you might have known as a boy has approached the police . . . us . . . with some information. He insists on discretion, and I've promised him he'll get it. I trust him, we once worked on a TV series about unsolved homicides. He's not some . . . sensation seeker."

"A *murder series*?" The realm's number two sounded skeptical.

"Yes—like that. He's a TV editor. His name is Verner Jensen."

The name triggered a visible reaction from both powerful men. Their shoulders lifted and their eyes narrowed—like something out of one of the comic books all three men collected in their youth.

"You know him." It wasn't a question.

"He went to our high school." The minister of justice sounded both clumsy and cautious.

"Yes. I understand that. But there were others at that high school, and Verner Jensen thinks there might be good reason to look a little more closely at some of them."

Neither of the two men reacted.

"There was an episode . . . about a girl who was attacked."

Poul Blegman nodded. "Yes, but that was sheer nonsense. There were no witnesses and no evidence. And we both had alibis. It was just a stupid story." The two brothers had obviously been prepped for a direct line of questioning about this specific rumor. The minister of justice had recited his little defense without his usual anger and condescension.

"I'm not going to get into that—that case is ancient history."

"If there *was* a case—and there wasn't." The rage was creeping back into Poul Blegman's voice.

"No, but there was a girl who *claimed* that she was attacked and who later married one of your high school classmates—Ove Nilsen."

"Most people know his name. He's even been in my office." Judging by the expression on the minister of justice's face, it wasn't one of the highlights of his time in office.

Now the prime minister jumped in. Placing his powerful bear paws on his thighs and leaning forward in his chair, he towered over the policeman. "Yes, you're digging, you're digging into the past—and you have no idea what you're doing. What the hell is so interesting about two high school sweethearts from before . . ." He was searching for the right word, but it didn't come.

"What might be interesting"—the investigator leaned back as if to escape the Bear's reach—"is that *both of them* work at the nursing home—and both in your mother's section. That's a coincidence we need to look into."

He avoided the last and most important piece of information, about the brothers' bad relationship with their mother, which he knew would have resulted in a violent outburst. Both Ove and Agnes had seen the family animosity firsthand. Agnes had even signed the new and undoubtedly altered will.

The two brothers sat in silence for a moment before the youngest spoke. "And you've just discovered this connection now—after digging into our past for over a week? Lovely. Really clever police work."

Inside, the Homicide Boss cringed under the minister's accusation, because it was true. But that wasn't really relevant to the case. They had to push on. "No, but now we know. And we really had no reason to track down and question every student who went to high school in those years. It would have been—"

"—a lot of work? Yes, exactly. And that's why you've had *every* resource you needed at your disposal. It's *incompetence!*"

"At any time have you ever had any threats from Ove Nilsen or Agnes?"

"No." The answer was simple and cold.

The Homicide Boss nodded. "Good. We'll look into it. They may have been tempted. They have a motive. Verner Jensen says that they never had any children. Maybe they talked about the Widow when they met her later in life—and got the idea for revenge."

"What do children have to do with this case?"

"There are tons of pictures of children on the Widow's walls . . . your children, her grandchildren. According to Verner, Agnes believes that when she was attacked, it left her childless."

"You're implying . . . *aggravated assault*." That sounded like a quote from one of the Criminal Code's most serious paragraphs. "Maybe you're even talking about *rape*?"

"That was the rumor that went around," the Homicide Boss said.

"A rumor that your source—Verner Jensen—was already spreading around. And now he's been lucky enough to bring it back to life."

The Homicide Boss could see the end of his interview looming. He didn't have much time left. Apparently the two brothers were more concerned with reinforcing their spotless reputation than with solving the case, so they could receive their inheritance from the Widow and win the next election.

The mystery of their mother's death involved two violent threats to their reputations: it could both ruin them and knock them off the powerful pedestals they'd spent their entire lives constructing.

"Viggo Larssen." That was all the Homicide Boss said.

"Viggo—who?" The minister of justice was lying. Of course he knew whom the Homicide Boss was referring to.

"He lives in a lighthouse now, but you knew him when he was a child. He was your neighbor—on Death's Highway. It was his grandfather who ran down your little brother."

Time seemed to stand still in the large office—there in power's innermost chamber, where heads of state had watched over their people for generations.

The Homicide Boss's use of the nickname for that fatal stretch of road and his lack of any elaboration signaled that he didn't want to waste his last syllables. No one moved. No one even blinked.

"He had a visitor. Recently. A woman who also worked in your mother's section, as a night guard. She cosigned your mother's new will. The one that has disappeared."

Now both brothers straightened up in their Hans Wegner chairs, and the slender constructions groaned simultaneously beneath their weight.

"The other cosigner was Agnes."

The groans of the two chairs reached a new level, and the chief of police leaned as far back as he possibly could. The Bear sprang up on his enormous back legs. The man who led the most important investigation in the nation's history thought that he was seconds away from being tossed out of both the office and his own career by one of the Bear's infamous blows.

It didn't happen.

"The guard on night duty—her name was Malin . . ."

"I don't give a shit what her name was—*fuck Malin*—just find that will and bring it to this office, if it even exists. It's mine. It belongs to the *state*."

The Homicide Boss refused to stop staring at the prime minister. But out of the corner of his eye, he caught the minister of justice's nervousness, a slight start triggered by that last word. All this talk about the will was dangerous, and to connect it to the state—when it was so deeply personal—was idiotic. The whole thing seemed like a setup in one of those Agatha Christie novels his mother had given him as a child. If something other than what people believed appeared in the will, then you'd know who the murderer was.

Or at least where to look.

Palle Blegman slid back into his seat.

Poul Blegman exhaled slowly.

The Homicide Boss held the two brothers' gaze.

Their final answer came in unison—yet with an uncertainty usually foreign to such formidable tyrants: "*Malin*—we don't know her."

He could see that they were telling the truth.

But he could also see their fear. And fear never lied. When it blinked, it was only to make people believe that it didn't exist.

***

Teis from Søborg
Tuesday, January 13, morning

He looked just like what he was, a stooped-over, somewhat unworldly scientist, who met us with a slight scowl, as if our very presence was making him uncomfortable. Or maybe *guarded* was the right word.

If only the Blegman brothers hadn't insisted on eliminating his entire department, he might have been a little less hunched over. The government had demanded that all his studies of rare diseases be excised from the university's budget. Teis Hanson was asked to take an early retirement. Much too early.

The shining star of the first generation of DNA pioneers had been kicked to the curb, sacrificed on a political altar that had nothing to do with actual research. Of course he was bitter.

Although his condo was on the third floor, with large windows facing the gardens of Rosenborg Castle, it was strangely dim inside, even on such a sunny morning. We'd spent the night at the Cabinn Metro Hotel—each in our own monklike cell—across from the old DBC headquarters. I caught Viggo Larssen staring at the place that was the scene of his ultimate breakdown.

At breakfast I cautiously questioned Viggo about his old friend Teis Hanson, the chubby boy who had finally crawled out from under Ove's thumb and who, apparently, hadn't seen him since. The two boys had shared a strangely symbiotic relationship in which Ove's ridicule of Teis also united them as friends—so much so that they sometimes completely forgot the humiliations and lopsided friendship. Stockholm syndrome for children. From the perspective of so many years, it seemed as if future spin doctor Ove Nilsen had been practicing on Teis, the naïve boy with the thick thighs and waddling legs. Teis, meanwhile, took refuge in a world where chromosomes and strings of DNA—so strange and magical that they revolutionized an entire world—lay waiting for him. Early in his career, Teis had enjoyed a high status. He had been the newspapers' favorite source in several scientific areas, including a few he really had no access to as a researcher.

Today he was—in the blunt words of several newspapers—a little batty. He'd become involved in a group of scientists who, in addition to accepting many other conspiracy theories, believed that the American government had blown up the Twin Towers to create the necessary pretext for an invasion of oil-rich Iraq.

Now, Teis Hanson would argue that scientific reality was wilder than any fantasy the human mind could conjure up. For a time after his abrupt firing from the institute, he had been studying near-death experiences based on the notion that death had never been scientifically proven. He pursued subjects as diverse as superstrands and astrophysics and read popular articles on Easter Island and Stonehenge, David Deutsch's many-worlds theory, wormholes, time travel, the Einstein-Rosen bridge, and Schrödinger's maladjusted cat vacillating eternally between life and death.

So naturally, Viggo had sent his first letter to Teis.

"You were crying by the bog," Teis now said. Not quite the hello either of us had expected. "Back when your mother died."

Teis Hanson was not much taller than me. He made some coffee, which he placed on the dining room table.

"You wrote about her," he explained, "in the letter. Ove and I were spying on you. From the banks of that creek. That's how Ove was. I think he was born a spy—even back then. I haven't seen him since. But you can certainly read a lot about him. He's one of those people who devour others' livelihoods to make themselves rich. Very, very rich."

I could sense the anger lurking beneath the casual character assessment.

Then he changed the subject. "I remember Adda . . ."

Viggo still didn't respond.

"Now they're married. A damn farce—even for God's chosen few."

That was elegantly worded, though a bit malicious. Maybe he had learned something from Ove during those childhood excursions to the bog.

In his own way, Teis had the darkest character of all of them, and his scientific career would have made him the perfect murder suspect in a classic British detective novel. He had known the brothers, he was permanently disabled by the eldest, and they'd given him an actual motive with their devastating cuts to the research he loved. Their maneuvering had turned him into a court jester, a conspiracy theorist who was both scorned and ridiculed—and not by just one tormentor, but by everyone.

"At school they called me Gene-Teis," he said, splashing milk from a cracked cup into his coffee. "I never got to know anyone. I was probably too weird."

I could picture him, waddling around the halls of the University of Copenhagen, all the while mumbling about the human genome.

"Later, the genome became common knowledge. Things got a little better. I became popular. I even had a girlfriend. But we never had any children. Then she just disappeared." As he stared out at Rosenborg Castle Gardens, I got the impression that it was the last place he'd seen her, somewhere among the bushes, as he tried in vain to reach out and stop her escape. "Her bed is still here."

That was a strange comment. As if it still connected two separate worlds that no amount of miracles could ever reunite.

"They wanted to focus on the commercial winners. Drugs for cancer, Alzheimer's, all that. Research into rare genetic diseases wasn't as profitable—the patient groups weren't large enough. My specialty was extremely rare lung diseases. The pharmaceutical industry had far more important goals. My area became simply . . . obsolete." He flicked his coffee cup with a fingernail, so that the last word was underscored by a hollow snap. "Obsolete, huh? The oldest thing in the history of the universe had become obsolete." He laughed.

Some people's laughter sounds more like crying. It's a strange phenomenon. I discovered that early on as a child. I used to think that the crying laughers, as I would call them (though never out loud), possessed much greater sensitivity than other people. The idea was that laughter meant going too far, saying too much, maybe even hurting the people who weren't laughing, who couldn't see that there was anything to laugh about.

With Teis, maybe he laughed because the tyranny of childhood insisted that you laugh, even when you're being tortured and persecuted and are always on guard.

"The police have contacted me." The assertion came just as abruptly as the end of his brief laughter.

Viggo Larssen simply repeated the words. "The police?"

"Yes, about the Blegman affair. And about when Palle attacked me in high school. They found it very interesting. I don't think they know that he also destroyed the institute." Teis Hanson shook his head at the unscientific approach to their investigation. "They also asked about you. I didn't tell them you had contacted me."

"What—" I stopped myself. I wasn't really the one who should be talking. But Teis, who had barely even noticed my presence until now, answered as if I had completed the question.

"They asked me if you were . . . a little strange. Well, they didn't use those words, naturally. They wanted to know if you were obsessed with the Blegman brothers. I said no. Then they asked if you had some kind of special interest in death. That last part was really quite amusing. I said no. Which was even more amusing."

Viggo didn't react to the sarcasm in the scientist's voice.

"I've done research into near-death experiences—into life and death. As a geneticist, I've always been interested in the basic building blocks of life." Teis Hanson's voice had taken on a ceremonious tone. "Nothing is impossible, although what you're suggesting . . . it sounds a bit"—he searched for the word—"unbelievable." That was funny coming from a man who suspected the American president of mass-murdering his own people. "Still, many unbelievable things occur. I've never encountered this particular theory before, though, and it is a strange one. If you're right—if the documents are real—someone should have come across . . . *something* . . . long before now, no?"

"I can certainly see that." Viggo spoke low, almost in a whisper. After all, Teis was his best shot on this trip. "But you'd need luck—we're talking about coincidences here—and then you'd have to be able to spot the connection, the *weirdness*, and be interested in it." That was the most Viggo Larssen had spoken in the entire half hour we'd been in the apartment.

Teis flicked his cup again, this time only for show, without any sound. "Certainly anything is possible," he said, half to himself. "But even if your theory is true"—he looked up—"remember that everything, even what dies, may simply turn into something else. We live in eleven dimensions—maybe even more—that's the lesson of quantum mechanics and superstring theory. And if you believe in the theory of parallel universes, as many of today's leading physicists do, we live in an infinite number of worlds . . ." His eyes were shining, and this time he flicked his cup so hard that it nearly overturned.

Viggo Larssen did not seem to understand the connection to the letter he had sent. I could see the disappointment in his eyes.

"Your mother, Aunt Jenny, the Spanish resistance fighter, the sailor from the shipwrecked schooner—maybe they've all simply disappeared into a new world, one we don't know about. That would certainly offer an explanation for some of what you are imagining. Your visions."

"They're not visions."

"Dreams."

"They're not my dreams."

"No, or else you'd be dead now." The dethroned scientist giggled slightly, and I could see from the twitch in Viggo's left eye that this meeting would end shortly. He hadn't come here to be made a fool of. This man they had all mocked as children—the man who now saw conspiracies everywhere he looked—seized the opportunity to mock an even weirder newcomer. A classic power play in the worlds of both children and adults—and one that would never go out of style.

Teis continued. "As I wrote you, science and research are open to all possibilities. In some theories there's no such thing as *time*—time is merely an illusion. And if time and motion don't exist, then thought is the only element that has the notion of being alive, of the movement from birth to death. So the notion of death is also only an illusion, in which death affects every possible thought—yet in reality can never touch us, personally, experientially. We don't die. We see other people die, but we don't die ourselves. In reality no person has ever experienced his or her own death—only the death of others. When the near dead come back, they haven't been dead at all. No actually dead person has ever returned. None."

I could see that Viggo Larssen had long since abandoned any hope of having a rational conversation. Even I found the half-crazed scientist's ramblings a bit unnerving.

Teis traced the rim of his coffee cup with the tip of one fingernail. "It means that all of us *are*—and *have been—everywhere—at all times* . . ."

Viggo didn't respond, which was hardly surprising.

"Your letter will remain confidential, regardless. The police, and all the others . . . they can just fuck off."

I was sure the feeling was mutual.

The researcher prepared his fingers for another flick of his half-empty cup. "But that's why I can't help you. *You* have to come forward and prove your theory. If I were to come forward now and say something so"—he almost said *weird*—"I'd never get back on my feet. And that wouldn't be of any help to you at all."

Although Viggo stood up, I stayed in my seat a second longer. I was staring right at Teis Hanson's chubby little fingers. And I wasn't disappointed.

This time the flick was so strong that the cup toppled over, lying in a light brown puddle as we left the apartment.

***

We sat on a bench in the gardens of Rosenborg Castle, out of sight of the apartment and the childhood friend we had just left.

We had automatically chosen our same spots as on the bench outside the Lighthouse. My right shoulder next to his left.

He shook his head, though he said nothing, and we sat there in silence.

Viggo Larssen was a man who had been frightened out of his shell, shattered thanks to the Widow's death and his strange dreams. I'd seen his tics, and I'd seen all his childhood oddities, including the ones that haunted him in the following years. I'd seen all of them—or I thought I had that afternoon beneath the beech trees.

Before the trip was over, he'd have no more secrets—or so I believed.

CHAPTER 18

The country's two most powerful men were alone in the prime minister's office. Following that morning's orientation meeting, their ever-expanding army of spin doctors and special advisers had left them.

Poul Blegman saw that his brother was about to rise up in an impotent fit of rage behind his desk and tried to soothe him. "Look—as long as they haven't found anything, everything's good. We just need to wait."

The Bear slumped back into his throne. "Where the hell *is* it?"

"If there even is . . ."

His brother shook his enormous head. "I don't think she left any opportunities for misunderstanding. The will *exists* . . . and we're not in it. For all we know, she may have left the whole damn thing to a cat shelter."

An absurd thought crossed the minister of justice's mind: that last theory was impossible, since their mother loved birds.

"And we need it—all of it. If the dynasty's going to survive . . ." He stopped.

Poul Blegman knew what he meant. What with their failed investments, real estate disasters, luxury vacations for their children, games, gifts, debt—they needed the whole fortune.

"If they figure out—"

The minister of justice interrupted him. "No one's figuring anything out." Unspeakable scenarios should never be discussed—not even in this sanctuary against eavesdropping.

"But they're rummaging around in our private lives—in our finances."

"Well, maybe they are. But it's officially none of their business, as long as—" He paused for a moment, allowing the prime minister to complete his little brother's unpleasant thought.

"—as long as it doesn't affect our work. Or disgrace us in any way. And maybe that's what's happening. After all, it's our government's official position that everyone should be tightening their belts while we're in crisis mode. That's not exactly what we've been doing."

For a moment the minister of justice thought that his brother was going to laugh out loud at his own comment—and he hastened to add: "Don't you remember what father used to say? That living well is permissible as long as you make even greater sacrifices. And we haven't seen the public protesting against any of it. As father used to say—people almost expect it."

"Is it possible that the person who did it, who shut her up in the basement . . . ?"

". . . has removed the will? Yes, it's possible."

"But *why*?" The Bear made the question sound almost like a snarl, before it rose, threateningly, above the two men's heads. "Blackmail?"

"Then it's one patient soul."

"Maybe mother regretted everything and destroyed it herself. Maybe that's why she asked us to come over." The prime minister was grasping after the slightest bit of hope.

Poul Blegman shook his head. "No, I don't think so. I think she would have spoken to us first. Someone has taken it."

"What about the police's theory—about Ove and Agnes? Both of them work there, and Agnes has seen the will."

"Yes, but she hasn't read it." The minister of justice clarified his statement, as any good lawyer or prosecutor would. "Or so she says. But even so, I can't see the connection. I can't see *any* connection in all this. It's like looking into an underwater hall of mirrors, where everything is blurry and distorted . . . yet somehow it's all connected."

That incoherent remark wasn't going to calm down anyone.

***

Ove from Søborg
Wednesday, January 14, morning

We arrived by foot from Klampenborg station.

Walking around one corner of the house, we heard a sound coming from the backyard. Ove Nilsen was standing there, his legs spread apart, in a cluster of half-grown apple trees. His clothes were a leafy green color, he was wearing a camouflage cap, and in one hand he was holding a large bow, like Robin Hood. He had just strung an arrow. He turned slowly, without lowering his bow. I ducked, involuntarily. For a moment he stood there with the longbow raised high and pointing directly at us—and then he lowered it and laughed loudly.

"Uninvited guests in Sherwood Forest . . . the Sheriff of Nottingham and his companion!"

Neither Viggo nor I were laughing.

He placed his bow on the grass and walked out to meet us. "Maid Marian." He bowed. "You're Viggo's friend from the Lighthouse." He extended his hand, which had been holding the arrow on the taut string. It was small, chubby, and a little clammy. Was he nervous? Many men have weak handshakes—I remembered that from my childhood, when all the doctors, sociologists, pediatricians, and psychologists had to greet the little foster child who, for her part, always had to curtsy back for them. I was not feeling any urge to curtsy for Ove.

Viggo Larssen responded to the same hearty handshake with a guarded look on his face.

"Our bird flew away the other day—so now I don't have one to practice on!" He laughed again.

Ove Nilsen wasted no time showing us the house and gardens. "Agnes, my wife, will be here soon." He spoke as if Viggo didn't even know her.

A relatively small and broad-shouldered man, he reminded me a little of the toads that undoubtedly inhabited his garden—yet slightly friendlier.

"Agnes is the pastor at Søllerød Church, so she's busy getting ready for the Widow's funeral," he said, pouring white wine into a beautiful crystal decanter.

He placed three tall wineglasses on the low coffee table. "I once knew a man who researched *opinions* at Roskilde University Center, that haven for old-school Marxists. He was an *opinion researcher*—he separated opinions into classes, categorized them into columns and diagrams, and tried to extract from them a pattern that dyed-in-the-wool Marxists could use in their conversion of all of us nonbelievers." Even though it was early in the afternoon, Ove poured three generous glasses of wine.

"The point is that eventually he didn't have any opinions of his own. So . . . he became a journalist." The management consultant laughed heartily. I glanced at my friend from the lighthouse to see if he'd been offended. It didn't look like it.

Our host wrenched his lounge chair free from the polar bear's claws and yanked it over to the coffee table, where we were sitting.

"I could have been an artist myself—instead of just a half-baked advertising hack—if it hadn't all gone wrong." He laughed. "It was called the School of Decorative Art back then, and I had to submit some of my own artwork for the entrance exam. So I showed the admissions committee a black-and-white print that depicted a black sundial draped with skeleton heads all around the disc. They wanted to know what it *meant*, what I was *thinking*—but I was in my Salvador Dalí phase and I simply answered, *'Nothing.'* So I became an advertising major!"

He lifted his glass to toast us, then set his glass back on the table and turned toward Viggo. "We met again at the DBC. Quite a few years ago now. I reorganized that place *completely.*

"Still, it was a necessary operation. *Christ,* you were all up shit's creek. When you spoke about something as simple as cluster development management—or process implementation strategies—you were like a bunch of beavers caught in a flood. Everything you'd built was about to be washed out to sea and would have to be rebuilt."

"Or torn down completely." I couldn't stop my objection, as I could easily imagine what a restless pirate like Ove had achieved.

He didn't react. "Yes, the world was changing. And so was the media. I was one of those who saw it coming—and I've lived pretty well off it." He smiled. "It's a beautiful place here, isn't it? Agnes and I have always had an almost *romantic* penchant for historical places like this. It's become a kind of hobby for us to research and piece together the whole area's history. Did you know that a heated discussion once surfaced about the first bicyclists' duty to pay tolls at Strandvejen, where before there had only been carriages? It was one Sunday in the summer of 1897."

I stared at the somewhat powerful man sitting in the blue easy chair. Was he trying to play the deeply romantic cynic—or was he merely sitting there, taunting his earlier rival with his declarations of love for Agnes?

"Agnes found newspaper clippings. All the male editors decried the bicyclists' hunched-over position and pointed out that cycling, where you straddle the seat, was not *ladylike*. One of the doctors wrote in response that 'Women will get a more beautiful Buttocks from the new Exercise than from a sedentary life.' Excellent, isn't it?"

Ove suddenly laughed, loudly, and for some reason Viggo laughed, too. I didn't react. It was the dumbest story I'd heard in a long time.

"Think about living back then—when the only worry was a little dust on your clothes from people cycling along Strandvejen. Of course, we lived in a much simpler society. We had time to take care of each other . . . unlike now, when we put our elderly in nursing homes before they know what hit them. Bam! And they're out of the way." He poured more white wine into his glass. "That's my new area of interest. And I say that only to show that what is good and practical can go hand in hand. *Win-win*, as we say."

I could see that the whole bicycle story was nothing more than a pretext for him to boast about his visionary new business project—his unholy agreement to cash in on Death's monopoly in a person's final hours.

"Just look at Solbygaard Nursing Home, and forget about all that terrible business with the Widow. Look at this place that has been selected as the most promising development project for old people, with me as its"—for a second he searched for the right word—"catalyst."

Death's number one man, I thought.

For the first—and only—time, our insufferable host touched upon Viggo's letter, which must have surely gone over like a bad smell in this sylvan retreat. He looked straight at Viggo. "As you wrote in . . . your letter"—he placed a slightly disapproving emphasis on that last word—"naturally, it's a subject that interests a lot of people, though probably on a more mundane level than you indicate. I've never had such . . . dreams."

I had no doubts about that.

"Or strange visions."

I glanced at Viggo. He had anticipated his old friend's outright dismissal.

Ove, for his part, was past the point of distraction. Our only purpose here was to hear his story. He smiled again and poured another glass of wine. "First, I rearrange the seniors' daily lives—mentally and physically—and when they've regained some of their vigor, I send my people out to speak to them about their lives. That's the concept. Naturally, none of them has much time left—so it's urgent." Ove paused for a moment, but no one jumped in. "The goal is to capture the very narrative of their lives—what I call living wills. It's the story of their lives, captured on film. Those who want to can pay for the entire package—and there are a surprising number who will. Everyone else might think: Who wants to listen to a long, dull story about boring events, trivialities, routines, abandonments, losses, and terrible disappointments in CinemaScope, surround sound, and whatever else they call it? But in my form—this new form, preserved for all posterity—every individual's life will be elevated to an adventure, emphasizing everything that is beautiful, then presented as unique and life affirming. I say to them, *Leave your mark! You're worth it!*"

Ove smiled; you'd almost think he believed all of it. And maybe he did, though I could already imagine the fortunes he was coaxing out of decrepit seniors who had nothing else to do with their remaining days—yet who feared death and being forgotten more than anything else.

"It's nothing more than what happens every day on Facebook and Twitter—and the ever-increasing number of blogs. People want to leave their mark, all the time—always. I'm just broadening their range."

Beyond death, I thought. Clever. The millennials will love it.

"The first move is to bury them with as much pomp and splendor as possible. Large-format obituaries in beautiful colors—and don't worry, the newspapers can use the revenue in their death throes"—Ove laughed at the thought—"enthusiastic memorials written by my staff, a farewell ceremony worthy of St. Peter's Basilica. I'll record the whole thing for posterity. And the final phase is to ensure that the living wills are also used—that the narratives reach their audience, so to speak." He blinked at us. "That is where Eden's New Garden comes in." He hesitated, but only for a moment. "We're planning entire landscapes with all these destinies arranged so that everyone can come hear their stories. Virgin landscapes, meadows, river valleys, small forests, deer grazing—just like in Dyrehaven."

I could hear the wonderment in his voice. Was he crazy—or had he hit on a concept that might prove inexhaustible?

"The Widow is on board. She was one of the first. She signed a contract with us, with the Real Eden Foundation: Center of Unlimited Life." He lifted his glass as if he were toasting his own company—or maybe the deceased Blegman matriarch. "Now, unfortunately, she's disappeared . . . sorry, dead. It's a shame. But she'll get her place of honor. Right next to her little Arrow."

"Arrow?" It was Viggo who responded.

Ove blinked again and lifted his glass and waved his other hand dismissively. "Forget it—it's just a . . . trade secret. We all remember that little beast."

I could sense Viggo's rage and was about to place my hand on his arm.

"Yes, these are the services I offer in all modesty." Ove set down his glass.

"And to rake in the bucks." I discovered a half second too late that my thoughts had managed to slip out.

Our host lifted his square head, and for a moment I peered right into the soul that I knew was capable of both hate and envy. He must have been high on the list of suspects in the mystery of the Widow's disappearance. And Agnes must have been the only person in this whole wide world whom he loved.

I thought about Viggo, who had surrendered the love of his life to this emissary from the Courtyard of Death. I thought about Agnes, who had to hide her soul behind a kind of shatterproof glass to endure the double life she found herself in: the forger disguised as a worshipper, the robber masquerading as an artist; my head was full of angry, miserable, pointless similes. And you could see all of it in my eyes.

"Yes," he said. "Of course I raise money. So do morticians. Even ministers when they baptize our dear wee ones and welcome them to this life. So do *all* people, except the ones who . . . loaf off others."

Loaf, I wanted to hiss, but Viggo interrupted. "Yes," he said, "people's lives are different, as you just said."

He only said it to save me from embarrassment. A rare gesture—I had never seen him do that before. Of course Ove ignored it.

"Yes, some even move out to a lighthouse. But people . . . like *you two* . . . there aren't too damn many of."

The derision was palpable. The two rivals sat directly across from each other. All three of us heard a car engine turning off in the driveway.

"That must be Adda."

He purposely used her childhood nickname.

"Look, Viggo . . . the specter of your father, it means everything, and that's why you are the way you are."

I had no idea where he was going with this, but it couldn't be good. Especially since the management consultant might just be right.

"Look at us as a nation . . . we have a country, a society, where *everyone* is busy running around but still dreaming of finding form and beauty, for themselves, for their houses, their children. Just as we all learn at our jobs, more than half of a good product involves *design* and *packaging,* and the other half is a good working relationship and effective forms of organization. That's where people like me come in. I'm the *designer*—of the good life—for everyone who wants it. For everyone who no longer wants to be afraid of the future, afraid of change."

That was Ove's main product: the gift of gab about life's most central relationships in a form that sounded scientific, or maybe even just well thought-out. That was his business's core concept, and no one was better at it.

"Look at the young in this vacuous era—how do you think *they* feel? They don't want to hear lies, they want to see things clearly, but unless they get some help, there's *nothing* to see beyond a limitless and uncontrollable stream of information, most of which is meaningless. For them, there's only one incomprehensible, generous provider—the great global network, the Internet, the holy *spin*, in which all of the world's wealthy movers and shakers tumble around. Yet day by day that network will reveal itself more, until it finally becomes its ultimate self: one gigantic marketplace, driven by avarice and greed and unbridled trade. A breeding ground for a worldwide, totally spineless ambition that we must learn to accept."

Ove paused to sip his wine, but only briefly. I wondered whether his cynical observations weren't a kind of confession—or perhaps even a requiem—for the life he had lived.

"That's where I come in. I can frame existence instead of demolishing it. I can make room for opinions and feelings in the middle of this deluge of lust and greed, so that it all feels real. I can provide the sense that we're still flesh and blood. The hopelessly antiquated human cultivation of morals—as in the old fairy tales—suits my concepts perfectly. A realistic world where we can inspire and comfort each other—and where death above all else can't overtake *us*. That's the universe I offer my customers."

I glanced at Viggo. He was as shocked as I was. We heard a door slam somewhere in the house. Agnes had come in. Our host cast a quick glance my way, once again exposing his inner darkness to me.

He knew full well what he was up against. He'd seen it in my expression. One recognizing the other.

Ove stood up quickly and walked over to the window. "I think Agnes is home now," he said, his back to us. There was a strange tone in the way he pronounced his wife's name. I knew that they'd never had children, which must be a great sorrow.

Almost as if he'd read my mind, he said, "Our children are growing up with life's unconscious urge to imitate—without having anything of value worth imitating. They want to imitate their ancestors' revolutions, their forefathers' heroic deeds . . . it's just that there *aren't* any revolutions needed anymore, and there *aren't* any heroic deeds worth performing. There are only *sinners* left—but no sins that shock us anymore. We can watch people die screaming on live TV and it doesn't affect us in the least. The same with drowning in the Mediterranean on the way to the cradle of civilization. As long as there's a warning for viewer discretion!" Ove laughed briefly above his wineglass. It sounded like a bowlful of marbles dropping onto a cement floor.

I could still feel something else. Something deeper. As if—as Agnes got closer—all the armchair philosophical nonsense he'd been entertaining us with didn't really interest him at all.

He could read my mind—we were almost one . . .

At that moment Agnes stepped into the room. She was thin, bordering on emaciated, wearing a light gray dress that reached down to her knees. She looked like the abandoned bride in a Charles Dickens story—or Cathy in Steinbeck's Edenic novel.

I started to stand up, but she lifted a slender hand and waved me back into my seat. She made no attempt to touch Viggo, and she made no indication that she knew me.

Viggo Larssen got no opportunity to speak with her. Ove Nilsen ended our visit with a statement that sounded almost like a command. "My wife has to bury the nation's first lady—the Widow Blegman— tomorrow. She has to write a sermon and needs to rest." Once again he was talking about Agnes as if no one in the room knew each other.

If Viggo had wanted to ask about the letter—or Ove's failure to respond—he never got the chance, but I don't think it really mattered. He hadn't taken this trip to solve a mystery. Neither the Widow's nor his own. He'd traveled because he needed time to make his final decision. That was why he had taken me along as his escort. It took courage.

He had no way of knowing that the investigators' trail was about to blow his intentions right out from under him. And that Verner would do just as I'd feared.

***

That afternoon we took the train from the Central Station to Kalundborg, where we caught a bus to Ulstrup and traveled the remainder of the distance on foot, through the Sea Witch's forest, back to the Lighthouse and Hell's Deep.

Something strange happened along the way.

A little gray man got onto the train in Jyderup. He had gone to Søborg School, and Viggo told me afterward that he remembered him well. He was the only one who was even smaller than Viggo; the only one who was more silent and—possibly—even weirder. He sat next to Viggo in the lower grades.

It was like a sign from Heaven. I think that the God of Viggo's grandmother wasn't going to let her grandson make the trek home from that dreadful meeting with the Devil in Dyrehaven without a little encouragement.

He had to get off the train again in fifteen minutes. That's the way it is with miracles—they're gone within fifteen minutes. He was a poet, and that was his only means of income.

He was going to read four of his poems at the library in Udby-Nedre. He'd get three hundred crowns for that.

"I moved to Jyderup in 1995." He almost whispered it—as if the place were the last stop on humanity's final and irreversible journey into Nothingness.

"I've been trying to write a novel. I can't—" He stopped. "It's been fifteen years now, maybe even more." His eyes bugged out a little, like a bloated frog's, perhaps at his sense of all those wasted efforts. Then he livened up.

"I've finally figured out my big mistake. As a writer, that is. I'm simply too exacting. I want everything to be *perfect*, without seeking the *imperfect* first—maybe even *remaining in the imperfect*. You have to be able to tolerate being *brutally honest*—about everything. About sex and bowel movements, about the deepest urges, all the juices, feelings, and thoughts, and paint all of it in large, bloodred, smelly"—he hesitated for a moment—"strokes." Not a particularly grand finale.

"I've been working on a suicide note—I call it *The World's Longest Letter*—for many years now. It's going to fill an entire book, maybe even three volumes." He looked out the window for a moment.

"I've talked to my mentor about committing suicide when the book is published. It would be a convincing form of expression, but of course it's"—he couldn't quite figure out what it was—"maybe it's a bit too . . . wild. We haven't made the final decision—you can't force that kind of thing. True expression comes when it comes—once it's finished and in its *final* form. You can't force it. Only bestselling authors do that."

His frankness amazed me. Once again, this chance meeting made me think about our totally unsuccessful visit with Ove Nilsen.

Then the train stopped at Udby-Nedre, a little whistle-stop on the line, out in the middle of nowhere.

He said good-bye politely and shook our hands. We simply had to visit him, as soon as we got the time—an offer we all knew would evaporate before the next gust of wind blew across the platform. His hand was small and white, limp and almost spongy.

Could it even write?

And then—abruptly—right before he got off, he stopped and unbuttoned his bag. He stood hesitantly for a moment, holding a slightly crumpled piece of paper in his hand, took a few steps toward me, regretted it, and then took two steps in the opposite direction, before suddenly leaning toward Viggo and handing him the paper. "Look . . . it's a poem. Just keep it. It's a copy."

There was something strangely pleading about the meek little man's gesture; like watching a spider trapped in a corner go lightly down on its knees, faking its final escape, first to the left, then to the right, then stepping back abruptly—only to simply give up. And a moment later, to be sucked off the face of the earth by my foster mother's shiny vacuum cleaner.

On the bus to Ulstrup, Viggo read the paper carefully. He held it at an angle, away from my curious gaze.

Not until we were sitting on the lighthouse bench again, and he had opened the Rioja, did he hand me the piece of paper. I held it in my outstretched hand (even a sharp-eyed observer like me can be a bit farsighted).

> *Soon we must let all this world's fools*
> *rest*
> *and forget ourselves—for a while*
> *Soon we must let all this world's morning fools*
> *stand and smile*
> *while the day wanes—for a nap*
> *An eternity, when the moon and the stars simply*
> *rise*
> *on a sky of watercress, sadness and*
> *adulation*
> *For no reason—you've forgotten me at home*
> *Only the mashed potatoes are left—*
> *screaming*

I placed it on the bench and turned to Viggo. "Only the mashed pota-toes are left . . . screaming . . . ?"

He shrugged his shoulders so faintly that the movement was almost invisible.

I repeated the line mercilessly (it was his old classmate, after all): "Only the mashed potatoes are left . . . screaming . . . ?"

Now I could detect the movement a little more clearly, a slight shrug of the shoulders, but oddly enough his voice sounded moved. "Uffe was truly original . . . and strange."

A simple remark that contained unconditional solidarity.

My eyes welled up, and I quickly turned my head away.

He was nodding, as if he could hear my thoughts.

I looked down through the fog at that small piece of paper—at what may have been an aging poet's last hope. I could picture Uffe's boyhood face, blurry and distant like the tiny lines on that piece of paper.

In a way he, too, was preoccupied with death, and that was a com-fort to me, sitting here on the bench. This traveler from the past had not completely escaped her earthly connection.

CHAPTER 19

Tårbæk
Saturday, January 17, evening

In every way the Homicide Boss had stepped outside his comfort zone. It reminded him of an old cartoon in which Donald Duck looks down and discovers that he's walking over an open abyss. The problem isn't the absence of any foothold—it's that he *looked down* and realized it.

For a policeman to make it over this abyss, deep thoughts and heavy moral considerations were not an option.

The former police commissioner had invited him to this meeting.

Although retired, the former police commissioner made the untraditional invitation sound like an order. He was used to giving orders—both at work and now as a retiree with access to the powerful cabal of previous and current officials everyone knew of but few had gotten near.

"I thought you should come. It might prove interesting for you. There's complete discretion, of course."

Before retiring as police commissioner, he had been the permanent undersecretary in the Ministry of Justice. Wielding almost unlimited power, the ministry really meant something in those years, before a few scandals too many forced him out of the powerful position.

Close friends in power saw to it that it didn't end his career, however, and gave him the job as police commissioner in Copenhagen, where he finished his career.

Upon arriving in Tårbæk, the Homicide Boss had parked his Honda Civic, circa 1998, in front of the retired commissioner's seaside villa.

His host met him at the door, put a hand on his shoulder, and once again impressed upon him the unbreakable rules of these meetings. "What happens here—the next few hours—must never be discussed anywhere. Still, maybe you can use it. I just took out the beef tenderloin, so we should be eating in about twenty minutes."

Although he sounded like a conspirator in some dark Shakespearean play, the house was bright, with high ceilings, an enormous kitchen, and panoramic views of the Øresund. A sliding door led out to a small but beautiful backyard that ended in a strip of white sand and a wooden pier jutting out into the water.

The Homicide Boss was the last to arrive, and clearly he was not part of the usual group.

He recognized all of them—except one—and something in their fellowship and the way they were standing, each with a Czech beer in his hand, reminded him of a lodge. A very elegant one, that is, only for the chosen few—self-confident men accustomed to daily luxury, enjoying a cold pilsner straight from the fridge.

They were in the middle of discussing the Widow's funeral, which the Homicide Boss had also attended, not as an invited attendee but because everything concerning the Widow also concerned him. Every pew had been packed at Søllerød Church, and many everyday citizens had to stand outside.

Only one of the other seven men hadn't been there, and he was a bit of a surprise in this company; in the distant past, he'd been one of

Copenhagen's most promising young journalists. The Homicide Boss knew his name. He had since become head of the largest editorial office in the country, one that published three dailies with the stated aim of "nipping at the heels of the high and mighty."

"She could have been a little more personal in her comments. You'd think she hadn't even spoken to Poul and Palle."

They were talking about the pastor, and the group's old sage—a small man who used to be the permanent undersecretary in the office of the prime minister and was now a passionate art collector—was offering his assessment of the funeral service. They were standing in a circle by the garden door, their places obviously part of the ritual, before they sat down to eat and continue their conversation.

"She seemed nervous—not because of all the stylish people there—but just to be speaking."

Stylish people. That was a funny term to be using in this group, the poshest of all, thought the Homicide Boss. Not least of all the man speaking, the former ombudsman of Parliament.

"But such a beautiful woman—at least as much of her as you could see." It was the Ministry of Justice's current undersecretary, a thin, dark man with a sunburnt face (even though it was the dead of winter).

Everyone laughed.

"Our two . . . friends . . . seemed moved. But even that was a bit . . . lacking."

The comment, in all its ambiguity, hung in the air for a moment; it could only have been made by the group's (and thus the nation's) most powerful official, the permanent undersecretary in the Ministry of Finance. Even though he was once CFO of the Danish Broadcasting Corporation, his new appointment placed him in a position in which he was now orchestrating the realm's future—with an army of young officials beneath him.

There may have been a hint of irritation in the voice of the prime minister's undersecretary when he replied to his colleague. "Palle—and

Poul—can't just stand there sobbing all over the church floor. They knew that the place was filled to the rafters with journalists and photographers."

"Yes—and they had other things to worry about, naturally." Their host had wedged himself between the two and the tiff he feared was imminent.

"What do you *mean*?" The former police commissioner looked over at the newspaperman. "Do you think that *our friends* might use the sympathy they've gotten . . . going into the election?"

"No doubt about it. There's no reason not to. My people will be writing about it in tomorrow's paper." The editor made his somewhat pompous remark sound like the words of an oracle just flown in from Delphi. His face was friendly, with its slightly sharp, handsome features.

"She talked about loneliness and revenge . . . I wonder why." The former ombudsman returned to the subject of the pastor. The Homicide Boss had already discovered that the man knew Agnes Persen from church, where he played the recorder at special occasions.

"She talked about sacrifice, too," said the group's oldest member, the prime minister's former undersecretary. "It made me think of a painting by Velázquez or Goya." He stared ahead dreamily.

"I really liked her final words—that all people have the right to their own peculiarities." It was the prime minister's current undersecretary. "Maybe she was also referring to the brothers."

That was a brave comment, even coming from a former socialist.

"Shall we eat?" asked the host. "I'll take the potatoes out of the oven, and the beef tenderloin is done. I take it everyone likes theirs a little *rare*."

Once again, the Homicide Boss thought about the relaxed atmosphere that allowed these seven sworn companions to give their household help the day off and grill their own slabs of meat, which were sitting on the cutting board next to the ceramic range. They took theirs without anything as mundane as béarnaise sauce—just a dollop of butter with parsley and garlic, and the meat's own flowing juices. In copious amounts.

He thought again of his host's conspiratorial welcome, which had reminded him of a scene in Shakespeare, maybe *Julius Caesar*, which he'd always been fascinated by and had first seen at the Royal Danish Theatre when he was still just a cadet. He started as a street cop and went on to patrol Bakken amusement park on long summer evenings; later he found himself chasing thieves through the extensive network of courtyards in Nørrebro, an area now torn down and replaced by block after block of redbrick buildings. In this group he was a novice, an outsider who had never been involved in secret agreements or plotting networks; still, there had to be a reason he'd been invited. At least the seven men weren't lying around the table like their Roman predecessors but instead were seated around the enormous oak table, which was covered with nothing but plates and utensils—no tablecloth, candles, or flowers from the garden.

"When the pastor threw dirt on the coffin, you could almost hear the old lady groan from below. Everyone thought she would live forever." The retired police commissioner seemed pleased with his morbid observation as he sawed thick cuts off the beef tenderloin.

"What she said about death"—the former ombudsman paused solemnly to assure everyone's attention—"that *no one* is forgotten if they don't want to be . . . that everyone can have eternal life if they leave a lasting memory. It was thought provoking."

What was really thought provoking, thought the Homicide Boss, was that the remark had come from a pastor who just happened to be married to Ove Nilsen, a man who stood to make a fortune off that very idea.

"It was touching when she mentioned the son the Widow lost so many years ago. He had never been forgotten, because he was still living in his mother's heart."

The former ombudsman bowed his head for a moment, as if he were praying. His piety obviously tested the patience of the other attendees. As it had when he'd been working, too. The Homicide Boss wondered how he'd ever been accepted into this closed circle of friends. During his tenure as Parliament's so-called watchdog for abuses of power and misconduct, he had criticized several of the ministries represented at the table, and even a couple of the men here, too, by name. Of course nothing serious ever happened. They'd been admonished, sometimes severely, yet they'd still been promoted to powerful new positions. It was like a wheel, turning endlessly and inexorably; only the general public and the most idealistic journalists thought it would ever stop.

The Homicide Boss once heard the former police commissioner discussing a particularly toxic case with his successor at the Ministry of Justice—a minister and his top officials had interfered in the opposition's taxes—and he realized that men in these positions saw it as their duty to protect the general public from anything that might endanger people's belief in democracy. It was the one thing that must never happen—even if it meant discreetly sabotaging appointed commissioners, misleading the public, and massive cover-ups of mistakes, shoddy work, and manipulations.

"Yes," said the editorial director, whose editorials had often criticized the lack of any consequences for politicians and government officials bending the rules—or just plain breaking the law. "We've written about them and their little brother Arrow who died. That was a great tragedy."

"Arrow," grunted the Ministry of Finance's undersecretary, who still remembered his childhood songs and poems. "'I shot an arrow into the air.'" He laughed.

Even for this group, the remark seemed a bit insensitive, although most around the table were laughing. The Homicide Boss was painfully aware that he hadn't smiled and that they may have thought he was uneducated and unsophisticated, even about something as simple as an old children's poem.

Three bottles of the finest Italian Barolo arrived at the table and were passed around.

"Maybe they can use that phrase in their campaign materials," said the host, who came off as a bit vulgar with his slightly lumpy nose beneath watery blue eyes. He was the only one present who'd had to vacate his department involuntarily; he'd been caught staying at three rather expensive hotels at the taxpayers' expense when he traveled one winter in an official capacity. Apparently, that was the only offense that could shake the system's ruling elite and really get the news media to dig in.

The aging policeman had always been amazed that that's the way it was, in both the press and the realm's upper echelons (with whom he was now sharing a table). Whenever the country's finest deceived, betrayed, or were caught in blatant lies—whenever they destroyed telltale evidence to cover up their obvious abuses of power—they went free. Every single time.

The minister of justice's undersecretary didn't miss his cue. "A new election? I don't think so. They'll have to clear up this whole matter first."

Everyone turned toward the prime minister's own undersecretary, who was shaking his head slightly. He had no fear of anyone leaking anything said at the table. "There's no talk about any election—yet—but that's because the Bear is so irritated. You know, all these new parties . . ."

All of them knew what he was referring to: a small network of rebellious politicians had been collecting signatures to create entirely new parties. "It could lead to Armageddon," agreed the minister of finance's undersecretary. "Imagine if some . . . *ass* . . . with a party platform that consists of nothing more than whining about the environment and the way older politicians talk gets to influence the country's future. Try to picture such a person . . . the worst kind of shithead."

Several of those present looked at the group's old sage, the previous undersecretary for three prime ministers. He had just received the first serving directly from the cutting board, a thick slab of bloody meat that engulfed his plate. He declined the offer of a baked potato, sliced his first chunk of meat, and said, "Boat refugees . . . Muslim terrorism . . . Islamists in war-torn areas"—he took his first bite—"all great cards—if the game is played right and no one blinks. That kind of thing scares people . . ." He gulped down the large piece of meat almost without chewing. "Images of those things threaten our security. And when we feel threatened and frightened, we *don't* vote for new and uncertain parties."

His analysis was simple, and they all knew what he meant: in the end, democracy worked best if the responsible remained in power. No one at the table had any doubts. Even if it wrecked lives (quite literally) and meant cynical alliances.

"And that's why your editors might want to think twice before they write anything!" The former ombudsman's remark was directed at the editorial director, and everyone laughed—except the newspaperman. Maybe the remark veered a little too close to something ominous—something that should remain unsaid, even within this closed group. The host had filled everyone's plate, and conversation stopped for a moment. The Homicide Boss looked down at his mammoth serving of meat and wished that someone would sneak in and devour it for him. He thought about the old Donald Duck cartoon and lifted his knife. *Don't look down, no foolish thoughts, and above all else, don't act nervous.* Despite how he really felt.

The host raised his glass, and following his toast, said, "She never mentioned their father, the old patriarch—Peter Blegman—that was a little strange."

"He was the one pulling all the strings behind the scenes." Once again it was the group's oldest member who interrupted with his almost limitless knowledge, thanks to a lifetime spent in the halls of power. He'd been the government's number one man under an earlier Conservative-led coalition. "Without him we wouldn't have had that goddamned *case*." He almost spat out the word, and everyone knew what case he was talking about. "That's what started all these insufferable commissions and investigations we've had to put up with for decades now."

"Didn't he die following a newspaper article?" The ombudsman stared inquisitively at the editorial director. But it was their host, the former police commissioner and undersecretary in the Ministry of Justice, who replied.

"No, not a newspaper—it was a magazine, but I forget the name. The reporters had written a large feature on the Blegman family. A real exposé. He had a stroke on the same day and died shortly thereafter."

"So maybe he wasn't as tough as he thought."

"The brothers were furious. They pulled every possible string . . . *anything* that might lead anywhere. I was there—an inexperienced lawyer—when we attacked that magazine. Everyone loved it, but they didn't stand a chance. The editor was Verner Jensen, by the way, now the head of the news department at the DBC." The former police commissioner looked over at the Ministry of Finance's undersecretary.

"I didn't know him back then. We worked together on cutbacks at the DBC, and his work was impeccable. He managed to get the most cuts through, actually, without any strikes or employee upris-ings, because he had the kind of past they respected. He got them to swallow all these management consultants' inane buzzwords about developmental concepts and Christ knows what else. None of which anyone understood—even though they all acted like they did. That was the secret. No one dared say no, not even the bosses. In reality, they'd just hit on some very clever headlines and held up some charts with a few circles and boxes—and everyone hopped on board. Verner realized that, but he pulled it off. You've all probably done the same."

Everyone nodded—even the Homicide Boss. Every public workplace had been visited by management consultants—from McKinsey & Company to Kaospilot.

"They spent two months making all the employees at the DBC come up with 'key words' to describe where they'd already been working for years. When I left the DBC, I found the final report in the bottom drawer of some desk. The whole thing resulted in five words—and probably cost hundreds of thousands of man-hours—not to mention a gigantic fee for the company—and no one has used any of it ever since." He shook his head.

"In any case, Palle managed to destroy Verner Jensen's little gossip rag." Their host smiled. "Sometimes, when Palle was drunk, he'd stand in the middle of his office screaming, 'I have the biggest fucking *cock* in the world!' Maybe that's true. At least he has the highest post." The former police commissioner laughed.

Only the editorial director smiled—and that may have been out of politeness, because he was the youngest person there. The others clearly viewed the vulgar remarks as a bit embarrassing.

Coffee arrived in three French presses, along with a fine Larsen cognac. The Homicide Boss passed.

The editorial director excused himself and said his good-byes, explaining he had an early start at work the next morning. Their host followed him out, and when he came back, the Homicide Boss could see that his turn had come.

"We've invited you here"—his former boss paused for a moment— "we've invited you here because we really want to talk to you in private."

That was fairly obvious, thought the Homicide Boss.

"We've been following your investigation into the Blegman case, and we know it's not an easy task. It involves . . . well . . . powerful people."

True enough. And no one would know that better than the six men sitting around this table.

"We think you've stumbled upon . . . some information. We"—that must mean the closed group at this table, and the Homicide Boss suddenly understood why the newspaper man had left—"know that you've been looking into all of the family's background and their finances."

The magic word. Now the old policeman knew where the conspirators were headed with this. He didn't speak.

"What you've found, but haven't been able to—or had the chance to"—he meant *dared to*—"use until now is not just some minor infraction like overpaying for a hotel room during some exhausting mission. It's something else, something bigger—and more private."

The Homicide Boss couldn't agree more. But still he said nothing. So that's what all this was about. Don't lose your footing—and for Christ's sake, don't look down.

"What you've discovered apparently, is that they aren't doing so well . . . financially. As your sources have surely told you."

That was not a question.

The Homicide Boss didn't respond.

"They're bankrupt, goddamn it!"

That indelicate statement came from the former undersecretary to three men—all prime ministers. The party's old sage.

He'd cut to the chase, as he'd always done. The accusation hung in the air above the round table.

That was the Ministry of Finance's undersecretary's cue, as the responsible financial expert. "Yes, they are *bankrupt.*" A statement as raw as the meat they had just eaten. "They've spent everything—*everything.*

And if they don't get their inheritance *now*—within a few weeks—they're finished."

The comment rose above the table, like a death sentence.

"They've mortgaged their houses, spoiled their children, waited hand and foot on their party colleagues, gifted their mistresses—basically they've spent everything. All on private luxuries."

Now the party's oldest member spoke up again, and he stared right at the Homicide Boss as he spoke. "It's their top priority. To get their inheritance."

Everyone at the table sat in silence. Several with their hands folded.

"Once that's discovered," added the Ministry of Finance's boss, "the citizens will lose all faith in our leading politicians. How can I ever ask Danish families to sacrifice and save after that kind of scandal—without being crucified?"

"The will must be found. If she's disinherited them, that needs to come out—and as soon as possible." The group's oldest member held the Homicide Boss's gaze. "The only safe course is to tell people the truth. They've put us in an impossible situation. They've placed their own . . . debauchery . . . above democracy."

A deep silence fell over the round table. The Homicide Boss almost couldn't believe what he was hearing.

Maybe the six government officials were only pointing out that the two brothers would steamroll over anyone who stood between them and a solution to their own personal ruin.

That wasn't exactly news. They would never have summoned him if that were the only piece of information he'd be leaving with; they wouldn't care at all about some little policeman's feelings—or future. It couldn't be that.

He felt a chill run up his spine, which wasn't like him. Number Two was never going to find out about that.

Were these officials suggesting that the realm's two most powerful men had a motive—a motive for murder?

Or were they just using the suggestion to let him know, clandestinely, that he'd be safe if he went after the Blegman brothers? And brought them down? Or at the very least leaked information about their personal ruin.

It didn't help that cold feeling running up his spine. On the contrary.

Were the men sitting around this table so powerful—so clever with their finely woven invisible web—that they could say, *These politicians think they have the power, but we can take it from them whenever it suits us.*

And it suits us now.

At that moment he looked down; he was floating, free form, without a net, and so he did the only thing he could: he stood up so suddenly that his chair almost toppled over behind him.

Surely the most awkward and abrupt action in the history of this group—but he needed some fresh air. And he needed to get back on solid ground. Once he was sitting with his foot on the accelerator in his old Honda Civic, his hands and feet calmed down again. His host had followed him out, neither of them saying a word. They both knew that the die was cast and the trap had shut. The two brothers, who were preparing for a major election with the nation's welfare and future as their key talking points, had lost control of their private affairs. The noble knights he'd just left had all the ammunition—from the tax authorities to knowledge of where the brothers hid their finances. But only the Homicide Boss could leak it.

He could refuse . . .

. . . but the six vultures sitting in that villa in Tårbæk would flay him in a public bloodbath. He understood full well what had happened.

He had looked down.

He left the six men, the nation's true engine of power, sitting behind drawn curtains. As he rolled out onto Tårbæk Strandvej and turned around, the kitchen light had been turned off. There were no lights on in the house.

***

The Lighthouse on the Cape
Saturday, January 17, shortly before midnight

The day after my return, the fox was sitting on the hillside as if waiting to welcome me, its long tongue hanging out as if smiling at me.

Its furry red coat was almost hidden in the brown and reddish leaves among the tree trunks in the clearing below. I grasped the symbolism, probably arranged by some higher power.

Agnes had buried the Widow—I heard it on the evening news—and I was expecting her call. I could picture her; she probably went outside with her phone. Ove must never know what his gentle pastor-wife was hiding.

"It's Agnes . . ."

I didn't respond.

"Have you hidden it . . . they're on their way."

She was talking about the will, and "they" were the police—and the Blegman family.

"Yes."

"Are you sure it's hidden?" Her voice sounded a bit nervous.

"Yes," I said. It was easy to guess what she'd say next.

"It will destroy them."

"Yes."

"Provided it turns up—and they don't manage to destroy it first. They have a lot of power . . ."

"Yes." I repeated my contribution to the conversation in the same tone of voice.

"You don't need to stay there anymore, now that the old lady is dead."

"I realize that."

"So are you leaving?"

"No."

A long pause. Then her voice reached across Sjælland to me, standing on the hillside by the rickety house. "What is it you're really looking for?"

My gaze turned back toward Hell's Deep. I didn't answer her.

"You've met him. Now he won't inherit anything."

"No." I was about to break my own record for monosyllabic answers.

"I'm going to the seminary in Kalundborg on Tuesday." This was the real reason she had called. "I'll stop by your place. If they find those . . . papers . . . if anyone finds them now, then they'll disappear for good." She paused for a moment. "Everything will have been in vain. And we—" She stopped herself.

I knew why. She was about to mention her husband's name—the name that had appeared in the final version of the Widow's will. The reason why the Widow had suddenly become so kind in the twilight of her life, why she had succumbed to Ove's temptation, to Eden's New Garden.

If you believe in this vision, then there are no limits. I can make your son live again.

Little Arrow would come back. Eternal life. What could be more just?

The Widow had kept some old 16 mm film. Ove said he could transfer the flickering images to a hard disc and clean it all up, make it like new. Her son would be remembered; he would reappear . . .

I'll make your pictures live, so that everyone can see your boy and you can tell us all about him.

I knew what he'd said. He had no scruples. All that mattered was his and Adda's future.

You're going to sleep side by side in paradise.

That was true—at least in Ove's version of paradise—and she fell for it. It was all there in the will.

Agnes returned from the borderland of fear she'd just flown through on her innocent, God-given wings. "We'll be able to talk for an hour about the whole thing."

"Yes," I said.

Suddenly she laughed. Perhaps as she had in her childhood, long before I knew her.

CHAPTER 20

Office of the Prime Minister
Monday, January 19, morning

The press release lay on the enormous desk that separated the two brothers.

Next to it lay the morning newspapers and a small stack of magazines, their covers plastered with pictures of the Widow and life among the Blegmans. Many had been taken from a distance, through wrought iron gates, over high walls, from places no photographer should ever have access to. Almost as if the lady and her family were lawless renegades being hunted—like outlaws in the woods in one of the brothers' old Robin Hood comics.

The two men—the hugest pair of brothers ever, as one tabloid had joked—were furious.

"First, following your *advice*, we published this"—the Bear slammed an oversize index finger down on a piece of paper on his desk—"and then all *hell* breaks loose. Everyone wants to know where that damn will is. Some people even think we hid it ourselves and then burned it. Why in the world would we do that?"

The Homicide Boss couldn't help thinking about what he'd heard two days earlier at the villa in Tårbæk, when the veil had been lifted from his eyes. He said, "Before we find it—or don't find it—we can't move forward . . . or even begin the inheritance process."

He didn't know where those last few words came from—it certainly wasn't anything approved by the cadre of lawyers now populating police headquarters.

He'd suggested that on Sunday evening they should inform the public about the missing will—and he'd received immediate support from both the prime minister's and the minister of justice's undersecretaries. That left a bad taste in his mouth; he was now part of a secret game, arranged at the table in Tårbæk. He couldn't back out; his second in command would be dumped along with him.

He'd inquired discreetly and heard from a retired prosecutor that the Tårbæk Club's existence was well known. Such powerful men would never be so stupid as to keep it a secret that they got together. Yet to outsiders, they were merely casual social gatherings sprinkled with a little professional sparring. The prosecutor had heard that the small but powerful circle had started with the alternative name of *January '93*—and that the group had existed since then, the founders alluding to the so-called Tamil case, which had brought down an entire administration and discredited a number of top officials.

Now, the missing will had become the day's top story, and the two brothers were about to meet the media wolves with only a half hour of preparation.

The office was teeming with counselors and top officials, and the Bear looked like he was on the verge of a breakdown.

The minister of justice's handsome undersecretary was functioning as a moderator. His respectful mien was a perfect mask for feigning humility and loyalty. The same could be said for the former socialist standing tall and proud by Palle Blegman's side.

If it were up to them (and how many others in the room?) this case would drive the two heartless emperors far from the realm's finest chambers. It was surreal; he almost said the word aloud, a word he'd heard his daughter use when she started studying law at college.

The Bear stood up. Here it comes—and no one would be able to hold him back.

Only a young, eager adviser missed the warning signs.

The Homicide Boss perceived just the hint of a smile on the moderator's face. The would-be spin doctor stepped foolishly into the ring, the way young people do when they think they're much older than they are: "We have to see to it that the press really sets the right tone . . . in one sense the old woman was robbed of her life's work—at the very *moment of her death* . . ." The Homicide Boss couldn't believe his ears, and the undersecretary's mouth started to quiver, like right before swallowing a chunk of beef tenderloin, but the young spin doctor was oblivious. "And someone has seized control of her last will and testament, someone wants to take advantage of a vulnerable situation for both the bereaved and all of—"

That's as far as he got.

The Bear reached the slender adviser in three enormous steps and knocked him to the thickly carpeted floor with one fell swoop of a bear claw.

"We're not talking about some *fucking . . . old . . . woman.*" Spit fell in a stream onto the prostrate man. "Her name is *the Widow Blegman*—and no fucking . . . *idiot* . . . is going to be dancing on her grave . . ." He stopped, short of breath, and the tall undersecretary took his prime minister almost gently by the arm and led him back to his desk.

The young would-be spin doctor was carried, half unconscious, from the office.

The two undersecretaries cleared the room of the gaggle of advisers, leaving only themselves and the Homicide Boss with the two Blegman brothers (who had moved their heavy bodies over to the guest sofa).

The Homicide Boss knew exactly where things stood.

The brothers were in crisis. The country was in crisis. His investigation was in impending crisis. And if the Tårbæk Club got what it wanted, then he was merely a pawn in the craftiest game ever devised.

The men in that villa would think the same thing he and Number Two had thought: because the will was changed shortly before the Widow's death—with two complete strangers as witnesses and no input whatsoever from the Blegman clan's lawyer—something must have been completely altered.

The investigation had revealed bad blood between the old lady and the two brothers, but they never thought that their behavior would have any consequences.

He shook his head. Maybe they'd disinherited themselves. Of course, they'd always inherit something, but not enough to save their empire.

"There's one more detail we need to discuss," said the prime minister's undersecretary, looking mistrustfully at the man with whom he had eaten steak and drunk the finest Barolo wine only two days before. The Homicide Boss lowered his head slightly; after their meeting at the round table, he had told the powerful official everything the police knew.

The Homicide Boss told the two brothers about the live bird in the cage.

The Bear was half lying, half sitting on the elegant sofa next to his brother. The three others present sat creaking slightly in the stiff-backed Wegner chairs.

"So what!" The prime minister was getting his second wind. "What the hell else would she use a birdcage for!"

"You're not allowed to have birds at the nursing home." The police-man bent his head, as if he were sitting on a perch, without any wings, and pondering the heights.

"Our mother loved canaries." It was the minister of justice. "I think that maybe . . . it might have reminded her of little Arrow. He had a—"

"Fuck Arrow," interrupted the Bear, "and his pathetic bird!"

Both undersecretaries looked at the Homicide Boss. There was no turning back now.

He returned to his point. "The thing is that she didn't have any bird. Not in the past year—not *just* before—and . . ."

He stopped for a moment, preparing for the semirecumbent man's reaction, then continued, "She took the cage with her to the nursing home as a memento. But it just sat there. She was *absolutely* not allowed to have a canary."

"And yet it was there." The minister of justice laughed, a bit nervously.

"Exactly." The Homicide Boss shifted focus to his ultimate superior. "So where did it come from?"

For a long moment the two brothers sat in silence, blinking blankly at some unsolvable problem.

Palle reacted first. "So, you're saying someone put it there . . ." He paused.

"Yes, that's what I'm saying . . . but we don't know why."

"I don't understand." Poul Blegman shook his head. "I don't understand."

"Apparently, the person we're searching for left the bird in the cage when your mother . . . it might indicate a reference to something in the past. I know I've asked before, but is there anything at all you two can think of?" He waited almost thirty seconds but got no answer. "The boys in the neighborhood?"

No answer.

"Someone from high school?"

The prime minister glanced at his younger brother, who had completely collapsed on the uncomfortable sofa, and said: "Christ, there could be hundreds . . . all kinds of people who want revenge."

Surprisingly enough, that confession was delivered quite calmly. He might just as well have said, "We've basically tyrannized every living being we could on our way through life, so *everyone* around us has a reason to hate us." But of course he didn't.

The two undersecretaries looked at the Homicide Boss again.

He couldn't avoid the final revelation—and he knew that the Bear would never understand the investigative decisions they'd had to make.

"There was something else in the basement . . . where she was found. Something by her feet. She must have been holding it when she died."

"Something . . . ?"

"Yes. A book."

"A book?" Poul Blegman shook his head slightly.

"*The Little Prince*—by the French author, Antoine de Saint-Exupéry."

The minister of justice's eyes looked like two marbles, shining, but completely opaque.

His big brother stood up and walked slowly over to the desk; his enormous hand brushed aside both the press release and the newspapers, scattering them in a fluttering jumble all over the floor.

"You've kept all this *secret*!" He turned toward the Homicide Boss. "You've kept it *hidden* that there were other clues . . . you kept that bird . . . we saw it . . . you let us think it was supposed to be there?" Palle Blegman was not speaking clearly. His undersecretary quietly got up out of his chair. Either to escape or to prevent an unwanted close encounter.

"Yes, first and foremost, I'm a policeman." The Homicide Boss had prepared his defense—and it was a surprisingly brief one. Seven words in all.

The prime minister suddenly shifted from his expected rage to an almost pleading tone, which struck everyone in the office as strange. "But what does it *mean*? A book? And a bird . . . ?" He let his large body plop down onto the buffalo-leather chair, which creaked ominously.

"Yes," said the Homicide Boss. "To find a living bird in a cage . . . in a cage that had been empty for a lifetime . . . yes, that's pretty damn strange. And that's why we didn't want to make it public."

The Homicide Boss had explained his defense in a formal, almost monotone voice.

"My God," said the prime minister, "so this is some *crazy* person . . ."

"Yes," said the Blegman case's lead investigator, standing up. "Or maybe, it isn't. Or else . . ." He left that sentence incomplete as he left the room.

". . . or else what?" The Bear's final question took a long, silent lap around the elegant office.

But none of the remaining guests could answer him.

CHAPTER 21

The Lighthouse on the Cape
Tuesday, January 29, afternoon

I spent the entire night and the following morning pondering my next step before I made my decision. For the last few hours, the fox had been sitting there, his green eyes staring intently at the house.

As if it were waiting, waiting for something to break out of the Sea Witch's old house—something unavoidable and uncontrollable— something I had never had any control over.

If the little prince were standing there invisible by its side, wearing those wide pants and that innocent expression in those boyish blue eyes, it wouldn't have surprised me.

Was what had happened a form of sacrifice—or the exact opposite? I wasn't sure.

Pride has never been one of my virtues. Joy over your own achieve- ments is a false emotion—treason committed by your soul on behalf of Satan. In any case, I lost that illusion back in the orphanage when my foster mother forced me to smile and wave at those who were leaving. For their benefit.

In the end humiliation was all that was left. I don't recall anyone ever waving back.

Agnes was sitting in my room. Her car was parked down on the gravel road, and she had crawled up the cliff while calling my name.

I didn't answer until she was really close—a bit scratched up from shoving aside the crooked trunks with their outstretched branches, which one could easily mistake for the final desperate movements of the dead—a gesture from Hell's playground.

That's the kind of thought Agnes would never have; she would just climb past it. Obstacles were for overcoming.

"You have it . . . someplace safe."

She had looked around the little room. It was not easy to connect this rickety house with any kind of safe place. On the other hand, it wasn't a question.

"Yes—in a way it's buried. No one will be able to find it, before we—"

"Publish it." She fell silent.

And that was the problem. The Widow had asked me to take care of the will—she had encouraged me to take it with me to the cape when I left. Of course she knew that the altered contents were so earth-shattering that she didn't dare entrust it to the family lawyer. Which made sense. After all, surely he'd support the realm's most powerful men; with a stroke of his pen, she could be deemed legally incompetent or her final version of the will might suddenly disappear. Those kinds of things happened.

Agnes had discovered her hiding place at the nursing home—it was almost pathetic—under the tray in the bottom of the old birdcage.

Even the most incompetent thief would look there first.

I took her final will with me.

The problem was that she disappeared after that—and then we hesitated.

And at the moment she was found, our hesitation turned to indecision, almost to panic.

How were we going to explain that we'd just found the will after the police had ransacked the entire place without finding it?

How could either of us suddenly show up with the nation's most sought-after document—like a knife we'd been hiding in the folds of a toga—so long afterward?

We sat in the Sea Witch's old house for maybe five minutes without talking. Listening to the gusting wind, we pondered our real problem. The will had to be made public—the police were searching for it, and it was the point of no return for the Blegman brothers' descent into the abyss. We didn't envy them.

We'd set the whole thing in motion, and now we had to find a solution. I could see the desperation in her eyes. It was odd that she didn't understand me better—that she couldn't see through my plan. There was only one solution, and I had found it long before she'd crawled past the skeletal branches on the steep slope.

"Come with me."

We left the house. It seemed about to collapse as we stepped off the porch, as if it were considering its last plaintive tremor before crashing into the sea—but changed its mind at the last second.

I turned around. It was still standing.

We passed the Giant's Footprint and struggled farther up the cliff, that last little stretch to the stone bench and the lighthouse door. We sat down.

"It's here . . ."

"Yes."

"It's a beautiful place."

I wasn't sure she meant it.

"And deserted . . ."

"As are most places by the sea. He'll be here in a moment."

She nodded.

Letting Viggo meet Adda again is the oddest decision I've ever made. Sometimes I don't understand my own choices. I wonder if everyone feels like that. We think one thing and do another, and sometimes one is dark and inexplicable, whereas the other is bright and completely understandable—as if the mind is suddenly ripped apart by some invisible force. Sometimes, it's the other way around.

Back from the cliff, Viggo was standing across from the lighthouse steps, out of breath after climbing the crooked steps up from the rocky coast.

The two of them stared at each other. He walked over to us.

"Good day." I repeated my very first greeting to him, the one that says so much and yet nothing at all.

"Good day." He only had eyes for Agnes.

If I ever had a chance, I relinquished it there. She was just as beautiful as the first—and only—time they kissed. Viggo went into the lighthouse and fetched his little three-legged stool. He placed it in the gravel, facing us.

My only thought, curiously enough, was that he had finally let the little prince sail his own sea without any landfall.

We told him about the Widow; we told him all about my role. We told him I had come to the Lighthouse and the cape to procure him a place in her will—the will that her own sons were no longer a part of.

He nodded.

But we also told him the real reason for our involvement.

"It was their father who killed your mother," said Agnes. As a pastor she was used to delivering difficult news.

Viggo Larssen sat on his stool; his expression didn't change a bit, no sound came from his throat or his chest, nothing. He was frozen in shock. He could just as well be dead.

"Peter Blegman from the Yellow House ran over your mother that Midsummer Eve, in 1971. And he got away with it," I said.

He still didn't say anything,

"The Widow told us that when we signed her will." I glanced at Agnes. "That was the main reason why she . . . wanted to make things right again. If you can ever really do that."

No one can make everything right again.

"You received an anonymous letter—it was from me—telling you to look more closely at the family in the Yellow House, at the Blegmans, in connection with your mother's death. Then you went to Copenhagen to talk to her."

This time he nodded at me.

I mentally nudged him as forcefully as possible, and he spoke.

"I don't know if the police know that yet. She was the only one I saw, and the whole thing ended quite awkwardly. She cried, and in the end I just stood there, yelling. She wouldn't admit to knowing . . . anything."

"When she saw you, she lost her nerve. A failure I had not anticipated. I spoke to her afterward. We agreed . . . it wasn't right and it had to be rectified."

I could feel Agnes moving restlessly next to me. There were things she didn't know about me—and Agnes Persen didn't like being kept in the dark or meeting someone who could match her cool perspective—something she saw only in the Supreme Being, the God who asked his earthly children to turn the other cheek when they were struck, to walk another mile, or to give their shirt to the thief who'd only asked for a coat.

I'd said what I had to say; I stood up and offered him my spot next to Agnes.

The wind had picked up as I walked back across the Giant's Footprint; the rustling in the trees would make it impossible to hear her go back to her car and drive away. It meant nothing to me.

If the fox was following me up the cliff to the house, I didn't see it. I laughed a little to myself. Maybe it was offended by my prolonged absence.

What you tame you never lose.

***

I fell asleep and I dreamed.

Love is found only in the darkness.

I learned that from Magdalene, my disabled friend from another cliff, far from here.

As we'd looked out at the Swedish coast, she taught me that the bones that stretch and grow and later shrink and decay might possess unimaginable strength in another world and another time . . .

. . . in a lighthouse, in the dark, where it should have been too late for everything . . .

. . . in a mirror, in my dreams—on the other side of the breaking surf . . .

. . . in the first light of day, when the sun's rays would strike the lighthouse wall . . .

. . . in the light that clings to us—and is always there . . .

. . . as lovers . . .

. . . in one simultaneous motion . . .

CHAPTER 22

The Lighthouse on the Cape
Wednesday, January 21, afternoon

Maybe it was an expression of sheer calculation.

I should have understood that when he turned to me the day after his reunion with Adda. She had been his last hope—that was why I'd brought them together—and it had failed.

I was all that was left. He was ready to reveal what he had hidden from the world for so long. The strangest thing in his life.

"Maybe you're just as odd . . ." He stopped for a moment, but I knew what was coming.

". . . as me?"

It was a bold claim. But I pretended it didn't matter.

"None of my . . . old friends . . . can really understand it . . . or they just don't have the time." His voice sounded a bit sad, like when a child is left out of a game and doesn't know why.

Surprisingly enough, he stood up. "Let's go in."

I was dumbstruck. He would never have said those words before.

"I want you to see something, something no one else has seen." He opened the door. "Malin." He spoke the name I had chosen for myself, and it sounded right. "You're the only one I dare show this to. I know you'll understand it . . . without thinking . . ."

I knew what he wanted to say: *Without thinking I'm stark raving mad* . . .

Though on some level, that's just what I was thinking.

He had it all laid out on the living room table. In the order he thought was logical.

Seven documents in all—seven "pieces of evidence," I was sure he'd call them.

Some of them I recognized, naturally: his mother's diary, the Spanish journal, the old ship's log, and Aunt Jenny's letter. There also was a thin envelope there, and a couple of pieces of paper in a protective folder.

He fetched the three-legged stool, and I sat down on the chair across from him. He reached for his mother's journal as his first piece of evidence. It was her third and last one—the one I'd never read, because it had stayed locked in the glass cabinet. *My journal* was written in gold letters, along with the start date—1970—with no end date. But I knew the end date: just before Midsummer's Eve, 1971.

He leafed through to that section and opened it to the last written page. "Read it . . . it's her final entry . . ."

I took the book, and it gave me an involuntary start. I saw it immediately. *The woman, the water, the hands, the serpent.* The description was short and precise—and in that moment I could physically feel the fear in that cold lighthouse room.

> *I had a strange dream tonight, and I have never had such*
> *a dream before. I dreamt that my mother was coming*
> *toward me—she was wearing a black dress—and she was*

*reaching her hands out to me, as if she wanted to hug me
or invite me along to some unknown place. But it frightened me. Her skin was pale, almost chalk white, and I
sensed that she was no longer living. Still, she wanted me
to come with her. Then I realized that we were standing
in a desert, yet it couldn't be a desert—there was water.
My mother was surrounded by a large sea that stretched
behind her as far as I could see. The strange thing was
that the water was alive, or that's how it looked. As if
the water was moving around her feet and her bare legs.
When I looked down, I saw the serpent—and right then
it lifted its head up out of the sea. I knew that the whole
dream was really about me. My mother wanted me to
come with her—she knew that I was going to die. It's the
most terrifying dream I've ever had . . .*

. . . she never wrote another word.

I read the whole thing again, and Viggo Larssen let me read until
he was certain I was finished.

He lifted the book carefully out of my hands, closed it, and placed
it back on the table. Then he took the green book I had seen so often—
and read, mystified—before I understood its meaning for him.

He opened to the last page in the small book and handed it to
me. They were the last words written by the Spanish Civil War volunteer. I'd read that short section many times, and I knew—shuddering
slightly—what was coming and exactly what Viggo Larssen had seen. I
felt a numbness in my hands and forearms when I grasped the leather-
bound journal. Viggo Larssen was either crazier than I'd imagined or he
had spotted a correlation that even I couldn't explain.

This is how the fighter for Spain had concluded his final page, his
last observations:

Morning. The sun has just come up. The others are still sleeping. The night would have been a good one, if not for the strange dream I had. My mother was standing before me and reaching out her arms, as if she wanted to say something. The strange thing is that she was standing in water, like a large ocean, maybe it was the Øresund, whereas everything here is bone-dry and completely withered. Not much grows in this hell. Her legs were bare and there was a golden glow all around her, although her hands were totally white. Suddenly a serpent's head shot up out of the water in a large, foamy white pillar. The serpent was behind her, and she either did not see it or else it did not mean anything. At that moment I felt as if it represented something terrible. We are still some miles from the front, and as Halfdan would have said, "Calm and steady, my friend—to preserve our courage to the very end." Even when he is banal, he can rhyme, and of course he is right.

I looked up.

I looked at Viggo.

"I researched it. There was a large battle near the Ebro that same day. Many of the Danish volunteers were killed. Including him."

I nodded. I'd never had any interest in wars happening elsewhere in the world.

He carefully placed the book on the table next to his mother's journal. Then he handed me the next item—the Christmas letter from his grandmother's friend Jenny. I'd seen it before. I knew with ice-cold clarity what was coming.

"This was my third discovery—from when my grandmother died— a letter from one of her childhood friends."

I took the letter carefully, as if it might crumble in my fingers, and read what had been written more than forty years ago.

> *I had such a strange dream last night. In the dream my mother was standing in front of me and reaching her hands toward me. I wanted to grab them but I knew that something was wrong. She had a dark dress on, and she was standing in water, in the middle of a great ocean. Suddenly a huge serpent came up out of the water by her side. It looked as if it was whipping up the water with its tail or its body. Although I became very frightened, she didn't seem to notice. She reached her bare arms out toward me, and I thought that she wanted to save me, that I should follow after her. I had the feeling that she wanted to say something to me. And still I was afraid, like a small child. Well, that's not a very nice story for a Christmas letter. So, I'll just close now with yet another wish for a very Merry Christmas and all the best in the New Year. You deserve it more than anyone.*
> *Yours—"Aunt Jenny."*

I placed the letter between us and thought about the woman in the black dress in the water, which all three had described. I tried to picture my foster mother standing and reaching out to me—but it was impossible. She would never have reached out her hands; she would have just yelled, *Jump, Marie—the water will hold you up!*

And then she would have laughed loudly at my fear, while I kept standing on the pier, just as I always did. While all the other children jumped in. But I would still be standing there, the last one, like some crooked reed, swaying in the wind.

He folded up Aunt Jenny's letter and placed it back in the blue envelope with the Christmas seals on it. But the man in the Lighthouse wasn't finished, even though he must have known how uncomfortable I felt. I was either involved in some half-baked comedy or else I needed to take these messages from the past seriously—without knowing why.

He lifted yet another envelope off the table, one I hadn't seen before. "I got this one from a woman I took one of Ove's seminars with—just before I got fired from the DBC." Suddenly he smiled, as that implied some kind of competition—with Ove playing the losing role.

"It was at a Danish vacation center in Gilleleje. Her father had just died, and we started talking."

He lifted two pieces of light blue paper out of the square envelope and handed them to me. "I'd listened to her, and at one point asked her whether his last letter mentioned a dream . . . she seemed shaken . . . because it did."

I felt as if I were locked in a room without any air. For a moment I tried to picture Viggo Larssen engrossed in conversation with a stranger—and I almost felt an absurd twinge of jealousy. I took a deep breath.

Dear Linda, the letter began. I read the dying man's intimate farewell with a certain discomfort, read about his sorrow over losing everything, but most of all, his daughter.

> *Your mother appeared to me last night, at least I think it was her. It was a woman in a long black dress reaching out to me, and at first I had the feeling it might be my own mother. There was something mild and peaceful about the whole thing—like when your mother was still living. Behind her was the ocean, and I think she wanted me to come with her. I think she was calling to me. The only thing that scared me was a shadow in the water behind her, like a large snake, but right at that moment the nurse woke me up.*

I placed the letter on the table, and he slid the two pages back into the envelope, carefully, trying not to bend the corners.

"It's the same dream. Four almost identical descriptions. All four of them died on the very day they had that dream, only a few hours later."

He spoke matter-of-factly, as if he were placing an order at the Daily Market in Ulstrup.

He took out a clear plastic folder with a single piece of paper in it. "This is number five—I discovered it in connection with the DBC, in 2002, while researching a radio documentary on near-death experiences. I never managed to finish it." Again that strange little smile, and I had no doubt that he was picturing his executioner in front of him: Ove. Perhaps with some help from Verner.

"It's the transcript of a tape recording. I interviewed several people, maybe five or six, who had been dead and then brought back to life again. But only one of them had had the exact experience I was searching for. Or the others just couldn't remember it."

He handed me a sheet of letter-size paper with the DBC's logo on it. "The dream was interrupted—and that makes perfect sense, since he didn't die."

I nodded as if that were the most logical claim in the world and read:

> "*Since you asked, something strange actually did happen the night before my heart attack. It was in a dream . . . I was standing out in the water . . . no, my mother, who'd been dead for many years, was standing in the water, looking at me. I think I was standing on land, maybe back on the shore. Maybe I was a small boy again . . . because she was reaching out to me and calling to me. Well, she wasn't actually calling, because there weren't any words. It just felt like she was calling. As I was about to step out into the water to grab her hand, I saw something*

moving in the water . . . and I became very frightened.
But right then I woke up."
"You saw something in the water?" It was the interview-
er's question (Viggo, but younger). *"By her feet?"*
A long pause followed, indicated by over one and a
half lines of periods.
Then the man spoke again. *"No, but I recall that the*
water around her seemed a little restless. Even the sea
behind her was gray and completely still."
"Restless?"
"Yes. I'm not certain. But there was something . . . otherwise
she was standing perfectly still."
"What do you think it meant?"
"I don't know . . . well . . . [slight grin] . . . the trite read-
ing is easy enough. I had my heart attack the very next
day. She was calling me to her. But it . . ."

The transcript ended there.

He placed it back in the clear plastic folder and took a new one
off the table. "Here's number six. I found it at a secondhand dealer on
Ryesgade—there are a lot of small shops on that street. I was always
looking for bargains there. It was just a piece of paper attached to an
article on dream interpretations, lying in a box. The dealer said the box
had just come in with other items from an estate." Viggo stopped talking and handed me a torn, crumpled piece of loose-leaf paper.

"The article was only two weeks old, so I decided to investigate the
matter. It was a 'John Doe'—a person who had died with no relatives—
his body was found in an attic somewhere in Guldbergsgade. The people
at the church office couldn't tell me anything. They could only confirm
that he was dead and that they'd found the note and the newspaper article
on him. For a long time after that I would look for obituaries where they
were searching for relatives and cut them out of the newspaper. Sometimes

I'd manage to get their home address from my friend at the church office and"—Viggo Larssen hesitated—"and if it wasn't too hard, I'd break in and investigate the place before any belongings were removed." He bowed his head, a bit shamefully, I could tell. "I never found anything."

I almost laughed, both at his facial expression and from sheer relief. I, who had been breaking into his home for several months now, had found a surprising partner in crime.

The sixth omen consisted of the shortest description yet—but a shiver still ran up my spine. The crooked handwriting was clearly authentic and offered the same vision in a shortened form, the one I now knew by heart. At the top was written *To be investigated,* and just below it:

> *Strange dream last night. Woman in black. My mother?*
> *Water, sea. She was reaching out her hands. Water foam-*
> *ing around her. Until it all turns white. It's a serpent. I*
> *want to run away but it's too late. She's calling to me.*

We sat in silence for a long time.

Then he reached out and placed his hand on the last object in front of us: a small, somewhat shrunken black book.

It was the logbook I had seen before, the one that had washed ashore along with all the other wreckage when the good people of the cape—one cold, hungry winter—had turned to poaching after luring the distressed ship onto the rocky reef and to its demise out in Hell's Deep.

The old lighthouse keeper had carefully hidden the book in a hollow in the wall, where Viggo had found it that New Year's night.

"I had decided to simply live with the knowledge I had accidentally acquired, to live with these omens . . . these dreams. A man with my reputation as"—he was about to say "strange" but kept going—"no one would ever believe me. And I had no idea where it was all leading. I'd spent time in a mental hospital and now I was on disability and could only get a little occasional freelance work."

I nodded, and for some reason I placed my hand on top of his, which was still lying on the old ship's log. My heart skipped a few beats out of fear, but he didn't respond—he didn't pull his fingers away abruptly or suddenly get up and leave.

"My friend Verner—from high school—visited me a few times. He'd become a big deal by then at the DBC. Head of the news bureau. Yet he still had . . ."

". . . a soft spot," I suggested. "For you."

His fingers trembled for a moment beneath mine. "Yes. A real softy . . ." Was he describing himself or Verner Jensen? ". . . and he knew from my work—on our magazine and on the documentaries—that I had an interest in death and . . ." He paused again.

". . . that kind of thing," I prompted.

"Yes. And one day he said that he could find me a place to relax, to think and write—I think he believed I was going crazy again. I was drinking a little too much, rambling on about the old days . . . about . . ."

". . . death."

"Yes. Verner said he came from a famous old family out on Røsnæs and that he could get me a lighthouse to stay in. And that's just what he did. I arrived on May first." He smiled, as if it were a clever joke to spend the old workers' day of solidarity on moving out to hell. Alone.

I didn't say that out loud, however.

"I've only been back two times. When we went the other day—and then in August, after I got that anonymous letter that you sent about the Widow. I went back to talk to her—this was in the middle of August—I don't know if the police know that yet. She was the only one I saw, and the whole thing ended quite awkwardly. She cried, and I think in the end I just stood there yelling. She wouldn't admit to any knowledge . . .

about anything. Suddenly she started talking about little Arrow. It's strange because there was an empty birdcage on her windowsill."

"You haven't left here since then?" I asked carefully.

"No."

"Not even to . . . celebrate New Year's with your old friends?" It was a stupid question, I know that, but I had my reasons.

"No."

He took his hand off the old logbook. "But on New Year's Eve I got the worst shock of all." He looked lost, like a person who can't see his way out of the abyss, and I was about to reach out to him again. "I thought I'd finally escaped it . . . my fixation on death, or whatever you want to call it, the omens I'd stumbled upon. As if I were the only one. As if I'd been chosen. And then I found this one . . ."

He handed me the old logbook.

I carefully opened it.

"It was written right before the shipwreck. I know the date because locals still remember it. It's a silent, terrible secret—a feeling of guilt that people on the cape have shared for generations. It's one hundred and fifty years old."

"Where . . ." I didn't need to finish the logical question.

"Here." He pointed under the table. "Right here. I was a little drunk. It was New Year's Eve, late in the afternoon. I had my reading glasses on, and suddenly the left lens fell out. It does that frequently. Always the left one. I don't know why."

I nodded as if it were the most natural thing in the world.

"It fell on the floor, so I started crawling around looking for it. Suddenly I noticed something strange about the wall, right above the baseboard. There was a loose stone. I pried it out, and there was a rather large space behind it. The book was in there. The old lighthouse keeper must have been in on luring the ship onto the reef—that's how he found the book. It's bad luck to destroy a dying man's last words—everyone knows that—so he hid it, someplace where no one would ever find it."

Viggo looked up. "But I found it. It was a terrible shock. Death—or whatever the hell it is—had found me, even way out here . . . at the end of the world." He stopped for a moment.

It wasn't like him to talk so intensely. And he usually never cursed.

"I only read the ending, but that was enough. I think I sat there in the dark all night long. I didn't fall asleep until it was getting light—and when I did wake up, I heard about the Widow's disappearance."

That last comment seemed to have no connection to the rest of his story—unless he had connected the two things subconsciously.

I didn't dare ask.

"This was written by a ship's mate. A poor wretch. Right before the ship went down and he drowned."

I leafed slowly, page by page, through the beautiful old logbook. About midway through, the entries ended—on May 17, 1872. That must have been the day his ship—a three-mast schooner—was lured into running aground near the Lighthouse.

I knew where the shipwrecked mate's final words were leading me.

> *I must have eaten too much, because I had the strangest dream last night. My dear mother was standing in a black dress a little out in the water. She was waving and calling to me, as if she wanted me to come to her. At some point the sea became very rough, like in a fairy tale, and the water was whipping up around her legs as if it were alive. A large serpent rose up behind her, and for a moment I thought it would coil around her, but the only thing it did was stare at me, and my mother started reaching her hands toward me again. I want to tell Elise about it. She can usually interpret that kind of*

thing. I miss her and am going up to the bridge now. The weather is rough and we are in danger of hitting a reef. If we miss even one flash of the lighthouse, it will be fatal on a night like this.

I sat for a long time, staring at the open book.

At some point the sea became very rough, like in a fairy tale, and the water was whipping up around her legs as if it were alive.

On top of the previous descriptions, the unlucky sailor's words were enough to make my heart beat hard and fast.

This time it was Viggo who placed his hand on mine, still lying on the logbook.

"You're the first person I've shown all of this to."

I sat motionless, breathing heavily, my heart beating fast.

"Seven people's statements, with decades between them. Men and women who were nowhere near each other—who didn't even know of each other's existence. Yet they all describe the exact same thing, a dream vision, with the exact same images . . . and all of them die the very next day. Some of them even have the feeling that it *is* an omen of death."

He made the whole thing sound so dramatic that I could almost hear him as the young reporter who used to rave about conspiracies and plane crashes and the Palme assassination.

Yet the seven descriptions in front of me didn't seem fake. I could always sense that kind of thing—a skill I'd acquired from the ladies in the foster home where I'd grown up by the sea.

Viggo Larssen had stumbled onto something no one had ever seen.

I took another look at Viggo Larssen's seven documents. Books, letters, a discarded piece of paper.

Releasing my hand, he gathered up the papers. "Number eight—that's me. I had half of the dream as a child, but without the most important part . . . the serpent." Viggo Larssen wasn't even smiling. "But I certainly don't need to wait for it. I don't need any more proof. A warning exists, a strange omen of death—that I have accidentally stumbled upon."

"Have you tried—"

"—telling anyone? Yes, I talked about it at Sankt Hans—to the psychiatrist—and of course I wound up with some psychologist rambling on about delusions and obsessions and involuntary muscular movements, and about all the visions I had as a child. And all of that's certainly true. No one knows better than I do." He stared out the lighthouse window for a moment. "As I child I was always walking around with my face contorted . . . every other moment my eyes would be squinting, and I couldn't help it. You've seen people with those kinds of facial tics. You have to experience it to understand it." He paused for a moment. "I managed to stop it—even almost hide it—but it just vanished into myself. This is the only tangible explanation I've ever come up with. And no psychiatrist can conjure it away." He placed his left hand on the small pile of books, papers, and letters, all of which contained what Viggo Larssen called the *Omen of Death*.

I wanted to touch him again, but I didn't. It reminded me of my own dreams, where I was always wandering on the edge of a cliff, on a footpath so narrow that only a child could walk on it without falling down.

"It's all incomprehensible—if it's really true," I said, hating the matter-of-fact tone of my voice. "If people . . . believe . . . that . . ."

". . . that they're getting a warning about their own death—and that the warning is conclusive . . ."

". . . all kinds of panic would ensue." I finished the chain of thought.

"That's why I don't know what to do. That's what I wanted to ask Teis and the others about—but apparently none of them took it seriously. If it's true, then I've discovered something of the utmost importance . . . maybe even something that, as Teis would say, unites all dimensions—or stems from the theory of everything, the belief that everything exists forever and that's why—" He stopped, hopelessly.

I understood why. But I had to warn him. "You absolutely can *not* ask some sworn conspiracy theorist to help you explain any of this—"

"Unless he's right—about the towers."

I closed my eyes.

He could feel my desperation. "Yes, I understand the problem. But to claim, in any way, that people receive warnings about their own deaths . . . even if it's true . . . might result in mass panic. Many people will believe it. I believe it myself."

For a brief second he looked almost apologetic. It was absurd.

"Who else have you told about this . . . theory?" I couldn't bring myself to call it anything even resembling actual fact.

"You," he said.

"Other than me?"

"I've contacted those three—Verner, Ove, and Teis—and I told Adda when she was here. Otherwise, no one."

"But your letters may have been read . . . or passed on to the police. You know the Blegman brothers, you knew the Widow. You chose the very same day she disappeared to start ranting about death omens and doomsday theories in the letters you sent and—" I stopped. He didn't deserve my anger, which stemmed from frustration, which stemmed from concern, which stemmed from something even deeper, something I never wanted to articulate.

He had the greatest motive of all of them. And maybe he also had the soul of a madman.

He was trapped—even if he thought he was safe in his lighthouse on the cape at the End of the World. That was merely an illusion in our society of surveillance, which the Blegman brothers had practically invented. Surely Viggo Larssen's telephone had already been tapped.

And his mail was probably being read, too. In fact, satellites might be pointed right at us at this very second. The old paranoia, a remnant of the Left's heyday, had turned out to be much worse than anyone had ever imagined.

At that moment I had no doubts: they'd be coming to get him in just a few hours—and they'd be taking a good hard look at me at the same time.

They couldn't figure out the web of coincidences. How the children from Søborg were connected—and what had really happened.

Yet they could see the threads as clearly as the connections in a Facebook group, and they were coming for us. Of course they were.

"The police will say you're crazy. And they'll find out that Peter Blegman ran down your mother."

That's all I needed to say. But he'd already thought that for a long time now.

PART V

Vengeance

CHAPTER 23

The Lighthouse on the Cape
Friday, January 23, late morning

You can't just hop across the Giant's Footprint.

One time I counted my steps, and it took me forty-four steps to traverse the entire width of the foot.

I stopped abruptly and let myself sink behind the shrubs, as I'd done before when I wanted to observe Viggo Larssen without him knowing it.

They'll be here today. I'm never wrong about that kind of thing. I met a high-ranking chief of police once before in my life, and I had no doubts; they all think alike, whether they wind up as heroes or villains in their own tales and legends.

I thought about Viggo.

Everyone has a secret life, a deep dark cave inhabited by strange shadows, filled with terrifying thoughts and feelings. We don't tell anyone else about it. We carry it with us from birth to death, and at times we think we're the only ones with such warped imaginings.

During our four years working together at the nursing home, Agnes told me some of the strange stories she had encountered.

> *As a pastor, I met a woman who promised her child they would die at the same time. The girl had lymphoma—she was six years old. They had to tell her that she wasn't going to survive. So the mother lay down next to her daughter and held her frightened body and promised to die with her so that she'd never be alone. The child died. But the mother lacked the courage to fulfill her promise. She lost it when it really mattered. And so today she suffers from a constant feeling of guilt. In a way, she's also dead.*

The girl from Søborg had been fascinated by all the strange stories she encountered, and she became an expert at telling them. I could see why the boys were so fascinated with her in Søborg—Viggo and Verner and Ove and Palle and Poul and maybe even Teis—as well as all those government officials who had watched her bury the Widow the other day.

She once told me about an older man who had promised his much younger wife that he'd commit suicide if he ever became incurably sick and in need of constant care. He did get sick, but in the end he reneged. So she sat by his deathbed and told him off, because he had betrayed his sacred promise.

I was shaken. What were these dark sides people revealed when they felt safe in the midst of faith?

I've never understood people who doubt the existence of God.

Darkness. The final curtain. Nothingness.

No person could have thought that up.

It seems to me that even the most objective person must acknowledge that everything is possible in this universe we inhabit. Especially since no one can answer the most simple, basic questions of existence: Where do we come from—and where are we going?

Only the deluded would claim that they understand why an ordinary planet in an ordinary solar system in a totally ordinary galaxy settled into the exact point in space and time that the cosmological expanse had provided for life. I could understand why millions of people felt the need to find something more, something greater, than the disappointing explanation for life (and death) we've been given—even though their quest often ends in catastrophe. Just look at Christianity, which is always preaching kindness and yet has gone off the rails countless times throughout history. We're merely following the lead of an endless row of players that started with the fable about those two escape artists banished from the Garden of Eden when things got too tough. That paradise in which the snake was warning not of an ending but a beginning.

Viggo Larssen's curious vision was the closest I'd come to what might exist somewhere else . . .

. . . some kind of connection, a link between past and future, a pattern. Of course it had to exist somewhere, if you only looked hard enough. God and his two henchmen would never let such an opportunity for amusement slip by . . .

. . . the first glimpse of such an unknown world would have to be astonishing, almost incomprehensible.

CHAPTER 24

The Lighthouse on the Cape
Friday, January 23, afternoon

I wanted to ask, *Are you still in love with Agnes?*

But I couldn't get the words out.

We walked together out to the cliff, along the rocky beach, across the jetty, with our wet shoes and chilly fingers; I'd never walked side by side with him before.

We were silent; it was, quite literally, the calm before the storm.

Guests were on their way.

***

The Homicide Boss arrived on foot, which didn't surprise me.

He stood there waiting for us as we climbed up the steep steps from the beach.

We sat at the small round table in the living room, just inside the lighthouse door, and the Homicide Boss looked around inquisitively. Like a hunter investigating his prey's territory.

He asked me only three short questions, though he must have known he wasn't getting any real answer to any of them.

I hadn't read the will.

I didn't know where it was.

I just happened to be a night watch at the nursing home. I didn't know the Widow at all.

No one is better at lying.

He ended the conversation with two more questions—also without getting any real answers. "Why have you moved to Røsnæs . . . do you know each other?"

Of course not. It's just a coincidence. Some might call it Destiny.

Behind my harmless, somewhat flippant remark, I was half paralyzed by fear that the policeman might start asking me for some form of identification or about my earlier life. But so far he'd been satisfied to place me at the nursing home simply as a former night watch. And that was definitely a mistake.

As he turned toward Viggo Larssen, I sensed something sharp in the air, an impending fear coming from the man who had always been a bit strange, both as a child and as an adult.

I immediately came to his recue: "I'm sorry, I forgot your name . . . ?"

Caught right on the cusp of his first question, the Homicide Boss turned toward me. "No one ever calls me anything but the Homicide Boss."

"But surely you must have a name?" I knew I had him. To say no would sound stupid. To remain silent would be the same as running away. And he was the hunter, after all.

He sat there for a moment. Then he said his name, and I stared at him.

He'd replied: "Jens Olsen."

For some reason, I was shaken.

"Yes. Nothing too strange. Only the cases are strange."

All three of us laughed—at least I think we did—I didn't actually hear a sound.

"Viggo Larssen, how well do you know . . . or *did you know* . . . the Widow?" The Homicide Boss wasn't allowing any more diversions. He had stepped out into the open landscape, lifted his bow, and taken direct aim at his victim.

I could see Viggo's thoughts fly from his head in one crystal clear and unavoidable realization: he would never manage to escape, not this time. He was already a wounded man, a man fixated on death, and for that reason alone an obvious suspect in the case the policeman had come to investigate—and possibly solve.

He didn't respond. The policeman knew the answer.

"You recently sent letters to three of your oldest friends from Søborg, letters in which you"—he let the question hang in the air for a moment, just as a true hunter would enjoy watching the arc of his arrow's flight in slow motion—"mention the Widow and fantasize about visions and omens of death. Why?"

Viggo didn't respond. The chief of police nodded, as if even this answer would have lacked any newsworthiness.

"I've read the letters. You visited the Widow. You saw her on the eighteenth of August in 2014. Why?"

If Viggo was wondering about the Homicide Boss's knowledge, he didn't show it; anyway, his response was only an extension of the other missing answers.

"I know this from the employees—from the home's chaplain, Agnes Persen, who saw you go in. Do you deny it?"

Viggo Larssen shook his head. I could read the enormous shock in his eyes. The hunted knew that something was seriously wrong but could no longer see where the shot might come from.

"Have you visited her before . . . have you ever seen her since your childhood?" Once again the Homicide Boss had asked two questions in a row, and Viggo shook his head to both.

"So why now?"

"I got a letter."

"A letter?"

The man in the Lighthouse told him about the anonymous letter that had connected the Yellow House with his mother's death.

"Do you still have this letter?"

"No."

"We know about that case. The perpetrator was never found. Did the Widow know anything?"

"Nothing."

"Have you been there since?"

"No."

"You're lying. You were there on the first of January. Except that time you were lucky enough not to be seen—but you were there. You kidnapped the Widow—and then left her to her fate."

Viggo Larssen stared at his captor. "No." He glanced at me, as if looking for support where none was to be found.

The Homicide Boss leaned across the small table. "I'm investigating a murder in a family you have every reason to despise. You've been at the nursing home, you think the Widow had something to do with your mother's death—and your sending letters with death fantasies in them in the days following her disappearance is the icing on the cake."

Viggo was here both New Year's Eve and New Year's Day. That was all I needed to say. But then they'd start looking into my background, and they'd find out about my past. My testimony would be smashed to pieces, like the kindling lying scattered over the Sea Witch's forest. All of it worthless.

Also, I didn't really know that he was here.

"Agnes—the chaplain—says that you read *The Little Prince* all the time as a child. That you were obsessed with that book."

Viggo stared at him uncomprehendingly.

"We found *The Little Prince* in the basement, right by the Widow's feet. She'd had it in her bookcase. The murderer took it down there with him."

Viggo Larssen bent his head and closed his eyes—his one and only answer. And in that moment I noticed, paradoxically enough, hesitation in the aging detective, something instinctive, perhaps some learned wisdom, something that had enabled him to stick to his decision to investigate the two most powerful men in the realm in connection with their mother's death. He hesitated. For only a tenth of a second. Though Viggo didn't notice.

Right then we heard a car pull up. This time Viggo's almost supernatural senses hadn't warned him—not of the sudden arrest nor of the patrol car as it rounded the Lighthouse, stopping right outside the door, as if to prevent any sudden attempts to escape.

Viggo and I stood up at the same time.

The Homicide Boss remained calmly in his seat. I couldn't understand how he'd been able to time this whole thing so precisely—and so dramatically. The four policemen in the vehicle had arrived at the very second the chief of police arrested the man in the Lighthouse.

***

Office of the Prime Minister
Friday, January 23, evening

The prime minister was sitting behind his desk, his brother standing by the window, staring out at the city's spires and red-tile roofs.

The Homicide Boss stood by the door with his hands behind his back.

"He's crazy," said the Homicide Boss, "but that's not the same as being homicidal—or a murderer. He's totally fixated on death, but so are many other people . . ."

He was interrupted by the head of state. "First you arrest a man in some fucking lighthouse with pomp and circumstance . . . and then you say that it may not be him after all?"

"I'm saying he *denies* having been at the nursing home. We have no eyewitnesses, no actual traces of anything connecting him to Solbygaard on Thursday, January first. All we have is his possible interest in the Widow and his fantasies about death and omens—and *The Little Prince*, which he has been reading all his life. But who hasn't?" The policeman shook his head. "I may be the only one who's never read it . . . but I'm reading it now." He shrugged his shoulders. "A little long-winded, not exactly Stieg Larsson."

The prime minister scowled as if the chief of police had made a bad joke.

His brother turned away from the window. "This man, Viggo Larssen . . . he talks about some fucking *omen* that all people will get one day—about their own *death*—that is *not* normal!"

"No," said the Homicide Boss. "But it's not any kind of—recognizable—motive for murder." There was a hint of sarcasm in his voice, which Number Two would have appreciated. "In a way, we can't even prove it's a lie. If it exists, it would be a secret people take with them to their graves. And we can't interrogate the dead."

The prime minister pounded his enormous fist down onto the desk. "Don't make a fucking joke out of this! You need to find the . . . the . . . *shithead* who has done this to her!"

The Homicide Boss was unimpressed by this outburst. Taking two steps closer to the desk, he wished that Number Two were by his side—like in Bakken, when they were young (not that he'd say anything—he rarely did—but just as backup).

"Tell me—one more time—about the accident with your little brother. Maglegårds Allé, 1963," he said.

For a moment both men stared blankly at him. "What in the *world* does that have to do with this case?" The minister of justice's voice sounded like a whisper from somewhere deep in Hell.

"The gate was open that day . . . it usually wasn't. That's what people in the neighborhood told my officers. It's not gossip—or more accurately, it's the *kind* of gossip that rests on the truth. The gate was open, and it normally never was."

"You're saying . . ." The head of state placed both hands on the shiny wood in front of him.

"I'm not saying anything. I'm laying out the facts as they exist—and maybe we'll find a pattern by working together." He was flirting with his own dismissal, which would almost come as a relief at this point. For the first time in his long career as a policeman, he perceived an undefinable shadow. It was, to say the least, something beyond drunk Swedes and burglars in the alleys of Copenhagen. Something different from all his other cases.

"You're implying that someone . . ."

"I'm implying . . . that it's possible . . . and you must have thought so yourselves, a long time ago. Someone who really knew your little brother's habits may have opened that gate—and that got him killed. Maybe it's the same person we're looking for today."

They stared back like two boys on a raft in the open sea.

"At the time the case was investigated, quite discreetly, and I trust that investigation, because it was led by my current second in command. He found nothing."

"So it's possible that—" Palle Blegman stopped. Clearly, the enormity of what needed to be said couldn't find enough air in the large body that had collapsed into the desk chair.

"That someone did it willfully, yes." The Homicide Boss nodded.

"And you think . . ."

"I don't think. I'm laying out the pieces of the puzzle until—"

"—until you solve the goddamned puzzle! Stop rummaging around in our family's affairs. We know what you suspect . . . we know that you've been asking about the will, the inheritance. Right now you think that gives *us* a motive, don't you? We might as well all just be insane . . ." The prime minister stopped there.

The Homicide Boss resisted the temptation to nod. The minister of justice stood motionless, unable to speak. "It might also give someone a motive to take vengeance on behalf of Viggo's mother. When the opportunity presented itself. But we don't have any proof of that."

The room was silent for a long time. It might have lasted several minutes—or perhaps time stood still for what seemed like an eternity.

Naturally, the roar of the bear broke the silence. The prime minister hammered his paw yet again on the desk, and for a moment the whole office seemed to shake before the policeman's eyes. "It's irrelevant— completely *irrelevant*—and it's completely, totally *insane!*"

The Homicide Boss let the two Blegman brothers sense his growing suspicion. For several minutes the younger Blegman had been ghostly white, an almost-invisible presence in the room. The policeman could hear him breathing heavily by his right shoulder.

Now Poul Blegman returned to the land of the living. "You're sick in the head," he hissed.

"Yes, I'm the head of homicide." He didn't even try to stifle his response—actually, he thought it wasn't the worst trait for someone hunting a beast.

"I'll get you fucking *fired* for this." The minister of justice was still hissing.

The Homicide Boss had severed his last lifeline and was now walking directly over the abyss. In many ways it felt like a relief. "You can fire me. But it won't look good . . . and who's to say what I might decide to do in the boredom of my retirement?"

Had Number Two been there, he would have been shocked to hear the deep anger in his boss's voice. He was almost always able to keep his true self in the background, to hide Jens Olsen completely and just be the Homicide Boss. The prime minister waved his arm defensively; surely he realized that firing the policeman would be impossible as long as the two brothers were in such a vulnerable position. To do so before the Homicide Boss had declared that the will had disappeared and couldn't be found would be a catastrophe.

Instead the Bear said, "I take it that all this will remain confidential as long as there's no indication of any . . . verifiable . . . pattern."

The policeman nodded. "Yes, that's where we now stand. Yes." The Homicide Boss wasn't quite sure what the prime minister meant.

Without saying a word, the minister of justice opened the door for the man he had just threatened to fire.

The last thing the Homicide Boss noticed—and told Number Two about in their office a little later, behind a closed door—was the look the two powerful ministers exchanged behind his back. Of course he'd seen it. Heads of homicide aren't just sick in their heads—they also have eyes in the back of them.

What he'd perceived was a flash of guilt, though it might also have been something else: a fear triggered by what he had told them.

Two powerful men who, in their mutual silence, might have realized that they had no idea exactly where they stood.

"And that was your goal"—Number Two sounded quite impressed—"to plant suspicion in both men—suspicion of each other."

The Homicide Boss didn't need to answer. After all, the two men used to go out on patrol together.

***

Verner from Søborg
Tuesday, January 27, afternoon

It was Tuesday afternoon. The stage was set.

And it had changed completely.

On Monday morning the Homicide Boss released Viggo Larssen without asking the court to uphold his three-day arrest.

He simply announced—via the news agency Ritzau—that they were continuing the investigation but had no reason to hold Viggo Larssen in custody.

I understood that his visit to the lighthouse, along with that sudden, almost brutal arrest, had been an attempt to scare Viggo into a confession. It didn't work. They hadn't found anything of consequence during the search, and they returned all confiscated materials upon his release (except for *The Little Prince*).

But Verner Jensen was not going to miss his big chance. He was the closest friend of Viggo Larssen, Denmark's most talked-about man—a man with a story that would captivate the nation. The story about the omens of death, the warnings that had been central to the police's decision to arrest him.

Verner Jensen must have made his decision at the very moment Viggo became Denmark's most famous—or was that infamous?—citizen.

He had smiled at his assistants. He'd found the perfect blend of something totally concrete and totally fantastical—something that struck at the very heart of what had always preoccupied most people: their fear of death, a fear that was only escalating in wealthy societies, along with a thousand new possibilities for healing and prolonging life. Never had so many followed the authorities' ever-stricter dietary guidelines and wellness campaigns; never had so many monitored and checked their health; never had so many allowed themselves to be screened and examined, from head to toe, several times a year in the hope of postponing the inevitable.

Never before had death—the death of others, that is—sold so well on film, in books, and in news broadcasts: the more terrifying, bloody, and bestial, the more the terror triggered responses from those unaffected but content to look on in quivering, crippled fascination. Macabre but inescapable.

Viggo's omens would fit snugly into that movement, predicted Verner Jensen.

So the DBC had hastily arranged a press conference at their head-quarters on Amager—and Verner, along with the company lawyers, had prepared a flawless, analytical examination of Viggo Larssen's documents, one by one.

Three specialists were present in the press hall: an interpreter of dreams, a graphologist, and an expert in forgery from the National Museum. All three had reviewed the material, and all could confirm that they'd found no errors in what had been presented. Their statements had already been taped and would be shown on a large screen at the meeting. Viggo's story would be presented as pure, groundbreaking truth: *People were dreaming of their own deaths.* It would become a sensation, on par with the first visit from an alien planet.

"But isn't this going a *bit* too far?" the chairman of DBC's governing board had asked carefully, framing his concern almost as a warning.

"We're simply presenting the facts. We have the experts. *No one* can explain how such similar descriptions of dreams—the last dream that people have had, people who've never known each other and who've lived in three different centuries—can be so *similar*." That's what Verner's people had written in the press release that would be distributed to all news bureaus, newspapers, and radio and TV stations—and be reported to all social media—when the press conference started. The chairman of the board had refrained from shaking his head, although he felt a bit groggy. It was like being trapped between a dream and reality, this place where the media found itself as it hunted for customers; in his earlier career he'd been head of the Royal Danish Theatre, and he knew the feeling of creating illusions for an enormous public.

Verner Jensen had invited Viggo Larssen's closest friends to the press conference: the three friends he'd sent letters to and, of course, Agnes and me. We were there to protect the man from the Lighthouse from another breakdown and to demonstrate that we believed in him—in his story. The same story the police wanted to use against him to prove he was insane.

But it had backfired. The little man with the enormous theory. All of the drama's compelling aspects, scenes, and speeches were in place.

Less than a day ago, we were sitting in Verner Jensen's mammoth kitchen at his villa in Frederiksberg. On the long oak table in front of us were the letters Viggo had sent. And next to them the seven omens the police had released. Maybe someone in the Ministry of Justice was hoping that their contents would strengthen the case against the man in the Lighthouse, as the newspapers had christened him.

The mood was strangely jubilant. Neither Viggo nor Agnes said a word to each other, and of course I was totally silent. If Ove knew anything about our meeting and what had happened, he didn't show it.

Verner had examined the journals, the letters, the piece of paper, and Viggo's transcript of the documentary interview—all of them containing almost identical descriptions. I couldn't tell if he actually believed the idea that people received a warning about their own deaths.

But no one at the table had said anything about the truth of the idea, either for or against. I could see that had strengthened Verner's decision about the sensational revelation. We had functioned as a mini–focus group; had we immediately turned against Viggo's discovery—with blunt declarations of fraud or madness—so would many other Danes. Our reaction, hesitant or maybe just cautious, showed that despite every-thing, the material was so convincing that you had to think twice before disavowing it.

This wasn't Area 51, the Twin Towers, the Abominable Snowman, the Loch Ness monster, or those enormous boulders on Easter Island (which some said were tossed out of UFOs).

This was far more tangible, all of it lying on Verner's table, right before our eyes.

Wasting no time, he'd gotten experts from both the National Museum and the Royal Library to vouch for their authenticity. He'd received estimates from several accomplished chemists on the age of the two oldest documents: the ship's logbook and the diary from the Spanish Civil War. Both ink and paper were genuine and originated in the time periods indicated; according to the hastily summoned graphologists, none of the handwritten documents had been drafted by the same person.

It meant, beyond any doubt, that the omens were written by seven people who had never known each other, over a span of at least one hundred and thirty years.

Verner had looked at each and every one of us at the table. "I think the authorities will try to prevent this discovery from ever reaching the rest of the world. Maybe with an injunction—so we have to act fast. The press conference is Tuesday afternoon, and we're broadcasting direct—on all channels.

"I think that a story like this might seriously scare people. But there's nothing to do about that—you can't repress the truth. Viggo could wind up a hero, and that's the last thing the Blegman brothers want. They'd much rather have you strung up on murder charges."

He nodded, smiling at Viggo, as if he'd just shown encouragement. Then he got serious again.

"Finally, there's the possibility that the authorities already know about the existence of a death omen . . . and are trying to hide it."

He waved his hand dismissively.

"I can tell what you're thinking: it's far-fetched . . . but it's *not* far-fetched when shrewd officials believe the government can be *blamed* for it. That's the way it's been for decades with all the great conspiracy theories. People believe Bush brought down the Twin Towers. People believe there are aliens living in the desert, underground, in Area 51. Millions of people even believe the moon landing was a hoax created by the authorities. And in the thirties, a dramatized radio report about Martians invading Earth created total panic in the US."

"Like if the little prince came down to Earth and started talking about . . . sheep?" That was my voice. I must have spoken. It frightened me a little. As if I were caught between a fantasy about weird death omens and my knowledge about the boy who had always been weird, maybe even weirder than myself. The boy who had become the center of the weirdest story ever told . . .

Verner didn't respond. At that point—only twenty hours before the press conference—I don't think he had any clear idea how he was going to handle everything. I almost felt I needed to warn him against constructing a huge theory about death that, despite the strange similarities in the documents before us, might just as well be nonsense.

I was up against forces that couldn't be contained: the media's need for stories to feed every agenda—and make the entire country breathless—and also perhaps vengeance. Viggo's innocence would turn the arrow in midair—back toward the two brothers; in the last twenty-four hours, high-ranking anonymous police sources had begun revealing details about the brothers' precarious economic situation. They were going to lose the upcoming election, despite the sympathy they had garnered since New Year's Day. They might even be ousted before then. No Danish journalists had ever been able to derail two top officials at once.

After his first glass of red wine, Ove—almost giggling—said that death had already provided a life-giving source of income for both him and Agnes. So he totally understood Verner's gamble.

Agnes had bowed her head slightly, as in prayer.

Verner, who'd had a sip—or two—and was already intoxicated by the prospect of the sensation he was creating, said, "In a way, the typical

TV viewer is already dead—so he needs to be brought back to life. And that's what we're doing here. We're all dead . . . suffocating on welfare . . . and security. The television has become the absolute center of most families. Boredom is now the greatest sin of all"—he poured more red wine in all six glasses on the table, though mostly in his own— "because boredom means that we aren't *loving* . . . that we can't even *see each other*. That's why those in power, like Palle and Poul, garner the citizens' forgiveness—all they have to do is *perform*, tell their enormous lies on live television. Now we're answering them back. Now the fuckers will get something to go with their evening coffee . . ."

It sounded like the worst kind of armchair philosophy. On the other hand, he was head of the country's largest news organization; he had "muscle," as they'd say at the DBC.

Actually, I never believed he'd dare publicize his crazy theory. But then I remembered a detail Viggo had once confided to me. The staff of the high school magazine used to call him "Jules Verner"—after the author of such tales as *From the Earth to the Moon*, *Twenty Thousand Leagues Under the Sea*, and *Around the World in Eighty Days*—precisely because of his rather strong affection for adventure stories.

***

He stood at the podium in his red sweater.

There were at least a hundred journalists in the hall, correspondents from all the Nordic countries and from Germany, France, England, and the United States.

Verner's little PR army had done its job well.

He began with a glowing defense of his old friend, then fired up his PowerPoint.

One by one, all of Viggo's documents appeared on a gigantic white screen.

First came Viggo's mother's journal.

Then the diary from the Spanish War volunteer.

Then the letter from Aunt Jenny.

After that came the letter from his DBC colleague, Linda.

Then the near-death account.

Followed by the discovery at the secondhand dealer.

And finally—as the grand finale—the logbook from the ship's mate, whose words looked chilling on the enormous screen.

All seven omens of death were up there on the screen. It was overwhelming—impossible to explain away or trivialize in any convincing manner.

The response was the same as what had happened in Verner's kitchen. Absolute silence. No one dared contradict such a crazy theory without having some specific objection. And they didn't—Verner's presentation hadn't left any room for that possibility. Those present had no access to the original material. Almost magically, the very intensity of the theory turned into its justification.

One obvious protest would have been to accuse the DBC of blatant fraud—of falsifying all those materials. The only logical thing was to ask for more proof of authenticity, which would send a signal that they'd already at least considered the notion—that everyone in the hall had, in some way, been bowled over by the documentation.

Verner flashed his trump cards on the screen: the cadre of experts who had confirmed the materials' authenticity, even if they hadn't endorsed the overall conclusion.

People would have to make their own decisions about that.

The serious-looking men—they were all men—had stressed the authenticity of the journals, their age, the writing, and the strange coincidences.

A shiver ran through the room. Verner had been right.

From my seat in the back row, I could clearly sense the discomfort the experts' unassailable statements had caused.

Verner was standing at the podium and smiling.

The most important experts would appear in a large, live TV broad-cast that evening in prime time. In less than three hours.

He promised the attendance of a psychologist, a couple of museum curators, a linguist, a graphologist, a dream interpreter, and a specialist in paranormal phenomena, along with researchers from several natural science faculties.

Irreproachable experts in every field.

***

Panic began to build in the hour following the press conference.

That's the speed with which news travels, which social media had ensured.

The general public was allowed to study the seven texts, all of them separated by time and space but sharing one common trait: someone had noticed the connection that might have been evident since the origin of writing, if only others had had the same luck—or clarity of vision.

"Why shouldn't we be able to sense that kind of thing—and in some cases even dream it?" said a psychologist (who'd been paid a hefty fee) on the evening news.

A neuroscientist added: "The brain is still, on the whole, an unex-plored area. A person's thoughts may possess potential we don't know about—yet."

A physicist specializing in superstrings and black holes said, "The Einstein-Rosen bridge has shown us that we can move through time. More and more scientists now accept the existence of at least eleven dimensions, whereof seven are invisible to our senses—creating the pos-sibility of parallel universes. Anything is possible."

A researcher in paranormal activity said, "Paranormal events are increasingly accepted. Mind reading is a clear example. Quantum mechanics allows for simultaneous occurrences with billions of light-years' distance between them. Nothing is unthinkable anymore."

Verner then appeared on the screen and hinted at the possibility of a conspiracy against the man who had discovered something that the authorities, fearing widespread panic, did not want to share with the public. As if Danes couldn't think for themselves. As if free democratic people needed to be protected from reality. And the truth.

Verner was then interviewed by a famous news anchor who asked the evening's only crucial question: "But couldn't it *all* just be one big coincidence?"

The moment had been timed impeccably.

"Of course it could," said Verner Jensen, bowing his head. A masterful maneuver—and one intended to extinguish all doubts.

CHAPTER 25

Denmark, the next day
late January 2015

At first, news of the sensational story about the Dream, the Sign, the Warning, the Omen of Death (every media outlet had its own name for the phenomenon) split the population in two: the rational, who called Viggo's examples pure bunk—although they couldn't produce any concrete reasoning—and the growing band of uncertain and frightened souls who were easy prey for the examples' similarities and the chosen experts' trustworthiness. That wasn't really so strange, I thought, in a country where faith in authority sets a world record, in an era when all kinds of crazy claims could achieve validity, from wild dietary guidelines to totally undocumented management concepts. Verner's experts had found the only area no one had ever gained control of or packaged as a trendy concept: death.

Over the next few days, there were dramatic developments that even Verner hadn't imagined. He had never suspected that underneath its controlled facade, modern humanity's fear of death ran so deep. Even among the world's happiest people.

Many Danes became terrified. There were reports that several pharmacies in the greater Copenhagen area were already reporting a decline in the sales of sleeping pills. As if people had become afraid to sleep and perchance to dream. As if you could live forever if you could just avoid dreaming.

Even though people were bombarded daily with images of death and destruction, only a small number ever talked to each other about death—and rarely about their own. Not even on the cusp of old age or in the middle of a serious illness. We postponed it, ignored it, suppressed it, and shoved it far out onto the horizon, like a distant cloud formation that would hopefully pass by. Despite our undeniable certainty otherwise.

Some people started to confirm Viggo's documentation with purportedly authentic examples from old journals and accounts from the long-since deceased. Like in the seventies, when TV viewers all over the country suddenly claimed that they could bend spoons and forks just like the Israeli illusionist Uri Geller, who performed his strange tricks on live television.

In those first few days of the dream crisis, any timid voices warning against such a mass psychosis didn't appear until the end of the news. All the TV executives sensed what was unfolding: that people from the land of fairy tales needed fairy tales. The Dream. Even if it were a more gruesome sort of tale than those they'd been raised on.

One skeptic compared the Danes' reaction to the belief that a circle of people could make a drinking glass dance across a table and spell out messages from the spirit world; but the deliberately condescending comparison had the opposite effect, as many Danes actually believed in the spirit in the glass. Also, as Verner Jensen remarked, Danes loved the spirit in the glass in the same way that they loved their monarch. It didn't matter whether or not it was real.

I thought about Jesus, who, according to all documentation, could walk on water, turn water to wine, and make the blind see. All religions were based on such miracles.

The Homicide Boss had called Verner Jensen, whom he knew from a TV series about unsolved murders, and asked him to tone down the drama. He'd sounded a bit shaken, which wasn't like him.

"Don't you believe it?" The news editor had said challengingly.

There was a short pause. "I'm a detective. I deal in facts. Someone playing the lottery can hit seven specific numbers out of almost infinite possibilities—at the same time and almost miraculously—as you certainly know. You see it every week on your television."

"But these aren't *numbers*. They're words. It's the same as teaching seven apes to write and then having them writing the exact same thing. It's impossible."

The Homicide Boss sighed deeply. "Maybe people sometimes dream the same thing for a reason we don't yet understand. Maybe it actually isn't so strange when you think about the billions of people who may have dreamed something totally different—or nothing at all—before they died. Unfortunately, your old friend stumbled upon some very precise coincidences."

The Homicide Boss had placed a slight emphasis on *old friend*.

On the crisis's most dramatic day, several competing media outlets reported about people who'd dreamed about the Omen of Death yet survived in the best of health to tell their stories. Many people saw the dream crisis as their chance for two minutes of television fame, which didn't make determining authenticity any easier. Confusion spread.

I had anticipated that—and Verner must have too; he knew the media's impact, and I knew the power of people's imaginations, not to mention their dreams of being famous.

On the other hand, additional staff had been added to hospital wards for the seriously ill, where anxiety about the dangerous dream had created panic among both patients and caregivers.

The same uncertainty struck the nursing home, and Ove Nilsen was quickly summoned to Solbygaard to calm down several seniors who, with nothing else to do but watch television, had been following the developing story with horror.

Other countries were hesitant to respond. I think they viewed most of what occurred in the land of Hans Christian Andersen with some skepticism. The world's safest, happiest people had been prepping for this new form of self-centered paranoia for about two decades, in their fear of the outside world and their cultivation of the Danish candle, glowing carefree in the middle of the burning world.

As an apology, we would send an F-16 fighter, sometimes even two, to those places we'd rather not visit. The reaction might be called typical for the swans who still felt like ugly ducklings—or who had never actually become swans.

Maybe the other countries' delayed reaction was due to the fact that the reproduced texts, once translated, lacked the same impact as the originals. "People in this little fairy tale land have gone totally berserk," said one news anchor on CNN, and the BBC only made passing reference to the story at the very end of a broadcast. Since people couldn't actually research the visions of long-since-dead people, public opinion leaned heavily toward doubt—thanks to Anglo-Saxon faith in the power of documentation—and the story fell totally out of the news rotation.

On the other hand, the Middle East reacted—through Al Jazeera—with almost resignation over this strange little country and its persistently ungodly behavior. First the Muhammad cartoons and now this theory, perfect for deriding all the world's true and holy writings. In Yemen all Danish dairy products were ripped off supermarket shelves, but then the excitement died down again.

The Swedish prime minister's humor was noticeably worse. He was head of a people who had always been rational, bordering on arrogant, but who had also created a welfare state that believed in trolls and gnomes and small boys who could fly on the back of a goose to the mountains of Kebnekaise and back again. "Someone must be able to kill this ridiculous story . . . *a death omen* . . . a crazy man's *deranged fantasies* . . . *come on*," he said while TV cameras whirred. "Hans Christian Andersen's compatriots have had a collective *stroke*," he hissed, dropping all pretense of Swedish politeness. Like his Nordic colleagues, he feared a mass panic that might affect the well-greased wheels of society and maybe even make the wheels of production turn more slowly. If people were afraid to sleep—or spent half their work hours discussing terrifying stories on social media—it would be felt. And the story hit at the worst possible time—just as the financial crisis was about to turn around.

For days, the seven omens were shared on Facebook and Twitter, revealing their collective electronic power. While the authorities and established media outlets were trying to tamp the excitement down to an acceptable level, the strange story with its dramatic texts and mystical undertones was perfect for sharing, forwarding, and embellishing. Facebook groups with names like *The Death Omen Lives* and *Apocalypse Now* sprang up at lightning speed, and a huge petition demanded immediate answers from governments.

YouTube ran a clip of a TV news editor who, according to his own colleagues, had laughed at Viggo Larssen's Omen of Death at a morning editorial meeting—saying that he'd had the same dream the night before. His candor had come as a relief, and everyone had laughed along with him. Three hours later, a heavy projector fell without warning from the ceiling of a studio and struck the editor, who died on the spot.

No one was laughing now.

Two hours later the video turned out to be a fake, created by a fourteen-year-old boy.

The blessings of the modern age.

Anything could be true—but was just as often false.

***

On the fourth day the Danish government finally took charge of a relatively effective counterattack.

Officials from the top government ministries formed a task force consisting of a bevy of experts stating that Viggo Larssen's examples had been falsified. That anyone could tell that the same person had created them in a relatively short span of time. That the language in the older documents had clearly been constructed recently. Think of all that nonsense about Hitler's diaries, which had been published in *Der Spiegel* but had been painstakingly manufactured. And just look at Viggo Larssen's past, with his hospitalizations and neurosis. He'd been weird since childhood. A band of his old schoolmates had confirmed it. Also, because the DBC had exclusive rights to the story from the very beginning, the counter-response received favorable coverage in a wide swath of competing outlets, with TV 2 leading the way.

It also helped bolster the counter-response when Teis Hanson, the former geneticist and current conspiracy theorist, came forward—not to counter the claims but in blatant defense of his childhood friend's theory. "If we in Denmark cannot accept that there's more between heaven and earth than moths and bumblebees"—no one knew where that came from—"then we are ill off." Only the oldest Danes recognized that last turn of phrase from World War II. "My old friend Viggo is right—but those in power have manipulated our thoughts, so that we can no longer recognize the truth," he said.

He should never have said that. People want to be led but they don't want to hear they've been seduced. And certainly not by a known seducer with bizarre theories.

Teis Hanson's statement was the last straw; the skeptics received ample coverage in the following days. The country's elite had reacted a bit slowly at first, but after Teis's remark they regained control of the nation's slightly eccentric population.

The Tårbæk Club's three highest-ranking officials had proposed a crisis management group, and Palle Blegman quickly agreed. The new task force held its first meeting at the villa in Tårbæk, with the Homicide Boss in attendance, and the same seven men who had been there before. No food or drink was served, and that in itself reflected the dire nature of the meeting.

The retired police commissioner was furious. "Shut that totally crazy story down!"

As usual the prime minister's previous undersecretary led the charge. "We can't allow this . . . this dream crisis, as the press calls it"—he glanced at the editorial director of the largest newspapers in the country—"to escalate. It might hurt our society."

Of course, thought the Homicide Boss, and it could also hurt the campaign against the two Blegman despots, which he had been chosen to execute within the next few days. The story of the Death Omen was an impediment not only to solving the case, but also to finishing off the two brothers.

"People are bat-shit crazy. *Dream omens* . . ." The aging former top official had almost spit all over the same table where they had previously enjoyed those bloodred steaks. "No one's putting me in the goddamned grave because of some fucking *dream* that's never even really happened."

The Homicide Boss thought that was an oddly illogical conclusion.

"We need experts . . ." Now the editorial director was speaking, naturally. In any highly civilized society, people can mobilize experts espousing exactly what they needed to espouse. Any news editor can tell you that.

"We're just a tad late out of the starting gate," said the Ministry of Finance's undersecretary.

The Ministry of Justice's undersecretary defined the Homicide Boss's role, which came as no surprise. "You've had the papers in your hands—these so-called warnings. And as the lead investigator, you have the most credibility, even if the Blegman affair is a tricky one."

The Homicide Boss almost wanted to clap.

The former ombudsman took over. "You're going to appear in prime time, and in all the large newspapers"—he nodded benevolently at the newsman—"and say the whole thing is nonsense. And that you never would have released the material if you thought there was *anything whatsoever* to it."

The Homicide Boss could hear the irritation in his voice; it flew across the table like the beating wings of some invisible bird. These powerful men, who'd been controlling the country for half a generation, didn't understand his (in their eyes) naïveté. Had it been up to them, they would have immediately arranged for the destruction of the idiotic letters and ridiculous journals. Even if they'd documented the origin of the world.

The prime minister's current undersecretary folded his hands calmly. "It's up to you to kick-start the campaign. Your statement is crucial."

He did as they said.

Two hours later he was interviewed by the news boss's in-depth reporters, and three hours later he appeared live on the nightly news.

The mobilization of skeptical experts—from physicians and psychologists to TV celebrities and beloved artists, all of whom called the whole thing a fantastic stand-up comedy routine—worked. More and more stories emerged from the masses and circulated on Facebook and Twitter with the glad tidings that everyone applauded.

I had the dream but nothing happened.

The Homicide Boss was fully aware that his next task—the most important one of all—would need to proceed at the same pace that the dream crisis abated.

***

The Lighthouse on the Cape
Tuesday, February 3, afternoon

The first few days we followed developments from Verner's villa in Frederiksberg.

He was at work most of the time, so Viggo and I had the house—and his enormous flat-screen TV—all to ourselves. Viggo had been advised by the Homicide Boss not to return home, because they feared an aggressive siege of the Lighthouse. Everyone knew its location, and it could become a destination for unknown fanatics: both those who wanted to kill him and his ungodly visions, and those who wanted to praise him as the new messiah with his wonderful revelation.

But now we were back at the cape on Sjælland's westernmost point, in the lighthouse that leaned slightly to the east above us.

I sat in Viggo Larssen's little living room. The door stood open on this sunny morning, clouds passing over the cape and Hell's Deep. Strange people had been spotted all over the cape in recent days. They'd even wandered across the Giant's Footprint; I could see the imprints of their shoes. It was a wonder no one had broken into my house. Maybe even these strange beings—seeking the very epicenter of strange predictions—had noticed my residence's increasingly threatening tilt. The Sea Witch's house beneath the fir trees wouldn't last much longer—not that it needed to—and I knew that better than anyone.

Out in the Lighthouse's parking lot sat two Danish Security and Intelligence agents, who looked like they were freezing, despite their large hunter-green jackets, as they cast despondent glances out over Hell's Deep. These officers had identified the disciples of the new prophet and chased them away. Now they simply guarded the barrier that blocked any cars from driving down the gravel road to Viggo's home.

Exactly a week had passed since the dream crisis began—and a good month since the Widow Blegman's disappearance had alarmed an entire nation.

The man sitting across from me had been at the center of both events. Yet sitting in this tiny seaside residence, I couldn't see any distinct connection between the two cases. The death omens and the Widow's death. Unless . . . and that was a thought I didn't want to pursue, at least until I was alone.

Of course the Homicide Boss had thought the same thing. But so far he had given up on the idea of connecting Viggo Larssen to the Widow's death. I had a weird feeling that might change soon—and a long life had taught me never to underestimate my weird feelings.

Sitting close together, neither of us said anything. That was as it should be. We had never been people of many words.

I thought back to New Year's Eve, when, in a rare fit of confidence—the opposite of my usual patience—I had taken a flashlight and clambered up the cliff to the lighthouse. But there'd been no light anywhere—inside or out. I returned the next morning, and there was still no sign of life.

I tried a third time, late that afternoon—it must have been just as the Widow's disappearance was discovered, sparking alarm in Copenhagen—and the silence was the same. I couldn't sense his presence.

He told me that he had found the journal that afternoon and that the discovery had frightened him so much that he'd sat awake all night. And then he fell asleep. That might be the explanation . . . but of course there was another, simpler one.

He wasn't there.

***

Just like the last time, we had all the time in the world—and yet no time at all.

Maybe that's the feeling lovers have in those seconds when they become one—like two small sparks at the origin of Life.

Viggo and I were made of something different than women and men like Ove and Agnes, a darker substance, like the one that makes the universe expand and contract endlessly. Love never breathes more deeply or more freely than where the darkness is thickest—as the poets have written in untold songs and poems—but that is also the hardest place to find. At least in the real world.

That's what Magdalene had taught me. My disabled childhood friend. She had found me on the cusp of adolescence, and she had used my name, the name no one had heard since, and she said . . .

I've never held a lover in my arms, and that's the most difficult thing of all . . .

I remember that still, after all these years.

Never more than now . . .

. . . on the edge of Hell's Deep, where for centuries the only significant sound has been the screams of those who drowned.

***

I don't know what the DSI agents were thinking, sitting in a Ford Fiesta outside the lighthouse at the end of the world, twiddling their thumbs, their heads nodding . . .

. . . or maybe they thought it just another example of this strange place's weird events . . . seagulls screeching in the night . . .

. . . it shouldn't be possible.

CHAPTER 26

The Lighthouse on the Cape
Wednesday, February 4, morning

I could see the red house in the middle of the clearing in my mind's eye. Like something out of a fairy tale. Agnes and Ove's home.

On such a cool, clear February day, Dyrehaven would be as beautiful as it had been for centuries, looking like a child's drawing, the sun at the very top right corner behind a little marshmallow cloud, smiling down on a fawn nibbling peacefully at a hazelnut bush.

Paradise.

Based on that simplistic first impression, I'd originally pictured the two of them in black-and-white terms: Ove as the cynical and calculating businessman. Agnes as the compassionate, selfless spiritual guide.

That's how I'd defined their respective callings: one forced people into systems and boxes, sucking the very joy out of them, making them mistrust their closest relatives; the other led those seeking more into the fold and held God's very word to be boundless, forgiving, without guile.

But it was never quite that simple.

At the nursing home, she told me all about Ove's plans—his new concept for people's departure from life—which I didn't fully understand. The Widow was selected to play a very special role, and little Adda from the neighborhood offered a glimpse of the cynicism she also possessed—and that may have been there since her earliest childhood. I could imagine her standing there by the hedge when a small boy on a tricycle rode down those concrete steps, her blue eyes fixated on that Donald Duck comic book lying in the basket.

She had helped her husband persuade the Widow in the twilight of her years at that dreary place; they had an almost invincible weapon at their disposal: Arrow.

They needed only one good shot—and of course they hit their mark. The rich old woman had added Eden's New Garden to her will.

Through Ove's foundation, where she held a governing seat, a large part of her considerable fortune would serve as a solid guarantee for realizing the grand project. The greatest expense would not necessarily be the purchase of land at Dyrehaven for construction of a gigantic graveyard but instead it would be for creation of the living wills in a quality and form that would quite literally be eternal.

The very soul of the project. And, in its own way, much more spectacular than Viggo Larssen's death fixation and dreamy omens.

Ove Nilsen wanted to replicate all Danes' life stories in sounds and pictures and in writing—the idea of a "living will" taking on a much greater and far more encompassing meaning than the way people had previously understood it.

In this way, the deceased would be willing their entire existence to all earthly beings, for all time.

The idea was so simple that Ove couldn't stop smiling.

Ove would simply amass all relevant documents about each person's life—from black-and-white photos and old slides to 16 mm films, tape recordings, video, and writings—and supplement all of it with new interviews and footage offering a retrospective of the existence that was about to end—exactly as the old or dying person wanted it described.

He would hire the best journalists and storytellers for that task and then transfer the edited and finished portrait of the deceased's life to a microchip that skilled masons, with help from computer technicians, would embed into the very gravestone, which would be covered with a paper-thin plasma screen attached to the surface like a dense, invisible skin.

The deceased would rest beneath the most beautiful stone with the most beautiful flowers in the most beautiful surroundings, their life preserved in the most beautiful images, writings, and sounds—emanating from a plasma screen and built-in microspeakers.

The entire experience could be activated by anyone—relatives, accidental wanderers, anyone looking for a good story—simply by pushing the small deep blue heart, Ove's logo, placed in the top right corner of the gravestone.

Right where the sun sat on every child's drawing.

Arrow would be lying next to the Widow—and on his stone you would see old black-and-white photos along with 16 mm films. In the final section of his experience, the Widow would talk about her boy; that work had only just begun when she disappeared.

The Widow's will was essential—for Ove, the brothers, and the police. Maybe we all knew that.

But only Agnes and I knew just how destructive it was: we had signed it as witnesses late one morning last August.

She had written her two sons out of her will.

She left most of the fortune they believed was theirs to Ove's concept, to her dream of lying side by side with Arrow, for all eternity. It was a devastating turn of events. Once the will turned up, everything would change.

As the sun slowly rose over the Lighthouse, I saw the fox sitting in the clearing, half hidden behind the broken birch trunks, white before red, death before living, just as it had always been. I recalled the Widow

Blegman's expression when she asked me to make sure everything would go as planned. Six months had passed since the signing of her will that Saturday in August.

Viggo had visited her just a few days earlier—after receiving the anonymous letter I wrote in frustration.

She hadn't slept well since then.

I accepted the mission, and she agreed to pay for everything. I was supposed to find a place to live near the Lighthouse and get to know him. I was supposed to write up a report for her, and then she'd make her final decision. She didn't want to go to her grave without knowing whether she could find absolution on her dead husband's behalf. Both on earth and with God. I understood her well.

I'd hesitated when she handed me the will. I didn't want to take it with me on my trip to the cape. Then she told me why, and I finally took it.

Now, it was sitting in front of me in the Sea Witch's house on day thirty-five after the Widow's disappearance. Such a valuable document should never have landed in a house that was about to crash into the deep and take everything with it.

I thought about the Homicide Boss, who would give anything to have that document, and I had no doubt that something was about to go wrong (I've always been able to sense that kind of thing).

Some evil demon had broken through the first of the barricades we thought were protecting us.

Who was it?

. . . I had no concrete idea.

Where would the attack come from?

. . . I wasn't sure.

How could we stop it?

. . . I had an answer to that last question and could almost hear the fox laughing. The way foxes do.

***

Office of the Prime Minister
Wednesday, February 4, morning

Both Palle Blegman and his little brother had the same feeling. They were at war. They'd known that feeling before, and they had always won.

There was just one difference that they both sensed this time. One difference from all the other times—since their childhood in Søborg and their high school days in Gladsaxe. Their enemy was far greater and stranger than ever before and had no intentions whatsoever of coming forward. It wanted to remain invisible, hidden in the shadows.

Panic across the nation following publication of Viggo's omen had miraculously subsided. Maybe it was that collective survival instinct that surfaces when most needed. Who could live with a potential death sentence hanging over them, day and night? The Danes understood that. For once, we all agreed to reject the fantastical, the supernatural, the easy solutions, and the miraculous concepts.

Rejection of Viggo's dream-visions had been like one massive sigh, slowly releasing all tensions, followed by a feeling of collective embarrassment about the way they'd let it happen—almost accepting death as something that could be foreseen and scheduled.

A pair of formidable warriors, Palle and Poul stood shoulder to shoulder, side by side. When the attack came, they would protect each other, sidestep, block, whirl around, fall to their knees—each parry executed perfectly. And normally they'd survive. But they hadn't even gotten a glimpse of this enemy. Someone had leaked information about their ruined finances to a select group of reporters. Someone had that will, which could destroy them.

Both men were at a loss. Sitting next to each other on that uncomfortable sofa, they looked like two wounded bears no longer capable of standing up. They wanted to crawl away on all fours while waiting for the decisive blow. And if you were searching for even the most indistinct thoughts, there weren't any.

They had run out of ideas.

***

The Lighthouse on the Cape
Wednesday, February 4, a little past noon

I'd made my decision.

But he could never know about it.

We were sitting on the bench, by the open door, where we'd first met, as planned. As usual, he was sitting with his back leaning against the white stone wall. If he was thinking the same thing I was, he didn't say so. We had known each other for just over four months, and I knew that soon we would have to part. And that's the most difficult thing of all.

I took his hand in mine, and he let me, but of course he couldn't answer the question I didn't ask.

Instead I said, "The soul is . . . like a black hole." I took a deep breath. "They exist, but are invisible, swallowing everything around them."

He didn't react to my banal observation.

I wanted to stand up—to wander restlessly, like a ghost, and invoke all his childhood demons—eventually summoning all those ship-wrecked souls out there on the reef, every last one of them, in the hope that they would be able to break through his silence. But I couldn't.

I wanted to say, *People are an endless chaos of peculiarities, fused at the point we call normal.* It might have comforted him.

He wouldn't have answered.

I could have tried to add something a bit more down-to-earth: "Just look at the human body . . . the way it's formed . . . the ears, nose, and toes . . . the absurdly thin neck between massive shoulders and grotesquely large heads . . . just look at the rickety, misshapen body, arms and legs flailing about senselessly."

At best, he would have remained sitting for another moment. And then he would have stood up.

I could have played my final trump card, knowing full well it would never work.

Look at our feet, pointing straight out from our legs, protruding at a totally impossible angle, much too short, much too small, good for nothing but knocking us over at the slightest shove. I would have looked right at him and held his gaze. *It doesn't make any sense, there's nothing about us that really makes sense, and yet we humans can still manage to fall in love with such a construction.*

I released his hand. Although he didn't know it, that was my good-bye. I was his friend.

"May I take your omens home with me? There's something I want to do."

He sat for a long time before he nodded.

"I'll get them myself," I said, standing up.

I needed to be alone in the Lighthouse, just for a moment.

CHAPTER 27

Office of the Homicide Boss
Wednesday, February 4, afternoon

Number Two had never seen his boss so confused.

A word you'd normally never apply to Jens Olsen, who'd left both his real name and his youthful naïveté back at Bakken amusement park and in Copenhagen's darkened alleys.

"I just don't understand how we could have missed it."

On the desk before them lay a blue folder, a dossier, as the police call it. The Homicide Boss's restless fingers danced across it.

A woman, a small girl—a ghost, thought Number Two, *a visitor from Hell.* They should have seen it.

"She was the daughter . . . the foster daughter . . . of the old headmistress. Viggo Larssen's mother knew the headmistress, because as a young single mother, she received help from the Council for Unwed Mothers."

"Viggo's mother was there Midsummer's Eve, June 23, 1971." Number Two nodded somberly. "And she was struck by a hit-and-run driver on her way home. A driver who was never found."

"But most important"—the Homicide Boss's finger drummed on the thick folder—"is the daughter's part in an old case involving the death of at least three old women. She may have killed a neighbor, her own mother, and her foster mother."

". . . and then disappeared." Number Two nodded again. "She had the most innocent name a Danish girl could hope for—Marie."

"Now she calls herself Malin." The Homicide Boss's fingers stopped moving. Number Two knew what he was thinking: they could change their names but never who they were, no matter how much the Creator pulled on the reins. You're chasing and trapping a beast.

The youngest detective in their squad had found the old case file. A search in the electronic database revealed neither the birthdate nor the birthplace of the former night watch at the nursing home—the one who was now living at the Sea Witch's house. Her first name, Malin, appeared in a passport issued in late 2011, but prior to that date it didn't appear in any of the databases the government had so generously supplied to the police.

Not even in the National Registry.

That the youngest detective had found the solution was all the more embarrassing, thought the Homicide Boss. He was the only one who had abandoned all the modern technology and search engines and gone down into a storage room to leaf through old murder files involving elderly women. He'd gone back almost seven years when he hit the jackpot.

The case occurred in Skodsborg, north of Copenhagen. The former headmistress at a famous oceanfront orphanage had been found dead in her apartment. For a long time, the police had only one suspect: the woman's own foster daughter.

At some point she had disappeared from the face of the earth. No one had seen her since, and the case was dropped.

They found pictures and compared fingerprints. There was no doubt.

Marie and Malin were the same person.

"She was clever . . . she devised a whole new identity."

Number Two nodded yet again. "She must have had help. She seemed to know how to play the entire system ever since she could crawl. The Council for Unwed Mothers, social services, government agencies, the National Registry . . ."

"All those records gone. Living in a small apartment in the basement under the administration building at Solbygaard. It couldn't possibly be a coincidence."

"But what's her—" Number Two stopped. *Motive* was such a powerless word; you used it when you didn't have a clue about the truth.

"Well, she obviously has some kind of problem with older women . . ." Once again the Homicide Boss's fingers crawled across the old case file. Nothing but that one similarity matched the new case. No fingerprints, no trace of DNA, no witnesses.

Number Two read his thoughts. "No one ever saw her at the crime scene."

"No one has seen anyone."

"Not Viggo, either."

The Homicide Boss lifted his hand off the old file folder. It said: *Marie Ladegaard.* A name that no longer existed. He understood what his deputy meant about no one seeing Viggo. They'd reinterviewed everyone at the nursing home. This time, holding the copy of *The Little Prince* they'd found next to the dead woman.

No new information had come out of it. But it played a role.

"Viggo got a copy of the book from his mother when Mrs. Blegman's son died in that car accident. Then his own mother was killed by a hit-and-run driver. He's been almost obsessed with death, just like the prince in the book. You could say he's just as strange and lonely."

"He went to the home. He visited her. Back in August. Something happened between them. Our witnesses say that he seemed quite upset when he left. The Widow never talked about it."

The Homicide Boss nodded. "But . . . which one?"

"Viggo or Malin?"

There was no way back. If they sat on their hands, doing nothing— and that got out—it would be worse than making a mistake. The brothers would be furious, and the media would crucify them.

They had to make a decision.

The Homicide Boss sighed. "The sheep has eaten the flower . . . or maybe not . . ."

Number Two stared at his boss. He'd had his face in that little book they'd found by the Widow's feet for too long now.

They stood up at the same time, an ingrained, inexplicable habit among men who have covered each other's backs for so many years. That's why they didn't need to speak. Or even nod to each other.

***

The Lighthouse on the Cape
Thursday, February 5, early morning

All night long the storm had raged, shaking the Sea Witch's house on the cliff. Every single piece of wood creaked and rattled, and at one point I was afraid the north wind would actually toss me out of bed and onto the floor—if it didn't take my whole home down with me.

As dawn rose I caught a glimpse of the foamy white breakers out on the reef, as the wind came barreling in across the cape with a sound like widows moaning for their long-dead sailors. Of course that was all pure nonsense.

Only a madman—or a refugee like me—would spend the night in such a place and still manage to sleep and dream without any fear. I'd seen dead people, I'd met dead people who were still living, and none of them made any sound. A fact you couldn't simply dismiss. The wind from the deep that struck the house meant life. It would stop soon enough. That I knew.

I turned on my old cell phone and called my new friend. The Homicide Boss.

He got the message he'd been dreaming of getting for almost five weeks. A name . . .

. . . for the beast he'd been hunting.

***

The fox didn't like what it saw. A slipping, sliding human on a neck-breaking crusade across its private hillside, headed straight for its hole. It wasn't that tame.

It recognized me—and it knew what was about to happen. Of course it did.

I destroyed its home with the same determination my foster mother had always sensed in me and feared. The only thing that had stopped her from putting me up for adoption before she died was her fear of what I might do. That a pilot somewhere might lift a hat and see what it hid. Not an elephant—but the creature that had swallowed the elephant.

I stomped all over both of its exits—or entrances—as I watched the fox seek refuge behind the birch trunk farther down the hollow.

The storm had toppled the birch over during the night. It was almost symbolic, lying there like a white arrow across the dark, rotten leaves. Maybe, like the flower in Viggo's book, it was telling me to leave—to go away.

I strode over it, without looking back.

***

Police cars rolled into the Lighthouse parking lot. They swarmed in, as my childhood comic books would have described it.

The Homicide Boss and his Number Two didn't know that they'd arrived too late. Yet again. Viggo said, "She's not here. She may have gone out for a walk." And he pointed, as in a dream, in the right direction. Out toward the deep, out toward the reef.

They found everything I'd left for them on the beach. No more, no less. I'd planned my exit, just as I'd always done.

They found my note with the Homicide Boss's name on it. They found my clothes, my shoes, my jacket of genuine reindeer leather, which my foster mother's assistant had given me when I left the foster home (in addition to my name and my freedom), all folded neatly together, then a trail of footprints in the sand among the rocks (just like in the movies), leading out into the water, directly toward Hell's Deep.

Where else?

The will was lying in a plastic bag that, as a precaution, I had tied shut with three pieces of twine. All quite simple. With a rock on top of it. No one could have hidden the truth from so many witnesses—the beach was swarming with police technicians and detectives in both white lab coats and black uniforms. The Bear would rise up on his back legs, and that useless roar would dissolve into the air, in a comic book on a nightstand in a yellow house many years ago . . .

But cartoon bears don't roar. Only men do.

***

I'm sure that after the police interrogated him, Viggo Larssen hiked across the Giant's Footprint, and over the toppled birch trunk. They had only one theory in the case against him but no evidence, whereas in the case against me they had a confession that was only a few hours old. Written, quite neatly, by hand.

Of course he didn't see the fox's trampled lair, and he'd never know what was hidden there. Still, when he reached that point, he must have wondered where the Sea Witch's house was.

Or—more accurately—should have been.

Apparently, the house had barreled down, at rapidly increasing speed, directly into the place where the surf from Hell's Deep slams the coast. By the time Viggo reached the top of the cliff, all the lumber had been smashed to smithereens, engulfed in all those dead sailors' final breaths. It couldn't be more symbolic—and it satisfied me more than anyone could know.

He probably stood there for some time until the truth finally hit him. His omens were gone for good. I had asked for them, and I had released him from them—they were gone, once and for all.

He trudged back up the slope to the Lighthouse. Only the two DSI agents were still there, sitting in their Ford Fiesta. A sign that the Homicide Boss wasn't quite ready to set him free.

He had walked right over to them and asked them to leave. They rolled down the window but didn't respond.

He leaned forward. "You know everything now." He gesticulated up toward the place where the Sea Witch's house should have been. "She's gone—she's not here anymore. She was spying on me—just as you are—I've always known that. So now . . ." He leaned his forehead against the upper edge of the window, as if there were a kind of intimacy about the metal and hard plastic. "So now I'd like to be alone."

His right eye twitched three times, a sign of what lay ahead in the coming days. Having trained in the Homicide Boss's unit, they understood. They made one phone call—and they didn't need to make any others.

Ten minutes later the Fiesta drove quietly away, disappearing into the woods.

***

My guess is that Viggo was in a state of doubt about everything in those days. Who isn't?

He made his treks out to Bavnebjerg's Cliff and back mechanically, like a cartoon character who has lost his creator. He missed me and sat on the bench, silently, unthinking.

What was he supposed to think? What was he supposed to say?

Every time he tried to describe what had happened, his thoughts changed direction and all logic vanished. Are we ruled solely by chance, or does someone have a hand in it—even just a tiny one?

Viggo's cell phone had rung, and the first words could have been God's if he hadn't had other more divine channels at his disposal: "We know everything."

Know was a very large word, even coming from the head of homicide. *Everything* even more imposing. Viggo Larssen said nothing. Just like the pilot in the desert when the little prince predicted his own death, the snake lying in the sand by his bare ankle.

"We've read her letter . . . it was all very simple."

He said nothing.

"She committed suicide. That was what she wanted."

At that moment Viggo must have sensed who the pilot was and known that the fox on the cliff had never really existed. Only the snake in the sand meant anything.

His mother had circled that short passage about the little prince's death in pencil. How he was motionless and did not cry out—how he fell gently, the way a tree falls.

"We believe she has killed before . . . at an orphanage north of Copenhagen."

The pilot had said he wouldn't leave the little prince.

"We expect her body to wash up on the coast, somewhere in Sejerø Bay, in a few weeks. In the meantime we are working on a psychological profile. We're getting help from the FBI. They're experts at that kind of thing."

The Homicide Boss sounded confident, even a bit proud, and Viggo Larssen understood his logic.

"Her motive was revenge—on your behalf. She had signed the Widow's will, along with the minister at Solbygaard, Agnes Persen. The old woman told them a terrible story about her own husband . . . that he killed your mother. He ran her down that Midsummer's Eve in 1971 and then fled the scene. As revenge for little Arrow's death. First Malin wrote you an anonymous letter in which she hinted at the truth—but obviously it wasn't enough. So she traveled to the cape to tell you the whole story, and she took the will with her. The Widow had been hiding it, because she was afraid the brothers would find it . . . and destroy it."

There was a slight hesitation.

"It's a very special document."

Yet another pause—this one seemed to last forever.

"She couldn't figure out how to tell you the truth, so she took matters into her own hands. New Year's Day at the nursing home . . . in the basement, which she knew better than anyone because she used to live right next door. She knew the old woman would never survive down there, and she wanted to destroy both her and her two sons."

Viggo said nothing.

"A terrible story—from beginning to end." The Homicide Boss hung up.

Viggo Larssen remained sitting with his back against the cold lighthouse wall. He missed her. Suddenly it seemed as if he could smell her clothes and her skin. She always smelled like a mix of seaweed and sand, he thought. Or maybe that was just the sentimental, half-faded memory of an abandoned man.

He'd never thought of himself as sentimental.

He could see the bushes on the edge of the cliff above the Giant's Footprint, where Malin used to crouch in hiding. He'd spotted her there on the very first day. He was just waiting for her to find her own time—and now that time had passed before she'd ever found it.

He sat on the bench and stared into Hell's Deep. He missed her with an intensity he didn't understand. Why did she do it—to save him?

He knew she hadn't killed anyone. Maybe herself, but not the Widow at Solbygaard. She couldn't have—she was on the cape at that time. He'd heard her in the thicket—the wind was in the east—late in the evening.

Some children dream mild dreams, as in the book about the prince; they dream about a flower or a friend who can ultimately be tamed, but they don't ever move on. Others dream about a world much larger than the small planet the pilot describes in the book. Eventually, they will fall over the cliff, just like Malin, just like the doomed Sea Witch's house. If it had ever even existed.

***

Office of the Homicide Boss
Thursday, February 5, afternoon

The Homicide Boss had just spoken to the man in the Lighthouse on the red phone with the top secret number. He hung up and turned toward Number Two.

They still hadn't published the Widow's final testament. Of course not. Here, behind closed doors, they were both puzzled. Not for the first (or last) time, but in an oddly united way.

They had a motive—a violent yet logical motive—and they had a murder.

But something didn't quite make sense.

There was something . . . something that they couldn't see.

"We have her letter . . . it was lying there on the beach."

The beach wasn't really a beach. Just a pile of sharp rocks driven into the perpetually wet sand. But that's where it had been found.

"And we know that in an earlier life she was suspected"—the pause was quite long—"of having killed other elderly women."

All people are left alone in the end. With no way out, like the fox's smashed lair and the nursing home's airtight cellar. Closed in for all eternity. If I could have taken part in the conversation, I would have said so.

"It never came out . . . what really happened back then."

"But she vanished."

His deputy couldn't deny that fact. It appeared in the files about the Kongslund Affair, so-named after the orphanage where the mysterious incidents had occurred.

The Homicide Boss frowned. Something was still wrong. He leaned over the old folder with the mysterious woman's dossier. Something was missing.

***

The Lighthouse on the Cape
Friday, February 6, noon

He was cold, really cold—as he had been on that very first day when she'd appeared out of the woods and sat down next to him on the bench.

He just didn't know who was playing the pilot and who was playing the prince. They thought they had all the time in the world. Who doesn't—here at the end of the world?

His friend Verner had taken the bus to Ulstrup and then walked the rest of the way, through the Sea Witch's forest and out to the Lighthouse. Maybe, in his fall from grace, he rediscovered a much younger version of himself. The DBC had suspended him. Later the word was changed to *released*. Men like Ove take care of those kinds of details. By mutual agreement. Far greater powers than Verner's had signaled his impending demise; he'd frightened the entire nation—so much so that the Blegman brothers had almost emerged as heroes.

"It was Teis who did it, wasn't it?"

For a second Viggo thought his friend was talking about the Widow's murder.

"Teis who killed the story"—that was a journalist's expression that Viggo understood—"like the coward he is . . . and always has been."

Teis had gone to all the Danish media when the counterattack began.

"There's this thing called . . . the Tårbæk Club . . ."

Viggo turned toward Verner. He'd been out of the business for a long time.

"It's a group of top government officials—old and new—a totally informal group, naturally, but no less powerful. They would never accept the nation divided, neither the living nor the dead. So they paid our old friend Teis to come forward."

Viggo didn't respond. He remembered the fat, teased boy as odd—and that was a kind of comfort. He didn't view him as powerful.

"I know this from . . . sources who would never say so openly." Verner looked up, as if all journalists' sources had a divine character. "They knew that his support would send your story right back . . . where it came from . . . out into the stratosphere."

"Maybe he's the only truly interesting one out of the five of us from the neighborhood—because he *gave up*—after he tried."

"Tried?"

"He defended another student in sophomore year—don't you remember? And he got beaten up for it." Verner shrugged his shoulders. "By Palle. But it was Ove who took care of the rest of it. He broke him. Simple logic."

Viggo didn't respond.

Almost a minute passed. "Of course Teis became a traitor—to his own friends. How else could it go?" Verner shrugged again. "Anyway, he hated you in that way one weird kid hates another. So there's really nothing that strange about it."

They sat in total silence for a while on the bench—or maybe Viggo had never actually spoken, because Verner suddenly turned toward him and said, "What . . ."

It's the wild who are innocent, and that's where we make a mistake. The tame become vain and calculating, and they can no longer see beyond themselves.

Did Viggo actually say that out loud? Maybe a fissure had developed in one of his thoughts, and certain words just slipped out. His tics had gotten much worse.

Afterward they walked out to the water's edge, just as they did when they were boys, strolling along the beach at Hornbæk in front of the high school girls.

"What . . . ," repeated Verner, as if being fired had, in one fell swoop, robbed him of any clear thought process.

This time Viggo must have spoken. Mostly to himself, but still. He looked up at the Lighthouse on the cliff; they were on their way back. "It was just something she often said. I don't know why . . ."

"She must have meant the Lighthouse." Verner had resumed his role as rational observer.

"Yes."

"Her childhood home was certainly nothing to write home about."

Viggo was referring to the orphanage by the Øresund. About the mysterious dead women. All of which the Homicide Boss had told him. Still, he thought Verner's remark seemed a bit clipped.

"Her house out here was nothing to brag about, either."

Glancing at his friend, Viggo said, "She thought so. She always said, 'I'm living between Paradise and Hell, and that's as it should be.' She meant Hell's Deep and—"

"—and the white tower where her prince lived. Were you screwing her . . . I mean . . . were you two together?"

A typical remark in that world Viggo had left but that Verner was still in—even when he was walking on a cape in a forest a king had cursed. The simple questions were always the most important.

"She certainly had the right to expect something. A man in a big, impressive lighthouse. Alone. Did you think she was pretty?"

Viggo didn't say anything.

They walked up the steps to the garden in front of the lighthouse.

"I think she loved me." Carried by the wind, his voice betrayed him.

Verner stopped on the next to the last step and turned around. He looked as surprised as Viggo had sounded. "You miss her . . ."

That wasn't a question, and Viggo didn't need to respond.

They sat on the lighthouse bench, a bottle of Rioja between them. Verner poured his own wine when his glass was empty. Which was often. Viggo went to get a new bottle. Corks were scattered on the gravel by their feet.

Finally Verner said, "Do you really believe in . . . all that . . . with the death omens?"

"Yes . . . I believe in it." It was a double answer.

"Do you still have them?"

"No."

"Where are they?"

Viggo Larssen let a faint twitch run across his left eye, like he did when he was a child. "I think the fox took them."

Verner Jensen didn't reply. For him, that was enough of an answer. He had never really believed in Viggo's tale. But a good story is a good story, and when it's as good as Viggo's was, no one in his profession—his former profession—could blame him for pursuing it.

"Neither rain, nor snow, nor sleet."

"What . . ." This time it was Viggo.

"Donald Duck."

That was enough of an answer for both of them.

***

Office of the Homicide Boss
Friday, February 6, a little past noon

For once the Homicide Boss was sitting in his office without Number Two. His guest had made that request—and he understood why. He knew what was coming.

The only irritating thing was that the minister of justice was sitting in the chair where his best investigator usually sat. Right across from him.

They hadn't wasted any time.

"I'm leaving my office . . . you know . . . health." Again, the strange wording.

The Homicide Boss nodded, just as Number Two would have. Without saying a word.

"I'm handing it over to . . . someone younger."

"If the current government wins the election." The words came out before he could stop them. Although there was no longer any danger in them.

"Yes."

Then he took a deep breath. "Was it true, what she said . . ." The woman he was talking about had suddenly become nameless. ". . . what she wrote in her suicide note?"

"That my father ran down Viggo Larssen's mother?"

"Yes."

"No." No hesitation.

The Homicide Boss squinted. "No?"

"Yes." Danish was a wonderful language to converse in.

Still, the police chief knew what he meant. Poul Blegman had denied Malin's critical piece of information. Once again he felt as if he were tottering out on the edge of that damn cliff. Floating in space. What in the world had gone wrong?

CHAPTER 28

The Lighthouse on the Cape
Saturday, February 7, morning

Verner had left first thing in the morning. This time he called for a taxi. He was on his way back to civilization.

Viggo didn't feel sorry for him. In Verner's world, being fired wasn't really a big problem. If he wanted to, he could live off his pension—or he could simply take advantage of the favors so many others owed him: politicians, colleagues, business people. He could even go work for Ove Nilsen. It might be a fresh start, a much-needed change of scenery. He might become a brilliant PR man for Eden's New Garden.

Something suddenly compelled Viggo to bend down, crawl under the table, and loosen the stone from the hiding place the police had never found, where the old lighthouse keeper had hidden that logbook from Hell.

She had found it. In the end, nothing in his life had been a secret to her.

He stuck his hand in, and felt around. Sure enough, a little farther in, he found her letter. The real letter, the one that the Homicide Boss and his Number Two would never see.

She had tricked them. Naturally. That was the least of her skills.

Dear Viggo. I don't exactly know how you've managed.
But when you read this, I will have done the only thing
I could do, which may have always been my intention.
I believe that, because I only had one option.

He turned on the light above the bench and went outside. He leaned over the words. They had been handwritten in blue ink on unlined paper.

As you know, I sent you that anonymous letter six months
ago about Peter Blegman being responsible for your moth-
er's death. You visited the Widow, but she didn't dare
admit the truth to you, although I know that your sorrow
left a deep impression. In a way that's why we got to know
each other. And I haven't regretted it.

Viggo Larssen sat for a moment, motionless, and then continued reading.

It all started when she wrote her will—her new will—or
more accurately it started long before that, back when
little Arrow was run down on that dangerous road by
your grandfather. It's a strange story. The gate was open.
Agnes was also there when we signed the will, and it
seemed as if she wanted forgiveness for her actions. As if
she had been the one who let the boy out of the garden—
on purpose. Yet that makes no sense at all.

Viggo Larssen turned to the next page.

> *Then some years passed. Arrow died in 1963—your mother in 1971. She had gone to the Midsummer's Eve party, at the orphanage where I grew up, the night she died. We met each other at her funeral, because I was with my foster mother, but you didn't see me. All of that would have been forgotten long ago if the Widow, in the twilight of her life, hadn't decided to resurrect Arrow and write her two oldest sons out of her will.*

Viggo Larssen looked up. It was almost dark. The country's two most powerful men had been brought down by their own mother. It was absurd.

> *In 1988 her husband—old man Blegman—died, which you know all about because you had written a wicked though accurate portrait of him and his dynasty. On his deathbed he confessed to his wife what she must have suspected all those years. That he was the one who had killed your mother. She never told anyone about it—not until she became sick and knew she was going to die soon. Both Agnes and your friend Ove were seeing her at that time— Adda as her pastor and Ove as a consultant for the nursing home. She was quite fond of Agnes, and she believed in Ove's idea. Nothing preoccupies modern people more than death. The thought of being forgotten is the worst one of all.*

Anyone watching Viggo Larssen would almost believe that he smiled.

> *In April of 2014, she had a serious relapse, so she finally decided to rewrite her will. Her two oldest sons never*

visited her—they didn't have the time. Over the years they had pissed away their entire share of their father's inheritance. With a stroke of a pen, she disinherited them. Agnes and I were present. It was one morning in August. We were her witnesses. Then she told us about her husband and said that was the real reason, that it had to be atoned for. Nothing could justify taking one life for another. I wrote that anonymous letter to you on the same day (Agnes found out where you were living from Ove and Verner). Of course I've regretted doing so, as I had no idea you would react as you did . . .

Viggo Larssen frowned and turned to the third page.

. . . I only wanted to give you some peace. So you could hear it from the Widow's own mouth. Your visit frightened her. She probably couldn't take any more. She sent you away empty handed, and I reproached her for it. What else could I do? She became frightfully sad and maybe it was her idea—or maybe I convinced her—because we decided to make amends. She wanted to give you part of the inheritance as compensation for your loss. But she wanted to be certain about how you would react (and that you wouldn't go on a spending spree!). She made me a very generous offer to take a leave of absence and move out to the cape, where you were living. My task was simple. I had to get to know you and report back to her. I think that in the fog of old age, you had become an incarnation of her lost son, and I didn't deny her that illusion. In the fullness of time—those were the words she used—as gently as possible, I was supposed to tell you the story about your mother and how she died . . . about the evil that exists in

*this world. I never got to that last part. I don't know why
it dragged on . . .*

He turned the page over.

>*. . . I think it was because I fell in love with you, but it's
>hard for a woman who had never before seriously touched
>a man. It's the hardest thing of all. You on that bench.
>You and your walks, back and forth, along the deserted
>coast. You and your burlap-wrapped bottle of wine, on
>the bench, in the late afternoon. How could anyone love
>such a man? You and your little prince, your journals,
>your fantasies about the death that some higher power
>had sent to Earth in the shape of your mother and planted
>out in Hell's Deep, with the serpent from your mother's
>favorite book as the final omen. How could anyone love
>such a man? I thought I was the strangest being on earth,
>but you had me beat, out there on the cape. And you had
>lived with it your whole life without going under.*

Viggo Larssen shook his head. It was the strangest thing he'd ever read.

>*I didn't see you in the Lighthouse on New Year's Eve or the
>following day—and I had to live with that knowledge,
>because that was when the Widow disappeared.*

Viggo Larssen shook his head again. That was the night he found the
logbook. And then fell asleep.

>*Once I realized that the Homicide Boss was never going
>to let you go—and at some point would expose you—I
>made my decision. In one way it wasn't difficult. For*

people like us, time only exists in short, precisely measured lengths, when it really matters. I wrote that "confession" that was left on the beach along with the Widow's will. Then I wrote this letter, which I'm going to put in the only place I can think of where you'll find it. When I leave you for the last time, I'll be taking your omens with me, your dreams about death—and you'll never see them again.

Viggo Larssen had reached the last page.

Here, at the story's end, there isn't much left to say. The will is going to destroy the dynasty, and you'll live on. I think that you, like the Widow, figured it all out a long time ago. Of course it wasn't an accident that both her son and your mother were killed in traffic accidents. I think you had already realized that their father was guilty of your mother's death, and I think you've tried to put it all behind you. In a way I'm the one who brought the evil back to life. I'm going from Paradise to Hell—but at least the Sea Witch's house didn't manage to get me. I went on my own . . .

Viggo Larssen blinked; that restless twitch was something he'd lived with his whole life. The lighthouse bench felt cold beneath him.

I think, and hope, that after a while you will forget me. As you know, forgetting is the only hope we humans have. I'd like to think that you will sleep soundly now, like children do, smiling in the dark when no fear disturbs them . . .

The twitching ran down his cheek, turning into the sound in his throat that he knew so well—a kind of snort behind the bridge of his nose that spread down, making people think he was laughing. But once it reached your heart, you were dead.

> *When the flower in the book cries, it's vanity. If a fox does it—or even threatens to do it—it's affected. When people do it, it's silent.*

The twitching had reached down into his chest, and he had to move away from the strange letter.

> *You shouldn't be carrying around so much guilt, not for anyone, because guilt makes your mistakes possible again and again.*

The sins of the fathers—and the mothers. He understood what she meant, and he turned to walk back into the house.

> *There are phases of existence when we believe we have finally exhausted our pursuers, and we think we can see an end to our attempts at escape: a bright summer day in a garden where an old man is sitting in the shade beneath a blue umbrella, waiting for death. Waiting for someone to take him by the hand.*

He opened the door to the lighthouse.

> *Don't think about the Widow. And don't think about what has happened. Death isn't—as many people believe—some bony, slack jawed, noseless monster; it's only a thought that someone has about someone other than themselves.*

He walked into the house.

No one will ever know.

He could still sense her presence . . .

No one will ever find you.

Beneath the name, which should have told him everything, she had circled the last line in thin blue pencil, just as his own mother would have.

Will the sheep eat the flower . . .

The dots were Malin's. She hadn't written any more.
But her parting shot made no sense.
Did she really believe that he had murdered the Widow?

***

Office of the Prime Minister
Saturday, February 7, afternoon

Palle and Poul were alone in the country's finest—though not most beautiful—office.
The view was depressing and the furniture uncomfortable.
With one powerful flip of his hand, the Bear could have shoved all of it out the window. He would have enjoyed doing so, too.
On this morning, however, it wouldn't have made much of a difference.
"I take it you've told that little *shit* that we are going to resign and hand over the reins?"

The oldest Blegman brother was referring to the Homicide Boss. He'd been on them since their mother died—and they knew he was never going to let up. He had to be the one representing their faceless enemy.

"No. I only told him about myself."

Palle Blegman stood up, and in his hunched-over position, his massive form resembled a question mark.

"You have to make your own decisions," said his brother in an oddly rebellious tone of voice.

"My own decisions . . . ?"

Poul Blegman didn't respond.

"It was you, wasn't it?"

That gave the slightly smaller man sitting in the Hans Wegner chair a bit of a start; if he was stalling, it was admirably brief. "Yes. What gave it away . . . ?"

"Nothing. I've always known."

Poul Blegman stood up halfway, without speaking.

"Sit down. At the hospital before he died, I heard father tell mother all about it. They didn't see me, I was standing in the doorway. Afterward it didn't matter. He was dead—you were living. So what really happened?"

"Father called home. He had been at the midsummer festival with the Conservative Party in Bernstorff Park, and it was a little before midnight. Everyone else had gone to bed. He was plastered . . . he wanted mother to drive him home . . . he was worried about hitting . . . something . . . but I didn't want to wake her up. So I took the old car—the one in the garage—and drove over to get him. It was dark."

That last bit of information seemed pointless. The Bear ignored it. "And?"

"She was on her bike . . . suddenly she turned left, right in front of us, without signaling."

As if that was an excuse—or merely an explanation.

"So he was drunk. What else?" It may have been the shortest—and most loaded—question ever posed in a prime minister's office.

"'Drive!' he yelled."

Palle could hear his father's voice. He could hear the engine of their old Saab speed up on the highway, sending the car lurching forward in one sudden, destructive motion.

"I stepped on the gas. There was a thud—and she was gone."

"Gone?" His incredulous tone matched the absurd situation.

"There were some red spots on the windshield."

"I can fucking believe it."

The country's highest-ranking official sat motionless for a moment, thinking about what had just been said. A life for a life.

"Father took the wheel . . ." The outgoing minister of justice was speaking in a strangely formal manner. ". . . and we drove home. Father parked the car in the garage, and the next day he fetched the Jaguar. He impressed on me that I could *never* talk about the car in the garage again. That it no longer existed."

"Yes, when I heard the story . . . at the hospital . . . it was . . ."

Poul Blegman looked up. Surely his powerful and decisive big brother wasn't fumbling for words.

". . . like when he shot those damned cats . . . some things just have to be done."

"Are you also resigning?"

Palle Blegman ignored the question and turned toward his little brother. "Listen to me. Father was lying there with all those tubes and machines and *shit*—and suddenly he looked up at mother and he said, 'I killed her. I fucking killed her!' But it wasn't actually me. Do you remember how I washed the old Saab the next day . . . that was her blood . . . blood for blood . . . *her* blood for your beloved little Arrow's. But I couldn't remove the dents, and the police would find out if I asked a mechanic to fix them. They searched and searched. So I let it sit in the garage, and that's why we moved to Gentofte the next year. I got some junkyard to come get it, nothing strange about that. They took it, with her hair and her blood and her father's cursed genes, anything I hadn't washed away. And your son—your son Poul, who's your youngest now—is a murderer, just like me—and you. You left the gate open that day. You let Arrow run out into the world.'"

"Out into the world . . . ?" Poul Blegman stared at his brother.

Palle Blegman sat down in his chair for the last time. "Yes, for Christ's sake . . . *out* . . . do I really have to spell everything out for you?"

***

Office of the Homicide Boss
Sunday, February 8, morning

The Homicide Boss was sitting across from Number Two, just as he had every single day for five weeks now, ever since the Widow had disappeared on New Year's Day.

He told him about the meeting at the round table in the house in Tårbæk, on the most glorious coast a king could imagine—and Frederik VII, the last of Denmark's absolute monarchs, had indeed loved it.

He had fulfilled the promise they had demanded of him that night he fell into their trap and learned their plan.

They'd been relentless.

He met them for the last time the night before.

The will lay on the round table. There wasn't a sound, no acknowledgment of its appearance. The will was lying there because—one way or another—men like that always get support from those in power.

"Exit Blegman."

The group's old sage didn't even need to say, "the Blegman dynasty." It went without saying. The whole family would vanish into the urban version of Hell's Deep.

The prime minister's current permanent undersecretary had lifted the gray folder with his long thin fingers and nodded. Malin would have said it's the only real difference between men and women, perhaps the reason for all of the planet's belligerence and decay: men nod when they shouldn't—regardless of whether or not they then also respond with real or imagined armies.

He turned the will around. A pointless maneuver, and he knew it, but a clear signal to the seven conspirators—and the homicide detective who had procured this crucial weapon for them—of the final outcome. Final procedure, voting, sentence. Endgame. If the Blegman brothers tried to resist, the will would be made public in its present form—but if they avoided that fatal mistake and relinquished power, the document in the folder would alter, quite imperceptibly, just enough so they would inherit enough money to sweeten their old age.

No one could resist such an offer. The decision was unanimous. Men like this placed the people's trust in democracy above all else. The unwashed masses didn't need to know that their fearless leader had been a crook, as they say in America, a spendthrift and a small-time swindler (as they'd call it out in the sticks).

"Why didn't Malin write about it . . . ?" The Homicide Boss's thoughts flew back from Tårbæk—and his own fall from grace—to the present.

That mistake—or oversight—meant that the two investigators, ultimately, had seen the wrong thing. Or not seen anything at all. As if someone had raised a hand and made reality disappear.

Number Two was the only one who would dare take part in such a deliberation. He would always be there for the Homicide Boss—just as he'd been there in Bakken and in the alleys of Nørrebro.

"Why didn't she say anything about the bird in the cage?"

Number Two said nothing.

"It wasn't her," said the Homicide Boss.

Number Two had his back. Without saying a word.

"She would have *told us* about the bird in the cage . . . she would have written about it . . . that canary we found in the Widow's empty cage . . . *The Little Prince* on the basement floor . . . who in the world would have put the bird there—and why? That would have convinced us completely . . . so why didn't she do it?"

His deputy was still silent—no one ever had more reliable support.

There was only one explanation: "Because it wasn't her."

The Homicide Boss repressed a sigh no one should hear.

What did they miss?

Neither detective understood it. They were the best in their profession—but they'd lost their bearings.

EPILOGUE

THE FINAL SERMON

Agnes from Søborg
Sunday, February 8

We call the second Sunday in February *Sexagesima* because it falls on the sixtieth day before Easter—and because we preach about the parable of the seeds, as described in the Holy Gospel.

After Malin's disappearance and death, no sermon could be more appropriate. I heard about her suicide from Verner, who'd gotten his information from the Homicide Boss himself.

Some people lose their chance to carry on God's will in a blindness I both loathe and can only marvel at—just what the apostle Mark writes about and stresses more clearly than anything else:

> *And he began again to teach by the sea side: and there was*
> *gathered unto him a great multitude, so that he entered into*
> *a ship, and sat in the sea; and the whole multitude was by*
> *the sea on the land.*

Jesus looked out over both the innocent and the guilty and said,

Hearken; Behold, there went out a sower to sow: And it came to pass, as he sowed, some fell by the way side, and the fowls of the air came and devoured it up. And some fell on stony ground, where it had not much earth; and immediately it sprang up, because it had no depth of earth: But when the sun was up, it was scorched; and because it had no root, it withered away. And some fell among thorns, and the thorns grew up, and choked it, and it yielded no fruit. And other fell on good ground, and did yield fruit that sprang up and increased; and brought forth, some thirty, and some sixty, and some a hundred.

And Jesus said to them:

And these are they likewise which are sown on stony ground; who, when they have heard the word, immediately receive it with gladness; And have no root in themselves, and so endure but for a time: afterward, when affliction or persecution ariseth for the word's sake, immediately they are offended. And these are they which are sown among thorns; such as hear the word, And the cares of this world, and the deceitfulness of riches, and the lusts of other things entering in, choke the word, and it becometh unfruitful. And these are they which are sown on good ground; such as hear the word, and receive it, and bring forth fruit, some thirtyfold, some sixty, and some an hundred.

***

I don't know why Malin chose this way to exit her strange life—and in such a godforsaken place. Perhaps it's symbolic that she disappeared into what the simple people on the cape for centuries have called Hell's Deep.

I don't know what she was thinking; we didn't share a destiny.

Still, she managed to play her role and carry out the errand I'd chosen for her, and she left the will for the authorities to find in such a clever way that the police wouldn't dare keep it hidden. Within twenty-four hours it would become public knowledge, and the Blegman family would be destroyed.

Exactly what I've been dreaming of for half a century.

The fact that Ove's dream of building his paradise on earth will get financed—I hope the Good Lord is forgiving—is merely an added bonus. We aren't in any financial need, and we never have been.

Malin, a deeply naïve soul, never discovered the truth that set our plot in motion. Of course, she'd never heard the Widow's entire story. She only knew the part about little Arrow and Viggo and the Widow's remorse for her husband's vengeance on Viggo's mother. A life for a life.

And it was even worse. Her husband had used their son as his weapon: Poul had been driving the car that killed her. Yet there was more.

The part that really mattered was only meant for my ears. And if she hadn't been crying so bitterly while she begged for my forgiveness, she would have seen the shadow run past her eyes, the shadow no prayer or confession could erase.

She forgot that there's one thing greater than forgiveness in both a person's life and in the oldest book:

> *Oh Lord, thou knowest: remember me, and visit me, and revenge me of my persecutors; take me not away in thy longsuffering: know that for thy sake I have suffered rebuke.*

Yes, I carry the shame. And in that moment she looked up at me—and I smiled back and blessed her—I had been chosen as his instrument. No one could be better suited for the job.

She asked me to stay when Malin left, right after we witnessed the new will, and I can still remember the tone in her voice. We were alone.

"Yes . . . ?" Maybe I already sensed the terrible thing she wanted to say.

"When it happened . . ."

At that moment I knew what she wanted to tell me.

"Palle . . ."

Of course.

"He raped you . . ."

The Good Lord looked down on us, but even he could not fend off her words: "I knew it."

She was on her own now—there was no way back—but she didn't realize it.

"He came home . . . his pants torn, with dirt and leaves . . . on the knees."

Yes, I thought, he came home from the Garden of Eden, soiled with my terror.

"I threw it all into the washing machine . . ."

That remark was so grotesque that I couldn't comprehend it. It described my world for all those years afterward. If anything went wrong, even if all the world's unhappiness crashes in on humanity, the right tools will take care of it. Eyes can be shut, innocence restored, and sons' mothers can go on living.

". . . before the police came . . ."

Before the police came. Naturally.

". . . and then I lied to them. I said he was already at home, long before you were assaulted."

Assaulted. She had already reduced Palle Blegman's crime to a word that contained no trace of remorse. She was crying.

I was sitting across from her, but she couldn't see me with those watery red eyes.

"I couldn't let them take my oldest son."

I should have known. She was using another to assuage her own guilt. A few seconds passed before she said the words I knew no God could ever forgive.

"I can understand why you chose never to have children . . . the sorrow that they bring . . . like Arrow . . . like my two sons."

She should have never used that word. *Sorrow* is like a broken tree left standing in the ground, one that died a long time ago.

Her sons were responsible for everything. I'd had an abortion, and they had sewn me back together with the news that it could never happen again. Life would not be coming back. He had taken the act of Creation from me—and she had let him, without any punishment. My father had looked at me with the eyes that belong to all fathers whose only wish for their daughters (and themselves) is that a fog will settle over the wilderness that no one can make their way through.

I was afraid that someone would find the Widow's new will, which Malin and I had signed as witnesses one August day at Solbygaard.

If Palle Blegman found it, it would disappear or be rewritten before she died. She might even tell him to—that's how widows of that ilk are . . .

I came up with a solution after Viggo visited the nursing home in August, after he received Malin's anonymous letter. She should never have sent it—I was furious when she told me about it—but when I saw Viggo leave, empty handed yet again, while the Widow sat there inconsolable, it suddenly turned into an advantage.

Malin never understood that she was merely a pawn in a game that involved hiding the will. No one could solve the problem better than she could.

For atonement, you can write Viggo into your will, I'd said to the Blegman matriarch; he'll know why, but no one else will ever know the real reason. She nodded eagerly. Malin will go out there first, as your ambassador, and she'll prepare the way for practical matters—and for forgiveness. The only thing you must do is give her the will, so no one can stumble upon it in the coming months.

The Widow had nodded again. Of course. She was dying; I could hear it in her breathing and see it in her eyes. Only the waiting remained.

Right before Christmas she looked at me with those watery red eyes I couldn't stand and said, "I need to talk to my sons about the new will . . . it's not *right* to keep them in the dark."

I stiffened, though she didn't see it. The brothers would find out what we had done; they would discover who the witnesses were and what the will now contained—and they would do so while the Widow was still living and could change it again. She would be weak and regret her decision. In the end, they were her sons, and the country's most powerful men, and that's what they would be until the will resulted in their ruin.

She had lost her bearing—like when Jesus distorted the Lord's message with these words:

> *And unto him that smiteth thee on the one cheek offer also the other; and him that taketh away thy cloke forbid not to take thy coat also. Give to every man that asketh of thee; and of him that taketh away thy goods ask them not again.*

When it truly mattered, God didn't fail me. I said, "Ask them to come see you on the first day of the new year—but don't tell anyone about it."

We scheduled the Blegman clan's reconciliation for the first of January, at six in the evening. The timing was perfect. Everyone at the nursing home would be watching her son—the prime minister—give his New Year's address on TV. That would give me plenty of time to carry out my plan unseen by the staff, which on that day would consist of only two care interns. In the late afternoon they would be busy with heating up the community's prepackaged meals in the large kitchen on the floor above the Widow. It was my best chance.

The two brothers would sound the alarm when the Widow wasn't there, without realizing they were smack in the middle of the crime scene.

When I knocked on her door at five that evening, the entire floor was empty.

Invisibility was my most important ally; even if I were seen, it would be very difficult to cast suspicion on a spiritual adviser like me.

Surprised, she stared at me. Her sons were supposed to come to visit her. She wasn't expecting to see me.

That day I had a sudden impulse I've never regretted, although it was reckless. Maybe I wanted to leave one last living message for her beloved son who had run out onto the street, out to his own death. And one for her, too. As it is described in the Apocalypse of John:

And I saw an angel standing in the sun; and he cried with a loud voice, saying to all the fowls that fly in the midst of heaven, Come and gather yourselves together unto the supper of the great God; That ye may eat the flesh of kings, and the flesh of captains, and the flesh of mighty men, and the flesh of horses, and of them that sit on them, and the flesh of all men, both free and bond, both small and great.

"I have a gift for you," I said.

"A gift?" Her bloodshot, old-woman eyes suddenly looked curious.

Maybe she wondered why I wasn't taking off my black gloves inside, although a cold front had rolled in and the temperature was close to freezing.

"Do you remember this?"

She didn't answer.

I opened the fingers of my right hand, and she looked down at the yellow piece of plastic lying there, almost covering my entire palm.

If it had been a nature film, you would have seen the snake take its first bite, then the paralysis, her realization that she was trapped and would never be able to stand up again.

Of course she knew what it was. She kept a piece just like it lying under her pillow. She'd had it for years, ever since Arrow's death.

Surely we'd found the two pieces of plastic in the same place, after the accident, fluttering around on Maglegårds Allé during the paramedics' vain attempt to cut the raincoat off the bleeding boy, in the hope of averting death. But only God can do that. And he was nowhere in sight.

I tossed the yellow clump on the windowsill between the porcelain figures of those two great Danes, Kierkegaard and Hans Christian Andersen.

Then she heard a sound coming from the box I was holding in my other hand.

It was a white shoebox with three holes cut into the lid.

The sound of a canary, chirping nervously in the darkness.

Surely she'd heard that song the day she let Arrow's soul loose to atone for her own guilt.

> For it is the vengeance of the Lord: take vengeance upon her;
> as she hath done, do unto her.

The bird would fly up to Heaven and follow Arrow's soul.

I lifted my little yellow companion out of the box and opened the door to the empty cage she'd kept on the windowsill. The police would never be able to figure it out—the two brothers wouldn't even notice it—and it made me feel secure about what I had planned.

It wasn't until Ove told Verner and Malin that our canary had flown away that I became nervous. Had the detectives publicized the discovery, cooler heads would have connected the two pieces of information. The Widow understood immediately.

> *For as the rain cometh down, and the snow from heaven, and returneth not thither, but watereth the earth, and maketh it bring forth and bud, that it may give the seed to the sower, and bread to the eater: So shall my word be that goeth forth out of my mouth; it shall not return unto me void, but it shall accomplish that which I please, and it shall prosper in the thing whereto I sent it.*

The Little Prince. I took that damn book off her bookcase, and suddenly it hit me.

She could sit and read it in her final hours.

She didn't so much as whimper when I led her out into the hall and onto the elevator, which stopped in the basement. I still had on my black gloves. She looked at me with her eternally weeping eyes right before I shut the door and left her. The book was lying in her lap.

Maybe she knew—I think so at that point—that either shock or a lack of oxygen would kill her long before midnight.

I never imagined the police would bungle their own investigation, or that it would take so many days before they looked into the rooms in the basement. It took almost the same number of days as the creation of the world before they found her.

Still, it was dangerous when I decided to tell the Homicide Boss about Viggo. Nothing came of it, but I felt as if there were no other possibility. I thought my first tip would be enough to trap him, but they let him go. I had to find another solution—or Ove might suddenly become the focus of their investigation.

I was an unlikely murder suspect, and I decided to say that I had tried to cover for an old childhood friend. I would tell the two policemen that

Viggo was at the nursing home the day the Widow disappeared and that I, in my misguided loyalty, had kept it a secret. That would be enough.

But Malin must have sensed it, though I don't know how. She managed to derail my plan with her foolish "confession"—as if she were trying to play God—or maybe because she was just as weird as Viggo. The two of them on that bench beneath the white lighthouse.

It seemed totally ridiculous.

I knew that deep inside Viggo blamed me for his mother's death. Because he visited me that night. It wasn't his profession of love, or even his attempt at kissing me—but rather that I had been right there, in his life, on the very night when he should have been home with his mother. Because he didn't prevent the accident that came barreling down from above and knocked her to the ground. If I had never lived, she wouldn't have died.

How simple the world looks to one who counts seconds, adding and subtracting, without understanding that God's very role is to predict everything. There was no gap between past and present that night. No accidental wrinkle in time. Peter Blegman had, single-handedly, advanced time by yelling at his son: "Drive!" Viggo's mother would never have escaped.

What else can I say before I cast my own words into the flames?

> For the preaching of the cross is to them that perish foolishness; but unto us which are saved it is the power of God. For it is written, I will destroy the wisdom of the wise, and will bring to nothing the understanding of the prudent.

I know the difference between good and evil when I see evil.

In my work, which I share with the Creator, there's no excuse for dodging one's responsibility.

I understood that the night Palle's mother closed her eyes to her son's deeds. Innocence paves the way for Vengeance. The entire God story is about that—and nothing else.

But none of it matters now.

Thank God that Viggo's strange talk about death omens came to nothing. It was a relief when Malin could report that the man in the Lighthouse had returned to his bench. At that moment I was happy about my decision, the day I killed the Widow Blegman.

I had opened her drawer to place the date of Viggo's mother's death in there, more proof of what I knew was true and would destroy the dynasty (how could I know the two homicide detectives would be that slow-witted and spend so much time on something that simple). And then I found a strange handwritten note, a couple of odd sentences in the Widow's own handwriting . . .

. . . which I burned in our fireplace at Dyrehaven before Ove came home. Her last words would never be found.

Right before I tossed them into the fire, I read them for the third time.

The living word belongs to God, not people, and no one would ever know what the Widow was suggesting. A foolish old woman's last dream, one she had written down when she woke up.

What amazes me is her description of something that, in a biblical sense, might resemble an omen about her own death. That day it seemed baroque to me, since that was precisely what would happen. She was standing on a beach, looking out at the horizon, out over the ocean . . . Out in the water she spotted a woman dressed in black, standing motionless, her hands reaching toward her . . . As if she were calling to her . . . In the dream she knew that the woman was her mother . . . At the moment the old widow decided to answer her mother's call, the water around the woman's feet turned into a bubbling white vortex, and a serpent appeared out of the sea with its head raised . . . The second it struck she understood what her mother's call meant . . . She was going to die . . .

When your mother calls, you follow—and you don't look back. The person who had been with her at the beginning of life would follow her to the very end.

Watching the dream turn to ashes, I felt relieved. No living soul should ever know about it.

ABOUT THE AUTHOR

Copenhagen native Erik Valeur has been an award-winning journalist for Denmark's most influential media outlets for the past twenty-five years. *The Man in the Lighthouse* is his second novel. His first, *The Seventh Child*, was released in Denmark in 2011 and has since been published in twelve other countries. This international bestseller has garnered numerous awards across Europe, including the prestigious Glass Key award given by the members of the Crime Writers of Scandinavia.

ABOUT THE TRANSLATOR

Mark Mussari has his PhD in Scandinavian Languages and Literature from the University of Washington in Seattle. He has translated Danish novels, short stories, and nonfiction for publication, including Dan Turèll's seminal crime novel *Murder in the Dark*. His nonfiction translations include *Finn Juhl and His House*, *Wegner: Just One Good Chair*, and *Børge Mogensen: Simplicity and Function*. A scholar of Danish literature, art, and design, he is also the author of numerous academic journal articles and the book *Danish Modern: Between Art and Design*. Mussari is also the author of numerous educational books, including books on Haruki Murakami and Amy Tan, Shakespeare's *Othello* and sonnets, and popular culture.